Shades of Love

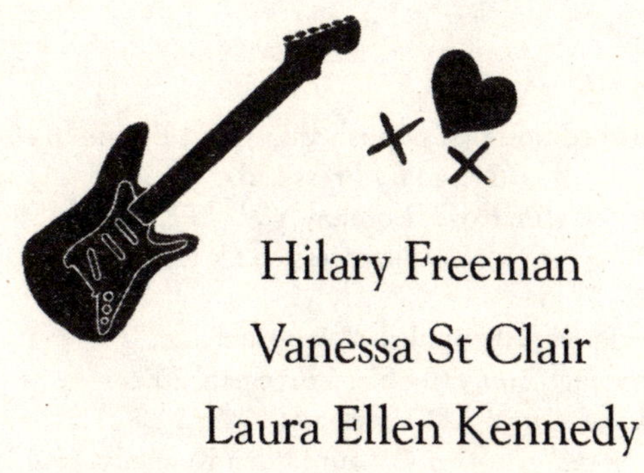

Hilary Freeman

Vanessa St Clair

Laura Ellen Kennedy

Shades of Love

Piccadilly Press • London

This combined edition first published in Great Britain in 2010
by Piccadilly Press Ltd,
5 Castle Road, London NW1 8PR
www.piccadillypress.co.uk

Previously published seperately as:
Loving Danny © Hilary Freeman, 2006
Love, Divided © Vanessa St Clair, 2008
My Best Friend's Brother © Laura Ellen Kennedy, 2007

A catalogue record for this book is available
from the British Library

ISBN: 978 1 84812 062 4 (paperback)

1 3 5 7 9 10 8 6 4 2

Printed in the UK by CPI Bookmarque Ltd, Croydon, CR0 4TD
Cover design by Patrick Knowles and Simon Davis
Cover illustrations by Sue Hellard

Loving DANNY

To Steve, for believing

HILARY FREEMAN

Chapter 1

The day I met Danny I had a hole in my tights. It appeared that morning, when I snagged them with the corner of a jagged fingernail as I pulled them up, and worked its way southwards as the day went on. By six p.m., when I made my way home from work, it had eaten its way past the hem of my skirt and stalled just above the cuff of my left, knee-high boot. No amount of skirt rearranging, leg crossing or bag repositioning could hide the hole from public view.

I mention this because it's one of the few things I remember about that day. I can't tell you what the weather was like or what I ate for breakfast. I have no idea what was on the news or what came in the post. Work is a blur. Before I met Danny, all I remember about that day is thinking how my mother would call me a trollop for wearing laddered tights to work, and cursing myself for still biting my nails, especially as I'd spent a fortune on expensive nail polish at Boots.

Isn't it weird how the truly significant days of your life often begin as the most banal? There you are, just minding your own business, doing something boring and ordinary like buying a Kit Kat or, in my case, catching the number 29 bus home from work and – boom! – the most momentous and life-changing event happens to you. You don't have time to rehearse or prepare or compose yourself. You don't even have time to change your tights.

My life-changing moment occurred shortly after ten past six, which was the last time I'd checked my watch. Danny (or the guy whose name I would later find out was Danny) got on the bus halfway up the high street. I was sitting at the back where there's more leg room, so I didn't notice him until he'd squeezed his way past the pushchairs and the strap-hangers and the men who territorially stretch their legs into the aisle, and made his way to the row of seats facing mine.

It was hardly the most romantic of beginnings. The very first words he said to me were, 'Uh, sorry,' as the bus choked and spluttered and sent him stumbling forwards on to my foot. I muttered something back and leaned down to brush his dusty footprint off my suede boot. When I looked up again he'd settled into his seat and was putting in some earphones.

I didn't want him to see me staring, so I turned to look out of the window. It was October and the nights were drawing in. Although it had been light when I left work, the sky was now the deep navy blue of dusk and the harsh lights on the bus were beginning to transform its windows into mirrors, reflecting everything inside. Soon, I could clearly see both my reflection and his.

He was fiddling with an iPod inside his jacket pocket. I tried to work out what type of music he'd be into. He was a wearing a beaten-up, vintage leather jacket, so old that the black looked almost brown, ripped jeans and a tour T-shirt for some obscure American band I'd only vaguely heard of. His hair was dark and almost shoulder-length and it looked as if he hadn't shaved for a day or two. He'd obviously tried hard to look like he wasn't trying too hard. But somehow, it worked.

I thought, *I bet he's listening to indie music.*

A few seconds later a familiar guitar riff began to bleed from his earphones. I smiled to myself; I was right.

It took me a moment to realise he was smiling too. He had very white, very even teeth and I liked the way his eyes crinkled up in the corners. Then, to my horror, I realised he was smiling at ME. I'd forgotten that when you look at somebody in a mirror they can see you too. It's like when you're a child and you close your eyes and really believe you've become invisible, but of course you haven't.

I watched my reflection turn crimson with embarrassment and I turned away from the window as quickly as I could, fumbling in my bag for something that wasn't there. I've never been any good at flirting. If someone makes eye contact with me I always feel so uncomfortable that I have to look away at once. If I try to smile I end up making an ugly grimace. It's even more discomforting if the person staring at me is cute. And he certainly was cute.

I also felt self-conscious about my clothes. Not the hole in my tights, which I was sure wouldn't bother him (it matched his tattered jeans, after all), but my boring wool coat, white shirt and navy, A-line skirt, which had actually belonged to my old school uniform.

I had started working at a solicitor's office just a week

after I'd finished my A-level exams and I still hadn't got round to shopping for new work clothes. To be honest, I hadn't really been bothered. I was saving all my money for university the following autumn, and, if I earned enough, a spot of travelling later in the year, before term started. Why waste money on drab suits to please my conservative boss, when I already had a wardrobe full of great clothes? I hadn't factored in wanting to impress a cool-looking guy on the way home.

There's only a limited period of time that you can pretend to be searching for something urgently, and remain convincing. Mine was running out fast. I was, however, aware that the moment I stopped peering in my bag my gaze would inevitably meet his. If I looked out of either window I'd see his mirror image; if I looked straight ahead, I'd be looking directly at the real him.

'Have you lost something?' he said.

Oh God.

'Um, yes, my . . . er . . . mobile,' I replied, my voice cracking with embarrassment and the knowledge of my lie. I'm almost as bad at lying as I am at flirting. My phone was, of course, beside me on my seat, tucked between my thigh and the armrest. I'd placed it there earlier for easy access.

I dared myself to look up at him, crossing my legs and smoothing my skirt down as I did so, in the hope that it would better conceal my phone. I felt certain everybody on the bus was looking at us; people don't talk to each other on public transport – it's one of those unwritten, universal rules that we must all be born knowing.

'Bummer,' he said. 'I'm always losing mine.'

His voice was deep and cigarette-croaky and he had a strange accent, which made him sound as if he was both well spoken and common at the same time.

'Yeah,' I said, playing along with my own story. 'I don't have half my numbers written down anywhere. My life is stored in that phone.'

He smiled again and shrugged his shoulders. I decided that he looked even more attractive in the flesh than in reflection. It might have been because of the slight bend of his nose. It's funny how different people can look when their features are reversed. I think it has something to do with how symmetrical you are. I'm always surprised when I see photos of myself and they don't look anything like the me I see in the mirror.

While we'd been talking I'd stopped looking at the road. Usually, I pressed the bell as soon as I saw the second-hand furniture shop at the end of my street. But on that fateful evening, by the time I noticed I was at my stop the bus doors were already open.

I leapt out of my seat, grabbing my bag and pushing past the other commuters who blocked the aisle, creating an obstacle course made up of bodies, umbrellas, briefcases and rucksacks. I reached the doors just as they slammed shut. Somebody pressed the bell urgently on my behalf and the doors flew open again, giving me just enough time to step on to the pavement before they closed emphatically behind me. Then, without pausing for breath, I turned into my street and broke into a half-walk, half-jog.

'Excuse me!'

The male voice came from behind me. I quickened my pace. It was now completely dark and the lighting on my street was notoriously poor – my dad had even written to the council about it. Whoever owned the voice could only be a beggar asking for change, or worse, a mugger or a rapist.

'Excuse me! *Hello!*'

Something about the voice sounded familiar.

'SLOW DOWN!' he shouted. 'I'VE GOT YOUR PHONE!'

Still walking, I swung round, at the same time feeling for my phone inside my bag. It wasn't there. In my hurry, I hadn't picked it up off the seat. Panic turned to relief then to embarrassment as I was struck by a second realisation: the voice belonged to HIM.

If I'd been a cartoon character, like the ones I grew up watching every Saturday morning when my parents were still in bed, I would have screeched to a halt, leaving track-lines in the pavement behind me. Instead, I clumsily stumbled, tripping over my feet as I came to an unplanned stop.

'God, you don't half walk fast,' he said, finally catching up with me. 'Who did you think I was, some mad axe-man?'

'No, of course not,' I said, with little conviction. The truth was, he was a stranger on a bus. We'd had a thirty-second conversation. He *could* have been a mad axe murderer for all I knew, albeit a very cute one.

He handed me my phone. 'It must have been on your seat all along,' he said, smiling so broadly and cheekily that

I knew he had caught me out. I felt myself reddening. 'I saw it when you rushed off. Lucky, that.'

There was a pause. It was, in retrospect, a very important pause, the ideal chance for him to say goodbye and walk away and never see me again. If he had taken advantage of the opportunity that pause afforded him, he'd have been forever just 'the guy on the bus who kindly gave me back my lost phone' – a bit-part player instead of the lead actor.

But he didn't. Still sporting that mischievous, dazzling grin, he said, 'My name's Danny, by the way. And you are?'

'I'm, er, Naomi.' Until I actually said it, I hadn't been sure if I'd give him my real name or a made-up one.

'So where are you off to in such a hurry, Naomi?'

I really liked the way he pronounced my name, emphasising the 'o' and not the 'a', like most people do. When your name has as many vowel sounds as mine, there's a big margin for error.

'I'm just going home,' I said, remembering again that he was a stranger. I didn't want him to know where I lived. I rearranged my bag on my shoulder, to indicate that I was about to start walking again.

He understood. 'Sure,' he said. He reached into his jacket pocket and pulled something out. It was a piece of paper. 'I'm playing a gig at The Bunker, next Thursday – why don't you come along? Bring a friend, if you like. I'll put your name down on the door.'

He pressed the paper into my hand. His fingers were long and the tips rough – a guitarist's fingers.

'See you, Naomi,' he said, with the self-assurance of

someone who knew that he would. 'I'd better get going – you made me get off the bus about four stops early.'

He smiled, playfully, then turned and walked away. I opened my mouth to shout 'goodbye' or 'thank you' after him, but he was too quick for me. Soon he had vanished into the darkness.

I unfolded the piece of paper. It was a flyer.

New Band Night at The Bunker
Thursday, October 28th @ 7p.m.
Live on Stage:
The Ring Pulls
Collateral Damage
Billy Franklin and the Hot Press
The Wonderfulls
Dandelion
Tickets £5 in advance – available from
www.bunkermusic.co.uk
or £7 on the door

He hasn't told me the name of his band, I thought, unzipping my bag and placing the flyer inside.

It would probably have remained there for weeks, nestling amongst the receipts, crumbs and grubby, loose mints, if it hadn't been for one thing: from that moment on, I couldn't stop thinking about Danny.

Chapter 2

When I reached the house I noticed that Mum's car was parked in the drive. I didn't feel like recounting my boring day at work – just living it was tedious enough – so I let myself in as quietly as I could, hung up my coat, unzipped my boots and crept straight upstairs to my bedroom.

I had slept in that room since I was six months old, but it didn't feel like mine any more. It belonged to someone younger, someone who liked pink, fluffy cushions and curled-up posters of faded pop stars whose names I had all but forgotten. That naïve and unsophisticated girl enjoyed skipping and Scrabble and playing with dolls. She had become an embarrassment; I didn't want to share my space with her. Now I wanted a room with freshly painted white walls, neat blinds and a sofa. But there was no point redecorating – my bedroom had no place in my plans for the future. Why waste my energy? I'd be leaving home for university in under a year.

I peeled off my tights (or what was left of them) and dropped them into the bin under my desk, watching as the lid swung back and forth in rhythmic applause. I couldn't wait to get out of my work clothes and into my jeans. Only four months into my placement and I was already beginning to wonder whether I really wanted a future career in law. Still, Dad had used his contacts to get me a gap-year job with a reputable firm and I knew I should be grateful. 'It's a great opportunity,' he had said, in his most headmaster-like voice. 'You'll be streets ahead of the other students and it will help you get a job after university.' But I didn't feel grateful. I felt trapped, as though my life's path had been laid out in front of me and I would have to walk along it, without any say in its direction.

'Naomi? Is that you?' Mum was coming up the stairs, the sensible heels of her court shoes clip-clopping on the wooden slats.

'I'm just getting changed,' I shouted back, willing her not to come in. I could sense her loitering outside the door, her hand poised above the door handle.

'All right, then.' She sounded disappointed. 'But make sure you come down for dinner. Dad will be home soon.'

'Sure.'

I couldn't hide my lack of enthusiasm. Over the past few years family dinners had become an ordeal – and it had nothing to do with Mum's cooking. My parents didn't believe in eating in front of the TV. We had to sit around the table all together, making polite small talk about our school or work days and offering 'intelligent' comments on the day's news. I think Mum and Dad saw it as some sort of family-bonding exercise, a way of ensuring my younger sister Emily, who was sixteen, and I confided in them. Of course, we never, ever told them anything interesting or important about our lives.

And that night, I had absolutely no intention of telling Mum and Dad that I'd met a guy named Danny on the number 29.

But I did want to tell someone. I was already beginning to forget what Danny looked like and what he'd said. Talking about him would make him real again. I felt for his flyer in my bag and unfolded it, brushing off the crumbs. It was just a meaningless list of band names. Reading it three times didn't help either.

'What's that?'

I jumped. Emily had come into my room. She never knocked. Usually, I'd have been irritated, but this time I was glad of the opportunity to talk.

'It's a flyer. For a gig.'

'Cool. Who's playing?'

I handed her the piece of paper and she studied it for a second, chewing her lip and then frowning dismissively.

'Never heard of any of them. Where did you get it?'

'A guy gave it to me. He's in one of the bands. I met him on the bus.'

Now she was interested. She sat down on my bed, crossing her legs. 'Really? What was he like?'

'He was cute.' I felt myself reddening. 'I didn't speak to him for long. Er, he was nice,' I said and smiled, unintentionally. 'He had something about him. I'm not sure if he'd have been your type. Scruffy – you know, an indie boy. He was looking at me and I was embarrassed. So I sort of lost my phone – even though I really did know where it was – and he found it and gave it back to me.'

'God Naomi, anyone would think you'd never met a guy before. You gonna go to the gig, then?'

I shrugged, trying to regain my composure. Why do I always ramble like that when I'm nervous? 'Maybe.'

'You've got to go. You never go out any more.'

It was true. Since my best mate Debbie had gone to university in Manchester and Natasha, Holly and my other friends had gone travelling, my social life had all but disappeared. Even my parents were beginning to take pity on me, offering me tickets to theatre performances and saying I could join them for bridge games (which, I must point out, I declined, and not always politely). Taking a gap year had seemed like such a good idea when all I'd thought about was the money I'd earn and the work experience I'd gain. I hadn't anticipated the loneliness, the sense that I was the one missing out. How could I have let my parents persuade me to turn down a round-the-world airline ticket for a bus pass and a day job? Still, I didn't want my suddenly sophisticated little sister, with her diary full of parties and youth clubs and sleepovers, reminding me of how boring I'd become.

'OK, I'll go. Do you want to come?'

'I suppose,' she said, trying not to sound too keen. She flicked her perfectly straight, blond hair. Why hadn't she inherited the 'frizz gene' like me? 'Yeah, all right. If I'm not busy.'

I didn't like her superior tone. 'It's on a school night, Emily,' I said, bitchily. I wanted to make it clear that I was still her big sister, still more worldly and mature. 'You'll have to ask Mum and Dad for permission. What was it you came in for, anyway?'

She looked hurt. Awkwardly, she climbed off my bed, unsure where to put herself. Now she was sheepish. 'Doesn't matter.'

'No, really. Did you want something?' I tried to make my voice as warm as possible. I hadn't meant to sound so mean. I really wanted to go to Danny's gig and I knew I couldn't – or wouldn't – go alone. I needed her to come with me. It might even be fun. Emily may have been a poor replacement for Debbie or Natasha or any of my other friends, but the fact was my friends weren't around. Given my circumstances, she was my only choice. And she knew it.

'You know that black halter-neck top you've got, the vintage one?'

I stiffened, certain of what was coming next.

'Can I borrow it for Andy's party on Saturday? I reckon it will look cool with my new trousers.'

She was, if you'll pardon the pun, trying it on. That top was my favourite – the most unique and flattering item in my wardrobe. I'd found it at an antiques market a year earlier and had bargained the stallholder down until I could just about afford it (it had cleaned out my Saturday job savings). It was made from the softest silk, with jet beading on the halter part and, because of the way it was cut – I think they call it 'on the bias' – it made my waist look tiny.

Emily could have asked to borrow any other piece of clothing and I would have been more than happy to oblige. But not that top. And not for a sixteenth birthday party. It would inevitably come back covered in beer (and maybe vomit) and reeking of cigarette smoke. What's more, the top wouldn't even suit Emily. It was designed to be worn by a woman with boobs and curves like me, not one as angular and flat chested as my sister.

'Of course you can borrow it,' I said, smiling through gritted teeth. If it meant that much to her, I could give in, just this once. 'But please be careful with it. And get it cleaned afterwards.'

'Thanks, Nay!' Emily beamed at me, enjoying her little victory. She was well aware that I don't like being called 'Nay', but all her friends shortened each other's names and now doing the same to mine had become an unbreakable habit. She walked back over to the bed and made herself comfortable again. 'So, what are you going to wear to this gig, then?'

'God knows. I haven't given it any thought. Maybe my black halter neck, if,' I hammered home my point, 'if it's still in one piece!'

'Let's face it, Nay. If he liked you in your work gear he's gonna be pleasantly surprised whatever you wear next time.'

'Perhaps I'll borrow something of yours,' I teased. I never borrowed Emily's clothes. Aside from the fact that most of them were too tight, I didn't much like her style. She dressed to show off her midriff and her legs – neither of which were my best features – and she wore lots of slogan T-shirts in bright colours, which I thought looked cheap.

'If you want,' she said, without irony.

Downstairs, the front door slammed shut. Dad was

home. I knew that in exactly two minutes Mum would be calling us down for dinner. I could have set my watch by it. Emily pushed herself up. 'Suppose we'd better go down,' she said, sighing. 'Get it over with.'

I rolled my eyes at her. 'OK, but don't mention anything about the gig. I'm not in the mood for an interrogation tonight.'

We went downstairs together. Dad was already sitting at the kitchen table. He'd taken off his glasses and was rubbing his eyes with the side of his hand. His bald scalp gleamed under the fluorescent strip lighting.

'Hello, girls,' he said, without looking up. 'Did you have a productive day?'

His question wasn't addressed to anyone in particular, so we both muttered affirmatively.

'I'm just going to help Mum,' I said, sensing an opportunity for escape. Emily screwed up her face at me. She hadn't been quick enough, this time.

Mum was juggling steaming pots and pans at the other end of our L-shaped kitchen. 'Ah, Naomi,' she said, gratefully. 'Would you help me serve the food and take it in?'

She had cooked spaghetti, with bolognese sauce for herself and Dad, and a vegetable sauce for me and Emily. I'd been vegetarian since I was eleven; Emily was just a fussy eater and didn't like mince.

Dinner passed without incident. Between mouthfuls, Dad told us what he thought was a funny anecdote about a man in the accounts department at work who'd left his travelcard on the train and had been fined, or something like that. I'm afraid I wasn't listening properly, so I can't repeat the story. Mum told Emily off for getting a C in her maths test and informed her she wouldn't be allowed out the night before a test again. She also told us she'd got a new piano pupil, whom she'd be teaching on Tuesday evenings at six. Dad asked after Mr Stevens, my boss and his occasional golf partner. I said I hadn't spoken to him that day, as I'd been left in the photocopying room on my own with a waist-high pile of folders to work my way through. I moaned that I could still see the flash of the machine every time I closed my eyes and now probably had radiation poisoning. Dad tutted, 'Well, we all have to start somewhere.'

My mind kept drifting to Danny. I wondered if he was eating dinner somewhere too, and with whom. He seemed too self-assured to live with his parents. Did he live on his own or did he share a flat with mates? I pictured him sitting in a bedsit, surrounded by guitars and CDs. I wished I hadn't been so keen to rush off. Perhaps he would have asked me if I fancied a coffee, there and then. We would have gone to the greasy spoon on the corner of Murray Street and talked till it closed. Then—

'Naomi, I said did you want some fruit? Naomi!' Mum looked exasperated. I shook my head.

'Don't worry about Naomi, Mum,' Emily said, smiling cryptically. 'She's got a lot on her mind. Isn't that right, Nay?'

'Shut up, Em,' I muttered, under my breath. I felt foolish. Danny probably hadn't given me another thought. I was merely a potential audience member for his gig, a clumsy girl who couldn't even manage to get off a bus without forgetting her phone. He almost certainly had a girlfriend, or a string of beautiful girlfriends. I was angry with myself for reading so much into nothing. How had my life become so mundane, so empty, that a momentary encounter with an attractive guy could make me fantasise about a future together?

I excused myself from the table and went back upstairs, leaving Emily to help with the washing-up. There were at least three hours to fill before bedtime. It was strange how long the evenings seemed now; last year, with homework to complete and friends to see, I'd felt I never had enough time. It was as if I'd been running on a treadmill that had suddenly stopped, sending me flying aimlessly. Maybe, it now occurred to me, I hadn't been as in control of my life as I'd believed. All my agendas, all my goals, had been set by school or by my friends. My social life had been handed to me on a plate. I had never had to be proactive. But if I was going to get through the next year I'd have to take risks, find things I enjoyed, and force myself to go out and be more independent. The only problem was I didn't know where to start.

There was nothing on TV, so I decided to listen to some music. I put on my favourite CD, a compilation that an ex-boyfriend, Mark, had made for me in the summer after our GCSEs. It was an eclectic mixture of songs that he'd downloaded or copied from his own collection: contemporary guitar bands plus some 1960s folk, 80s pop and 90s dance music. Unfortunately for Mark, I'd enjoyed listening to his CD far more than spending time with him.

For about an hour, I lay on my bed with my eyes closed. Downstairs, my family were going about their routines. Emily had popped out to a friend's house. Dad was in his study, doing paperwork. Mum was giving a piano lesson to a neighbour's very unmusical child. The cacophonous notes kept bleeding through the ceiling, jarring with the melodies on my CD. Mum must have been seething with frustration; she was such a perfectionist, especially when it came to music. At least she was busy. It seemed that everyone else had something to do, a purpose. Everyone except me.

Shut up, Naomi. I had to stop feeling sorry for myself – it wasn't an appealing trait and I knew it wouldn't get me anywhere. I sat up and gazed at the photo on my bedside table. It showed me, Debbie, Natasha and Holly, all grinning broadly, our arms wrapped around each other. Funny to think it had only been taken a few months before. We were inseparable. Now, Debbie was in Manchester, Natasha in New York, and as for Holly, who knew? Her last e-mail, which I'd received a month before, had come from Sydney. In it she said she had met a guy and was planning to travel to Indonesia with him.

Debbie hadn't called me for a few days. When she'd left for Manchester we agreed that we'd take it in turns to phone each other on alternate nights, but it hadn't worked out that way. We were on such different schedules, she might as well have been on the other side of the world too. I was up at seven a.m., she rarely went to bed before three or four. I had to be asleep by eleven, not long after she'd gone out for the night. She got up during my lunch hour.

Although strictly it was Debbie's turn to ring, I wanted

to talk to her that minute. It was nine o'clock; she might still be in her room. I took my mobile out of my bag and dialled. I didn't even have to look what I was doing – she was number one on speed-dial.

Her phone rang at least ten times before she picked up. 'Naomi, hi!' There was so much background noise, I could hardly hear her. 'I'm in the Union bar. Hold on a sec.' I heard her apologising to someone, then the background noise subsided and she came back on the line.

'Sorry, just had to go outside. What are you up to?' she asked.

'Oh, you know, this and that.' I tried to hide how world-weary I felt. 'What about you?'

She sounded excited. 'I'm just having a few drinks in the Union, then me and some of my mates from Hall are going clubbing in town. There's this great place that basically has a happy hour till midnight. And girls get in half price. Maybe we can go when you come up to stay. Hold on a second . . .'

I heard her saying hello to someone and then she must have hugged them because their voices suddenly sounded muffled. 'Sorry about that. Just this guy from my tutorial group. I think he's had a few too many. So, what have you been doing again?'

I knew I had nothing to tell her except that I'd met Danny. But she was meeting new guys every day; my brief encounter wouldn't impress her.

'I sort of met a guy today,' I volunteered, after a long pause. 'He's called Danny.'

'Oh, Naomi! That's great!' she cried. 'Are you going to see him again?' I'd left out the part about the bus and she'd concluded we'd already been on a date.

'Yes,' I half lied. 'We're going out next Thursday. Well, I'm going to see his band play.'

'That's great, Naomi,' she said again. I could tell she was only half-concentrating. 'Listen, I've got to go now. But I promise I'll call you tomorrow. You can tell me all about him then.'

I'd hardly managed to say goodbye before she hung up. I felt a little annoyed that she hadn't had time for me. But, if I was honest with myself, I knew that I'd be the same if I were in her position. Why on earth, I asked myself again, had I chosen to take a gap year? Why hadn't I realised I'd be left behind? The truth was I was jealous that Debbie was having such a good time, and scared that she'd replace me with a new best friend. I felt this more acutely every time we spoke, every time she mentioned someone she'd met in the coffee bar or in the queue for a lecture. I was so self-conscious about my lack of interesting news I was sure she'd soon discover what a boring person I really was.

Even if I'd known where to go to meet new people, I've never been the sort of person who can walk into a room, march up to a stranger and introduce myself. I don't know what to talk about, or how much eye contact to make and I'm not very good at judging when to move on to someone else. Always too polite, I usually end up getting stuck all night with the creepy, sweaty-palmed guy who nobody else wants to talk to. I had hoped that I might make some new friends at work, but although everyone was friendly enough, they were all much older than me and many of them were married with children. They treated me like the 'work experience girl', which, of course, I was.

I've got other friends, I told myself. OK, maybe they weren't such close friends, but I could still call them, couldn't I? What about Dee? She had been in my class at school and, like me, had stayed in London. But unlike me, it wasn't out of choice: poor Dee had got such bad marks in her A-levels that she was having to retake. Knowing there was someone worse off than me made me feel a little better. I believe my old German teacher would have called that feeling *Schadenfreude*.

I didn't have Dee's number on speed-dial, so I had to look in my phone's address book for it. Nonchalantly, I started scrolling through the Ds: Dad, mobile; Dad, work; Danny; Debbie . . .

Danny? I didn't know anyone called Danny. Did I? My heart began to pound. The cartoon 'me' did an exaggerated double-take, reacting with bug-eyed, wide-jawed surprise.

No, it couldn't be . . . could it?

There was only one possible explanation. Somehow, in the short time between chasing me from the bus and giving me back my phone, Danny had typed his name and number into my address book. He could only have done it because he wanted me to know he liked me. Maybe he even wanted me to call him. For an instant, I thought about doing it and then, just as quickly, decided against it. I told myself it was because I didn't want to appear too keen, but I knew, really, that it was fear that stopped me: fear of a stilted, silence-laden conversation; fear of spoiling the delicious anticipation of what might be.

I never did get around to calling Dee.

And I didn't sleep a wink that night.

Chapter 3

From the outside, The Bunker looks just like any other old pub on any high street in Britain. Its brickwork is decorated with overlapping graffiti, which nobody will ever be able to wash off entirely, and the bright green paintwork on the windows and doors is now chipped and peeling, exposing the wood beneath. A long time ago, someone – a landlord hoping for a different sort of clientele, perhaps – hung flower baskets along its frontage. But that landlord has clearly long since gone and the flowers have withered and died, leaving a mess of weeds and straw, which partially obscure the pub sign.

Strictly speaking, the pub is named The King's Arms, but it has become known for the music venue in its bowels and now everybody calls it 'The Bunker'. You don't even have to go into the main part of the pub to get to the venue (only old men drink in the pub); The Bunker has its own door at the side. Then it's down a long flight of stairs, which reek of stale beer and urine, to a dimly lit basement where you'll find another bar and a cavernous room with a stage at the far end.

I'd been to The Bunker many times before, but I'd never noticed just how dilapidated it was until the night of Danny's gig. That's probably because I'd never spent so much time standing outside it. Emily and I arrived unfashionably early, at seven p.m. It was Danny's fault (and mine too, for not having the guts to call or even text and ask); he hadn't told me which band he was in, so I had to be there for the start. The doors had not yet opened, so we loitered in the street outside, shuffling from foot to foot and repeatedly checking our watches and our mobile phones to make it look as though we were waiting for someone. I was on high alert with nerves, jumping every time a car drew up or a group of people walked past. If anybody even half resembling Danny approached in the distance, my stomach lurched.

I hadn't got much work done that day. I'd daydreamed my way through the filing and the photocopying, barely saying a word to anyone. I had left the office the moment I could, running for the bus and cursing every time it stopped at the traffic lights or stayed too long at a stop. I knew I only had half an hour to get changed, do my make-up and rush out again.

Fortunately, I had laid out my chosen outfit on my bed that morning. It had taken me the whole of the previous evening to decide what to wear. I'd modelled every garment in my wardrobe for Emily, calling her in and out of my room until she was so frustrated that she would have endorsed an orange shellsuit. It seemed as if everything I possessed was either too tight, too baggy, too warm or too revealing for the gig. My halter neck looked too dressy, jeans and a T-shirt too casual. We'd settled on black jeans and a green camisole top, with a black cotton cardigan to hide my chubby arms. Of course, it still didn't feel right, but it would have to do.

Hanging round outside the bunker, Emily was bored.

She pulled out a packet of cigarettes from her bag and lit one up. She expected me to looked shocked and say, 'I didn't know you smoked!' I think that's half the reason she did it – to provoke a reaction. Instead, I called her bluff and asked if I could have one too.

'I thought you had given up, Nay,' she said, annoyed that she had failed in her attempt to impress.

'Yes, I have, sort of. But I need something to do to try and calm my nerves,' I replied. 'And it's bloody freezing out here. I smiled, patting her arm. 'Don't worry, I'll buy you some more later.'

She beamed. I wasn't going to tell on her. We were becoming allies, friends even.

In the end, it had been surprisingly easy to persuade my parents to allow Emily to come with me. I'd cornered Mum when Dad wasn't around, knowing that she'd approve of any outing involving music. The conversation had gone something like this:

Me, in my sweetest tone: 'Mum, I really fancy hearing some music and a band I like is playing on Thursday night.'

Mum, falling for it: 'That's a lovely idea, Naomi. What's the band called?'

Me, worried that she might invite herself along: 'You wouldn't have heard of them. They're new.'

Mum, disappointed: 'Oh. Are you going with some friends from work?'

Me, looking mournful: 'No, it's not really their scene. Could Emily come with me? I'll make sure she does her homework first and we won't be late.'

Mum, looking pleased: 'It's nice that the two of you want to spend some time together. I'm sure it'll be OK with your dad.'

See? Easy. Emily hadn't done her homework, but we'd worry about that another day.

Three cigarettes later, at quarter to eight, somebody finally unlocked the doors to The Bunker. We loitered a little longer, so as not to appear too eager, then made our way down the stairs. A guy with greasy blond hair was manning the front desk, a makeshift table which blocked the way to the bar. Obviously worried about the night's takings, he looked happy to see us.

'We're on the guest list,' said Emily brightly.

'Name?' asked the blond guy.

'Naomi,' I said, pushing myself in front of Emily. I wasn't sure if she was too young to be there and I didn't want her drawing attention to herself. 'Plus one. Danny said he'd put us down.'

'Danny Evans?'

I had no more idea what Danny's surname was than what band he was in. 'Um, yes,' I muttered, hoping I'd got the right Danny.

The blond guy picked up a biro and scrolled his way down the typed list in front of him. Then he scrolled back up again. For a moment I feared humiliation. Had Danny forgotten about me? Was I supposed to have rung him to say I was coming?

'Ah, yes. You must be "the lovely Naomi",' he said,

smirking, as he turned the sheet of paper around so that I could see it too. There, in black type, were the words *the lovely Naomi*. A burning wave of crimson spread upwards from my neck, to my cheeks and to my ears.

'How cheesy,' tutted Emily, under her breath. *Or cheeky*, I thought to myself, secretly delighted that Danny thought me 'lovely' and didn't care who knew it. *There's a fine line*.

'Um, thanks,' I spluttered to the guy on the desk, glad it was so dark in there. I tried to push my way past the table.

'Hang on, I need to stamp you!' The blond guy smiled again, this time more kindly. He grabbed my hand, clumsily, and impressed it with an inked rubber stamp. Now the word *Bunker* was indelibly printed across my knuckles. I knew it would take at least three days of scrubbing to wash it off.

'The Wonderfulls won't be on till about ten,' he said. 'Go and get yourselves a drink.'

The bar was empty, so for once I didn't have to jump up and down to attract attention. Barmen never notice me; I grow bored of waiting to be served, lose eye contact and end up people-watching instead. I bought myself a glass of white wine and a Diet Coke for Emily. When I gave it to her she looked dismissive, but she didn't say anything. We could both tell that the barman had seen beneath the layers of make-up that she'd so expertly applied and clocked that she was underage.

As we sipped our drinks the bar slowly filled up. There were lots of overweight, balding, middle-aged men with ponytails and tattoos, several skinheads and a big group of indie kids with hennaed hair and second-hand leather jackets – the sort of odd mix of people that could only ever come together in one place on a 'new band' night.

'I haven't seen this many ponytails since the *Horse of the Year show*,' I joked.

To amuse ourselves, we played 'spot the fan', using my crumpled flyer to try to match the people in the bar to the band names. We decided that the ponytails followed Billy Franklin and the Hot Press, the skinheads were there for Collateral Damage, and the indie kids either The Wonderfulls or Dandelion. As for the poor Ring Pulls, we concluded that their fans must have deserted them.

By the time the first band came on and we were ushered next door to the room with the stage, I felt much more relaxed. It had a little to do with the wine, of course, but it was nice to be out, and Emily was actually quite good company. Every time I started fretting about Danny, she'd wink and refer to me as 'the lovely Naomi', making me crack up. She was also better than me at dissuading guys from joining us at our table. She'd just give them a withering look and they'd be off.

Once the music started, however, the evening went downhill. The Ring Pulls were dreadful – their entire set sounded as if each member of the band was playing a different song, simultaneously. When Collateral Damage came on – a thrash metal outfit whose shaved heads matched their fans' – we had to flee for the safety of the bar, or risk losing our hearing for ever. We didn't even bother to go back in for Billy Franklin and the Hot Press.

'Maybe this was a bad idea,' I said. I was beginning to feel anxious again. I also half feared that The Wonderfulls might be as bad as the other groups. 'I'm ready to go, if you are.'

'You are joking, aren't you?' said Emily. 'You've chewed my ear off about Danny for the past week, made me stand outside like an idiot, sit through two hours of hell, and now, a few minutes before he comes on stage, you want to leave. No way. Even if you don't want to stay to see Danny, I most certainly do.'

'Wow, that told me,' I conceded. 'OK, we'll stay. But don't blame me if The Wonderfulls are, er, terrible.'

Part of me – the cowardly part – actually wanted Danny's band to be an embarrassment. That way, Emily and I could leave halfway through his set and I wouldn't have to face him afterwards. I could delete his name from my phone, tear up his flyer and forget I'd ever bumped into him. Life would continue as normal. Normal and uncomplicated.

In truth, I feared Danny would be disappointed. I was afraid that the reality of me would not live up to his memory of me, just as I feared that the image of Danny, which I had stored in my mind since our meeting, had been enhanced by hope and expectation. I suppose it's not really possible to be nostalgic about something that has not yet happened. But that's the closest I can get to describing how I felt.

There was a sudden exodus of indie kids from the bar. 'Come on, then,' Emily said, dragging me up from my seat. 'It's show time!'

'Don't make me stand near the front, please, Em,' I

begged. I needn't have worried – we couldn't get near the stage. *I* might never have heard of The Wonderfulls before, but they appeared to have collected a large and loyal following. I felt a stab of jealousy when I realised that most of the fans were girls.

The lights dimmed and four male silhouettes appeared on the stage. The crowd whooped. There was a drummer, a keyboard player, a bass guitarist and a lead guitarist. For a second, I was confused: neither of the guitarists resembled Danny. Had he cut his hair? Was he shorter than I remembered? Then, as a spotlight hit the stage, a lone figure walked out to the front, a guitar slung over his shoulder, and took his place at the microphone. The crowd whooped again, louder this time. There could be no mistake: Danny was standing before me.

Emily nudged me. 'Is that him?' she mouthed above the cheering. 'He's gorgeous.'

My stomach was in knots, but I couldn't help grinning. 'Yes, that's him.'

Emily poked me in the ribs, as if to signal her approval and, perhaps, her surprise that someone so good-looking and charismatic might be interested in her older sister. I could barely believe it myself.

I had been carrying a single, blurry picture of Danny around in my mind ever since we'd met on the bus – a snapshot of a cute but slightly scruffy guy. Looking up at him on the stage gave me a whole new perspective. His legs were longer than I recalled, and his jaw squarer. Perhaps it was the well-cut, striped suit jacket that he was wearing over his

T-shirt, but his shoulders looked broader too. Standing in front of me was a rock star, as unobtainable as the ones in the pictures in my old magazines. Although I fancied Danny even more than I had expected to, he had become a total stranger again and it unnerved me.

Watching Danny perform, it was clear that he was in his element. He commanded the stage, moving from one side to the other with an effortless grace. It was his territory; the bands that had played earlier were merely his warm-up. Each time the crowd roared his eyes lit up. He knew he had every one of us – men and women alike – eating out of the palm of his hand. And the knowledge empowered him. He was no longer six feet tall – he was a giant, as high and wide as the room itself. I'd never really understood what stage presence meant until I watched Danny that night.

His voice, too, was a revelation. Nothing like the low drawl of his speaking voice, it was strong and raw and rich, with a haunting lilt. He sang effortlessly, soaring between the high and low notes, never running out of breath even when he flung his body about the stage. His voice was an untrained tenor, a rock voice – the type my mother would have loved to mould and shape – but, to my ears, all the better for its crudeness. I couldn't make out all the lyrics, but the songs were dark – full of allusions to love, death and loss. Most began gently, with a melodic keyboard or guitar riff, building up into a fantastic frenzy of thrashing guitars and crashing drums.

And all the while, I felt as if Danny was singing only to me. I knew it wasn't rational – the lights were out and I was in the middle of a packed crowd, squashed up to Emily on one side, my face pressed into a stranger's back – but wherever he stood on the stage he seemed to be looking directly into my eyes. No one else existed.

The Wonderfulls' set lasted forty-five minutes. Usually when I see a band I don't know, I start fidgeting and checking my watch, hoping every song is the last. When you don't recognise any of the songs, they all tend to blend into one. But I was so mesmerised by Danny that when he said, 'This is our final song,' and his loyal fans cheered at the opening chords, I actually felt a tinge of disappointment.

When the last cheers had died down and The Wonderfulls had disappeared backstage, the lights came on and Emily said, 'We'd better get to the bar, then, and talk to Danny.' For a few seconds I stood rooted to the spot, unable – and unwilling – to break out of my trance. She nudged me. 'Come on, that's what we're here for.' I let her lead me through the remnants of the crowd. She was excited and star-struck, keen to meet Danny and pleased to have a reason to do so.

'Can we go to the loos first, please, Em?' I asked, my voice hoarse from shouting over the din. I felt sick with nerves, vulnerable and unattractive. I was sure that my make-up had run and that my hair was lank and frizzy.

Emily sighed. She could read my mind. 'OK, but you look great, honestly,' she said.

As always, there was a queue outside the Ladies. By the time we came out – freshly powdered, our lip-gloss reapplied – the bar was starting to clear out for the final act.

The coward in me prayed that Danny had already left, but I saw him at once, standing in the far corner with a bottle of beer in his hand. He was surrounded by a group of girls, each one prettier than the last. One of them was standing tight up against him and he was smiling at her, nodding his head and occasionally laughing. Another girl, dark and petite, rushed up to him and kissed him on both cheeks. Someone else tugged playfully at his T-shirt.

I hung back, waiting for my moment, ignoring Emily's nudges.

'You're going to miss your chance. What are you playing at?' she moaned. I was irritated, as much with myself as with Emily. I knew I didn't have the courage to walk up to Danny and say hello, and I felt stupid standing there without a drink, exposed. But my feet were glued to the floor, my mouth so dry that my lips were sticking to my teeth.

'I'm sorry Emily, but I just can't do this,' I said finally. The rest of The Wonderfulls had joined Danny's party and he was now engrossed in conversation with the bass player.

Emily looked defeated. 'Don't blame me when you wake up tomorrow and you realise you've blown your chance with him,' she said, refusing to look me in the eye. She turned and made for the exit, not caring if I was behind her. I paused for a moment, and then began to follow.

'Naomi!'

I stopped dead. It was Danny's unmistakable voice.

'Naomi, wait!' he shouted. Before I could turn round his hand was on my shoulder. 'You're always rushing off, aren't you?' he said, smiling. His face glistened with sweat from his performance and his eyes were bright with exhilaration. 'Am I going to have to chase after you all the time? You do know, it's really not my style.'

'I'm sorry,' I stuttered, unsure what to say or do. I was paralysed, my body still headed for the door, my neck twisted round so my face could meet his. Emily had disappeared up the stairs and would be waiting for me outside, annoyed and impatient.

Danny's eyes bore into mine with an intensity that thrilled me, but at the same time made me uncomfortable. I felt vulnerable, as if I was naked, and I had to look away, momentarily. When I looked back Danny's gaze was unbroken.

'I'm so glad you came,' he said, gently removing his hand. 'Did you enjoy it?'

'Oh, yes,' I said, awkwardly moving my body so that I was standing straight in front of him. He was unbearably close and my heart was beating rapidly, my face glowing red. 'You were great, really great.' I instantly regretted using the word 'great'. Like 'nice', it was just a meaningless platitude. But my entire vocabulary seemed to have vanished into a chasm in my brain.

He didn't appear to notice. 'Why didn't you come and find me? I saw you standing there with your friend. I thought you'd come over.'

'She's my sister,' I said, embarrassed. 'You had so many people around you . . . your band . . . all those girls.'

He looked as if he was about to laugh. 'Ah. But none of those girls has my number in their phone.'

I felt an involuntary smile spreading across my face at

the memory of what he'd done. 'Really? Oh.'

'It was hardly subtle now, was it, Naomi?'

'No.' I laughed. 'You're lucky I had to call someone beginning with 'D', or I might never have found it.'

There was an uncomfortable silence, as we both fumbled for something to say next. I was aware that Danny's drummer had come up behind me and was motioning to his watch. Danny brushed him off; he wouldn't take his eyes off me. 'Hang on a second, Pete,' he said. He smiled at me again. 'Listen, I've got to help the guys pack up our stuff. What are you doing tomorrow night?'

Nothing, I thought, with absolute certainty. A few months ago it would have been a very different story. Back then, my schedule was so full with parties and shopping trips and study that I had been forced to become an expert at juggling times and people.

'I think I'm free,' I said, looking up to the ceiling as though I was picturing a full diary and wondering if I could fit him into it. I didn't want him to know about my non-existent social life. 'Yes, I'm free,' I repeated.

'Well, if you fancy a drink – just me, no groupies – meet me at Yellow at eight. You know it?'

'Yes,' I said, trying not to sound surprised at his choice. Yellow was a trendy and expensive wine bar quite near to my house, frequented by City slickers and C-list celebrities. I'd never actually been inside, but I couldn't imagine Danny there. 'Yes, I'll meet you.'

He grinned. 'Guess I'll see you there, then, Naomi.'

With that, he turned and was gone. I stood motionless

for a second, trying to compose myself. I wanted to jump up and down and scream. Then I ran up the stairs, my body suddenly so weightless that it felt as if my legs were floating above each step.

Emily was waiting for me outside. She was grumpy. 'Where have you been?' she demanded.

'You're not going to believe it, Em!' I was as excited as a small child, my voice high-pitched and breathless. 'I've got a date. With Danny!'

'Oh my God! That's fantastic!' She grasped my hand and beamed at me. 'Oh my God!' Suddenly, the smile vanished and she looked crestfallen. 'But I never even got to meet him.'

Chapter 4

Danny was late. Twenty minutes late. I didn't know then that it was his trademark. Our relationship was still a blank slate, like a brand new diary on January First, clean and smelling of freshly milled paper. And, like every new diary, within months it would become a mess of torn edges, smudged writing and scratchings out, its pages filled with adventures and secrets not yet imagined. Beginnings are always perfect: ripe to be spoiled.

I, of course, was ten minutes early. I'd left myself far too long to get ready and had found myself sitting on my bed with nothing to do but stare at my bedside clock and endlessly re-powder my nose in a vain attempt to quell my nerves. What had made it worse was that my parents were downstairs, circling like sharks. They were after information. It was my fault – I hadn't told them where I was going. It wasn't because I thought they would disapprove, or because I was afraid that they would try to stop me, I simply wasn't ready to divulge anything about Danny. Talking about him would bestow the date with a significance it hadn't yet earned. What if the evening turned out to be a disaster? I'd want to keep the details to myself.

Typically, Dad wouldn't let it drop. He was a born worrier – Mum sometimes called him 'an old woman'. He couldn't rest until he was sure he knew every detail of everybody's schedule. It irritated all of us.

'I'm eighteen,' I'd said earlier, when he'd pressed me. 'I could be at university now, in another city, and you wouldn't have a clue what I was doing. I'm sure Debbie doesn't ring her parents every Friday night to give them a breakdown of her evening ahead.'

He couldn't argue with my logic, but he didn't like it. 'But you're not at university, Naomi,' he had argued. 'You're still at home, living under our roof – and we want to know who you're with and that you're safe.'

'I'll be safe,' I'd promised. 'Just trust me, for once.'

'It's not you we don't trust,' Dad had said, perhaps visualising a world full of con men, rapists and murderers out to hurt or maim his daughter.

'Then trust me to use my judgement,' I'd barked. 'I'm not stupid.'

So, at seven-forty, I'd run downstairs, shouted goodbye through the living-room door and let myself out before Dad could start questioning me again. Now I was sitting at Yellow's bar, wondering if Danny would show. It wasn't a bad place to wait alone; Yellow's patrons were too trendy and self-obsessed to hit on a single girl they didn't know, and I had plenty to read. All the day's newspapers were piled up in front of me and there was an extensive wine list and food menu to peruse. My stomach growled as I contemplated the merits of a Thai curry or a goat's cheese salad. I hadn't eaten dinner at home – I was too nervous and I didn't want my tummy to look bloated. My black pencil skirt was far too tight already. And, if I'm honest, I was hopeful that Danny would ask me to eat with him later. The food at Yellow was supposed to be good, if rather over-priced. Would he want to pay or would we go Dutch? Would he stay for just one drink, then tell me he had to leave? What would we talk about? Would I bore him? Would he, for that matter, turn up at all?

For God's sake, chill out, Naomi, I said to myself. *He's been chasing you since you met – why would he suddenly go off you?* I wished I could reach into my brain and stop the cogs from grinding round and round. I ordered a glass of wine and a bowl of olives to keep my hunger pangs at bay. As I popped a couple into my mouth I realised they were marinated in a dressing that tasted strongly of garlic. *Great start, Naomi*, I thought. I rummaged for a mint in my bag. It was covered in fluff, but it would have to do. I swirled it between my teeth until it dissolved, then took a swig of wine. The combination tasted foul.

'Can I get you anything else?' asked the barman politely. It was now ten past eight and I was beginning to look con-spicuous, perched on my bar stool, silent and alone. People don't go to Yellow on their own, they go in big, air-kissing groups.

'No thanks, I'm just waiting for someone.'

The barman smiled. *Poor love*, I read in his eyes. *Have you been stood up?*

I'll give Danny five more minutes, I thought. *Or maybe ten . . .*

When Danny walked in, I didn't notice him. I'd given up on the menu and was now thumbing through a newspaper, devouring a kiss-and-tell story about some footballer. Dad only got the *Financial Times* at home, so reading the tabloids felt like a guilty pleasure.

'Has he been at it again, then?' said Danny dryly, over my shoulder. Flustered, I dropped the paper on to the bar, losing the middle section beneath my stool. Danny bent down to pick it up, pausing a little longer than was necessary as he took in my patterned tights and kitten heels. Smiling cheekily, he handed it back to me. 'Hello, Naomi,' he said. 'Sorry I'm late. Have you been here long?'

'No,' I lied. 'It's fine.' Sitting on the bar stool lent me almost an extra foot and my face was at the same level as his. He looked amazing. His hair was freshly washed and less messy than I'd seen it, curling gently into the nape of his neck. He'd obviously just shaved and, for the first time, I noticed a cute dimple in his chin.

He leaned in towards me and kissed me on the cheek. His musky scent and the warmth of his breath on my neck made me tingle. Then he smiled again and delicately touched my top lip with his thumb and forefinger. The intimacy of this gesture made me feel uncomfortable, until I realised he had merely removed a piece of fluff, which had stuck to my lip-gloss. Seeing me blush, he chose not to comment on it. Evidently, he was a gentleman.

'What are you drinking?' he asked, picking up my wine glass and taking a sip. 'Mmm, I'll order a bottle, shall I?'

I nodded. Danny's confident manner made me feel shy

and nervous, and I worried that if I spoke I might say something stupid.

'Hey, John,' he called out. The barman came over. He winked at Danny, then glanced at me with renewed respect. So Danny was a regular, then? It still seemed incongruous.

'All right, Danny, mate. What can I do for you?'

'Can I have a bottle of Pinot Grigio, please?' he asked. I could have sworn that the posh element of his curious, hybrid accent became a trifle more pronounced. 'Put it on my tab.'

I hadn't expected Danny to know about wine – it didn't fit in with his scruffy, rock-and-roll image. I'd simply ordered one of the few wines that came by the glass in Yellow.

'Why don't we go and sit somewhere more comfortable?' Danny asked when the wine had been brought over. He held out his hand to help me off the stool. I took it, shyly, aware that the feel of his skin on mine was making my heart beat faster and that sparks of electricity were shooting up my arm and into my body. I was conscious too that my own hand was clammy and that I wasn't able to pull down my skirt. Danny didn't appear to notice. He led me through the bar to a table and some plush brown sofas, only letting go of my hand when I sat down. The cushions were softer than I'd expected and I fell back into the sofa, jarring my back. He waited until I'd rearranged my clothes, then sat himself down next to me. His leg touched mine, expectantly.

'That's better,' he said.

'Yes, thanks,' I replied, unsure what to say next, and terribly aware of the proximity of Danny's leg. I hoped he couldn't tell that my legs were trembling. *Think, Naomi, think*, I repeated to myself like a mantra. 'The gig was good,' I volunteered. 'You were good.'

'I'm glad you liked it,' he said. 'We were trying out some new material. It seemed to go down all right.' There was an awkward pause. 'Anyway, enough about me. Tell me about you, Naomi.'

My insecurities came flooding back. I was no good at small talk and, it now transpired, neither was he. His question highlighted the fact that he knew nothing about me, nothing at all. He was out with me because he liked the way I looked, because I'd dared to turn up to his gig and said I liked his music. What was there about me that would interest him?

'What do you want to know?' I managed, buying myself time to think. Danny's motive was genuine – to get to know me – but his question had made me feel self-conscious, anxious that my personality would be scrutinised for flaws. Whatever I said now might make or break our potential relationship.

'I want to know everything.' He laughed, leaning in towards me. 'The name, I've got. How old are you? What's your shoe size? What music do you like – apart from mine, of course? What do you care about? What do you dream about? What do you want to be?'

'OK,' I said, taking a deep breath. 'Stop me when I bore you. My full name – which you don't know – is Naomi Jessica Waterman. I'm eighteen, I have one sister – whom you've seen – called Emily. She's sixteen going on twenty-five. My shoe size is a very average five; I'm five foot five and,' I paused for breath, deciding not to draw attention to my figure by giving him my dress size, 'and I like good music: pop, soul, folk, R & B, indie, jazz, classical, country – anything, so long as it's good. My mum's a music teacher, so we've got about a million CDs at home. She says there are only two types of music: good music and bad music. I have to say I agree with her on that one.'

Danny smiled. He had been nodding, approvingly, throughout my monologue. 'You mum sounds like a very wise woman. Continue.'

Excellent. I'd won a few brownie points. My confidence was growing and I even managed to smile back at him. 'All right. What was your next question? What do I care about? I care about people, my family, my friends, people I don't know. I care about not hurting anyone. I care about animals – I'm vegetarian. I care about the environment. Yes, I know, I sound like a cliché now.' I looked at Danny, expecting him to have grown tired of my rambling. He was concentrating intently, his turquoise eyes wide and piercing.

'Go on . . .'

'I dream about the most bizarre things. Doesn't everyone? I dream about places I've never been, where I meet people I don't know. I dream about being on ships, at fairgrounds, things I've read about or seen in films. I dream in colour, usually, and nearly every night. Sometimes I dream about shoes. Shallow, I know, but I am a girl.'

He laughed again. Now I was starting to relax and enjoy myself.

'What do I want to be? That's a tough one. I thought I wanted to be a lawyer, but now I think that's just what my parents want me to be. I'm on my gap year, working for a law firm and I'm hating every minute of it. All I know is that I want to be somebody, to do something special and important, something that people remember me for. Not tabloid famous – history book famous. God, now I sound like some kind of megalomaniac. Please make me stop before you have to get the men in white coats to carry me out!'

'They'll be coming for me too, then,' he said, suddenly serious. 'I want everything you want. The fame, the glory – plus a bit of adulation too. Of course, when I'm a famous rock star the tabloids will be full of me, but that's part of the job these days, I'm afraid.'

'From what I saw you already have the adulation,' I teased. 'All those girls at The Bunker?'

'No.' He frowned. 'Not the groupies. They only care what I look like and they want to tell their mates they've met me, just in case I make it. I could stand on stage and howl like a wolf and they'd still tell me I was wonderful . . . until the next band comes along. I want respect, I want people to quote my lyrics, I want people to play my records in years to come. Oh God, now who sounds like a megalomaniac?'

'No,' I reassured him. I was smiling automatically now, liking Danny more and more. 'It's good to be ambitious. I hate people who are apathetic and don't have any passion.' I felt a twinge of guilt – wasn't that just how I had been behaving lately? I pushed it away and continued. 'That's what's wrong with my dad. He's so happy being mediocre, going to work every day, like just another ant.'

'Sounds like my dad,' said Danny. 'Except he's got all the ants working for him. Pardon the mixed metaphor, but he's the big cheese: Mr John Evans, MBE, head of Evans Inc, purveyor of plastics to the world.'

'Wow,' I said, 'I'm impressed. He sounds important.' So that was where the posh vowels in Danny's voice came from! Nobody in my family had letters after their name. The more I found out about Danny, the more of a mystery he became.

Danny shrugged. 'Don't be. He's not important to me.' He voice sounded flat and his body seemed to crumple inwards. The sparkle in his eyes had dimmed noticeably. It made me feel uncomfortable, like I'd intruded on something private.

'Hey,' I said, brightly, trying to lift his spirits. 'You know loads about me now. What about you, Danny Evans?'

'Daniel, ahem, Hector, ahem, Evans,' he said, with a mock-bashful look. I decided it was all right to laugh.

'I know, I know,' he sighed. 'I was named after my grandfather. That's how people with bad names get back at the world – they pass them on to their descendants. It's a cruel trick.'

'It could have been worse,' I ventured.

'Not much,' he said.

'Actually, you might be right,' I teased.

'Enough now,' said Danny, playfully slapping my leg. I felt the jolt of electricity again and found myself wishing he would leave his hand there. 'You don't know me well enough to take the piss.'

The funny thing is, I felt like I did. We'd only been chatting for fifteen minutes or so, yet it seemed as if I'd known him for years. I'd never felt so comfortable, so quickly, with anybody. With Danny I could be one hundred per cent myself.

Apparently fearing he'd offended me, he qualified his remark. 'Yet,' he stated.

'Does that mean you're planning to stick around?' I asked, surprised at my boldness.

'Absolutely, Naomi. I'm not going anywhere. Are you?'

The next hour passed in an instant. I was never any good at physics at school, but things like time travel and black holes in space have always made a kind of sense to me. Time is a strange concept – it's divided neatly into seconds, minutes and hours, but they're purely artificial; they don't really mean anything. A few minutes can seem like an eternity when you're a small child desperate to arrive at your destination, and likewise when you're grown up and unhappy or in pain. But whole hours can vanish inexplicably when you're immersed in conversation, drunk or enjoying yourself. When old people say they don't know where the years have gone, I genuinely understand what they mean.

I learned that Danny was twenty and an only child. He had gone to Oxford straight after A-levels to study English literature, but had dropped out, disillusioned, at the end of his first year. Presently, he was concentrating on The Wonderfulls, determined to make his band a success. He had done odd jobs for pocket money – waiting at tables, a stint behind a bar and in a record shop. Now that The Wonderfulls were regularly playing paid gigs he spent most of the week rehearsing and recording in the studio he'd built in the basement of his parents' house. His mother, an ex-model, filled her time organising charity functions and lunching with her friends. She left him to his own devices. He said she was cold and distant – like an icy blonde in a Hitchcock film. I didn't dare to ask about his father again.

'Do you fancy some food?' he asked, when I came back from a visit to the Ladies and there was a natural lull in our conversation. It was a quarter to ten and I was starting to feel weak and dizzy. While it's true that I hadn't eaten for hours and my empty stomach was now swimming in alcohol, I can't deny that my giddiness was in no small part due to the sheer adrenaline rush of being with Danny.

'Yes,' I said, with rather more enthusiasm than I'd intended. 'I'm starving. They do food here, don't they?'

'They do, but I know somewhere much nicer. Trust me.'

'OK.' I smiled as he helped me put on my coat. I was all thumbs and elbows and, once again, his touch made me quiver. He stroked the fake fur collar, smoothing down the pile with the palm of his hand. 'Nice coat.'

'Thanks. I got it in a vintage shop. It's from the 1950s, I think.'

'You have great style, Naomi. Very individual. That's just one of the many things I'm beginning to like about you.'

He linked his arm through mine and took me to an Italian restaurant about half a mile up the road. La Casa Nostra was newly opened – it still smelled of fresh paint – and I'd read about in the newspaper. Its proprietor was an ex-footballer and it attracted the local celebrity crowd, those who didn't want to make the trip into central London. People went there to be seen, rather than to eat – although the chef was supposed to be excellent. It was the last place I had expected Danny to take me. Like Yellow, it didn't fit with his scruffy, musician's persona. I wondered if he was trying to impress me or whether this was the sort of place he went to all the time. And how could he afford it? Even regular gigs and stints behind a bar couldn't bring in that much.

I'd never have gone there without him; just walking through the front door was an intimidating experience. Even though I was 'nicely' brought up, posh, trendy restaurants make me feel insecure and clumsy. I don't know which cutlery to use or when to thank the waiter.

Danny must have noticed the anxiety in my face. 'Don't worry,' he said. 'They're really nice in here. I used to work in a pub with the guy behind the bar – he'll see you're all right.'

We were shown to a small table by the window, decorated with a thin glass vase containing a single orchid. As the waiter pulled out my chair he discreetly removed a 'Reserved' sign from the table. Danny saw that I'd noticed and smiled. 'I hope you don't mind. I was optimistic about tonight.'

'How did you know we'd get on?' I asked.

'I just knew,' he said, looking directly into my eyes with an intensity that seemed almost like sadness. 'There was something about you. Even on the bus, I just knew.'

I stared back at him, speechless. If anyone else had given

me this line, I'd have laughed at loud. But it wasn't corny when Danny said it because *I* knew too – because I felt exactly the same.

Even if I'd known how to respond, I didn't get the chance – the waiter arrived to take our order. When we received our meals, the portions were small, but the food was delicious. We each had a taste of one another's courses and Danny bemoaned the fact he hadn't ordered the same pasta dish as me – with asparagus, wild mushrooms and a saffron sauce. He insisted that we both have dessert, daring me not to agree that the chocolate mousse was the best I'd ever tasted.

'You win,' I conceded, as the last spoonful of creamy sweetness melted on my tongue.

'In that case,' he teased, his eyes twinkling, 'I get to choose my prize.'

'Yes . . . ?'

'Um,' he said, scratching his head comically. 'Let's see. I know . . . you let me take you out again.'

'What a cruel and unusual punishment!' I cried, playing along. 'OK, but I must let you know how painful it will be for me.'

'I know exactly how to torture a woman,' he said in a terrible imitation of a German accent. He laughed at himself. 'How about Sunday? Sunday daytime. I know just the place. But I'm not going to tell you where yet. You'd better give me your number so I can text you tomorrow . . . in code, of course.'

'I'm definitely free on Sunday,' I said. 'You're making it sound very mysterious, Mr Evans.'

He took out a chewed-up biro from his inside jacket pocket and handed it to me. 'Your number?' he asked. I rummaged inside my bag and found an old receipt, turned it over and wrote my details on the plain side. When I passed it to Danny he studied it intently, as if he was committing the digits to memory, before putting it away.

'Tell me,' I asked, 'What would you have done if you'd lost the bet?'

'I never lose,' he said, his tone unexpectedly serious. Then he winked and I laughed, but I still wasn't convinced that he'd said it in jest.

By the time the waiter had cleared away our coffee cups and brought the bill it was well after midnight. Danny insisted on paying, which was fortunate, as it came to almost my week's salary. *How can he afford it?* I asked myself, for the second time that evening. *I must not get used to living like this*, I noted. *Next year I'll be a student living on baked beans and pot noodles.*

As we were handed our coats I wondered what Danny had planned for Sunday – the excitement was rising within me and I didn't know how I'd get through the next day. Only a few hours before, Danny had been a virtual stranger. Now I couldn't imagine a full thirty-six hours without him. See, time *is* a crazy concept, isn't it?

Danny walked me home, slowly, with his arm draped around my shoulders. The difference in our heights meant that I fitted neatly into his side and I felt safe, as if I belonged there. Whenever we stopped to cross a road he'd take my hand, sliding each of his fingers between mine.

Every time he did it I felt my cheeks flush and I hoped that in the darkness he couldn't tell. We talked all the way, learning more about each other's CD collections and swapping stories about our travels. I'd never been further than Europe, but Danny told me he'd spent the previous summer travelling in Sri Lanka with a friend. He said it was the most beautiful place on earth and the people were the most friendly and hospitable he'd ever met. He'd promised himself he would go back one day, but first there were many other places to see, like Thailand, Australia and India.

He described his pride and joy to me: a Fender Telecaster guitar, which he'd received as an eighteenth birth-day present. Just thinking about it made him animated. He was like a small child – bright-eyed and breathless – unself-consciously imagining it in his arms and stroking it as if it were a treasured pet. His enthusiasm for it was so sweet, so infectious, that I had an urge to stop and hug him, right there in the middle of the street.

We were already beginning to create our own shared language, our own in-jokes. It seemed to happen organically. At some point in the evening, I don't remember when, he had re-christened me Omi and then I became Omi Wan Kenobi, after the character in *Star Wars*. On cue, I'd done my finest Alec Guinness impression, reciting, 'May the Force be with you.' Although I didn't particularly like the moniker, I loved the fact that Danny had given it to me. We laughed about a woman in the restaurant whose skirt was so tight that she could barely sit down. Danny did an impression of her struggling into her chair and then I, rather more used to negotiating clingy skirts and high heels, showed him how to do it properly.

All the way home I was aware of what was coming: the inevitable kiss, our first kiss. The anticipation was almost unbearable and at the same time, intensely pleasurable. Each time he touched my fingers, dwarfing my hand in his, I felt electric currents course throughout my body. I wanted the kiss to happen and I wanted it to be over. It hung over me like a cloud heavy with nerves; a good kiss would be a flawless ending to a wonderful evening, a clumsy one might spoil it all.

'This is me, then,' I said, hesitantly, as we arrived at my garden gate. My pulse was thundering in my ears and my teeth were chattering, even though I wasn't cold. All the lights in my house were off and, in the poor lamp light, I could barely see Danny's face. We stood silently for a second, looking at each other and then Danny took both my hands in his. I could feel him trembling too.

'Goodnight, Omi,' he said, softly. 'Thank you for a lovely evening.' Gently dropping my hands, he leaned towards me, placing his arms around me and drawing me into his body. He was so much taller than me that he had to stoop, and I instinctively cradled his face in my palms. And then he kissed me, tenderly at first, then more passionately. His lips were soft and full, his tongue warm and strong. I felt feather-light, as if my feet were hovering above the ground. It was the perfect kiss.

If only things could have remained that perfect. If only time could have stopped and Danny and I could still be standing outside my front door in the darkness, holding each other. If I could climb into a time machine right now, I'd go back to that moment. And stay there, forever.

<h1 style="text-align:center">Chapter 5</h1>

When Danny had disappeared up my street (he looked back twice – I counted, naturally), and the sensation of his kiss had faded from my lips, I realised there was nothing for it but to resume normality and go into my house. Assuming everybody was asleep, I turned my key in the lock as quietly as I could and closed the front door behind me with a gentle push.

I didn't want to go straight to bed, so I went into the living room and curled up on the sofa, arranging the cushions around my body like a cocoon. I wasn't really sure what I was doing there, or how long I'd stay, but it didn't seem right to end *this* day like any other, and I wasn't tired. In fact, I was wide awake with excitement. I went over and over the date in my mind, replaying every word of every conversation, every look and every touch. I felt the urge to write it all down, but thought better of it. It seemed too contrived. I didn't keep a diary; I'd tried several times when I was younger, always finding it too much effort to maintain for more than a few weeks.

I must have fallen asleep where I sat because when I next looked at my watch it was three a.m., I was cold and could feel a pull in my neck. 'Time for bed, Naomi,' I said, aloud, as I dragged my unwilling body up from the soft cushions. I stumbled on the stairs, going over on my ankle and banging my hand on the wooden banister as I tried to steady myself. I decided against going into the bathroom to take off my make-up and clean my teeth. It was too much effort and the sensation of water on my face would only wake me up. *One night won't hurt*, I told myself. A wise and sensible voice in my head said, *You'll only have yourself to blame if you wake up tomorrow with an enormous zit.* I chose to ignore it.

I opened my bedroom door, pulled off my clothes and left them where they fell. I intended to climb straight into bed, but then something – the half-conscious awareness of a presence in the room – made me jump. More alert now, with my eyes adjusting to the darkness, I could make out a silhouette, a figure, on my bed. For a brief moment I thought – or was it wished? – it might be Danny. Perhaps, not wanting our date to end, he had climbed in through my window and waited for me. But just as quickly, I knew the thought was ridiculous, the type of thing that only happens in books and films, and something which, in truth, would have terrified me. Of course, it could only be Emily.

She looked so peaceful, all curled up, with her fine hair fanned out on my pillow, that I didn't want to wake her. I thought about going to sleep in her room instead. But then she stirred and became aware that I was leaning over her. 'Nay?' she croaked, making an effort to sit up. Sleep still had a hold of her body and her coordination, and so she crumpled back down again.

'It's all right, Em,' I said softly. 'I'm home now. What are you doing here, on my bed? You silly thing – you're lucky I didn't squash you.'

My words jolted her awake. 'God, Nay,' she said, this time managing to prop herself up. 'Where have you been? I was so worried about you when you didn't call me, and I rang you so many times and you didn't pick up!'

Oh hell, now it was coming back to me. I'd promised Emily I'd go to the loo and ring her halfway through the date, to let her know I was OK and that Danny hadn't turned out to be some sort of weirdo. I was also supposed to tell her if I was bored and wanted her to call me and give me a random reason to leave – an escape plan. We'd even agreed on a code word, in case I couldn't find anywhere private. All I'd needed to say was, 'Is Simon over the chickenpox yet?' and she'd call back a few minutes later with a fictional emergency so pressing that I would have no option but to leave. How could I have forgotten? Because I was having such a great time with Danny, that's how.

'Oh Em, I'm so sorry. I just didn't think. I didn't need to call you and I didn't know you were trying to get hold of me.'

'It's all right. It's just that you're normally so reliable that I thought something must be up. So it was good, then? The date?'

I found myself smiling. 'Yes, it was amazing.'

'Really?' she gushed. 'Tell me all about it, right now. Every detail.'

Pleased to have an enthusiastic audience, I told Emily everything about the date, from the garlicky olives to the goodnight kiss. She 'oohed' and 'aahed' in all the right places, interrupting me to ask what I thought were trivial questions about which celebrities were in Yellow (none that I'd noticed), and whether I'd told Danny much about her (I lied and said he had asked when he could meet her properly). She also asked for rather more detail about the kiss than was strictly necessary. 'Pur-lease, Em,' I said when she began to get far too technical. 'If you want kissing tips, go and read a magazine.'

'Don't get all high and mighty with me,' she retorted, obviously embarrassed. 'I've kissed more boys than you.'

'Maybe so,' I conceded. 'But quality is more important than quantity, isn't it?'

'Charming!' she huffed, pouting at me. She yawned and stretched, then brought her arm round to her face and tried to make out the time from the dim fluorescent display on her watch. 'Blimey, Nay, it's four in the morning. I've got work tomorrow.'

'Sorry, Emily,' I said. 'Go to bed now. And thanks again.' I gave her a little hug, just like I'd done when she was little and had fallen over in the playground at our primary school, or one of the older girls had tried to bully her. We hadn't hugged for years – not since she was ten or eleven. After that, she'd seemed so disdainful of any physical contact with me. Now, she didn't seem to mind at all.

I slept fitfully, waking every hour or so. Consciousness brought with it the memory of the kiss. I'd lie in the dark, imagining Danny was kissing me again, giving myself butterflies and smiling until I could no longer keep my eyes open. When I finally awoke fully, it was midday. I could hear my parents moving about downstairs, murmuring to each other. They were probably discussing me, wondering when it would be late enough to come upstairs and drag me out of bed so they could grill me about my date. My ally, Emily, had long since gone out to her Saturday job. I would have to deal with them alone.

My clothes were scattered all over the bedroom floor. I stepped over them and went into the bathroom. When I peered into the mirror, the person who looked back was barely recognisable. She had hair the same colour as mine – chestnut brown with auburn streaks – but it was knotted and matted to her head on one side, frizzing over her shoulders on the other. Her eyes, like mine, were green, but they were puffy and half-closed, the lashes glued together with clumps of black mascara, which had also worked its way down her cheeks. Her nose was red, blotchy and shiny and her lips chapped and flaking. Looking at her appalled me.

After a shower, I felt more myself again. I made my way to the kitchen and poured myself a full pint of water from the tap, downing it in three gulps. My throat was dry and scratchy, like it is at the beginning of a cold. *All I need now is to get ill*, I thought to myself. *I've got to be on top form tomorrow. For Danny*. Just thinking his name made me smile.

Mum came into the kitchen and caught me grinning to myself. 'Good night?' she asked.

'Yes, thanks,' I said, unable to remove the smile.

'It must have been. You normally say, "It was all right," wherever you've been. So who is he? Emily said he was someone you met at work. Is he doing articles at the firm?'

So my parents had been fishing for information, then. Poor Emily. I had to admire her quick thinking – the story she'd come up with would surely have pleased Dad.

'What? Oh, no, Emily must have got confused. That's someone else.' There was no point perpetuating the lie. Now that I was to see Danny again – and hopefully not just the once – it would become too confusing in the long run. 'He's actually a musician.'

'Oh?' Mum was delighted. 'What does he play?'

'He's in the band I went to see the other night. He plays guitar and he sings. He's really good.'

'Who's good?' said Dad, appearing through the kitchen door. He made an exaggerated point of looking at his watch and then at me. 'Good morning!' he announced, sarcastically. 'So you're finally awake, then. Did you have a good night?'

'She did,' said Mum, smiling at me. I had her on side. 'She had a date with a musician.'

Dad looked perplexed for a moment. I could tell from the knot in his forehead that he was wondering whether the women in his house had once again conspired to keep him in the dark. 'Oh. And how old is he, this musician?'

'He's twenty,' I said, aware that my parents would consider this an acceptable age gap, since there were two years between them too.

'And what's his name?'

'He's called Danny. Danny Evans.' Knowing that Dad would be impressed by Danny's background, I continued: 'I think his dad is some sort of businessman. Plastics, or something. He's an MBE.'

'Ah,' said Dad, the tone of his voice changing from concerned to proud. 'John Evans. I know him. Very important man, gives a lot to charity. You know, Martha – he belongs to the Rotary club.'

Mum nodded, with disinterest. I had no doubt that she would rather hear about Danny's music.

'Well, well,' said Dad. 'So you're going out with John Evans's son.'

I didn't feel I should tell him that Danny didn't like his father – appeared to hate him even.

'So when do we get to meet this Danny, then?'

'Leave her alone, David,' Mum said, in the same voice she used to tell me and Emily off. 'She's only been on one date. I'm sure she'll let us meet him when she's ready.'

'Sure,' I said, already dreading that day. 'I don't want to scare him off. Maybe in a few weeks.'

Unlike Dad, Mum knew it was time for the cross-examination to end. 'Naomi, your dad and I are going into town to do some shopping. You're welcome to join us.'

'No thanks,' I said. 'I've got a few things to do myself.'

I had nothing to do, of course – just an afternoon to fill while I waited for Danny to text me about tomorrow's date. When my parents had left I went back up to my bedroom and tidied away my clothes. It took no time at all. After that, I decided to call Debbie, to tell her how the date had gone. I was a little disappointed that she hadn't called me first. I'd rung and told her how much I liked Danny and she knew it was my first date for many months. Wasn't she interested? I hoped that wasn't the case.

I couldn't find my phone and panicked, momentarily, until I remembered I'd left it in my coat pocket. The coat – which Danny had so admired – was hanging over the banister at the bottom of the stairs. *It is a beautiful coat*, I thought, stroking the collar, just as he had done. I was sure I could still make out the faint smell of his aftershave, or was that just dry-cleaning fluid?

I took out my phone and saw that it was switched off, just as Emily had said. I couldn't remember doing that. As soon as I switched it on it bleeped and shuddered violently; I had twenty missed calls and four messages – all from Emily. It was nice that she had been so concerned and, for the second time, I felt guilty that I hadn't called her. I played each message through before deleting it. Emily had started off with a cool, 'Hi, Nay, hope you're enjoying your date,' (giggle). 'Let me know who's in Yellow tonight'; progressing to a concerned, 'Are you all right, Nay? Please give me a call'; to 'Naomi – call me!'. Her last message was, 'I'm hoping you're OK, Naomi. I'm going to wait up for you.'

Debbie hadn't called once.

The phone rang about six times before Debbie picked up.

'Hi, Naomi,' she said. 'I was going to call you this afternoon. What are you up to?'

'Nothing much,' I said, annoyed that she appeared to have forgotten about my date. 'What about you?'

'I've got an essay to write. I should have done it last week, but you know what it's like.'

'What's it on?' I asked. I didn't care a jot, but it seemed the polite question.

'Something to do with the causes of the First World War. Pretty dull stuff. I'm hoping to get it done today because a group of us are going to head out on a trip tomorrow. Mike, the guy I told you about who lives in my halls, is driving us.'

'That's nice,' I said. I no longer felt like telling her about Danny and I wanted the conversation to be over as quickly as possible.

'So what's been happening with you? Oh yes, have you gone out with that guy yet?'

So she did remember.

'Yes, it was last night.'

'And?'

'And it was great. We had a really good time and I'm seeing him again tomorrow.' I left out all the detail because I could tell she didn't have time to hear it. The evening deserved to be more than an anecdote; I had hoped to give her a minute-by-minute account, so she'd be as excited about Danny as me.

'Are you upset with me, Naomi?' she asked, meekly. She knew it wasn't like me to be so concise.

'No,' I half-lied. I was upset, but I knew it wasn't entirely her fault. If only she wasn't so far away, then we could talk for hours, like we used to.

'Oh. You just don't sound like you, that's all.'

'Must be a bad line,' I said. 'Listen, I'd better go – I've

got to go and meet Emily. I'll call you tomorrow, after my date.'

'Please do!' she said, her voice rising an octave or two. She was trying to make up for her previous lack of enthusiasm. 'Actually, no, I'll call you – when we get back from our trip.'

'All right, then,' I said. 'Speak to you then.'

I put the phone down before she could finish saying goodbye. Was this what our friendship was going to be like from now on – snatched exchanges of headlines with no details? Then I had a little cry and decided to do the only thing that would cheer me up: I went shopping.

I was in the Topshop changing room, working my way through a pile of chocolate brown and khaki trousers, when my phone rang. Call me psychic, but I knew it was Danny before I saw his name come up on the screen. I had the butterflies to prove it.

'Naomi,' he said. I could only just hear him over the din of the music. 'How are you?' The intimacy we had shared the night before was gone and I was conscious once again of the odd inflections in his hybrid accent. We were strangers again, polite and nervous strangers.

'I'm good, thanks. How are you? Did you get home OK?'

'I'm good, yes, no hassle. Where are you? It's the middle of the afternoon, but if I didn't know better, I'd swear you'd gone clubbing.'

'You're almost right,' I said, laughing. 'I'm in Topshop.'

'Do you want to go outside? I can hardly hear you.'

'Um, yes, wait a minute.' I couldn't move. My trousers were round my ankles, my shoes buried under the reject-trouser pile. 'Actually, Danny, can I call you back in a few minutes? I'm in the changing room and I, er, need to get dressed first.'

'Oh, OK.' He sounded embarrassed. He wasn't the only one. 'Sorry.'

'I'll be literally two minutes, I promise.'

I pulled on my jeans and shoes as quickly as I could and rushed out of the changing room, handing a messy pile of trousers to the shop assistant. I hadn't put them back on their hangers and she tutted as I walked away. *Serves you right*, I thought, *for being so unhelpful when I asked for a different size.*

Once I was outside the store I paused to catch my breath. The high street was heaving with Saturday shoppers, and the roar of the traffic, with buses lined up end to end, was almost as loud as the music I'd escaped. I headed down a side street and found a small café with tables outside. Sitting myself down, I called Danny, using the 'Last Call Received' option. I wondered how long it would be before I knew his number off by heart. Would it be presumptuous of me – tempting fate – to put it on speed dial?

He picked up immediately. 'Hi there, I was beginning to think you'd changed your mind,' he said. 'Or are you wearing your entire wardrobe today?'

'I had to change into my Wonder Woman costume,' I joked. 'I'm out of practice. No, I thought I'd find somewhere I could actually hear you.'

'Good. Well, you know why I'm calling. It's about tomorrow.'

I felt a little sick. He wasn't going to cancel me, was he? Had he had second thoughts about me? 'Yes? Is it still all right? Weren't you going to text me?'

'I was,' he said. 'Well remembered. But I couldn't think of a clever enough code, so I gave up and thought I'd give you a call instead. I apologise.'

'Some spy you'd make, double-O Evans.' I cringed at my terrible joke. He kindly ignored it.

'So, if you still want to see me again, here's the plan. Meet me by the pond in King Edward's park at two p.m. And wear your Wonder Woman costume.'

'It's got to go to the dry cleaner's, I'm afraid. But two in the park sounds good. I'm intrigued. Are we going to feed the ducks?'

'Maybe,' he said. 'Maybe not. Enough questions – you'll have to wait and see. I'm looking forward to it.'

'Me too.' He had no idea how much. 'Bye, Danny. Take care.'

'Bye, Omi.'

And with a click, he was gone.

I went to bed early that night, but I couldn't sleep. Lying in so late and doing very little all day had left me with an excess of energy and no outlet for it. I tried to read for a while, but the words danced before my eyes. After scanning the same page three times, and absorbing none of it, I gave up. The truth was that I wasn't interested in the lives of the characters in the novel. I only wanted to know about Danny, to discover what the next day, the next chapter in *our* story, would bring.

Even then, I had an instinct that our burgeoning relationship was to be an important one for me, something that would mark and change me, that I would talk about in years to come. I'd had two 'serious' boyfriends before I met Danny, the first at fifteen and the second from sixteen to seventeen. I had cared for them both, but I had never really loved either of them, at least not in the way I believed love should feel. Both relationships had developed out of friendship, jogging along sweetly until I grew bored and felt it was kinder to put an end to things.

Mark, the boy who had made me the compilation CD, was the son of my parents' friends. We'd grown up together, spending summer Sunday afternoons at barbecues and evenings at each other's houses, ordered to play upstairs while our parents hosted dinner parties. By the time we'd turned fifteen, getting together seemed like the obvious thing to do; it would almost have been rude not to. It was the lazy option, so much easier for both of us than meeting a stranger at a party or youth club and enduring weeks of uncertainty, coded looks and gossip. To me, Mark represented familiarity and safety. We could practise kissing and fumbling with each other without any risk of getting hurt, or anybody else finding out.

The trouble was, I don't think I ever really fancied Mark – I thought of him as a mate and I assumed he felt the same way. It turned out that I was very wrong. When I broke up with him, one hot Tuesday afternoon in the summer holidays after our GCSEs (not long after he gave me the CD), he cried. He told me he'd thought we'd be together for years and that one day we'd get married. After that, he never spoke to me again.

My second proper relationship was with Jack, a guy who joined my school in the Sixth Form. We took the same classes and often found ourselves working on joint projects. We got together at his house while revising for a test and our relationship lasted the whole school year. I really fancied Jack – he had a mop of blond hair and an athletic build, a bit like David Beckham (though that's exaggerating his handsomeness). He was kind and sexy, but he was too much like hard work. He thought of himself as the strong, silent type – he rarely revealed what he was thinking or feeling and I'd have to drag it out of him. But what he had to say was never interesting enough to merit the effort. When he had his hair cut short, I did the same to our relationship.

Since Jack, there had been nobody special, just a few snogs at parties. I was impatient, ready for 'the real thing', for love and passion and excitement and intensity. And now, there was Danny, with his music and his dark lyrics and his ambition. You could say we were a perfect fit.

chapter 6

I've never been one for surprises – I don't like being thrown off guard and having to improvise. I always like to be prepared, to be wearing the right clothes and to have my things with me, just in case. What's more, I'm not a good actress – my real emotions are too transparent – and surprises are almost always a disappointment for me. Generally, I end up feeling guilty and the person who has gone to the trouble of surprising me wonders why they bothered.

So, while it was a lovely, romantic idea, Danny's surprise date had me fretting. You know where you are with a bar, restaurant, cinema or club – but a park? At the end of October? I had absolutely no idea what to wear (it might rain or be muddy), how much make-up to put on (bright sunshine can be unforgiving), and whether to shave my legs to the knee or all the way up. I was afraid I would be forced to do something I hated, like rollerblading, or something which might require me to take off my clothes and reveal my pale, untoned body, like swimming (which, I'll admit, was highly unlikely at that time of year). There were simply too many unknown quantities.

In the event, I left all my options open. I wore combats (hard-wearing, comfortable) and a pretty top (for glamour), draped a chunky, wool zip-up cardigan over my shoulders, and I packed my most compact umbrella in my shoulder bag, together with a swimming costume and a small towel – just in case – and my make-up bag. I shaved my legs from ankle to thigh, applied fake tan, waterproof mascara, concealer and long-lasting lipstick. I felt like a soldier, preparing myself for a campaign in a foreign country.

And, like every good soldier, I was on time, arriving at the park at fourteen-hundred hours prompt. Danny was late again – eighteen minutes and twenty three seconds late, if we're being (militarily) precise. On this occasion I had no doubt that he would turn up and I was merely annoyed. It may have been mid-afternoon, but I was alone in a wide open space and I felt vulnerable. I didn't even have anywhere to sit – there were no benches near the pond. It was a grey and sunless day, and I shivered, wishing I'd brought a coat. Still, waiting for Danny again, and now beginning to recognise that he had at least one flaw, made me less nervous about this, our second date.

I saw him before he saw me. He was walking up the path that leads from the main entrance of the park and snakes around its perimeter, branching off in several directions towards the pond or the tennis courts or the cricket pitch. He appeared to be carrying something heavy, which was causing him to stoop and making his progress uneven and slow. I wondered if I should run towards him and offer to help, but I didn't want to spoil his surprise. So I turned the other way and feigned intense interest in a family of swans swimming across the pond. When his footsteps drew close behind me, I pretended not to hear them and tried to stifle the smile that was involuntarily spreading across my face.

'Hello, Naomi,' he said, over my shoulder. He was panting. 'Are you ready for your surprise?'

Not as ready as I was twenty minutes ago, I felt like saying. He hadn't even apologised this time. But when I turned and looked at him, breathless and stiff-armed from carrying what was now obviously an enormous picnic basket, my irritation vanished. 'Absolutely,' I said, allowing him to kiss me on the cheek. The sensation of his lips on my skin again made my heart lurch. I ached for him to kiss me again, properly, like he had two nights before. 'Bring it on.'

'OK, but first you need to trust me. I'm going to blind-fold you. Is that all right?'

'Um, yes, OK.' I was nervous and excited at the same time. 'You're not going to push me in the pond, are you?'

'Not my style,' he said, smiling. 'Maybe it was, ten years ago, but no, what I've got planned does not involve dunking you.'

Danny placed his hands on my shoulders and I let him turn me around. Then I felt the caress of smooth fabric – it must have been silk – across my face, slipping over my ears and around the back of my head. He tied it loosely, smoothing down my hair with his palm. 'OK, now take my hand.'

We walked, awkwardly, for a few minutes, the picnic basket bashing into Danny's legs with each step. I humoured him by acting disoriented – it made him grasp my hand more tightly – but I could actually see the grass and the path through the bottom of my blindfold.

'We're here now,' he said, sighing with relief as he put down the picnic basket. 'You can stop.' He untied the blindfold, letting it drop to the floor at my feet. There, in front of me, was one of the most beautiful sights I had ever seen. The park's ancient gazebo had been decorated with multi-coloured flowers and ribbons and tinsel. There were even bunches of grapes hanging from its poles. It looked like something you'd see in an epic movie set in Roman times.

'Oh my God!' I exclaimed. Had Danny really done this just for me? When had he done it? I'd had no idea how thoughtful he was, how inventive. Worried that I might begin to cry, I hugged him, a little too tightly. Then, embarrassed, I pulled away.

'Do you like it?' he asked, trying to gauge my emotions from my perplexing expression.

'What do you think?' I laughed. 'It's beautiful. Thank you.'

Reassured, Danny then opened the enormous picnic basket, taking from it two large, green floor cushions, which he placed side by side within the gazebo. 'Now, if Madame would care to sit,' he suggested, bowing and waving his hand like a courtier. I stepped into the gazebo and sat myself down cross-legged, while he continued to unload the basket. He took from it two plates, two cups and two sets of plastic cutlery, which he spread out on a tartan blanket. Then he brought out the food, the majority of it in tiny portion-sized containers, which I recognised from the posh delicatessen on the high street. He must have spent a fortune. There were giant olives, feta cheese, a pasta salad, stuffed vine leaves, asparagus spears, sun-dried tomato bread, lemon hummus, rocket salad with parmesan shavings, Kettle Chips and honey-roasted almonds. For dessert there was an exotic fruit salad and strawberries dipped in chocolate. It was all my favourite food, everything I'd mentioned liking on our first date. There was even – somewhat incongruously – a bag of dolly mixtures, because I'd told him they were my favourite sweets when I was a child. I was so overwhelmed by his thoughtfulness and attention to detail that I couldn't speak.

'Is everything OK?' asked Danny, looking slightly anxious. 'Or would you rather we'd gone to McDonald's?'

'Very funny,' I said, resisting the urge to hug him again. 'It's gorgeous. Incredible. I just don't know what to say.'

He beamed. 'Don't say anything. Eat.'

As we enjoyed the food, Danny told me about The Wonderfulls' most important gig ever, which would take place in February at the 142 Club in town. 'There's going to be an A & R guy – a talent spotter – there from Excite Records,' he said. 'Word on the street is that they're looking to sign a band like us.'

'Wow,' I said. 'That's amazing.'

'It is, but we're going to have to get a hell of a lot of practice in between now and then.' He saw me looking downcast. 'Oh God, Omi, that didn't come out right. I didn't mean I won't be able to see you again. I want you to be part of it all and, with your extensive musical knowledge, you can give me feedback on some new songs.'

'Really?' I asked. 'Won't the others mind? I don't want to become some sort of Yoko Ono hate figure.'

'No,' he said. 'I'm the songwriter and the lead singer – it's my band, really. Don't worry about it. They're great guys – you'll like them. And they'll love you. As far as I'm concerned, from now on you're permanently on the guest list.'

We smiled coyly at each other, acknowledging that each of us saw a place for the other in our future, but not wanting to spell it out for fear of appearing too forward.

While we'd been in the park the sky had darkened considerably, and the clouds had brought with them an icy, damp wind. I didn't want to put my cardigan on properly because, suddenly self-conscious, I was sure the chunky wool made me look fat. Instead, I draped it over my shoulders and chided myself for not wearing a coat. Danny noticed me shivering. He was only wearing a T-shirt and thin leather jacket, yet he appeared immune to the cold, as men often seem to be. 'I've brought another blanket along,' he said. 'Why don't we wrap it around us?' He clambered up and went over to the basket, pulling out a soft, cream alpaca throw. I raised my eyebrows. If there was one thing I knew about, it was fabrics, and this was no picnic blanket.

'This is my mum's, actually,' Danny explained. 'She'd go mad if she knew I'd brought it, but she never uses it herself. Why waste it, eh?' He sat down next to me and draped the throw over us. It was only then I realised how much I'd been longing for this contact again. He was so close that I could feel the warmth of his body, and the anticipation of another kiss began to grow within me. I would have been happy to sit there with him like that for hours, but, within minutes, it had begun to drizzle, then to rain heavily. Fat droplets of water trickled through the sides of the gazebo, causing the ribbons, which Danny had so artfully arranged, to bleed red, blue and yellow.

'Shit!' he cried, as a globule of yellow water stained the throw. 'We'd better make a run for it! This rain is practically horizontal. There's a shelter over there. I'll come back for the picnic stuff later. Are you ready to go?'

'OK,' I said, picking up my bag and holding my cardigan together at my neck. He grabbed my hand and started running. His legs were so much longer than mine that I was being dragged along, my feet barely touching the ground.

'Stop a second,' he said, laughing at me. 'I've got an idea. Climb on my back.'

He bent over and I jumped on his back, flinging my arms around his neck as he grasped for my legs. I was aware that it was a long time since anybody had given me a piggy-back and, the last time, I'd been rather smaller and lighter. *I hope he doesn't think I'm a heifer*, I thought. As we moved, I was half on, half off, pulling Danny's T-shirt from his shoulder and accidentally kneeing him in the small of his back. Despite my discomfort, the sensation of his strong, muscular body beneath mine was tantalising. We were both giggling hysterically, becoming wetter and wetter and more bedraggled, and no longer caring.

Danny tipped me off his back at the entrance to the shelter. For a minute we just stood there laughing at each other. 'Whose stupid idea was it to have a picnic in October?' he said, raising his eyebrows in self-mockery. 'Now what do we do? We're both dripping wet, the food has gone swimming and I don't think there's much chance of getting served in here.'

We looked around us. The shelter was like a bus stop – a small metal hut with no front and a bench inside – except no buses would ever stop there.

'Hang on,' I said, as a realisation struck me. 'I've got a towel! See?' I pulled the towel from my bag and handed it to Danny. He took it gratefully, rubbing it over the top of his head and then across his face. He looked so cute wet, with his hair sticking out in all directions.

'Here, let me,' he said. He delicately pressed the towel to my face, wiping the droplets of water from my nose and my chin. The feel of his fingers on my face, even through the roughness of the towel, was thrilling and I stifled a sigh. Then he gathered my hair together at the back and wrapped the towel around it like a headdress.

He chuckled. 'Now you look like a nun,' he said. 'Which wasn't really my intention. Anyway, Naomi Waterman – an apt name if ever there was one, today at least – what sort of girl brings a towel on a date?'

'I used to be in the Brownies,' I said. 'You know, always be prepared.'

'I always am,' he said with a cheeky smile, as he moved closer.

What do two people on a second date do, alone in a shelter, while they wait for the rain to stop? They pick up where they left off at the end of the first date, of course. And so, at last, while the rain clattered on the roof, we kissed – for far longer and more ardently than the first time. It didn't seem possible, but it felt even better than I remembered. Our kiss on Friday had been a goodbye kiss to end our date. But this was a kiss that didn't have to end, a kiss full of expectation, of the promise of things to come. There was no awkwardness, no first-time nerves or fear of clashing teeth. We just fitted together, mouth on mouth. While we kissed, Danny stroked my neck and the small of my back, sending tingles down my spine. I had my hands up the sleeves of his jacket, caressing his strong arms and shoulders through his T-shirt.

Nothing mattered when I kissed Danny – not the fact that I was still damp and cold, or that the hard, wooden bench was bruising my bottom, or even that, from time to time, other people walked past us and stared. (In fact, I rather liked that. I felt proud to be seen with such a gorgeous guy.) When I closed my eyes and kissed him I was as warm and as comfortable as I could ever hope to be. We were alone together in our own little bubble.

Occasionally, we would break off to hold each other silently and gaze into each other's eyes, as if we were trying to see far beyond the iris and the pupil to somewhere deeper, to a place that was secret and hidden. Once, Danny said, 'You have the most beautiful eyes, Naomi. I've never seen eyes that green before.' And I, never very good at accepting a compliment, had to ruin the moment by looking away.

By the time it started to grow dark, shortly after five, the rain had virtually stopped. With his arms still wrapped around me, Danny said, 'Why don't you come back to my house? It's a lot warmer and drier there and I make a mean hot chocolate.'

'That sounds divine,' I said, looking up at him. I was still damp and my mouth was dry and sore from kissing. 'Is it far? You've never actually told me where you live.'

'No,' he said. 'It's just the other side of the park, and then a bit. And I've brought the car.'

I was expecting Danny to drive a beaten-up old Ford or, perhaps, a Mini. But the only car in the car park was a red two-door, convertible sports car. I know barely anything about cars, but even I could tell it was expensive and very flash.

'I apologise for the car,' said Danny, in advance of any comment. 'My dad got me this when I passed my driving test. I think it was some sort of tax dodge for him. I loathe it – it's pretentious and brash and totally not me. I'd rather take the bus than drive this. I only brought it today because that picnic basket – which I *will* go back for later – is so bloody heavy.'

First Yellow, then the swanky restaurant, and now this car? And yet Danny said it was pretentious and brash. But he still drove it? I was confused. Was he worried that his wealth would put me off him? But then why had he taken me to those places? He was nothing if not contradictory. But, then again, I liked his air of mystery, the challenge of putting the pieces of the puzzle together.

He held open the car door for me and I climbed in. I'd

never been in a fast, expensive car before and just sitting there made me feel special, older and more sophisticated. I imagined myself arriving at a film premiere, flash bulbs popping from every angle. But, after what he'd just said, it didn't seem prudent to share my fantasy with Danny. Instead, I said, 'Yes, it's a bit over the top. I can see why you don't like it.'

If the car had surprised me, Danny's house was an even bigger shock. I knew his dad was a successful businessman and therefore, by implication, wealthy, but I had still imagined that his house would look like mine: a three-bedroom, semi-detached, with a front and back garden and a small garage. Pretty much everyone I knew lived in houses like that – suburban town houses built for mums and dads and their two-point-four kids. The hedges, doors and windows may have differed slightly, but the homes of all my family and friends were variations on a theme.

Danny's house was built to a different tune altogether. It was on one of the most exclusive streets in the area, where the residents hired private security guards and put up electric fences and surveillance cameras. It was set back from the street, at the end of a drive with electronic gates, which opened when Danny's car approached. I tried not to gasp when his house came into view. It was huge – at least four times the size of mine – and three storeys high, with a garden almost as big as the park. There were at least four cars parked outside, one of them just like Danny's, but in electric blue.

'Don't say anything,' said Danny sharply. 'I know what you must be thinking – that I'm some spoiled little rich kid who doesn't know he was born. I don't like living here; I'd rather be in a bedsit any day. It's just convenient, till I make The Wonderfulls a success. I don't want anything else to do with my parents or their filthy money!'

It was the first time I'd seen Danny so defensive. 'It's OK,' I said nervously. 'I'm not going to judge you. I like you for you. I don't care about where you live or what car you drive. Honestly.'

That seemed to reassure him. He squeezed my hand and smiled. 'All right, Naomi,' he said, in a calmer, gentler voice. 'Come in and get warm and I'll make you a hot chocolate.'

Danny had his own kitchen, in his own 'granny flat' at the side of his parents' house. It was entirely separate from the rest of the house, except it didn't have its own front door – you had to go through the main hall to get to it.

While he made the chocolate, he sent me off to look around his flat. He also had his own living room, bathroom, study (which he used as a storage room for his guitars) and a very messy bedroom (he must have forgotten he'd neglected to tidy it). His studio, which I didn't see that day, was in the basement, accessed by a flight of stairs from the kitchen. I gave each room a cursory glance; I didn't enjoy looking around on my own because it felt intrusive.

'How long have you lived in here?' I asked, coming back into the kitchen.

'Since I was sixteen,' he said, without looking up. He was stirring vigorously. 'My parents got sick of my noise and having my friends traipsing through their house and getting mud on their cream carpets. So they set me up in here and left me to my own devices.'

'You're lucky,' I said. 'I don't have any privacy.'

He shrugged. 'Maybe.'

We sat close together on Danny's leather sofa and sipped our hot chocolate in blissful silence. It was delicious – nothing like the powdered stuff I had at home, but thick and creamy, like warm, liquid chocolate mousse. I dreaded to think how many calories it contained. When Danny had cleared our cups away he asked if I minded if he played his guitar. 'I want to play you a few songs,' he said. I told him I'd love to hear them.

For the next couple of hours, he serenaded me, playing a mixture of his own compositions and some covers – Bowie, Nirvana, Oasis and Coldplay. It was good to hear stark, acoustic versions of The Wonderfulls' songs, without the frenzied guitars and heavy drums. Some of them were actually quite beautiful and tugged at my emotions with their aching melodies in minor keys. Where I could, I joined in, singing the harmony parts. Danny said he was impressed, that I had a sweet voice.

'We should get you in the band, doing backing vocals,' he said. I wasn't sure how seriously to take him, so I just blushed and smiled. The idea of standing up on stage and singing horrified me. The last time I'd tried – in a school concert five years before – I'd had such terrible stage fright that I'd dried up entirely, standing fixed to the stage in silent terror until one of the teachers rescued me.

When Danny's fingers grew tired of playing, he put

down his guitar and went into the kitchen to make us toasted cheese sandwiches. After we'd eaten and wiped the globules of melted cheese from our chins, he dimmed the lights, lit some candles and put on a chill-out CD. Then he spread himself out on the sofa and motioned that I should join him. I snuggled into his body, resting my head on his chest and hooking my legs around his so that I didn't fall off the edge. He stroked my hair and my face, placing his other arm around my waist. Self-consciously, I held in my tummy for as long as I could. For a while we just lay there, listening to each other's breathing, our eyes closed. From time to time he would pull me up towards him, so that I was almost lying on top of him, and we would kiss.

It's almost impossible to describe how good I felt. 'Nice' or 'warm' or 'lovely' or 'wonderful' or 'content' just don't sum it up. When you're a child and you have a tummy-ache and someone asks you what type of pain it is, you can't say, because you don't have the words to explain it – so you just say 'it hurts'. It was the same with the pleasure I felt while I was with Danny. I simply don't have the words in my vocabulary to explain it. All I knew was that I really couldn't be happier, physically or emotionally.

We must both have fallen asleep because when I next opened my eyes the candles had burned themselves out and the CD had finished playing. Trying not to wake Danny, I sat up and looked at my watch. It was eleven o'clock. I tiptoed into the bathroom and splashed some water on my face. My hair was dishevelled, my lips slightly swollen, and the skin around them red from kissing.

I heard Danny coming into the bathroom behind me. 'Hello, Omi,' he said, smiling. He yawned and stretched, rubbing his eyes with his hand. The side of his face was imprinted with creases and lines from the sofa. 'Are you OK?'

'Yes,' I said. 'Apart from a bit of stubble rash.'

He grinned. 'Occupational hazard.'

'Have you seen the time?' I asked. 'My parents will be worrying about me.'

He looked down at his watch. 'It's too late to go home now,' he said. 'Why don't you stay on the sofa? Call home while I go and get you a duvet and pillow.'

I hesitated before pulling my mobile phone out of my bag. Was 'sleep on the sofa' a euphemism for something I wasn't ready for? No, Danny deserved the benefit of the doubt. He had given me no reason not to trust him; he was so gentle and thoughtful.

I decided against calling my parents – I knew they would already be in bed. So, I texted Emily instead. HI EM. IT'S L8 SO STAYING WITH D'S PARENTS. TL M+D NT 2 WORRY. C U 2MORROW. NX

I knew she'd received it because a few moments later my mobile beeped and there was a message in return. It read: OK B GOOD X

'Everything all right?' asked Danny. I hadn't noticed him come back in. I nodded, a little shyly. He was carrying a double duvet and two pillows, which he must have taken from his own bed. He also had with him a huge, white T-shirt. 'For you to sleep in,' he said, handing it to me.

I went into the bathroom to change and squeezed out some of Danny's toothpaste, which I swished around my mouth with my finger. Once again, I conceded that I wouldn't be able to remove my make-up. *Danny really isn't good for my skin*, I thought. *But who cares?* I would gladly have endured a faceful of zits if it meant that I could spend the whole night just a few feet from Danny. *Just a few feet* . . . The realisation made me feel uneasy and excited at the same time. Did he intend to stay in his room all night, or would he tiptoe in to join me in the early hours? *No*, I decided again, *from all the evidence I've seen today I'm certain that Danny really is the perfect gentleman.*

When I came back into the living room I saw that he had already made up the sofa. He pulled the duvet aside and waited for me to climb in, before smoothing the cover over me. Nobody had tucked me in like that since I was a little girl.

'Goodnight, Omi,' he said, leaning over to give me one last, lingering kiss. He paused, as if he couldn't make up his mind about something, and then stroked my cheek. 'I'll see you in the morning,' he whispered. 'Sweet dreams.'

'Good night,' I said, smiling up at him. I felt happy and warm and protected. Looking back, I think it was at exactly *that* moment that I started truly loving Danny.

Chapter 7

I came round to the sound of a distant vacuum cleaner. Danny was standing over me, holding a cup of tea. He was wearing just a T-shirt and boxer shorts and I couldn't help noticing how unexpectedly good his legs were – strong and toned, like a footballer's.

'Good morning,' he whispered. 'That's just the cleaning lady in the main house. Don't worry, she doesn't come in here on Mondays.'

'What time is it?' I croaked.

'About ten,' said Danny. 'Pretty early for me, actually.'

'Ten? Oh my God!' I sat up, forgetting for an instant how dreadful I must look and then wishing I could hide back under the duvet. 'It's Monday. I was supposed to be at work an hour ago!'

'Oh.' Danny sounded disappointed. 'I suppose I could drive you there if you want.'

'But I haven't got my work clothes with me.' Now I was panicking.

'Calm down, Omi. It's not the end of the world. Look, why don't you call in sick and we can spend the day together.'

'No, I can't. I mean I shouldn't. Oh, I don't know!'

'What are they going to do to you? Arrest you?' he

gently mocked. 'Hang you? I don't think so. Go on, live dangerously.'

I thought about it for a second and then realised Danny was right. Calling in sick was simpler than going home, getting changed and then being two hours late. How would I explain that? And what could they do to me, anyway? I hadn't taken any time off sick before, not even when I genuinely didn't feel well. Surely one day was acceptable. They probably wouldn't even miss me.

'OK, I'll do it,' I said, before I could change my mind again. 'Danny Evans, you are a bad influence.'

I insisted that Danny leave the room and sent him off to get dressed while I made the call. I was worried I'd burst out laughing if I saw his face. I'd previously told him that my boss, Mr Stevens, was a stickler for discipline and Danny had done a wicked impression, marching around the room like a sergeant major, shouting 'Attention!'.

As I'd anticipated, the phone was answered by Kathy, the office receptionist.

'Hello, Kathy,' I said, in the huskiest voice I could muster. 'I'm really sorry, but,' (cough) 'I'm not very well today.'

'Oh, you poor love,' said Kathy, with so much sympathy that I felt guilty. 'You sound terrible. Don't you worry, I'll tell Mr Stevens. Now go back to bed and we'll see you when you're better.'

'Thanks,' I whispered, adding another cough for effect. 'I'm sure I'll be much better tomorrow.'

I hung up, sighing deeply. Danny had been waiting just

outside the door and he now came back in, grinning broadly. 'See, it wasn't so bad,' he said. 'Now drink your tea and then we'll decide what to do with the day.'

Content, he sat down next to me, leaning back against the cushions and crossing his legs. It was the first time I had seen him close up and jacketless, in sunlight. He was wearing a clean grey T-shirt and faded black jeans, which still smelled of washing powder. His forearms were lean and muscular, with a light covering of dark hair, and I could see his veins protruding. And then, when he stretched out his left arm towards me – I think he was intending to take my hand – I saw something else: a long, spidery pinkish mark, like an old scar. Next to it, there were other marks, some redder, some whiter, etching up and down his arm like doodles in a sketchbook.

'What's that?' I asked.

'What?' he exclaimed, surprised, snatching back his arm as if from a fire.

'That,' I said, pointing to the big scar. 'Did you hurt yourself? Was there an accident?'

He furrowed his brow. 'Yes,' he said. 'That's right, I had an accident, at school, a long time ago. It was nothing.' He appeared to shrink back from me, pulling himself up straight and staring into the distance. The action told me: *I don't want to talk about this now.*

'Poor Danny,' I said. My instincts told me there was more to it, but I didn't want to spoil what promised to be a perfect day. 'Poor Danny.' I didn't know what else to say, so I left it at that.

* * *

We spent a wonderful day together. I said I'd prefer not to go out anywhere, in case I bumped into someone from work, so we stayed in, listening to music and chatting about our pasts and our friends. We were filling each other in on the background to our lives, swapping anecdotes and memories. That's the funny thing about new relationships – you feel closer to your lover than to anyone else and yet you know virtually nothing about them, or they you. I didn't know what Danny's favourite colour was (he said green, like my eyes, but I think he was trying to flatter me), or whether he could dance or swim (he claimed he could do both, and well). He didn't know that I had broken my leg on a school trip to France five years earlier, or that I had a pet rabbit that had died, leaving me heartbroken when I was seven. I found out that Danny had appeared in a TV advert for a breakfast cereal when he was four; he was too embarrassed to show me the video clip and made me promise never to mention it again.

Telling each other these things is very important – you never know when the knowledge might come in handy.

'I'll remember never to order rabbit, then, when we go out to eat,' said Danny, with a dark grin.

'And I won't mention porridge. Ever,' I said, giggling.

I told Danny about Debbie and Holly and Natasha, and how much I missed them. I said I was certain he'd like them too and that he must meet them when they came home. He agreed, but, looking back, he didn't seem all that interested. He didn't ask many questions about my friends – not like I did when we discussed his – he just nodded and 'uh-huhed' in all the right places. I put it down to his being a 'bloke', but, if I'm honest, I was feeling a little hurt. My friends were important to me; I wanted them to be important to Danny too.

At the start of the day I'd made Danny promise that he would drop me home by four in the afternoon, so I could shower and change before Mum got back. I'd already decided I would pretend I had been to work and had simply left early. So, at three-fifteen, while Danny was showing me around his studio, trying (and failing) to impress me by twiddling various knobs and pressing odd buttons, I said, 'Danny, I think I'd better go home now.'

'Oh, Omi,' he said. 'Stay a bit longer. Can't you?'

'No.' I was insistent. If Dad found out I had skipped work I would never hear the end of it. I didn't want to tell Danny my reasons – he might have thought me childish.

'Go on,' teased Danny, tickling me under my chin. 'Just a few minutes.'

I giggled and squirmed. 'No, please, Danny. Now. Anyway, you've got to go and pick up the picnic basket from the park. If it's still there, which I doubt.'

'OK,' he said, with the exaggerated pout of a petulant little boy. 'I'll go and get my jacket and keys and your stuff. Wait for me in the hall by the front door.'

Danny took ages. I paced up and down the hall, stopping to admire the paintings on the wall (all originals) and the vases and other ornaments displayed on the sideboard. In my house we had vases from IKEA and Habitat, but the ones in Danny's house looked like museum pieces. I was carefully turning one around, so I could admire the ornate decoration on its handle, when I thought I heard the front door creak open behind me.

'Hello,' said a woman, with a deep, throaty and rather posh voice. 'And who might you be?' I jumped and turned simultaneously, almost knocking over the vase. The woman was extremely tall and elegant, with blond, sculpted hair. She was wearing an expensive–looking navy trouser suit and her make-up was perfectly applied, from her brown, pencilled-in brows to her blood-red talons.

'I'm Naomi,' I said, only too conscious of my own dismal appearance. I was wearing yesterday's muddy combats and I'd finger-combed my hair and applied new make-up over the remnants of the old. 'Hello.'

I moved forward to shake her hand, but she ignored me. Then she looked at me with disgust, as if I were a creature who had just stepped out of a swamp.

'Naomi who?'

'Naomi Waterman.' As soon as I said it I realised she hadn't wanted my surname. 'Er, Danny's Naomi.'

'I see,' she said, smirking. 'Well, I'm Danny's mother, Caroline Evans. I take it Danny is with you, or have you just wandered into my house on your own?'

Now I was upset. Why was this woman being so horrible to me? My mother would never have treated my friends or a boyfriend like this. She wouldn't have treated *anyone* like this.

'Of course not. Danny's gone to get his jacket so he can take me home. Sorry, I guess you didn't know I was here.'

She smirked again. 'Danny doesn't tend to talk to me about his girlfriends.' Perhaps I was being oversensitive, but I was sure she emphasised the 's'. 'Or,' she continued, 'very much at all, these days. I think it's easier for both of us that way.'

She walked towards me, and, for a second, I thought she was going to touch me, but then it became apparent that she was making for the stairs. 'Goodbye, Naomi,' she said as she went past. 'I trust you enjoyed your visit to my home.'

I must have looked shell-shocked, because when Danny appeared a minute or so later, the first thing he said was, 'What's the matter, Naomi? Are you OK?'

'Yes,' I said. 'I just met your mother.'

He nodded. 'That explains it. Did she give you a hard time?'

'Not really, but she wasn't very friendly.'

'Like I told you,' Danny spat. 'She's a cold bitch.'

The rage behind his words was chilling; I had never felt hate like that, and certainly not for my mother. I thought, *She must really have hurt him. What on earth did she do?* I was suddenly aware how little I knew about Danny's past, that he had lived twenty whole years before he met me. It made me feel uneasy.

I laughed nervously. 'I'm sure she's not that bad. Come on, Danny, please take me home now.'

'Sure,' he said, opening the front door. He put his arm around me and kissed me on the top of my head. I saw that he was smiling, but only with his mouth. His eyes were focused somewhere else, somewhere dark and desolate.

Chapter 8

The next few months were blissful. Danny and I spent as much time together as we could. He would pick me up from work and take me out for meals (I started to insist on paying half, even though it meant dipping into my university savings), or we'd go to the cinema or to a bar. At weekends we'd go to markets or galleries or tiny festivals in venues I didn't know existed, to hear performers that he'd read about in some obscure magazine. He opened my eyes to the city I'd lived in all my life, pointing out curiosities I wouldn't have noticed alone – a piece of ancient Roman wall on a modern street or a bizarre wig shop run by a couple in their eighties. When I was with Danny I saw the world in technicolour; it was like putting on a pair of 3-D glasses.

Sometimes we'd just stay in at his flat, have a takeaway and talk until the early hours. Whenever we were apart we were constantly on the phone, chatting and texting at every opportunity. I'd wake up to a HELLO message (usually sent in the small hours) and go to sleep reading, SWEET DREAMS, OMI.

Every minute that I spent with Danny made me fall in love with him a little more. I loved his spontaneity. I loved the way he turned up his nose and pouted when he was confused or deep in thought. I loved his funny little habits – the way he drank his tea, always taking a sip when it was still too hot and then appearing genuinely surprised when, once again, it burned his lips. I loved knowing that he kept all my texts, refusing to delete even the most mundane one until his message box was full. I loved the fact that he didn't appear to notice my flaws; he'd tell me how beautiful I looked without make-up and that he thought my body was perfect. He even laughed at my feeble jokes and when I mixed up my words; to him they were idiosyncracies, not idiocies.

There were thoughtful gestures, too. When, for example, I mentioned how much I enjoyed photography, he dug out an old Brownie box camera from his parents' attic and asked me to show him how to use it. Weeks after a silly conversation about sweets, during which I'd told him how I liked yellow ones best, he presented me with a jam-jar full of miscellaneous yellow sweets: wine gums, fruit gums and fruit pastilles, jellies and boiled sweets. He said he'd collected them from every packet he'd eaten and joked about the huge price he'd soon have to pay in dental bills. I later discovered that he had, in fact, been to his local supermarket, bought sackfuls of every tube and packet available, and carefully removed all the yellow sweets one by one, before discarding the rest.

He'd sit through *Friends* with me, even if it was an episode he'd seen at least three times before. He would come with me to watch tacky, romantic films because I had nobody else to see them with and, afterwards, he'd try to think of something good to say about the plot or the actors.

He'd cut stories out of newspapers if he thought I'd find them interesting and he'd scout eBay for vintage clothes I might like to check out. When I had a cold he tucked me up on his sofa and brought me gallons of freshly squeezed orange juice and made me tomato soup and boiled eggs with soldiers because I'd told him that was my favourite comfort food.

I could go on and on. I could probably fill a whole book with lists of what I liked about Danny. But no amount of examples would sum up why I felt so strongly about him. What makes you love someone has little to do with the number of wonderful qualities they possess. It's about glimpsing something inside them that nobody else can see and realising you've always needed it, even though you didn't know you were looking. It's about inventing a reality that is true only for the two of you.

Meeting Danny on the bus no longer seemed like mere accident. It was fated: I had been meant to catch that particular bus because Danny would get on it. This belief was sealed when Danny told me that he'd seen another bus coming first, but had made a split-second decision not to run for it. It didn't occur to me that he might have felt too tired or too lazy to run; it was simply meant to be. I credited other coincidences with the same, irrational significance: the fact that we had matching birthmarks on our collarbones, for example, gave us a unique bond. I ignored the probability that thousands of other people probably had a birthmark in the same place.

Whenever I thought about Danny my heart beat faster

and it brought a strange sensation – half pleasure, half nausea – to the pit of my stomach. It made me smile to myself and flush all over. I knew that what I felt for Danny must be love – at least, this was how I'd always imagined love to be – but somehow I could never say it. Even though the things he said and did made me fairly certain he felt the same way, there was a tiny part of me that was afraid he might not say 'I love you' back. What if he were to laugh? Or say, 'Sorry, Naomi, I like you a lot, but I don't feel like that about you.' I didn't want to risk breaking the spell. Sometimes, we'd look at each other for long, silent minutes, and the words would be on the tip of my tongue, but I'd swallow them back down again. I needed to hear them from him first.

Christmas was an ordeal that year, because it meant four whole days away from Danny. He was spending it with friends and had invited me to join him, but I didn't even dare ask my parents. Missing our annual family celebration would be considered a crime almost on a par with mugging an old lady – so heinous that I might as well pack my bags and never return. So, as always, Dad drove us up to Nottingham to stay with my uncle's family. In the past I'd always looked forward to it. I'd enjoyed packing the car with presents to be opened on Christmas morning and I liked spending time with my younger cousins. But that year, every mile on the motorway was another mile further from Danny. I didn't care what my parents had bought me (even though I got the funky speakers for my iPod that I'd wanted for months), and I couldn't be bothered to help the little ones put batteries in their new toys. On Christmas Day, all I was interested in was having some time to myself, so I could open Danny's present.

I finally unwrapped it late in the afternoon, in the guest bedroom I shared with Emily, while the children were happily playing and my older relatives were dozing on the sofas. I was like a little girl all over again, fumbling at the shiny paper, desperate to see inside. Danny had bought me a gorgeous, sea-green cashmere sweater – the softest, most beautiful thing I'd ever seen, let alone owned. It was almost too nice to wear. For a while, I just hugged it, as if it were a teddy bear, thinking warm thoughts about Danny and giving myself butterflies.

Emily came into the room while I was trying it on. 'Wow!' she exclaimed enviously. 'It's lovely, Nay.' Then she peered at the label – from a posh, designer shop – and raised her eyebrows. 'How can he afford it?'

'I dunno,' I said. 'His gigs, maybe? Or his savings? I think he also got some money when his grandad died.' But the same thought had crossed my mind. I'd pushed it away, as I always did then. I had no time for such thoughts, for questions without resolution.

'What did you get him?'

'Some CDs and a really nice, leather-bound book for him to write his songs in.'

'Oh,' she said.

'I know.' I'd spent hours choosing Danny's presents, but now they seemed inadequate.

'God, Nay, he must really like you.'

'Do you think?' I asked, smiling. 'I really miss him. I know it's only for a few days, but it feels like forever.'

'Wow,' she said. 'You're really smitten.'

'I think he's the one, Em. He totally gets me, you know? I think he's my soulmate.'

Emily was embarrassed. We'd talked about Danny before, of course, but I hadn't gone this far with her. She wasn't a romantic like me and she preferred to keep her feelings hidden. 'I've never seen you like this,' she said, for once, apparently at a loss for words. 'I'll leave you alone, so you can call him.'

It was the first time I had articulated my feelings about Danny. Ever since I was little and had read about princes and princesses in fairy tales, I'd believed that there was someone out there who would complete me, my other half – my soulmate. It had never been clear what I was looking for – there were no criteria to cross off a list – but I was as certain as I could be that I had found him in Danny. I had only my feelings to go on, but what else is there?

The tedium of work no longer bothered me. I was happy to stand alone in the photocopying room, whiling away the hours daydreaming of Danny. I stopped asking for more interesting tasks and now rarely volunteered to sit in on case meetings as a note-taker. Late nights at Danny's meant that I often slept in and consequently arrived at work later than I should, and I never worked a minute past five-thirty. If my boss disapproved, I didn't notice. I had lost all interest in the legal practice; I may as well have been working in a super-market or on a factory production line.

When all my sentences began to start and end with 'Danny', my parents realised I must be serious about him and decided it was now time to invite him for Sunday lunch. To my relief, he arrived on time – which was a first – and he was dressed smartly, in a blue cotton sweater and grey trousers. He shook my parents' hands and called them 'Mr and Mrs Waterman' until they insisted they'd prefer David and Martha. He complimented my mother on her cooking and my father on his choice of wine. He even indulged my father by discussing share prices and the implications of the latest European directive. Emily shot me questioning looks and giggled behind her hand. After Danny had left, Dad said what a nice, intelligent young man he was, and Mum declared him 'charming'.

I must admit I found it all rather odd. The Danny I knew and loved – the scruffy, affectionate joker – was nowhere to be seen that day. He kissed me on the cheek when he came in, but after that, he didn't touch me all after-noon, and I could only surmise it was for fear of offending my parents. Even his voice was different, the lazy drawl replaced by clearly pronounced, public-school English. It was like dating Superman and then one day finding myself with Clark Kent instead. I wondered which was the real Danny and which the mask: this perfect gentleman or the edgy rock-and-roll dreamer? Could he really be both people, at the same time?

When I mentioned it on the phone later that evening, he didn't understand why I was perturbed.

'I was just being the person they wanted me to be,' he said, sounding a little annoyed. 'I'm the same guy and I feel exactly the same way about you as I always have. But I'm not exactly going to snog you in front of your parents, am I?'

'Of course not,' I said, frustrated. I was finding it hard to articulate my feelings, or to figure out why I was so bothered. How could I tell him that I feared I didn't know or understand him as well as I'd believed? How, when I didn't even want to admit it to myself? 'It's not that. I just wanted them to see what I see.'

'Look, they liked me and that's what you wanted. Or would you have preferred it if I'd come in half-loaded and ignored them?'

'No. It's just . . . Oh, it doesn't matter.'

I dropped the conversation. Perhaps I should have tried harder, but I didn't want to make a fuss. Somewhere, at the back of my mind, a subconscious feeling was beginning to form: the worry that if I pushed Danny too hard I might push him away. And it was easy enough to convince myself that he was right. Life would be so much simpler if my parents liked him. I decided I could learn to live with the clean-cut version of Danny, so long as he only appeared every couple of Sundays at my parents' house.

As Danny had promised, I became a regular at The Wonderfulls' gigs. They played various pubs and venues around North London and always got good write-ups in the local press. The groupies no longer worried me. As soon as Danny came off stage we'd disappear out of the back door together, leaving his gaggle of girl fans waiting, disappointed, in the bar.

Danny asked if I would help with The Wonderfulls' website, which featured photos, lyrics, snatches of songs to download and upcoming gig dates. I enjoyed typing in reviews and adding new pictures. I'd always liked taking photos and I became the group's unofficial photographer, snapping away at gigs and making everyone pose for portraits and group shots backstage. I kept the best portrait of Danny for myself, framing it and putting it on my bedside table so I could see him as soon as I woke up. Unlike the other pictures, which showed Danny in rock-star guise, pouting and preening for the camera, I felt that this photo captured 'my' Danny. In it he was looking away to the side, his eyes focused on a distant point and his lips slightly parted, as if he was about to speak. He said he didn't like the photo, but he would never explain why.

I was also invited to rehearsals, which usually took place at Danny's flat on Tuesday and Wednesday evenings. The other band members seemed to like me – or at least tolerate me – and I grew fond of Mike, the keyboard player, who always took the trouble to find out how I was and what I'd been doing. I wasn't so sure about the others. The drummer, Pete, was withdrawn and hard to talk to; the bass guitarist, Dylan, was a pot-head who didn't seem capable of intelligent conversation; and Andy, the lead guitarist, had been at school with Danny, and just seemed arrogant. I didn't like the way he tried to alter Danny's songs, imprinting them with his own arrangements and ideas, not because it improved them, but just so that he could make his mark.

I was always careful not to get in the way or to give my opinion when it wasn't wanted. Often, I'd make my excuses and go and sit in Danny's bedroom to watch TV or read. But Danny said he liked having me there; he called me his muse. The word filled me with pride. I had always looked at paintings in galleries and wondered about the artists' muses, their faces captured for all eternity. I didn't have the talent or the confidence then to create anything valuable myself, so being somebody else's inspiration seemed to me almost as great an accomplishment as being the artist.

From what I could see, The Wonderfulls didn't get much playing done at rehearsals. They'd sit around smoking and drinking, talking about other bands and football. I knew it wasn't my place to say anything, but I couldn't understand why I was the only person who seemed concerned. In a couple of weeks, they would be watched by an A & R guy, who had it in his power to give them a record contract. They might not have another chance. But what did I know?

chapter 9

ate one Wednesday night, when I'd arrived home from rehearsals at Danny's and I was getting ready to go to bed, my mobile rang. I knew it couldn't be Danny because it wasn't his ring (a tinny version of a Nirvana track which I'd downloaded from the Internet), and I thought about letting it go straight to my message box. The number didn't look familiar and I couldn't imagine who might be calling me so late. But although I didn't really feel like talking to anyone, curiosity got the better of me and I picked up.

It was Debbie. We'd spoken several times over the Christmas holidays, but she'd gone away with her family and we hadn't managed to see each other. Since she'd returned to university we'd fallen back into a pattern of irregular communication.

'Hi, Naomi,' she said. Her voice was quiet and she sounded anxious.

'Deb?' I said. 'Are you OK? I didn't recognise your number.'

'I'm using Sam's phone,' she said. I could tell she was on the brink of tears. 'I got mugged.'

'Oh no, that's awful! Are you OK?'

'Yes, I guess. I was just going into a club and I saw this guy coming towards me and he grabbed my bag and shoved me really hard. It all happened so fast I couldn't even scream.'

'Are you OK?' I asked again. We'd hardly spoken in weeks and even though I felt sorry for her I was very aware of the distance between us. I wanted to hug her, but she was in a different city so I couldn't. I couldn't even picture where she was or whom she was with, and I didn't know what to say to make her feel better.

'My bag had all my stuff in it – my mobile, keys, ID, all my cash . . .'

'What a nightmare. Have you told the police?'

'Yes, and I've cancelled my cards. I don't know, I guess I just wanted to hear a friendly voice. You don't mind me calling, do you?'

'Of course not,' I said, emphatically. I was pleased it was me she'd chosen to call.

'I think I'm going to come home at the weekend. I'm feeling a bit homesick. It would be really nice to see you.'

'Yes,' I said, recalling the plans I'd made with Danny for the weekend. He didn't have a gig and we were supposed to be driving down to Brighton to meet some friends of his. But I couldn't let Debbie down – and I did want to see her. Brighton would keep. 'Yes, it would be nice to see you too.'

'Maybe I could stay over on Saturday?' she asked tentatively. 'It would be like old times. We could get a DVD or something.'

'Sure,' I said. 'That would be lovely.'

'That's great,' she said, sounding more cheerful. 'I'm

looking forward to it. I'll give you a call when I get home on Friday.'

After we'd said our goodbyes I went to my wardrobe and took out my old photograph albums, which I stored on the top shelf behind my jumpers. I wanted to remind myself of the good times I'd shared with Debbie – the joint birthday parties and sleepovers and holidays abroad with her parents or mine. I couldn't remember a time when I hadn't known her. We'd met on the first day of primary school and had become firm friends at once, hugging each other and declaring proudly that we were 'best friends', in the possessive way that little girls do. Other friends had come and gone, groups had formed and splintered, but Debbie and I had remained solid, protecting one another from the bitching and the name-calling. She was the first person I told when I'd started my period; she'd bought me my first lip-gloss; we'd both enjoyed our first snogs during a game of spin the bottle at her thirteenth birthday party.

And here, in the tattered albums, was the documentary evidence of our friendship. There we were, at seven, standing in a playground somewhere, our arms wrapped around each other, grinning broadly. And there at fourteen, in crop tops and hipster jeans (which did nothing for either of us), with badly applied make-up and terrible hair. Here I was, last year, sitting on a beach in Greece in a bikini, my arms folded protectively over my belly, while Debbie stood next to me in a T-shirt because she'd sunburned her shoulders the day before.

Thumbing through the pages made me grin and cringe in

equal measures, as I witnessed my transformation from a sweet-looking, freckle-faced child to an awkward and self-conscious teenager. It was like viewing one of those computer programmes the police use to show what a toddler who'd disappeared ten years before might look like now. My face had visibly thinned and lengthened over the years, while my nose and chin had become more prominent. My hair, which had been through a remarkable range of styles, had darkened and curled, and my body had filled out. Debbie had changed too. She had always been thin and flat-chested, but in the past few years she'd become less of a tomboy, growing her hair and wearing skirts, and replacing her glasses with contact lenses. She said I was the pretty one, but I could never see it. I envied her long legs and flat tummy, the fact that her hair didn't frizz in the rain and that she never got zits. I wondered if she'd look different after a few of months away at university. It made me sad to think that now she would have new photographs in which I didn't feature, her arms around people I didn't recognise.

It niggled me that Debbie was only coming home because she'd been mugged. But maybe having something horrible happen to her had made her realise how much she missed me, that her real friends were the people she'd known for years. Maybe things would be just like they used to be. I looked forward to spending time with her, to staying up into the early hours and chatting until one of us fell asleep. Best of all, Danny would finally meet her and the three of us could hang out together, like a perfect triangle made up of the most important people in my life.

For the first time in months I went to sleep thinking not of Danny, but of Debbie. I dreamed that we were at her house, playing hide-and-seek. We'd locked ourselves into her bedroom and were cowering together behind her bed. Somebody – a faceless man with dark hair – was banging on the door, trying to get in. As he forced his way into the room, I woke up.

The following evening Danny and I went out for a curry. I kept meaning to tell him Debbie was coming home at the weekend, but the time never seemed right. He was in a particularly sweet and silly mood and I didn't want to spoil it. What do you do, interrupt a funny story to say, 'That's hysterical, Danny, and by the way, I can't go to Brighton'? Of course I knew even then that it was just an excuse. The truth was, I knew he'd be angry and I didn't want a fight. I've never been very good at arguing – I end up getting upset, then crying, which usually makes the other person feel even more frustrated.

So, it wasn't until later, when we were sitting in his car outside my house that I mentioned it.

'You know we were going to go to Brighton on Saturday?' I asked nervously. 'Well, would it be OK if we did it another weekend?'

'Why?' he said, smirking. 'You aren't shy about meeting my mates, are you?'

'No,' I said, laughing, although there was some truth in it. 'Actually, it's because of one of *my* mates. You know my best friend, Debbie? Well, she's coming home for the weekend.'

'I see,' he said, clearly irritated. 'And you want to see her instead?'

'No, not instead. I want you to come out with us too. But I do really want to spend some time with her.'

'But Brighton's all arranged. Can't you see her another weekend?'

'No, she's upset. She had her bag nicked. Look, I couldn't really say no.'

'You never can,' he muttered.

The comment was like a knife in my belly. Was that how he really saw me – weak and pliable? Or was he just trying to goad me?

'What's that supposed to mean?'

'Nothing.' He wasn't looking at me. 'Just that you've done nothing but bitch about her ever since you've known me and now you want to drop everything for her when she snaps her fingers. I thought you were stronger than that.'

'It's not like that, Danny,' I said, my voice beginning to break. I could feel tears welling up in my eyes. Danny and I had never before exchanged a cross word, but now I was receiving the icy treatment I had feared. He wouldn't even touch me. When I tried to put my hand on his arm he flinched and brushed it away. 'I was pissed off with her because she didn't seem to care as much as she used to. I was scared I was losing her. Now, she wants to come home and maybe if we spend some time together things will be how they were.'

'No, she wants to come home because she's a silly girl who didn't keep her eye on her bag and feels homesick.'

Hearing Danny echo my own niggling doubts made me feel defensive. 'That's not fair. You don't even know her. She's lovely. You'll see.'

'I'm not sure I can be arsed,' he stated harshly.

'What do you mean?' It was so important to me that Danny and Debbie got on. I was trying hard to stay cool, not to let myself cry. I felt shocked and angry and self-protective at the same time and I didn't know what to do with all those emotions.

'I mean I don't see the point of hanging round with you and your so-called best mate when I could be in Brighton having a great time.'

'Don't you want to meet my friends? I've met yours. I spend loads of time with the band.'

'That's different,' he snapped. 'And you know it. I do want to meet your friends, some time, but not when it means I have to cancel something we were both looking for-ward to.'

At last, he turned to look at me. Noticing that a fat tear was beginning to roll down my cheek, he softened. 'I'm sorry, Omi,' he said, wiping it away with his hand. 'I didn't mean to upset you.'

It wasn't enough. The worry that he wasn't really inter-ested in my friends had troubled me for many weeks. I made a point of turning my head away from him.

'But you have upset me,' I said. 'I'm sorry about Saturday, but Brighton's not about to fall into the sea – we can go another time. I just feel that you don't care about my friends. I know nobody's around at the moment and I must seem like Billy No-mates, but my friends are important to me and when they're here I want to see them. They're part of me. If you don't meet my friends, how can you really know me?'

Now *he* was upset. 'How can you say that? I know you better than anyone. I know everything about you and you know everything about me. I don't need to meet Debbie to know that.'

'But you do!' I cried. I opened the car door and put my left foot on the kerb. I didn't want him to see me sobbing and I could feel a gush of tears waiting to escape.

'You're being ridiculous,' he tutted, grabbing my arm in an attempt to stop me from getting out the car. 'You know what? Let's forget this weekend. You do whatever you want to do with Debbie and I'll go to Brighton.'

'Fine,' I barked, shaking him off me. 'Whatever.' I launched myself out of my seat and slammed the car door behind me. For a moment I thought he might follow me, but then I heard the roar of the engine and the squeal of tyres as he sped away up the street. Tears streaming down my face, I let myself into my house and, exhausted, went straight to bed. I cried myself to sleep.

So there it was: our first argument. My grandma once told me that nothing lasts, and nothing – good or bad – stays the same. I didn't really understand what she meant until that night. I'd genuinely believed that we would remain in our happy state forever. I saw us always laughing, always agreeing, always on the same page. It's naïve, I know, but I had never truly allowed myself to accept that Danny could be cruel to me – I'd hoped his feelings for me somehow granted me immunity. The argument brought me back to reality and, worse, it made me feel alone again.

There was no text from Danny when I awoke the next morning. I made myself go into work and do what needed to be done. I tried to spend as much time as I could with the other staff members, so I didn't have time to think about Danny. Whenever there was silence our argument began to replay over and over in my mind, like my dad's old vinyl records when they got stuck. But I couldn't ignore the nauseous feeling in the pit of my stomach that wouldn't go away. Surely this wasn't the end? It couldn't be. The thought of losing Danny terrified me and yet I couldn't bring myself to contact him first. All day, I toyed with the idea of calling or texting him, but what would I say? Sorry? I hadn't done anything wrong, so why should I apologise? Perhaps I should send him a jokey text pretending that nothing had happened. But that would just be letting him get away with it.

At three in the afternoon, Danny put me out of my misery by texting me. DECIDED 2 GO TO BTN 2DAY. HV GD TIME WIV D. DX. I read and reread the text countless times, trying to decide what it meant. There was no apology, no mention of the argument and he had stuck to his guns and gone to Brighton – and a day early too. Nothing had been resolved. Then again, he had wished me well and finished with a kiss – surely that was a positive sign?

It took me over an hour to reply. After deleting at least

ten possible messages, I settled on the concise: OK. SPK WHEN UR BACK. NX. Its brevity, in contrast to my usual messages – and the fact that I'd signed my name with an 'N', not an 'O' – showed I was still unhappy and hadn't entirely forgiven him, but it wasn't nasty and it left things open.

Emily agreed that I'd got the tone right. 'You don't want to let him think he's got away with it,' she said, angry on my behalf. It was lovely that she felt so protective of me. She'd made me run through the argument several times, punctuating the end of Danny's words with the occasional 'bastard' and 'selfish git' until she realised her vehemence was making me more upset.

'He'll come running back,' she said. 'Anyone can see how much he likes you. Just make him sweat a bit first.'

I wondered where she'd learned so much about guys. Wasn't I the big sister here? Still, I allowed myself to be reassured.

Now, I just had to get through the next two days.

Debbie came home that evening. She was spending Friday night with her parents and we'd arranged to meet on Saturday lunchtime at a coffee shop in town, and then do a bit of window shopping and come back to my house to watch a DVD. I was determined to have a good time with Debbie, to prove to myself that I could still have fun without Danny and, more importantly, to reassure myself that she was still my best friend.

I spent Friday night watching TV with my parents (Emily was at a friend's house). Anything was better than sitting alone in my bedroom, dwelling on what had happened. Mum and Dad seemed surprised that I wanted to be with them and even more surprised that I appeared happy to watch an hour-long documentary about medieval architecture. I was very quiet and Mum kept asking if I was all right. I told her Danny was at a family do and that I fancied an evening in because I was tired. I'm not sure she believed me, but she knew better than to pry.

I felt far less anxious in the morning, after a good night's dreamless sleep. I went into town early and wandered round the shops on my own, testing lip-gloss and blushers. Debbie was already drinking a cappuccino when I arrived at the café. She was dressed more scruffily than I'd seen her in years, in ripped jeans and a baggy jumper. Despite her concessions to the 'student' look, she still looked smart and polished, her hair a little too neat and glossy. It made me smile to myself. She hadn't changed, really.

'Naomi!' she cried, when she saw me come in. She bounded out of her chair and rushed over to kiss me hello. I was happy and reassured that she seemed so genuinely pleased to see me. I hugged her. When I put my arms around her I could feel the bones in her back.

'You've lost so much weight!' I exclaimed. 'Don't they feed you at university?'

'I know,' she said, embarrassed. 'It's terrible. That's what a diet of Pot Noodles and toasted sandwiches does to you. My mum was horrified. After Christmas she sent me back with a month's supply of nutritious food.' She looked me up and down. 'Hey, you look good, though.'

'Thanks.' I blushed. I was about to say, 'That's what being in love does for you', but given that Danny and I were barely on speaking terms, it didn't seem appropriate. Instead, I asked, 'So, do you want to hit the shops, then?'

'Great. I have absolutely no money and no plastic, so I won't be able to do any damage.'

'You can help me buy something,' I said, laughing.

We spent the afternoon trawling the rails of all the high street stores and chatting about everything under the sun. Although I was pleased that Debbie finally seemed interested in the details of my life, I wasn't in the mood for serious talk; every time she asked about me I deflected the conversation back to her. I had always been a good listener, so she didn't notice. She had so much news to tell me that a simple question, such as 'What's your accommodation like?' could elicit a ten-minute speech full of anecdotes involving copious amounts of alcohol and guys I'd never heard of.

To be honest, I was relieved that we were getting on so well. I felt comfortable in Debbie's company – it seemed almost as if she'd never been away. I decided to forgive her for her laxity in calling and her apparent disinterest in my life during our telephone conversations. It wasn't her fault, I told myself. She obviously didn't get much privacy in her hall of residence and it sounded like there was so much going on that she really didn't have any time. She'd simply stored thoughts of life back home in a little box at the back of her mind.

When our feet grew sore and our eyes bleary, we headed back to my house. Mum and Dad were delighted to see Debbie. They'd never told me directly, but I knew they thought she was a good influence. She was the sensible one, the one who'd always known what she wanted to do – to become a teacher – and hadn't wavered. She'd gone straight from school to university and, in four years' time, would come out with her teaching degree and, no doubt, step straight into a good job. She was intelligent and polite and reliable: the qualities my dad thought most important. Often, if I was rude or disagreed with him, he'd say, 'I bet Debbie doesn't talk like that to her father.' I found it irritating, especially as I knew Dad's opinion of Debbie was wrong. If she'd been as boring as he thought her, we would never have been friends. The Debbie I knew was fun, a bit of a bitch and a terrible flirt. She'd had far more boyfriends than me; guys liked her because not only did she have great legs, but she also loved football and could act like one of the lads.

My parents wanted us to join them for dinner, but we said we'd already agreed to get a Chinese takeaway – my treat. We escaped upstairs and ran into my bedroom, locking the door so that nobody could disturb us. Debbie perched on my bed, as she had done a thousand times before. 'Your room looks exactly the same,' she said. I wasn't sure if it was a criticism or a compliment.

'Course it does,' I replied. 'No point changing it now.'

'I guess not,' she said. 'It's weird sleeping in my bedroom at home. It doesn't feel like mine any more.' She glanced across me and her eyes came to rest on the photograph of Danny. 'Is that Danny, then?'

'Yes,' I said, with a mixture of pride and sadness. I looked at the picture and realised that I now knew every part of his face, every angle, almost as well as my own.

'Oh, he's not what I expected. He looks like a bit of a poser.'

Debbie had a tendency to be blunt – it often got her into trouble – but I hadn't expected her to be so unkind.

'What do you mean?' I asked, unable to conceal my defensiveness.

'Oh, you know, the designer stubble, the long hair and that faraway look in his eyes. He's not your normal type, is he?'

'And what's my normal type?'

'You know, like Mark or Jack – boyish, clean-cut, fair . . .'

'Actually, they *weren't* my type,' I snapped, irritated. 'They're more your type. I think Danny is gorgeous.'

'OK, sorry. Don't be so touchy. He is good-looking, just not what I imagined. So what's he doing tonight? I kind of thought – hoped – I might meet him.'

'He had to go to Brighton,' I said, trying desperately not to show that I was upset. 'I was supposed to go with him, but then you said you were coming home and I cancelled.'

'Oh Naomi, I'm sorry.' She sounded like she felt guilty.

I decided to tell her the whole story. 'Actually, we had an argument about it. It's pathetic, really, but we haven't spoken properly since. That's why I haven't said much about him today.'

'I didn't realise. You should have said.'

'It's OK. We can go to Brighton any time.'

'So why aren't you speaking?'

Now I wished I hadn't mentioned the argument. How could I tell her that Danny didn't want to meet her?

'You didn't give me much notice . . . and it all kind of got blown out of proportion.'

'Sorry,' she said, her tone sarcastic now. 'Next time I'm mugged I'll make sure Danny's informed well in advance.'

I laughed, but the damage was done. I'd wanted Debbie to be excited about Danny, to congratulate me on finding a wonderful, handsome, interesting guy. Instead, she appeared to dislike him already – and they hadn't even met.

Debbie took a deep breath. 'I'm sorry, Naomi,' she said. 'I'm your best mate. If I can't be honest with you, who can? I want you to be happy, and I know you really like Danny – you always seem so excited about him on the phone – but he sounds so intense and temperamental. I've known you forever and I've never seen you so moody and snappy. And he's got you caught up in his silly dream of being a pop star. Are you sure he's good for you?'

How could she say that? She must have had some idea how happy Danny made me, even if she hadn't seen us together. She didn't know how interesting our conversations were, how much he'd taught me about music and books and politics. Just *being* with Danny was a buzz.

'It's not a silly dream,' I said. 'He's talented and ambitious and creative . . .'

She interrupted me. 'Ambitious? You told me he dropped out of Oxford.'

'So? He left to follow his dream – that's pretty ambitious in my book. At least he was bright enough to get in.'

I knew my comment was cruel. Debbie had wanted to go to Oxford, but she hadn't achieved high enough grades in her A-levels. I had never worked as hard as her at school, but I always did better; it was something we never spoke about.

'Piss off,' she spat. 'That was below the belt. Anyway, I'm glad I didn't go to snobby Oxford now. I feel right at home at Manchester and from what I've heard, it's much more fun.'

We both sat silently for a few minutes, sulking. Yet another evening with somebody I cared about had turned into a bickering session. I appeared to have developed a talent for it.

'Sorry,' I said, eventually. 'I take it back. Look, let's call a truce. We'll go and get the takeaway and you can choose the film, OK?'

'OK,' she said. 'Nothing arty or French. I fancy a rom-com.'

'Deal.'

We made the best of the remainder of the night, eating too much and giggling at the movie, which was about a dumb, blonde American girl who gets herself into lots of scrapes, but – surprise, surprise – wins the gorgeous guy in the end. But my heart wasn't in it. I kept losing concentration and thinking about Danny and how much I loved being with him. I decided that when he arrived home I would call him and tell him I'd been stupid and that he was right about Debbie. My time with her had only confirmed what he'd said and what I'd feared: Debbie didn't really understand me any more. She didn't *get* me – not like he did.

At midnight, Debbie said, 'Do you mind if I call a cab? I know I was going to sleep over, but my parents want me to see my gran tomorrow and then I've got to get the train back.'

'Oh, Deb,' I said, aware that I was losing my last chance to make things right with her. 'It would have been fun,' I added, with little conviction, but it seemed the right thing to say.

'Yeah, but I'm knackered. I promise I'll come and see you again soon. And you've got to come up and stay with me too. We must arrange it.'

'Sure,' I said. 'That would be good.' We hugged each other, as we always had, but I felt no pleasure in it, no security or warmth. It was like hugging a distant relative at a funeral.

Emily arrived home a few minutes after Debbie had left. She came into my room and excitedly began to tell me about the party she'd been to and how the guy she'd really liked for ages had kissed her. I tried to feign interest, but then she noticed how sad I looked and stopped mid-sentence.

'Are you OK, Naomi? You seem so miserable. Where's Debbie? I thought she was staying.'

'She went home,' I said. 'I think we've grown apart.'

'But you've been, like, best mates for years.'

'Yes. I guess things change.'

She rubbed my arm affectionately. 'I'm sure you'll sort it out.'

'I don't think so. Maybe we were never as close as I thought and it took her going away to make me realise. And she doesn't like Danny.'

'What?' Emily cried. 'When did she meet him?'

'She hasn't. She didn't like his picture and she actually said she thought he was bad for me.'

'That's ridiculous! I think he's great, not to mention incredibly good-looking. I know you've had a bit of a barny and he was out of order and I called him a bastard, but I didn't mean it. You'll get it all sorted, I know you will.'

I really appreciated Emily's support. She may have been angry with Danny on my behalf the day before, but she genuinely cared about him. She had been out with us several times and Danny had been very sweet to her, letting her come backstage after a gig and introducing her to the band. She'd told me her school friends thought he was really cool which, by association, made her cool too. She'd even said that she looked forward to Sunday lunches now that he was a regular guest.

'I hope so,' I said.

'You're perfect for each other, Nay. Anyone can see that.'

'Thanks, Em,' I said. 'You've really made me feel better.'

And she had.

Chapter 10

Sunday was the longest day. I itched to call Danny, checking my mobile and my watch every few minutes, wondering if it was too soon to call, whether he would be home yet, if he would ring me. I ate lunch with my parents, went for a walk in the park, bought myself a glossy magazine and read it page by page. Still, I heard nothing. By five p.m., I was restless and sick with nerves, fussing with my hair and my clothes and chewing the skin around my fingernails. The words I had confidently planned – and rehearsed – to say to Danny no longer seemed appropriate. Like any words repeated too often, they had become meaningless, nonsensical, a jumble of syllables and sounds. '*Hi Danny,*' I had intended to say. '*I'm so glad you're back. Haven't we been a couple of idiots? I've missed you and can't wait to see you.*' But the longer I waited, the more my courage deserted me. I was afraid that if I dialled his number and he replied, all that would come out of my mouth was 'Dann*yyyyyyyyy . . .*'

The way things were, it would not have been sensible to send him another text. It's so hard to choose the right words, to make sure they don't have any other, unintended meanings. You can text something with one tone of voice in mind and it will be read in quite another. And, even at the best of times, Danny, always perceptive, had a tendency to analyse everything, to read between the lines. That day, even the inauspicious use of a question mark could have made things a hundred times worse.

Why hadn't he called? Surely he must be home by now. Had he met somebody else in Brighton? Had something happened – a fight, an accident? Was he lying in a hospital somewhere, alone and frightened, unable to call me? I knew I was letting my imagination run away with me, but the idea that he was injured seemed preferable to the alternative explanations: that he simply didn't want to talk to me, or worse, that he was over me.

At about seven in the evening, I put on my coat and told my parents I was going to the twenty-four-hour garage up the road to buy some cotton wool so I could paint my toe-nails. I couldn't think of any other reasonable-sounding excuse for going out on a cold and rainy Sunday evening. I figured that the walk would kill a good twenty minutes.

I was about to open the front door when I noticed a small, white envelope lying on the doormat. *That's odd*, I thought. *We don't get post on a Sunday.* It didn't look like a pizza-delivery flyer or a leaflet advertising window cleaning services. I bent down to pick it up and, on turning it over, saw that it was addressed to me. There was no stamp, just my name and address, handwritten. I recognised the writing immediately: it was Danny's. I had seen the same slanted, curly-topped lettering in the books of song lyrics he had let me read, and he had used the same purple ink.

Why had Danny written to me? When had he delivered this? He must have been here, at my house, while I sat in my bedroom upstairs. Why hadn't he rung the doorbell? I was breathing faster now, my heart beating loud and erratically against the wall of my chest. Still crouching in the hallway, my hands shaking, I ripped open the envelope. As I pulled out the three neatly folded sheets within, a five-pound note fluttered to the floor. I was confused. Why had Danny given me money? What did he have to say that he had to write down?

I don't have to try to remember the contents of the letter – I have kept it, to this day, with all my old photographs and mementoes, in a little trunk under my bed. Even now, it pains me to read it.

Dear Omi,

Please find enclosed the fiver you lent me the other night. I will give you back the books and CDs that I borrowed soon. It's two p.m. and I'm perfectly sober. Please bear with me for what follows – for once I'm thinking clearly and being very sensible.

I apologise if I ramble. All this stuff has been in my head since the other night, since our argument; and today more than ever. It's not fair on you that we keep on seeing each other. Let me explain my reasons. You want to enjoy yourself, see your friends, go shopping and clubbing, and I just get in your way. You're planning to go to university and have a great time next year – just like I did a couple of years ago.

There's nothing wrong with that. But that's not my world any more and I feel that I'm stopping you from doing all that stuff. I don't think I've got it in me to try to make conversation with Debbie and your other mates – we're from different worlds. I've got nothing to say to them and I don't think they'd like me. You understand me, but I don't think they would. It's not that I care what they think of me, just that I don't ever want you to feel that you have to apologise for me.

I feel like I've trespassed into your life. My only justification is the way I feel about you. I don't know if you feel the same, but even if you do, is that enough? You shouldn't have to make a choice between your friends and your work and me. It's not fair on you.

I'm ending our relationship now because every day I care for you more. Tomorrow, or the next day, I probably wouldn't be able to write this. I'm in so deep that if I go deeper I won't stay afloat without you. I care about you more than I have ever cared about anyone before. I love you. There, I've said it. I love you. And the more I love you, the more I want to be with you and only you.

It hurts to write this to you, but it must be written. If I tried to tell you to your face, or over the phone, it would all come out wrong. I'm putting my own *feelings last to protect yours. Because you're the important one. Don't be angry that I'm making this decision on your behalf. I hope you understand. I want you to be happy, I want you to have a wonderful, successful life, with great friends. I don't want to hold you back. You are the most special person I have ever met. You deserve better than me.*

I've gone on too long. I won't pick you up from work tomorrow. Don't come to rehearsal on Tuesday. Always remember the wonderful times we've shared and move on with your life.

Yours,
Danny x

I pulled myself upright, leaning on the door frame for support. The acid was rising from my stomach into my mouth and I thought I was going to vomit. I swallowed it down again, burning my throat and leaving an acrid taste in my mouth. From my first reading only five words had stayed with me, jumping out from the text and obscuring everything else: *I'm ending our relationship now.*

Danny was finishing with me. He was telling me he didn't want to see me again. He was leaving me. I was finding it hard to breathe, gasping for air, my ears filling with blood and a strange rushing sound. Was I having a heart attack? Was this what it was like to die? I tried to call out to my parents, but nothing came out of my mouth.

Focus, Naomi, focus, said a strange, calm voice inside my head. Although I had no control of my body, I managed to slump down into a sitting position. I closed my eyes and concentrated on breathing deeply, in and out, in and out. Then I read the letter again. This time different phrases leapt from the pages: *I love you. You are the most special person I have ever met.* Danny loved me. He loved me. So why was he dumping me? It didn't make sense. Because of Debbie? Because I was going to university in October? But I loved him too – didn't he realise? Didn't he understand that nothing and nobody else mattered? Now I was angry. How could he simultaneously tell me he loved me for the first time and finish with me? How could he make this decision on my behalf? Who did he think he was?

I dragged myself up again and opened the front door, drinking the cold, damp air into my lungs. I had only one purpose: whatever the outcome, I had to tell Danny that I loved him too. He HAD to know. My legs started to run of their own accord, pulling my body with them. Soon I was running faster than I'd ever run before, past houses and across roads, dodging traffic and pedestrians, uphill, downhill, through puddles and muddy grass and around sharp bends. I'd never been a very good athlete – I even hated running for the bus – but adrenaline was pumping through my body and fuelling my muscles, propelling me forward. I had no sense of time or distance; I might have been running for five minutes or an hour, covering a hundred metres or a hundred miles.

I didn't stop running until I was standing outside Danny's front door, breathing so fast that I thought my lungs would explode. I pressed the doorbell and left my finger on it, making it scream continuously until somebody came to let me in. I didn't care what anybody thought, didn't mind if I was disturbing the peace. I would have stood there all night if I'd had to.

'What the hell is going on?' Danny's mother was standing at the door. When she saw me her expression changed from anger to shock to alarm. 'Are you all right, Naomi? You look terrible – you're soaked through. What's happened?'

I was still hyperventilating, tears streaming down my face, my jeans and coat splattered with mud. 'Please, I need to see Danny. Please . . .'

Shaking her head, she let me pass her, stepping away from me so, I assume, I didn't stain her pristine dress.

'Danny's in his flat,' she said. 'You know the way.'

I didn't thank her – I was already banging on his door.

He opened it almost immediately. 'Naomi?' he said, bewildered. He had dark circles under his eyes and it looked as if he hadn't shaved for a couple of days. 'What are you doing here?' His mother was still loitering in the hall, curious. He nodded at her. 'It's all right, Mum, you can go now. I'll deal with this.'

He led me into his flat, locking the door behind us. 'What are you doing here?' he asked again. His arm twitched in my direction and I could tell he wanted to touch me, but he wouldn't let himself.

'Your letter . . . I . . . how could you? I don't understand.' I began to sob, huge, chest-filling sobs, like hiccoughs that I couldn't control.

'Sit down,' he said. 'Sit down and have a drink and then we'll talk.'

He made me a cup of tea and watched as I sipped it. Soon I had stopped shaking and my sobs had begun to subside. Suddenly self-aware, I felt foolish and then worried about what I must look like, with my hair plastered to my face and no make-up.

'I'm sorry, Omi. I didn't mean to upset you like this,' said Danny gently.

'I don't understand,' I repeated. 'You tell me that you love me and then you finish it. It doesn't make sense.'

'It made sense to me when I wrote it. I thought it was for the best. It is for the best.'

'But why? What about how *I* feel? I love you too. I didn't know how to tell you, but I do. And—'

'You what?' he exclaimed, his eyes growing wider.

'I love you,' I muttered, embarrassed.

His eyes pierced into mine. 'You do?'

'Yes, of course.'

'Say it again,' he demanded.

'OK, I love you.'

'Again!'

I was almost laughing now. 'I love you.'

'Again!' he cried. 'You have no idea how much I've wanted to hear you say that.'

'I love you, Danny,' I told him, frustrated that I couldn't infuse those three syllables with the colour and depth that lay behind them. 'I love you, I love you.'

'That's amazing,' he said, shaking his head. 'I can't tell

you how happy you've made me.'

He walked over to me and took my hands, pulling me up from my chair. Then he wrapped his arms around my back and pulled me tight into his body, kissing me so hard and so urgently that I was momentarily afraid I might be swallowed whole. Soon I was kissing him back, channelling all the emotions within me – all the words I should have said and the thoughts I couldn't articulate – into kisses. I was kissing him with my body and my mind and my soul. After that kiss, there was no going back for me, no escape. Danny had me. He was no longer just my boyfriend, he was part of me. We were one entity: NaomiandDanny, DannyandNaomi.

We never spoke about the letter again. I regret that now. I should have asked him why he had turned a small argument into such a big drama. Did a little bit of him enjoy it? Had he foreseen the effect that letter would have on me – was it all part of a clever game? And, most importantly, why would he try to protect me from himself?

I didn't ask because I was so caught up in the intensity of his feelings, and mine. In my half-formed dictionary of love, D-R-A-M-A was spelled P-A-S-S-I-O-N. The sad thing is, even if I *had* asked, I don't think he'd have had the answers.

Chapter 11

anny was on stage, singing to a crowd of about eighty people in a dingy room at the back of a pub. He had played in hundreds of venues just like it – dark, hot rooms that smelled of stale beer and cigarettes. But this night was different. Somewhere in the crowd stood an A&R man named Jed Wilson who had the power to change Danny's life forever. If he liked The Wonderfulls he could give them a record contract: the golden ticket that would take them out of local pubs, out of new band nights and poorly paid support slots, and put them on the bill at festivals and thousand-seater venues and even, one day, stadiums.

Danny wanted a record contract more than he wanted anything. There was no point fooling myself; no matter how much he declared that he loved me, if he'd had to choose between a record contract and me, I'm pretty sure I'd have been a poor runner-up. Music was his first love. Danny had spent his childhood imagining himself on stage at Wembley, a huge crowd mouthing along to his lyrics. Unlike most childhood dreams, which are drummed out of us by the realisation that we don't have the talent or the opportunity to fulfil them, Danny's had stayed with him, growing ever stronger. If you were to take away the deep voice and the stubble and the six-foot stature, you'd see he was still just a little boy playing air guitar in front of the mirror.

'You'll be fantastic,' I reassured him, as we drove to the venue for the soundcheck earlier that afternoon. 'The record company would be mad not to sign you.' I knew it was what he needed to hear and I wanted him to be successful because it meant so much to him. But part of me feared what might happen if The Wonderfulls achieved fame and fortune. Success would change him; it was inevitable. Would there be room in his life for me, what with recording sessions and tours and magazine interviews? And what about all the girls he'd meet, groupies who were prettier and more interesting than me?

No matter how much he told me that he loved me, that I was beautiful and funny and clever, nothing could erase the nagging doubt that I might not be good enough for him. I felt I'd lucked out and that one day Danny would wake up and realise that he'd made a mistake. I'd noticed the way some of the girl fans looked at me, and I imagined them whispering to their friends about my features or my figure, asking, 'What's he doing with her?' I sometimes asked myself the same question. I don't know where self-esteem comes from – perhaps you're born with it. My lack of it certainly wasn't my parents' fault; they'd always told me I was pretty and special, that I could be anything I wanted to be. It had just never seemed that way to me.

Seated at the side of the stage at a table covered in flyers and demo CDs, I looked into the crowd and tried to work out where Jed Wilson was standing. There were several men I didn't recognise, but they could equally have been there to see one of the other bands performing that night. Jed, I decided, would be alone and he'd probably be aloof and dressed a little too smartly, almost certainly in black. Danny had told me that most A & R men were terminally uncool, desperate to appear young and trendy and 'down with the kids', when in reality they were just overpaid businessmen heading towards middle age. There were a couple of guys who fitted the bill, one with a – presumably – 'ironic' mullet-type hairstyle and another whose jeans and T-shirt looked as though they might have been pressed. I watched them closely for a while; neither seemed to be enjoying himself much. If one of them was indeed Jed, it wasn't a good sign.

Although nobody would admit it openly, the band's rehearsals – which were disorganised at the best of times – had not been going well. Dylan had failed to turn up on several occasions and nobody had been able to contact him. Danny had taken his place, but the bass guitar wasn't his instrument and he'd found it hard to sing and play at the same time. When Dylan had finally resurfaced, he had offered few excuses for his absences and was not even apologetic. From his weary and unkempt demeanour it was obvious that he had been smoking far too much pot. He no longer seemed to care whether The Wonderfulls made it; he no longer cared about anything much at all. Worried that Dylan might leave altogether, the others kept their irritation to themselves, but the tension between them was palpable.

Still, the gig was as successful as anyone might hope. Danny was in fine voice, Dylan had got his act together and most of The Wonderfulls' fans had shown up to cheer them on. There had been a lot of buzz on the website about the possibility of a record deal and everybody appeared to like Danny's new songs. I watched the crowd's reactions as they heard them for the first time; they clapped and shouted their appreciation as much as they did for any of the old favourites. That gave me a warm feeling. I had seen the songs progress from scrawls in Danny's notebook to demos to full performances – I knew them as well as the band did. So when Danny said, 'This is a song for someone very special,' and looked directly at me, my heart leapt in to my mouth. I knew exactly what he was about to sing.

Not long after the letter incident, on Valentine's Day, Danny had sent me a cryptic text, inviting me to his flat that evening for 'a surprise'. I still found the idea of surprises rather unnerving but, since the picnic, I no longer dreaded them. I had no idea what it might be and I spent the whole day at work in a state of nervous excitement, imagining every possible scenario. He had already sent me a huge card and had flowers delivered to me at work – surprises enough, after he'd told me he thought Valentine's Day was just a commercial enterprise dreamed up by greeting card manufacturers. Foolishly, I'd taken him at his word and sent him nothing. Now I felt guilty and spoiled.

So what else did he have planned? Perhaps he was going to cook me a special meal, or present me with a gift, or even – if I let myself get carried away – whisk me off somewhere romantic, like Paris or Rome. Alone in the photocopying room I practised my reaction: a look of shock, followed by a tearful 'thank you'. As a child, I'd rehearsed my Oscar acceptance speech in much the same way, mouthing the words in the mirror and concentrating hard on sad things – in those days it was abandoned kittens – to conjure up genuine tears in my eyes. Now all I had to do was imagine not being with Danny.

I quickly changed in the toilets at work and took the bus straight to Danny's house, choosing a seat at the back so that nobody could watch me applying my make-up. When I arrived, he was standing in his drive waiting for me. I ran into his arms, letting him lift me up and cover my face with kisses.

'Are you ready for your surprise?' he asked. He was smiling, but he seemed a little agitated.

'Absolutely,' I replied, with as much enthusiasm as I could muster. His evident nerves had done nothing to calm my own.

He took my hand and led me into his flat, asking me to sit on the sofa while he disappeared into his bedroom to fetch my gift. When he came out he was carrying his guitar. For a moment, I thought, *He's giving me his guitar*, but it didn't make sense. He knew I couldn't really play and it was his prized possession. I tried hard not to look confused.

'OK,' he said. He hung back near the door. 'This is what I've been waiting to give you . . . I've written you a song. I hope you like it.'

Resting his leg on a footstool, he pulled his guitar strap

over his head and began to play a series of chords, which (thanks to years of school and Mum's music lessons) I could tell were in the key of G. He was so jittery that his fingers fumbled for the strings. Then he cleared his throat and, after a couple of false starts, he began to sing:

'Take it, take it now;
This precious moment will allow
Time to stop and heal all pain.
You are the sun that halts the rain.

And the dark clouds will disappear;
You are the calm that quells my fear;
Fate has cast the starring role,
So take the stage and save my soul.
Save my soul.

Take my hand, take my hand.
The best things in life are never planned.
That captured smile, two worlds collide,
My shooting star, my guiding light.

You will always be
The other half of me,
And if my world should fall apart
You would be there
To mend my heart.'

When he had finished, he put down his guitar and leaned against the door frame, waiting for a reaction. I didn't know what to say. I felt I needed to hear the song again before I could compose my thoughts. I was still scrolling through the song's lyrics, seeing them lined up in my mind, as though they were written on a screen. Danny had said I was his other half, that I could save his soul – he had sung of being with me forever. He'd said things in song that would have sounded over the top, scary even, in plain speech. But somehow, as lyrics, they worked. Whatever I said in response would seem trite. I felt as if I wanted to write a song back to him to express my feelings, but I didn't know how. So I sat there, in silence, overwhelmed by the words and the music and Danny's incredible voice, trying to compute it all.

'You didn't like it,' he said, hanging his head in resignation. Danny always assumed the worst.

'No, no, I loved it!' I said, hoping the tone of my voice would convey the emotions I couldn't articulate. 'I really, really loved it. I'm just stunned. Did you really write that for me?'

'Of course I did,' he said, laughing. Now he was perky, like a dog that has just been petted. He came over to sit beside me. 'Who else?'

'Angelina Jolie, perhaps?' I joked. 'Honestly, Danny, it's the best present you could have given me.'

And it was. Nobody else in the world had ever received this present and nobody would again; it had been created just for me. I didn't ask Danny about the detail of the lyrics. To be honest, I was a little embarrassed by the intensity of them. Instead, I said the only thing I could think of that seemed appropriate and would please him. I said, 'I love you, Danny.'

Ever since Danny and I had admitted that we loved one another, we hadn't been able to stop saying it. To me, the words 'I love you' were like a magic spell, and one which I was afraid would be broken if I didn't keep saying and hearing them. They made me tingle all over, sapped my appetite and cleared my mind of any other thoughts. They were also a useful silence-filler, a way to make up quickly if we disagreed, or to cheer each other up when we felt down. Now, as a response to Danny's song, they were shorthand for: 'Thank you, I'm not sure exactly what you're saying to me here, but, whatever it is, I feel the same.'

Hearing the song – *my* song – played at Danny's gig that night was just as special as the first time. It wasn't just because Danny looked deep into my eyes as he sang, sending warm shivers through my whole body. It was also because he was singing it in public – declaring his love for me in front of all his fans. Even though it was dark and the audience's attention was focused on the stage, I felt proud, as if all eyes were on me. I wondered if the crowd were listening to the words and imagining who they were about, who Danny's muse might be. I'd always envied girls who'd had songs written for them – they were usually beautiful models or actresses or tragic icons. How incredible that I, plain old Naomi Waterman, was now one of them. If The Wonderfulls made it big, 'my' song could be played on radios and CD players all over the world. How amazing would that be?

When he had finished singing the song and the whoops were building to a climax, Danny made a show of putting down his guitar and turning to walk off the stage. The others followed him. It's a ploy every band uses at the end of their set: whip the crowd up into a frenzy and then, when they are hoarse from cheering and tired from stomping and clapping, come back on stage to perform an encore. I often wondered what might happen if the crowd didn't behave as anticipated, and started walking out. But that night, as always, it worked a treat.

Two songs later, the lights came on to signal that the gig really was over. Danny threw down his guitar and jumped from the stage, rushing straight over to me. 'Is Jed here?' he said breathlessly. 'Did you see him?'

'I'm not sure,' I replied, looking back into the crowd, which was now dispersing. It was eleven o'clock and the pub staff were hurrying people to finish their drinks and leave the premises. There was no sign of mullet-man or the guy with pressed jeans. 'I thought I saw him earlier – or someone who might have been him,' I volunteered. 'I didn't notice him leave. Maybe he's in the loo or something?'

'Stay here,' said Danny. 'I'll just be a sec.'

He clambered back on stage and said something to a couple of the other band members. There was lots of head shaking and shoulder shrugging. Then he was off again, weaving his way through the crowd to find someone who might know the whereabouts of Jed Wilson. I saw him speaking to a guy I recognised from the website as one of The Wonderfulls' fans. I think he was called Simon. He was short and broad and his belly spilled over his jeans like milk boiling over from a pan. I watched as he gave Danny a bear hug, patting him on the back and whispering something into his ear. Danny gave him a quizzical look, then made his way back to me, deliberately dodging other fans, who had hung around to congratulate him on the gig. His body language had changed completely; he looked tired and dejected.

'He was here,' said Danny. 'But the bastard left halfway through the set, apparently.'

'That doesn't mean anything, does it?'

'Don't be naïve, Naomi. He obviously didn't dig us.'

'But you were great tonight. Really great.'

'Not great enough, it seems.'

'Maybe he'll give you a call tomorrow. Maybe he needed to talk to someone else first?'

'Maybe,' sighed Danny. 'But don't hold your breath. If he'd liked us, if he'd wanted to sign us, we'd know about it.'

I tried to hold his hand, but he brushed me away. When Danny was upset he found it hard to be affectionate. Seeing my hurt expression, he squeezed my shoulder and told me he'd meet me at the front of the pub once he'd helped the others to load up the equipment.

He drove in silence. He was deep in thought and I could tell he was torturing himself, wondering if he could have sung better or whether it was Dylan's fault, or if The Wonderfulls should have rehearsed more.

'There'll be other chances, Danny,' I said softly. 'I'm sure of it.'

'Maybe.'

I didn't want to leave him yet but he insisted on dropping me off at home. 'It's not you,' he promised. 'I won't be good company tonight. I want to be on my own. Come round tomorrow afternoon?'

'You were supposed to be coming for lunch, with my parents,' I reminded him.

'Oh shit. Look, can you tell them I'm really sorry. Make something up – I just don't feel like it, OK?'

'OK,' I said, disappointed. 'I'll come round after lunch, then.'

'That would be nice.' He smiled, sadly. I kissed him and for a moment he forgot himself and started to respond. But then he pulled away from me and leaned over to open the car door.

'I love you, Danny,' I said, hoping it might make him feel better.

'I love you too, Omi.' His voice was monotone.

Danny seemed in better spirits the next afternoon. He greeted me with a long, tender kiss, as if to make up for his lack of affection the previous night. 'I'm OK,' he assured me. 'I've had a chat with the others and we're going to record some more demos and send them out. We won't let the bastards get us down.'

I had told my parents that he'd missed lunch because he didn't feel very well and that I was going over later to look after him. They'd accepted my explanation without too much fuss and didn't question me further. Mum had even let me off dessert and asked, with genuine concern, if Danny needed anything. I'd almost quipped, 'A record deal,' but thought better of it.

We lounged around on Danny's sofa for a couple of hours, listening to music and watching rubbish television. I was always amazed how much trivia Danny kept in his head. He knew all the characters' names in the soaps, what the actors had been in before and what was going on in their private lives. But he was also well up on current affairs, able to fill me in on the latest developments in the Middle East and why a particular economic policy was bad news for the country. As for his knowledge of music, it was encyclopaedic. Whenever I said I liked a particular song, he'd say, 'You might like this, then,' and he'd go to his CD collection – which covered the wall of his living room – and pick out something by an obscure artist I'd never heard of. He was the same with books. His brain was like a sponge – if he was interested in something he had to know it all, to possess it.

'Do you fancy doing something – going somewhere, maybe?' I asked when the central heating began to make me feel drowsy.

'Sure,' he said. 'We could go into town, do a museum or gallery or something.'

I nodded. 'That would be nice.'

'I'd better get changed,' he said. He was wearing last night's long-sleeved, grey T-shirt, which now smelled of stale smoke and sweat. I watched as he peeled it over his head, admiring his slim torso and muscular shoulders. But as he pulled off the sleeves, I noticed a large, flesh-coloured plaster on his forearm. It hadn't been there yesterday.

'What happened to your arm, Danny?' I was curious and a little concerned.

'Hey?' His head was still caught on the top. He wriggled out of it.

'The plaster. Did you hurt yourself?'

He became suddenly modest, draping the T-shirt over himself and avoiding eye contact. 'Oh, that. It's nothing. I caught myself on a guitar string last night. Don't worry about it.'

But I was worried. I knew Danny well enough by now to know when he was lying. It seemed odd – more than coincidence, certainly – that a guitar string should have cut him on almost the same part of his arm as his old, schoolboy injury. Or, maybe that hadn't been an accident either. Could he have done it to himself? Were both wounds self-inflicted? Were they drug-related? Was Danny doing more than just smoking the odd spliff? Or had he been in a fight?

Before I could say anything else, Danny had scurried into the bedroom. When he returned, his top changed, he was smiling. 'Let's go, then.'

'All right,' I said, forcing myself to smile back.

I brushed my worries to the back of my mind – I was getting good at that. I hated myself for feeling suspicious of Danny and anyway, it didn't make sense. People only hurt themselves or picked fights when they were really troubled or depressed, didn't they? Last night hadn't gone well, but Danny didn't generally seem down, did he? If Danny was doing something destructive, it could only mean that there was something he wasn't telling me . . . that I wasn't making him happy. Didn't he feel close enough to me to confide in me? Wasn't I enough for him? Might it even be my fault? I couldn't face that possibility; it was far better for me to ignore my concerns and play dumb. I wasn't yet ready to open Pandora's box.

We caught the bus into town and walked around for a while, looking in the shop windows. Then we went to see a photographic exhibition, which I'd mentioned I fancied catching. I'd never had anyone to go to this type of exhibition with before – my friends thought them boring. But Danny encouraged my love of photography; he said I was talented and should dump law and make a career out of it. I was starting to think that it was a good idea. Danny had a lot of good ideas. They took me down avenues I'd never have visited on my own and made me aware that, if I wanted, I could skirt around the paths that I felt had been laid out for me.

chapter 12

Danny dropped me home late that night. I walked through the front door, smiling to myself, feeling that I was wrapped in the warm glow of happiness. I'd had a lovely time with Danny at the exhibition and we had followed it with a meal out and a hot chocolate back at his place.

But as I entered the hall I noticed that the kitchen light was on. I peered around the door to find Mum and Dad sitting at the kitchen table, waiting for me.

'Where have you been?' asked Dad in a nagging voice, which I knew meant trouble.

'You know where I've been – I've been at Danny's.' I was still smiling. 'We went to an exhibition – I've got some postcards – look.' I rummaged around in my bag. I'd bought some great images, portraits that had been taken using this cool technique called solarisation, which made them look like paintings. I was really excited by it.

'I thought he was ill,' said Mum, obviously hurt that I had lied.

I cursed myself silently for forgetting. Mum had seemed genuinely concerned about Danny and now I'd disappointed her and dropped him in it too. 'He was feeling better,' I said. I quickly changed the subject. 'Anyway, why are you up so late – isn't it past your bedtime?' I grinned, checking my watch. It was almost one in the morning.

'This is not the time to be cheeky,' said Dad flatly. 'We've been at a charity supper quiz. I'm sure that doesn't interest you. But what you might like to know is that Martin Stevens was there.'

'Oh.' Martin Stevens was, of course, my boss and an acquaintance of Dad's. 'How was he?'

'He was absolutely fine and so was his wife. However, he's under the impression that *you* haven't been too well of late.'

'Really?' I asked.

I hadn't expected the attack, wasn't prepared for it.

'You know exactly what I'm talking about, Naomi, don't deny it. Martin said you've had a few days off here and there, without notice, and that you've been coming in late rather too often. He's also noticed that you're not performing very well, that your mind doesn't seem to be on the job. Have you got anything to say to that?'

'No, not really,' I muttered.

'Well, is it true?'

'I guess, a bit.'

'Why, Naomi? You worked so hard to get that placement and it took no small amount of effort on my part, either. Why are you letting yourself down?'

'It's boring,' I said. 'It's not what I expected at all. They leave me alone half the day, doing stuff like filing and photocopying. I hate it.'

'What did you expect? You're hardly likely to be asked to represent people in court now, are you? For heaven's sake, Naomi, this is an opportunity to learn about how things work, to get some experience for your CV. It's invaluable for your degree and it could potentially lead to future work as a lawyer in that practice.'

'I'm not sure I want to be a lawyer,' I said quietly.

'Pardon?'

'I don't think I want to work in law after all.'

Dad got up from the table. 'What? You are joking, aren't you? You've got a place at one of the best universities in the country to read law next year and now you say you've changed your mind?'

'Yes,' I said. 'I've changed my mind. I'm going to pack in law and do photography instead. Danny thinks I'm a natural.' As I said it I thought, *Yes, that's what I want to do. I'll become a photographer.* Saying the words helped shaped the idea in my mind, made it a real option.

Dad exploded. 'You nincompoop!' It was such a funny word that I had to try hard not to laugh. Dad was always so worried about not swearing that he kept a collection of the most old-fashioned expressions in his head. He was the only person I knew who still said 'crikey' and 'good grief' and 'gosh'. 'Nincompoop' was his favourite when he thought someone was acting like an idiot. 'You fool!' he continued. 'After all your years of hard work you're now planning on throwing it all away. I'm very disappointed, Naomi. Very disappointed. You're just being . . . stupid!' His round face was red and puffy with anger, his cheeks swelling like a cooked tomato that was about to explode.

'I'm not being stupid!' I shouted. 'I'm just doing what I want for a change.'

'Are you?' interrupted Mum, in a calm, soft voice. She had kept quiet until now. She got up from the table and walked over to my side.

'Of course. What do you mean?'

'Are you doing what you really want or what Danny wants you to do?'

'They're the same thing,' I said. 'Danny knows me. He understands me.'

'But you never said you wanted to do photography before. You always had your heart set on becoming a lawyer.'

'I've always enjoyed photography, you know I have.'

'Yes, as a hobby, not a career. It just strikes me that it's Danny who's encouraged this. He's a nice, intelligent boy and we like him very much, but he has some crazy ideas.'

'What's crazy about photography?'

'That's not what I mean. We're not wealthy like Danny's family. We can't support you forever. We want you to have a career that will give you a happy, comfortable life. I don't think you've thought this through, Naomi. Have you?'

She was right. I hadn't. But I wasn't going to let her know that.

'Yes, I have. It's what I want to do and if you won't support me, that's fine. Danny will be there for me.'

'Don't be ridiculous!' Dad spluttered. 'You're eighteen

years old, he's – what – twenty? You might both feel differ-ently in a few years. Do you really think life is that easy?'

That hurt. I'd believed that Mum and Dad knew how serious I was about Danny. Now it transpired that they thought it was just a silly, teenage fling.

'But I love him,' I said. 'And he loves me. We're soul-mates.'

'Oh, Naomi,' said Mum. She came towards me and tried to hug me, but I left my arms hanging by my sides. 'I know you love him. But love doesn't pay the bills.'

'We'll work something out,' I said.

Mum tried another tack. 'Naomi, do you think that you would have changed your mind about law if it hadn't been for Danny?'

'I don't know,' I said. 'Maybe.'

She was hesitant. 'You know we like Danny . . . it's just that you seem to have been very influenced by him.'

'Influenced?'

'Yes. Ever since you started going out with him you've done nothing but talk about him and his band. You haven't seen any of your other friends – you hardly speak to Debbie any more. Now we find out you've missed work too. And today, you lied for him. He's a very strong char-acter. Where have you gone, Naomi?'

'This is me,' I said, pointing to my chest. 'This is the real me. Maybe I just didn't realise it before.'

Mum shook her head in exasperation. 'We're not trying to upset you, we're just worried about you. We don't want you to make any foolish mistakes.'

'I thought you liked him. You said you liked him!'

'We do, Naomi. But he doesn't seem the most respon-sible or stable person.'

She had touched a raw nerve, questioned the very things that had begun to worry me about Danny. Rather than admit that – to Mum or to myself – I reacted with anger. 'What?! I'm eighteen, I don't want stability or responsibility. You're so middle-aged.'

'Don't be rude to your mother,' said Dad protectively. 'We've got more life experience than you and we can see that you're risking making a mistake. Maybe you should take some time out for yourself . . . perhaps you should stop seeing Danny for a while, eh?'

'No!' I cried. I looked at Mum, pleading with my eyes. Surely she must understand. 'You can't ask me to do that. I love him.'

'I think it's for the best,' she said flatly, her eyes down-cast. 'Just for a little bit, while you have a think about things.'

I couldn't believe what I was hearing. She wasn't my rational, kind, understanding mother – she must be an alien replicant. She knew how happy Danny made me. How could she ask me to break up with him?

'I can't do it!' I shouted. 'I won't do it.'

'Can't do what?' None of us had noticed that Emily had wandered into the room. She was wearing her nightie and looked bleary-eyed.

'It's nothing, Emily,' said Mum. 'Go back to bed. You've got school in the morning.'

Emily didn't move. 'I woke up and heard raised voices,' she said, looking from Mum to Dad to me and then back to Mum again. 'Has something happened?'

'No,' said Mum. 'It's all OK.'

'Yes!' I cried, certain that Emily would understand and take my side. 'It's not OK. Mum and Dad want me to stop seeing Danny.'

Emily walked over to me and placed her hand on my shoulder. '*What? Why?*'

'They think he's a bad influence.'

Mum sighed. 'That's not exactly what we said, Naomi. We just said things were getting a bit out of hand and that maybe you should take some time to think about it all.'

I could feel my face growing red, the muscles in my jaw and forehead clenching. I stepped forward, unsure what I would do or say, my arms flailing in frustration.

'I'm sure there's another way,' said Emily, stroking my hair. She chewed her lip in thought. She had taken it upon herself to play the mediator. 'Naomi loves Danny – she's been so happy since she met him. Can't you give him another chance and then see?'

'For heaven's sake,' said Dad, irritated. 'This is getting silly. What we have suggested is very sensible – some time apart for Naomi to sort herself out.'

'I can't do it,' I repeated.

'It might not be your choice. You live under our roof,' said Dad firmly. I didn't like his insinuation.

'I'm eighteen, I'm an adult. If you don't want me to see Danny, I'll leave home.'

Dad laughed. 'And where exactly will you go?'

'To Danny's,' I stated. My hand was already reaching for the mobile phone in my coat pocket. 'I'm going to go round there now.'

'It's the middle of the night,' said Mum. I could tell she was anxious, worried that she and Dad had gone too far.

'Don't be silly, Nay,' said Emily. She tried to stroke my hair again, but I pushed her hand away. Her bottom lip began to quiver. I felt awful. She hated it when anybody argued and here she was, right in the middle of it, trying to appease all three of us and getting nowhere. 'Why don't you sleep on it and when everybody's calmed down we'll talk about it some more?' she added, her voice shaky.

I mulled over Emily's idea. 'Will you change your mind about Danny?' I asked Dad.

'Of course not,' he said stubbornly.

'Well, in that case, there's no point.' I started walking into the hall. I felt strangely exhilarated. 'I'm not going to change my mind about him either. So I might as well go now.'

'Naomi!' Mum shouted. 'Don't be silly. Come back!'

'Please don't go, Nay,' begged Emily, as tears began to roll down her face.

I was aware that she was following close behind me, but I didn't turn around – I quickened my pace. As I slammed the front door behind me I heard Mum and Emily still calling, 'Naomi! Naomi!'

I phoned Danny from the corner of my road. I prayed

he was not yet asleep and would pick up. I hid myself behind a hedge, in case my parents came out looking for me. Going home was not an option – I had left my keys in the hall and I couldn't face Mum and Dad's smug looks if I rang the doorbell in defeat. We'd never fallen out like this before and I wanted them to know how important Danny was to me. I was desperately upset, and not quite sure what I was doing, but one thing was certain – they deserved to sweat a little.

Thankfully, Danny answered the phone immediately.

'Please come and get me,' I sobbed, before he could say a word.

'What's happened, Omi? Are you OK? Where are you?'

'I'm at the end of my street. Please come and get me, Danny.'

'Of course I will,' he said, the tone of his voice coloured by a mixture of reassurance, confusion and concern. 'Give me five minutes.'

It seemed to take forever for Danny to arrive. Standing there, waiting alone in the darkness, I felt cold and vulnerable. Every time I heard the sound of a car I stepped out from the shadows, allowing myself to be illuminated by its headlights. None of them was Danny's. One car slowed down, causing my heart to beat wildly in terror. *All I need now*, I thought, *is to be abducted by some crazed sex attacker. My parents would think I was with Danny and nobody would report me missing for days.*

I recognised the sound of Danny's engine before I saw his car. For once I was pleased that he was speeding up my road; sod the speed limit – it meant he cared. As he screeched to a stop he flung open the passenger door for me.

'What's happened?' he asked again. I was shaking with cold, fear and anger and he looked panic-stricken.

'Oh Danny, I'm so pleased to see you!' I cried, leaning over and flinging my arms around him. 'Please take me back to your flat. I don't want my parents to see me.'

He clasped me so tightly that I couldn't breathe. 'For God's sake, what's happened?'

'It's my parents. We had a row. They don't want me to see you any more.'

'What?' he said, loosening his grip. 'I don't understand.'

'Nor do I,' I said. 'They think you're a bad influence.'

'What? I thought they liked me?'

'Please drive, Danny.'

'OK, but will you please tell me what's going on?'

As we drove I told Danny about how Dad had bumped into Martin Stevens and the argument it had caused. He listened intently, his expression growing stony cold with anger.

'Your idiot parents don't know what they're talking about,' he said. There was no longer concern in his voice, only indignation and spite.

'I think they mean well,' I said, trying to placate him. Angry as I was, I didn't like to hear him talk about my parents so hatefully. He didn't know them well enough to judge them. 'They're just overreacting.'

'They're trying to control your life, more like. What right have they to tell you not to see me?'

'None, Danny,' I said. 'They can't make me break up with you.'

'Damn right, they can't. I hope you told them that.'

'Of course I did. I don't think they believed it when I walked out.' I managed a shaky little laugh at my own gall. 'I've never done anything like this before.'

'Well, maybe you should have. You've let them push you around for too long. They don't understand you like I do – they're just trying to turn you into a clone of them. Listen, Omi, as far as I'm concerned, you can stay at mine as long as you like. Sod your parents.'

'Thanks,' I said, still uncomfortable with the way he was slating my parents. I was angry with them, sure, but they had their good points, and when it came down to it, I loved them. Why were Danny's emotions always so extreme? He saw everything in black and white. 'Maybe they'll calm down by the morning,' I suggested.

'It's already the morning,' Danny reminded me.

I looked at my watch. 'Damn, I'm due in the office in less than seven hours.'

'You hate that job. Why not pack it in right now? You don't want to be a lawyer anyway.'

'I need the money, Danny.'

'I've got enough money for both of us. I'll see you right.'

'Thanks, Danny, but I'm not sure.' I thought on the spot. 'I'm due a week off anyway. I'll call in tomorrow and tell them I need a few days' break now.'

'Great,' he said. 'We'll have a lovely time, you and me. Just you wait and see.'

Chapter 13

We did have a lovely time – for the first few days, at least. Being at Danny's, away from my parents and the stifling environment of my home, gave me a sense of freedom; it was like being on holiday. Arranging a break from work had been no trouble. By the time I called in – at ten o'clock on the morning after I'd left home – it was evident that Dad had already been in touch with Mr Stevens to smooth the way. He came on the line and, in a rather fatherly manner, told me that the practice had agreed to give me a couple of weeks leave 'to get your head together'. After that, I should come in to discuss my future. I had no idea whether or not I would go back; I honestly didn't care one way or the other.

It felt strange staying in such a big house, with its gated drive and huge garden. It could not have been more different from my house, where the walls and ceilings were thin and everybody knew each other's business. Danny's parents' house was so vast and so quiet; once I was shut safely away in his flat, there could have been a party going on in the main house and I wouldn't have known about it. I still hadn't met Mr Evans – he was away on another business trip – but Mrs Evans made me nervous and I dreaded bumping into her in the hall. Ever since our first meeting, when I'd almost knocked over her precious vase, she'd made me feel awkward and clumsy. And because she expected me to be clumsy, I succeeded in acting like it, tripping over my feet and banging into things whenever she was around me. When she spoke to me, I stuttered. It's funny how someone else's perception of you can have such a strong, unconscious effect on the way you behave.

Emily brought some of my stuff round on the second evening. She told me Mum was waiting in the car outside, so she couldn't stay long.

'She's really worried about you,' she said. 'Talk to her, Nay.'

'I can't. I'll ring her when I'm ready.'

'It's horrible at home. Mum and Dad have been arguing and dinner time is worse than ever. Come home, Nay. I'm sure you can sort things out.'

'I want to be with Danny,' I said, trying to sound stronger than I felt. 'Until Mum and Dad accept that, I'm staying put.'

Emily shrugged. She looked so sad that I felt guilty. I hadn't meant to make everybody miserable. As much as I loved being with Danny, I knew I wouldn't feel completely happy or settled until I had made things right with my parents.

After Emily had left I went downstairs to see Danny. He'd given me a key to his flat, but I still felt that I had to knock before I went in. Every time I did it he laughed at me. 'I do wish you'd chill out, Omi. The only person who knocks is the cleaning lady. Make yourself at home.'

'Sorry, Danny, I can't help it.'

'Stop apologising,' he said, playfully squeezing my cheeks. 'You seem really tense. What is it?'

'Oh, you know, it's just Emily coming round and thinking about all that stuff with my parents.'

'Your bloody parents again,' he hissed, rolling his eyes. Then, seeing that he had hurt me, his expression brightened. 'I just love having you here, Omi. I really hope you'll stay forever. Just you and me.'

He kissed me and everything felt better, instantly.

At first, Danny treated me like a princess, cooking me break-fast and dinner and generally fussing around me. He'd take me out wherever I wanted to go and buy me presents, like perfume and sweets. He even decided to take it upon himself to teach me to play the guitar, declaring me a natural when I mastered two chords at our first lesson. I'd never spent so much time with one person and I was surprised to find that we never irritated each other or ran out of things to talk about.

If I let myself ignore the situation with my parents, and the fact that this set-up could only be temporary, I could pretend that this was what it was like to be grown up and living with someone. Even mundane things, like going to the supermarket with Danny, made me feel closer to him. We'd walk down the aisles, hand in hand, and when other shop-pers looked at us I felt proud because we were 'a couple' and everyone knew it.

But for Danny, at least, the novelty of having me around

soon wore off. By Wednesday he had already started to lapse into his old routines and I found myself having to fit into them. Danny liked to spend a lot of time alone, strumming his guitar or reading in silence. I hadn't realised before how lazy he was; he rarely got up before twelve and he didn't go out until nightfall unless he had to. If I tried to wake him early he'd be grumpy and tetchy, so I learned to amuse myself until I knew it was safe to talk to him. I watched hours of morning television, painted my nails and practised guitar chords on an old acoustic that he had lent me. By the end of the first week, however, the lessons had all but dried up; it appeared that Danny had run out of patience for teaching me.

I didn't want to admit it to myself, but I was starting to feel bored and, strangely, lonely. I couldn't help wondering if Danny might be growing tired of me, and each time that thought crossed my mind I felt sick and panicky. I tried to come up with ways of making him fall in love with me again, dressing up in the clothes he liked best and taking time to do my hair and make-up. I even wrote myself lists of amusing anecdotes that I knew might make him laugh, so that I could reel them off at a moment's notice and he'd remember how much fun we had together.

But for every moment that I feared Danny might have cooled towards me, there was another when his words and actions suggested that he loved me as much as ever. Sometimes, he would gaze into my eyes and tell me how special I was, how much he needed me. He would start writing a song and tell me that I had inspired it, that having me around was making him more creative than ever. Or he'd present me with a gift or make me a fabulous meal for no reason at all. His behaviour was so erratic that I didn't know whether I was coming or going. Was I doing or saying something wrong sometimes to make him cross with me? Could it be something of which I wasn't even conscious?

If only I had been honest with myself I would have realised that I was not the problem – Danny was. And it wasn't only me – he no longer seemed to be absorbed by anything for long. The new demos he had talked about The Wonderfulls making never materialised and very few gigs were lined up. Band rehearsals still took place in his flat, but lately they were more shambolic than ever. Only half the band would turn up at any one time, so they couldn't ever get any real playing done. Instead, whoever had made it on that particular night would jam with Danny for a while, and then they'd get a takeaway and some six-packs of beer and sit around getting stoned until they crashed out.

I felt even more of a spare part than before. I've never been the sort of girl who's 'one of the lads' and Danny's mates made it perfectly clear that I was in the way. One evening, when I was in the kitchen getting myself a drink, I overheard Andy referring to me as 'her indoors' and then laughing. Danny didn't really defend me, he just laughed and told Andy I was 'no trouble'. I was hurt, but I couldn't show it. Was that what Danny really thought of me? Or was he just being blokey in front of his mates? Too upset to put on a front, I excused myself and went to bed. And by the next day, it was forgotten. Danny was in such a sweet, affection-ate mood that I chose not to say anything.

On an icy Monday afternoon, a week after I'd arrived, I asked Danny if I could borrow his laptop to work on the band's website. It hadn't been updated for a while and I was worried that the fans would begin to lose interest if there wasn't some new hype for them to talk about. He seemed reluctant to get it for me.

'Don't bother, Omi,' he said. 'There's nothing new to put up.'

'Yeah, but it's good to change it a bit anyway. I've got some pictures I haven't used.'

'If you can be arsed.'

'Danny . . .' I began, gently, worried about his reaction to the question I was about to ask. 'Is everything all right with The Wonderfulls? It's just since the gig, since you didn't get signed, you've seemed like you don't really care any more.'

'Of course I care,' he replied, turning away from me. I realised that he looked tired, older even, his eyes hollow and his skin blotchy.

'Yes, but you're not really playing or rehearsing. You were going to record some demos, get some more interest . . . You haven't even finished any new songs.'

'Musician's block,' he muttered. 'It happens.'

'Maybe I could help?'

He laughed at me. 'What, with your two chords?'

'That's cruel.' My mouth fell into an involuntary pout. I emphasised it comically so he wouldn't know how much his comment had hurt me. It was his fault that I hadn't pro-gressed with the guitar; he was a poor teacher. Playing came instinctively to Danny – he couldn't explain things clearly, had little patience when I complained that my fingertips were hurting and he had simply stopped bothering to teach me. I could have said, 'You're the one who gives up if things don't come easy, not me.' But I didn't want to fight.

'Yes, it is cruel,' he said, smiling apologetically. 'Look, I'm sorry, but you don't know what you're talking about.'

'Maybe not,' I continued, feeling the frustrations of the past few days welling up inside me. 'But I do know that sitting around drinking and getting stoned with your waste-of-space mates isn't going to help.' The instant the words were out, I knew I'd sounded just like my mother.

Danny sneered. 'Get off your high horse, Naomi. Sometimes you can be so prissy. If you don't like it, you can get back to your boring friends and oh-so-middle-class parents and your law firm.'

I flinched. The flip side of knowing someone intimately is that they recognise exactly which buttons to press to hurt you, and Danny had gone too far now. I was no longer prepared to pussyfoot around him. If he wanted a fight, he could have one. 'You know what?' I spat. 'Maybe I will.'

'Go on, then. If you don't want to be here with me, then go.'

He looked me dead in the eye, daring me to get up and walk out. I knew he didn't think I would actually do it. He expected me to crumble, to apologise and to ask him to hold me and kiss me until our disagreement was forgotten. But I couldn't bring myself to do that. I was angry, and, more to the point, I was in the right. Wasn't I?

Realising that I'd talked myself into a corner, there was nothing for it but to act on my words. I may not be someone who relishes confrontation, but I'm no walkover. I stood up, marched to the door, and, without turning back to look at Danny, I opened it and slammed it behind me. Then I grabbed my coat and my gloves and left the flat as quickly as I could. I was panicking slightly – I didn't have any idea where I would go; I didn't have my phone with me, so I couldn't call anyone, and home certainly wasn't an option. *My parents would love it*, I thought, *if I'd turned up, my tail between my legs, with nowhere else to go*. There was no way I wanted to give them that satisfaction.

For about ten minutes or so, I just walked, letting my feet take me wherever they wanted to go. The streets around Danny's house were unfamiliar and I worried that I might become lost. But I soon came upon a landmark that I recognised: the gates of the park where Danny and I had spent our second date. It seemed apt that I had found my way to this park, with its happy memories; it was as though I had been meant to find it.

There were very few people about, just a couple of dog-walkers and some young boys playing football. Walking alone in a wide-open space just a couple of hours before nightfall probably wasn't the most sensible idea, but that didn't occur to me. I felt safe in that park, protected by the same trees and the same grass that had hosted my lovely picnic with Danny only four months earlier. If I listened carefully I could almost hear our laughter still echoing in the breeze. Everything had been so simple then, before other people – and real life – had intervened.

I headed for the playground and, ignoring the sign that read *Under-12s Only*, sat down on one of the swings. My eighteen-year-old bottom was too wide for it and the metal joints dug into my flesh, making me wince. It didn't seem fair to me that only children were supposed to go on the swings. I had never grown out of it. I still loved the sensation of freedom – flying through the air, reaching higher and higher with each kick of my legs, my hair flowing behind me and the wind on my face, until I was in danger of going over the top. As soon as I had my own place with a garden, I decided, I would install a swing – just for me.

As I swung, my anger dissipated. I wondered if Danny would come looking for me. Surely he must have realised that I wouldn't have gone home and maybe he, too, would be drawn here. I imagined him coming up behind me and pushing me on the swing, refusing to stop until we were both laughing so much that we had forgotten what we had argued about.

But he didn't come. After an hour, I decided to return to his flat. In my mind, I knew exactly how the conversation would go: I planned to tell him that I was sorry and that I knew it wasn't my place to interfere in The Wonderfulls. Then he would apologise too, tell me he wanted me to stay and we'd kiss and make up. In my eagerness to create a perfect end to a horrible day, I'd forgotten that conversations never seem to pan out quite the way you've planned them.

Chapter 14

Danny's flat was unexpectedly dark and oddly quiet when I let myself back in. It made me wonder if he had gone out looking for me, but his car was still in the drive and his favourite leather jacket was hanging from a hook in the hall. I had never known the flat to be silent; Danny always had some sort of music playing – there was a stereo system or radio in every room bar the toilet. He also had a habit of leaving the light on in each room he entered, so the place was always well lit. I couldn't put my finger on it, but there was a peculiar atmosphere in the flat, the darkness as eerie as the silence.

Something – an instinct, a sixth sense perhaps – stopped me from calling out Danny's name or switching on the lights myself. With my coat still buttoned up, I made my way first into the kitchen and then into the living room. There was no trace of Danny in either room, no coffee cups, plates or papers providing any evidence of recent activity. He must be in his bedroom, I thought. But the door was shut tight and I could hear no movement behind it. Had Danny gone to bed? He couldn't have. It was only a few hours since he had got up. Was he ill? What could he be doing in there?

I grasped the handle and pushed the door, letting it open a fraction. 'Danny?' I said softly. 'Are you in there?' There was no response. I peered through the crack, tentatively pushing the door a little further. In the faint light I could just make out a shape, a human form in front of me on the floor. 'Danny?' Again, no answer. With my heart hammering against my chest, I inched my way closer. Now I could see that the figure was hunched over, its head between its legs, rocking gently back and forth. 'Danny, are you OK?' The figure began to whimper, its breathing laboured and wheezy. 'Danny, what's happened?' Still there was no reply.

'I'm going to turn the light on, OK?'

'OK,' he croaked.

I paused before I pressed the light switch, nervous at the thought of what I might see. But nothing I had imagined could have prepared me for the sight that met my eyes. Danny was crouched on the carpet, his arms folded around his lowered head, his knees pulled into his chest. He was shaking like a young bird that has fallen from its mother's nest. It made no sense to me, but his jeans were splattered with what appeared to be red paint, and there was a small pool of paint by his feet.

Then I saw the kitchen knife, lying just a metre away from Danny, and I knew that it wasn't paint; it was blood.

Danny's blood.

I thought I was going to be sick. My first instinct was to flee from the room, to run outside and pretend that this had never happened, but I couldn't move. I was cemented to the carpet, my legs numb and heavy, as if they were encased in a plaster cast. Seconds passed. I began to count: one . . . two . . . three . . .

'Oh my God, Danny, what have you done?' It was my voice, but it didn't belong to me – the words seemed to come from someone else's lips. The need to be practical had taken me over, it was driving me to action. I could feel the adrenaline coursing through my body, bringing my legs back to life and making my brain work in double time. Before I knew it I was at Danny's side, my arms around his back. 'Where are you hurt? Show me, Danny, show me.'

He looked up at me, his eyes watery and vacant. He opened his mouth, as if he were about to speak, and then closed it again. Then he sat up and unfolded his arms, and I could see that his left arm was wrapped in a makeshift bandage. He pointed to it. 'Here,' he said in a flat voice. 'Here.'

'Can I look?' I asked. He nodded. Afraid that I would hurt him, I unrolled the bandage as carefully as I could, praying that the bleeding had stopped. Part of the fabric had stuck to the wound and he winced as I pulled it away.

There were three gashes on his arm, two of them just scratches, but the third a long, deep slice in his flesh. The whole of his forearm was covered in dark, congealed blood. I didn't know anything about first aid, but I reasoned that if the bleeding had stopped it meant he didn't need stitches. He began to sob, deep, throaty sobs that made it difficult to catch his breath.

'I'm sorry, Omi, I'm so sorry,' he whimpered.

'It's OK, Danny, it's going to be OK,' I said. 'I'm here now.'

I fetched the first-aid kit from the bathroom cabinet and cleaned his wounds with antiseptic, bandaging them up again as best I could. Danny let me tend to him in silence, sitting still on the floor until I had finished. All his strength had gone; he was limp, like a giant baby.

When I had helped him change and put his clothes in the washing machine, I made him a cup of tea and told him to lie on the sofa and sip it slowly. I wished I'd made one for myself too. Now that the shock had passed I felt exhausted and my head was beginning to throb. I wanted to go to sleep, but I knew that I couldn't. I sat quietly for a while, Danny's head in my lap, trying to summon up the courage to talk about what had happened. The bloodstain on the bedroom carpet glared up at me through the open door and I knew that later I would have to get down on my hands and knees and scrub it away.

'It wasn't an accident, was it, Danny?' I asked, eventually, stating the obvious. We were now sitting side by side on the sofa, not quite touching. The inch of space between us felt like a yard. He shrugged and nodded.

'And the scars on your arm from before, they weren't an accident either?'

'No,' he said, hanging his head. He wouldn't meet my gaze.

So my half-formed suspicions, my instincts had been right. And yet, having them confirmed brought me no comfort, no relief at all, only more questions.

'I don't understand, Danny. Please help me understand.'

'It makes me feel better.'

'How?' I stroked his hair, as much to have something to do with my hands as to comfort him.

'It's hard to explain.' He sighed. 'It's like – when everything's getting to me, when I'm angry or upset – it makes the pain go away.'

'But doesn't it hurt?'

'No . . . yes . . . it's different. It hurts in a good way, because I'm making it happen. It's a buzz. And when the blood comes, it's like a release, it's like all my problems are draining away.'

'I don't understand. Is it my fault, Danny? Did I make you do it?'

'No,' he said, his voice cracking with frustration. Still, he wouldn't look at me. 'No, Omi, it's not you. You make everything better. When I'm around you I don't want to do it, I don't need to do it. Today, things just got out of control. I'm sorry, I'm really, really sorry.'

'It's OK,' I said, putting my arms around him. But it wasn't OK.

'I love you, Omi,' he whispered. He allowed me to hug him, but his arms remained limply in his lap.

'And I love you.'

Those three little words again. What did they mean, exactly? Speaking them required the same amount of breath, the same coordination of my lips and tongue as it had a thousand times before. They still sounded the same, were spelled the same. And yet, the words were now sticky with Danny's blood – imbued with a heaviness, a significance that they hadn't possessed before. What had I taken on by saying them? Only one thing was certain: I was in over my head. Way, way over my head.

Chapter 15

By the next morning Danny was his usual self again. He didn't want to talk about what had happened the day before – he seemed embarrassed about it, ashamed even – and he made me promise not to tell anyone. I agreed, reluctantly. I couldn't help feeling that *somebody* else should know. Fear, concern, pity, love, insecurity and a thousand other emotions I couldn't even name all swirled round and round in my head, swamping me like quicksand. I still couldn't comprehend what he had done; it made no sense. And if I didn't understand, how could I help him?

He larked around all day, telling me stupid jokes and trying to engage me in play fights, wrestling me on the sofa and then tickling me until I begged him to stop. Yesterday, he had revealed his weakest, most vulnerable side and now it was obvious to me that he was overcompensating, hoping that if he made me laugh I might forget what I had seen. But I couldn't forget. Images of his blood on the carpet kept flashing into my mind, each time jolting me with shock. I felt awkward around Danny, scared to say any-thing that might upset him and send him back over the edge again.

Mum had been ringing sporadically ever since I'd left home. She'd left pitiful-sounding messages on my voicemail, begging me to call her and sort things out. Guiltily, I had ignored all but the first, to which I'd sent a text in reply: DON'T WORRY ABOUT ME. I'LL CALL WHEN I'M READY.

That day, after what had happened with Danny, I felt differently. I actually wanted to see her. I needed a hug from somebody who could make me feel loved and protected. So when Danny was in the toilet, I texted her: CALL ME IF U WANT 2 TALK.

A few seconds later, my phone began to ring.

'Naomi, I'm so glad to hear from you,' Mum said breathlessly.

'You all right, Mum?'

'Yes, yes. And you?'

'I'm fine,' I lied.

'I'd really like to see you, Naomi. Would you think about coming home this afternoon? I promise you Dad's at work – it'll be just the two of us.'

I considered the offer. On the one hand, I welcomed the idea of some space from Danny so I could get my head straight, but on the other, I was frightened of how he would react and what he might do. I knew he saw my parents as a threat and I didn't want to risk angering him. And then there was the question of whether it was safe to leave him alone. Would he trust me not to reveal his secret? He had no cause to worry. Much as I needed to talk, I already knew I had no intention of betraying his confidence to Mum. I couldn't bear the thought of her pitying Danny or thinking of him as weak or ill.

'Hold on a sec, Mum,' I said. 'I'll ring you back.'

I knocked on the bathroom door. 'Danny – would you mind if I went out for a couple of hours? Mum's just called. I just want to keep the peace, you know?'

'Of course not,' he said, perhaps too brightly. 'I've had a great idea for a song. You go out and leave me to it.'

Allowing myself to be reassured, I called Mum back. 'OK,' I said. 'I'll come over. But just for an hour or so. I'm not staying.'

Mum was ever so formal when she opened the door to me – she greeted me almost like a stranger. Her jaw was clenched tight with nerves and her hands were sweaty and fidgety. *She's holding back because she's scared of me*, I thought, and I hated myself for it. The longed-for hug didn't materialise. I wanted to say, 'It's me, *Naomi*,' but I knew that if I let my guard down everything would all come pouring out. I had to stay strong, for Danny's sake.

When we were sitting together at the kitchen table Mum took a deep breath and began a conversation that she had evidently rehearsed several times in her head.

'I understand what you're going through – far more than you realise,' she began.

'What do you mean?' I asked nonchalantly. I sat stiffly, my arms folded on the table in front of me. My body language spoke volumes. 'Here we go,' it said. 'Another lecture.'

'Hear me out, Naomi. I understand, because I've been there myself. With someone a lot like Danny, actually. Before your dad.'

I studied her quizzically. As far as I was concerned,

Mum and Dad had been together since the year dot, since the Big Bang. I had never considered that Mum might have had a life – and relationships – before she met him.

'Yeah, right.' I managed a smirk. 'What, at nursery school?'

But she wasn't smiling. He expression was deadly serious.

'Stay there, Naomi,' she said. 'I'm just going to get something.'

She went upstairs and it sounded like she was moving furniture around. When she returned, looking flustered, she was carrying something in her hands. It was an old cardboard box. She rummaged around in it and pulled something out, which, after a moment's hesitation, she placed on the table in front of me.

'Look, Naomi.'

I looked. It was a photograph of two young people, their arms wrapped around each other. The image confused me. At first glance it appeared to be a picture of me, but I didn't recognise the guy or the hippie-style clothes I was wearing, and I knew I'd never grown my hair that long. It couldn't be me. And yet, something about the girl's smile was familiar.

I looked at Mum, then back at the photograph, and back at Mum again.

'It's you, isn't it?' I cried. I'd never seen Mum like this before – in all the photos she'd shown me she resembled a younger version of herself, with short, sensible, mousy hair, glasses and frumpy clothes. This was a period of her life I knew nothing about.

She laughed. 'Of course it's me. I wasn't born middle-aged, you know. Who else could it be?'

'Actually, you look like a lot like me,' I said. 'In horrible, polyester seventies' clothes. You look kind of cool, though,' Seeing her now, it was hard to believe that she had ever been young and pretty and – for the time – fashionable.

She laughed again. 'I guess I do. I was about your age there – a year or two older, perhaps.' Mum sighed. 'Hunky guy, isn't he? A bit of a dish?'

I hated it when Mum spoke like that; it was so embarrassing.

'He's not bad,' I conceded. 'If you take away the purple paisley flares. Nice eyes. Who is he?'

'His name was – and still is, I presume – Dominic Clearey, and,' she breathed deeply, 'he was the love of my life.'

I was shocked. 'What, more than Dad?'

'No, don't get me wrong, I love your Dad too. He's a wonderful man. But Dominic was my first love – my soulmate, as you put it. He was "the one".'

'Why are you telling me this?'

'Because I love you,' she said. 'And I think you need to hear it. I've never told anyone this before – not even your dad knows the full story. Please hear me out.'

I nodded, still sceptical that anything she said would make a difference, but intrigued nonetheless.

And this, more or less, is the story she told me:

Once upon a time there was a young girl named Martha Brookes who had an enormous musical talent.

People came from far and wide to hear her play the piano and she was awarded with prizes and scholarships to the country's top music schools. It was generally agreed that one day she would make her name as a world-renowned pianist. She practised hard, passed all her exams with flying colours and, at eighteen, took her place at the Royal Academy of Music.

But Martha was a dreamer. She dreamed of love and of passion with dark strangers from faraway lands. She was tired of practising hard, of playing the same phrases over and over again until her fingers ached. She longed for escape and adventure.

One night, at a concert, Martha met a man named Dominic Clearey. Half Irish, half Indian, he was the exotic, dark-eyed knight of her dreams. He swept her off her feet and made her feel that she was beautiful and special. Nobody had ever complimented her on anything but her piano playing and for the first time, she felt alive.

Dominic introduced her to new types of music, which weren't played in stuffy concert halls, and he took her to festivals all over the country in his camper van. The more time Martha spent with Dominic, the less she practised the piano. The accolades stopped coming and the invitations to give recitals dwindled, but Martha didn't care. All she wanted was to be with Dominic.

When Dominic asked Martha to move in with him she did so without a moment's thought. Her parents were horrified, but she ignored their advice. She dropped out of college, thinking that she could return in the future, when she was ready.

It soon transpired that Dominic was not the knight in shining armour she had imagined. He didn't want her to get a job, but criticised her housekeeping abilities, making her feel that nothing she did was good enough. He went out with his friends nearly every night, rolling in drunk in the early hours. And then, one night, he didn't come home at all. A few days later he rang Martha to tell her that he'd met somebody else, somebody more beautiful and more interesting. He told her to pack her things and to leave his house.

Martha was devastated. She returned home to her parents and began practising the piano again. But it was too late. There was no longer a scholarship or a place for her at the Royal Academy; younger and more prodigious talents had usurped her. So Martha put away her dreams of fame and of love, and trained as a teacher.

A few years later, she met David Waterman, the man who turned out to be her real white knight. He wasn't as passionate or exciting, but he was kind, hard-working and stable and all he wanted was to make Martha happy. Slowly, she let go of her feelings for Dominic and fell in love with David. Eventually, she married him, bore him two children and now, as everyone knows, they are living happily ever after.

When Mum had finished telling me her story she looked at the photograph again, smiled sadly, and then put it away in the box.

'Do you see, Naomi? Do you see?' she asked. 'I

thought Dominic was the only man for me, but in the end he didn't make me happy. If I hadn't met him I could have achieved so much more . . .' She paused, sighing deeply. 'And, even if things with Dominic had worked out, then I wouldn't have met your dad and I'd never have had you and Emily.'

'I'm sorry about what happened to you, but what has this got to do with me and Danny?' I asked. I wasn't stupid; I knew exactly why she had told me her cautionary tale, and that she wanted me to understand that she had once been young and idealistic, just like me – but I wasn't ready to accept it. So I played dumb.

'Oh, Naomi, can't you see? I just don't want you to make the same mistakes I did.'

'I'm me,' I said. 'And Danny's Danny. He's not Dominic. Just because you had a bad experience doesn't mean I will. I love Danny and I know he loves me.'

I may have sounded confident, but it was just an act. Underneath, I was a quivering wreck, desperate to tell her how worried I was about Danny, that he hurt himself and that I didn't know how to help him. I wanted to admit that being with him was no picnic, and that she might even be right about him. But I couldn't. I'd promised to keep Danny's secret. How could I betray him now? How could I let him down when he needed me most? I needed to be strong, for both of us.

'I know what I'm doing, Mum,' I said. 'I'm old enough to live my own life.' I almost added, 'and make my own mistakes,' but I didn't want to contemplate that possibility.

'You're right,' said Mum. 'You're old enough to make your own decisions. But please think about what I've said. Take your time, but think about it.'

'All right,' I agreed. I owed her that, at least. 'I'll give you a call in a couple of days.'

Chapter 16

I thought about what Mum had told me all the way back to Danny's. Her account really did seem like a fable or a fairy tale to me – a story with a moral, about someone I had never known. It was ironic, really. I had gone home to see Mum because I needed security and familiarity, and instead, I had found out that there was so much about her that I didn't know, that I only knew a little bit of her. She had lived a whole, other life in which Dad, Emily and I had played no part. Mum looked the same, spoke in the same voice, smelled of the same rose-tinged perfume, yet she had somehow changed. It unnerved me to realise that even the people you are closest to have secrets – memories, thoughts and dreams that they keep locked away from the world. It made me wonder if it was ever possible to know anyone completely. Even Danny. Could there be more secrets to uncover? The idea made me shudder.

Thinking about Mum loving anyone other than Dad made me feel uncomfortable too, as though I was being unfaithful to him. How horrible for Dad, I thought, that much as Mum loved him, she could describe somebody else as 'the one', that he was, unwittingly, second best. It made me realise, however, that what I had with Danny was unique to us. Mum had made herself get over Dominic, but her feelings for him hadn't vanished, they were and always would be tucked away at the back of her mind. Soulmates don't come along very often – once in a lifetime, if you're lucky. And only one person can ever be your 'first love'. If, as my parents wanted, I left Danny, I might never find love like this again. Mum hadn't – she'd admitted as much.

Mum had told me about her past because she wanted me to finish with Danny. I'm sure she hadn't anticipated that her revelations might backfire on her. Yet, backfire they did. By the time I reached Danny's front door I had convinced myself that, whatever his problems, I wanted to be with him, to help him. Our love was strong enough to overcome anything, I told myself. This was a once-in-a-lifetime relationship and I had to give it my all. I was only eighteen, there was no way I was ready to give up on him – on love – and settle for second best.

Whenever I pictured Danny in my mind's eye I saw him as he was on stage, at my first Wonderfulls gig: tall and power-ful and unfeasibly handsome. As I made my way back to his flat, I imagined that this was the Danny who would be wait-ing for me there. I would let myself in and then run straight into his arms, so I could tell him how much I loved him, how lucky I was to have him. Everything would be perfect again – of that I had no doubt.

But when I went into the living room and saw him – for real – all my hope and excitement drained away. He was lying on the sofa watching a kid's cartoon. He hadn't shaved or got dressed and his breakfast plate was still on the floor, where he'd left it. There was no sign that he'd done any songwriting; his guitar was in its case, leaning against the wall, just as it had been when I'd gone out. My pleasant fantasy melted into a pool of disappointment and, for a brief moment, I actually hated him.

'What have you been doing?' I asked, irritated.

'Oh, you know, this and that,' he said. He stretched out on the sofa. 'How was your mum?'

'She was good,' I snapped. I didn't want to talk about it. 'Are you going to get dressed today?'

He looked daggers at me. 'Where did that come from? Did your mum tell you to say that?'

I ignored him. 'It's after three, Danny. We could do something if you got dressed.'

'I don't feel like doing anything.'

'Maybe that's why you're so miserable. How can I help you if you won't let me?'

'I'm not miserable,' he barked. 'I'm perfectly happy sitting here. You're the one with the problem.'

'I'm going to lie down,' I said. I didn't want another argument. 'I'll see you later.'

I can honestly say that I have never been so confused in my life. My brain literally ached with it all. I absolutely, totally and utterly loved Danny. I loved his intelligence and his talent and his wit. I loved the way he looked. I loved talking to him, hearing him play and sing. I loved being in his arms, the way he made me feel. But maybe I wasn't in love with the real Danny. Maybe *this* was the real Danny: this lazy, depressive, aimless person, who hurt himself. Could I love this Danny? And if I couldn't, did that mean I didn't *really* love him after all? Did that make me selfish or shallow? Or was this just a phase, something that he would get over – something that I could help him through?

I needed somebody to talk to, somebody who could help and advise me. But who? Danny's mum plainly wasn't interested in her son and my parents had made their feelings clear. My friends weren't around (this wasn't something I wanted to talk about in a snatched phone conversation or by e-mail) and, anyway, I wasn't sure that Debbie, or anyone else, would understand. Emily wouldn't get it – she'd just think Danny was weird. As for Danny's friends, I didn't know any of them well enough to confide in. But even if there had been someone I could talk to, I had promised Danny that I wouldn't betray his confidence.

So there it was: I was utterly alone. There was only one person whom I felt was there for me completely, and that was Danny. But *he* was the problem. My brain whirred round and round and round, tangling my thoughts and feelings like a ball of wire wool, slicing deep into every nerve and every axon. Thinking was agonising, tortuous. Was this, I wondered, how Danny felt when he cut himself? I was beginning to see how physical pain might be preferable to mental torment. Perhaps it would work for me too. Perhaps if I experienced what he experienced everything would become clear.

I opened my overnight bag and took out my nail scissors, pulling them apart so that I could find the sharpest side.

Then, clenching my teeth, I held out my hand and ran the cold metal along my knuckles. I felt nothing but a sharp scratch; the scissors were too blunt to break the skin.

What are you doing, Naomi?

It was the first clear thought I'd had all day. I realised that my forehead was clammy and my limbs shaky – my body had begun to shut down, preparing itself for pain, for injury. I never had been able to deal with the sight of my own blood; if the scissors had done their nasty job I would have passed out. I took a deep breath. *Stupid, stupid girl.* Hurting myself wasn't going to help Danny and it certainly wouldn't help me. What I needed was space – time and space to think things through properly.

I went back downstairs. Danny was still sitting where I'd left him. He looked up at me, hopefully. 'Have you calmed down now?' he asked. 'Look, I'll get myself together and then we can go out somewhere, OK?'

'I don't think so, Danny,' I said. I swallowed hard, summoning my courage. I was aware that what I was about to say defied almost every instinct I possessed. 'I think I should go home, just for a week or so, to get my head sorted.'

He looked as if I'd kicked him in the stomach. 'What? You're leaving me?'

'No, just moving home for a bit. I still love you, Danny. But I'm so confused.'

'Love?' He pronounced it like the lash of a whip. 'You don't know the meaning of the word.'

If he had intended to inspire guilt, it worked. He couldn't possibly have known how much that comment

hurt me. The only thing I did know, clearly and unques-
tionably, was that I loved him. 'Please understand. I just
need some time.'

I walked over to him and put my arms around his neck.
I thought he was going to cry, but then his face hardened.

'Just go, Naomi,' he said, pushing me away. 'Go now.'

Chapter 17

I had no contact with Danny for three long weeks. Which was, I calculated, a total of twenty one days; five hundred and four hours; thirty thousand, two hundred and forty minutes; or one million, eight hundred and fourteen thousand, four hundred seconds. I was painfully aware that each moment that passed was another moment without him. And yet, conversely, time also stood still. I barely noticed that the days slipped into weeks because I was at a standstill, living the same empty day again and again, endlessly thinking the same thoughts and feeling the same contradictory emotions.

Three weeks of thinking left me no less muddled, no closer to finding the answers I needed. And three weeks alone did nothing to dull my feelings for Danny or to dispel the sense that, without him, I was lost, incomplete. I didn't want to experience anything new if he couldn't share it with me. Hearing a funny joke or reading an interesting story no longer gave me pleasure, because Danny wasn't there to enjoy it too. I'd often catch myself thinking, *I must show Danny that*, or, *Danny would love this*, and then I'd feel bereft because I couldn't tell him about it. Being apart from Danny was like having an itch beneath my skin that couldn't be scratched.

He didn't ring me; I'd asked him not to. That didn't stop me checking my mobile several times a day, hoping at the very least for a missed call. Sometimes I wondered if he was not calling because he was trying to punish me or because he didn't want to talk to me. I'd told him I would call when I was ready, but when would that be? Many times I had to force myself not to pick up the phone and tell him what a huge mistake I'd made. But until I was sure what I wanted, what was the point?

I wondered how long he would wait for me and worried that while I tried to decide what I wanted, he might make a decision for me. Images of his letter on my doormat after our first argument haunted me. Would he send another – a more cruelly worded one that couldn't be disregarded? Every morning, when I went downstairs, I had to steel myself in case a white envelope had appeared unnoticed while I slept. I knew that, this time, telling him I loved him wouldn't be enough. He didn't believe it, because he thought I had left him.

I couldn't bear to think of the relationship being over – and even worse, if it were over, it would be my fault. Fear gnawed constantly at my ribs. Surely our last kiss hadn't been our final kiss? It hadn't seemed special or significant at the time – I wished it had been. I tried to recall its every detail, how it had felt, how Danny had tasted. But as the days went by, my memory dulled and it was harder and harder to relive it. Soon it was only a shadow of a kiss, no more real to me than looking at an old photograph of two lovers embracing.

Guilt kept me awake at night. Had I been selfish and cruel? Did Danny think I had abandoned him? Was he now hurting himself because of me? That was the thought that most scared me: Danny bleeding, in pain, perhaps cutting too deep this time, and nobody knowing. Would he call me if that happened?

In practical terms, my life resumed as before. Mr Stevens allowed me to return to the law firm, on the condition that I applied myself and took no more days off. Pleased to have something to fill my time, I did my job on autopilot, performing every task that was demanded of me with a forced smile, so that nobody could complain about my attitude or my mood. I varnished my new conscientious image by staying late on several occasions. The truth was, I wanted to delay going home to nothing, and to avoid the small chance of bumping into Danny on the high street.

Evenings and weekends were interminable. I read I don't know how many novels to try to take my mind off Danny, but I couldn't absorb myself in the characters' lives. Every mention of love, every disagreement, made my mind jump to thoughts of my own situation. It didn't matter whether the hero was named John or Cal or even Siegfried; to me, they were all called Danny, and the title of every book, *Loving Danny*.

My parents had initially been delighted when I came home. But seeing how miserable I was did not make them happy. I wouldn't – couldn't – talk to them about my feelings, so they gave up and left me alone, whispering about me when they thought I was out of earshot. Concerned that I wasn't eating properly, Mum went out of her way to make my favourite dinners. That only made me feel guilty too.

I don't think I could have survived those weeks without Emily. She did everything she could to take my mind off Danny, offering to take me shopping and inviting me out with her friends. Knowing what bad company I would be, I rarely accepted. It was nice to be asked, though. In return, I helped her with her coursework and lent her my clothes. She was welcome to them; I didn't feel like dressing up any more.

But sympathetic as she was, Emily didn't really understand what I was going through. To her mind, you were either happy or sad; you either loved someone or you didn't. Day after day, she begged me for an explanation, wearing me down with her anxious stares and generous hugs. And so, a week after I'd returned home, having sworn her to secrecy, I finally told her that Danny cut himself.

'Really?' she exclaimed, her eyes growing wide with surprise. 'There's a girl in my class who does that. She burns herself with cigarettes too. It's weird.'

'I know,' I said. After keeping the information to myself for so long, just saying it out loud was a tremendous relief. I was surprised at how little guilt I felt.

'God, Nay, I can't even wax my own legs or pull off a plaster myself, because I'm scared it will hurt.'

'Me neither,' I said, ashamed at the memory of my failed attempt to cut myself with scissors.

'How long has he been doing it for?'

'I don't know.' I felt foolish. Should I have realised what Danny's scars meant the very first time I saw them? Would anyone else have know right away?

'Wow,' exclaimed Emily, for want of something better to

say. But I could tell that a little part of her was impressed. Cutting himself gave Danny some sort of cachet – she thought it was a cool, dangerous rock-star thing to do.

I rolled my eyes at her to make it clear she was way off track.

'So what are you going to do?'

'I don't know,' I said.

She hugged me. She didn't have any answers – I hadn't expected that she would. 'I'm sure it'll be all right,' she said. 'You'll work it out.'

I wasn't sure whether 'it' referred to Danny's problem or to our relationship and, whatever she meant, I wasn't convinced that I believed her. But it was good to hear.

One evening, when my mood was at its lowest, Debbie rang. I was surprised at how pleased I was to hear from her. Since her visit we had continued to speak once a week or so – out of habit, I suppose – but our conversations had been awkward and unsatisfying. I had self-edited any information about Danny because I felt she would judge him, so we'd stuck to safe subjects: our families, films and TV programmes and general small talk. Now that Danny and I were apart, I was aware just how much I missed the closeness we'd shared before she went away.

'Hi, Naomi,' she said warmly. 'Are you OK?'

'Yes, thanks, I'm fine,' I lied. 'How are you?'

'You don't sound fine,' she said tentatively. 'Your voice is weird. I know it sounds silly, but I've been thinking about you all day and worrying, and I just felt I had to ring you.'

We'd had this kind of 'telepathic' connection in the past – it's not uncommon between best friends. Often, I would pick up the phone to dial her number and she would already be on the line, having dialled me simultaneously. Was it possible that we still had it, despite everything?

'That's nice of you,' I said. I wasn't sure how to broach the subject of Danny. 'I've been better.'

'Has something happened with Danny?' she asked.

I hesitated. 'We're going through a bit of a rough patch. We're having a sort of break.'

'Oh, Naomi,' she said, with genuine concern. 'I know how much you love him. It must be horrible.'

That was the cue I needed to let it all come flooding out: the self-harm, my parents, my confusion. It was the second time I had betrayed Danny's confidence, but yet again I felt no guilt, only release. Debbie listened patiently, saying nothing until I had finished.

'Oh, Naomi,' she said again. 'Is there anything I can do? Do you want me to come down?'

'Thanks but no, Deb. There's no point. I've got to get my head straight.'

'It's a lot for you to deal with,' she said. 'I wish I had some useful advice, but I haven't got a clue what to suggest. All I can say is that Danny doesn't know how lucky he is to have you. You're so strong and kind and patient – anyone else would have fallen apart completely. What's happened isn't your fault, you know? Give yourself time and then do whatever you think is best. But remember to look after yourself too.'

There was no criticism, no 'I told you so' or 'you'd be better off out of it'. It occurred to me how foolish I had been to keep my distance from Debbie. She wasn't the enemy after all.

'Thanks, Debs,' I said, my voice beginning to crack with emotion. 'That means a lot.'

'Promise you'll call if you need me,' she said. 'If you want to talk about this more, any time, I'll be here for you. Really.'

I wasn't sure if I would call her, but now, at least, I felt that I could.

'I promise.'

On a dreary Sunday afternoon, three weeks after I'd come home, I decided to give in to temptation and log on to The Wonderfulls' website. I had avoided it for as long as I could, aware that the sight of my pictures would bring back troublesome memories. But I was sick of treading water and getting no closer to an answer; I felt I needed a tangible reminder of Danny.

I typed in the address – www.thewonderfulls.co.uk – and took a deep breath as I waited for the home page to load. I wondered if anybody had updated the site since I'd last worked on it, whether there was any band news, or if new gig dates had been posted. I hoped not; that was my job – I wasn't quite ready to give it up.

But there was no home page. All the pictures, all the text, all the links had vanished. Instead, there were just three enormous words, filling the screen:

I MISS YOU

I blinked hard. Were my eyes playing tricks on me? Had I typed in the wrong address?

But there was no mistake. Danny had sent me a message. I had told him not to contact me, so he had used the only forum open to him – a public one – to let me know how he felt. He missed me and he didn't care who knew it.

My brain went into overdrive. How long had the words been up there? How many other people had seen them before me and wondered what they meant? Did Danny think I had ignored them? Had he taken my silence as my response? He didn't know that I hadn't looked at the site until that day. What must he now be thinking – that I didn't love him, that I didn't care?

But I did care. The absolute knowledge of this hit me

like a sledgehammer. I cared about him more than anything –
I was a fool not to have realised it. Being away from him
hadn't made me happy and it had solved nothing. So what if
he was difficult? So what if he had problems? So what if my
parents thought he was a bad influence? So what! If he
needed help, I would help him. I wanted to be with him
regardless. I could actually feel my love for him flooding
back into my body, surging through my veins, hammering
on my heart and making my lungs expand. After weeks of
vacillation, Danny's message had made my decision for me.
It wasn't rational – something inside me had just clicked into
place.

I was a bundle of energy and excitement, unable to sit
still for a moment longer. I got up from the desk and ran
into the hall, banging on Emily's door with my fist. I had
to show her the website and tell her that I had decided
to get back together with Danny. I wanted to ask her
advice on what to say to him and to discuss the best way to
tell our parents. 'Wake up, Em!' I shouted. She didn't
respond. I pushed the door. 'I'm coming in – I hope you're
decent.'

I hadn't seen her all morning. She had gone to a party
the night before – another invitation that I'd declined – and
she still hadn't surfaced. I found her lying in her bed, her
eyes half-open. She didn't smile when she saw me.

'Wake up, lazy bones,' I said, bouncing on her bed. 'I've
got something to show you.' I was so animated that I could
hardly contain myself. I was jumping up and down, like a
dog ready to play ball.

'Go away, Nay,' she growled. 'I want to go back to sleep.'

'It's the middle of the afternoon. Must have been some party.'

She pulled herself up, rubbing her eyes. 'It was OK.'

'You've got to come into my room – I want to show you something.'

She didn't move. I took her arm, literally dragging her out of bed and pulling her through the door, across the hall and into my room. 'Look!' I cried. 'Look at this!'

When she saw the computer screen, she froze. She shook my hand from her arm and she dropped her head, her eyes beginning to fill with tears. It was not the reaction I had anticipated.

'What's wrong, Em? Can't you see? It's great! He loves me so much that he's done this. Isn't it great?'

'No,' she sobbed. 'No.'

'Emily, what's the matter?'

She gulped. 'I've got something to tell you, Nay. You're not going to like it.'

Chapter 18

'**D**anny kissed me.'

Danny kissed me. It was the last thing I'd expected her to say, absolutely the worst thing she could have said. My brain shut down with shock. I understood the words, but I couldn't process them.

'What? When?' We were still standing in front of the computer, the words 'I MISS YOU' shouting from the screen, like a cruel joke.

'He kissed me. At the party last night. He was there with some friends – I think he knew someone's brother.'

'Danny kissed you?'

She nodded. 'I'm so sorry, Nay.'

I felt as if I had been lifted off the ground and turned inside out. I was aware that I was involuntarily holding my breath, that I had stopped blinking and swallowing. This couldn't be real – it was like finding myself in an episode of a bad soap opera. Emily was my sister. I loved her, trusted her, confided in her. She knew everything there was to know about Danny. How could this have happened? How could she have let it happen?

Then my brain conjured up an image of Danny, his arms around Emily's slim neck, and I wanted to vomit. She had been wearing my top; it had still smelled of my perfume.

'Did you kiss him back? Was it a full-on snog?' The shock was speaking for me. I don't know why I asked that question – I didn't really want to know the answer.

'Not really.' She hesitated. 'Just for a second . . . a tiny bit.'

I remembered again my last kiss with Danny – it was what I had been grasping on to, our final intimate moment before everything fell apart. Now Emily, my confidante, my only support, had stolen even that from me. It was tainted, defiled. I had nothing left of him.

My shock turned to anger. 'You bitch!' I spat. 'Did you enjoy it?'

'Stop it, please.' She was crying so much she could hardly breathe. 'I'm sorry, Nay, I'm sorry. I'm being totally honest with you here – I don't want to lie to you. But it all happened so quickly. I'd had too much to drink, I wasn't thinking—'

'Oh, stop blubbing.' I'd had no idea I could be so cold, but I couldn't stop, couldn't help myself. 'Did you flirt with him? Did you want to look cool in front of all your friends? Did you?'

'No, Nay, I swear. It wasn't like that. We were just talking – about you, actually – and he looked so sad and I gave him a hug, and it just happened. I didn't plan it, honest.'

I'd seen the way Emily had looked at Danny, the way her friends looked at him. I thought, *She must have loved the attention – a gorgeous, older guy, wanting to talk to her, to kiss her. She lapped it up, didn't she?*

I said, 'I don't believe you.' But even as I said it, I knew

I didn't really mean it. I was thinking more clearly now. Blaming Emily was so much easier than allowing myself to blame Danny, shouting at her far less scary than the prospect of confronting him.

'You've got it all wrong. I was telling him you still loved him and that I thought you should get back together. I told him I thought he was great for you and that you'd work it out.'

'And so he kissed you? It doesn't make sense.'

'I know,' she said. 'I know. But I stopped him straight away – I promise. I told him it was wrong and that it shouldn't have happened.'

'And what did he say?'

'I can't really remember. He said not to tell you. I went to the loo with Katy and when we came back he'd just gone.'

'How convenient.'

Then a thought struck me. 'Were you going to tell me about this? If I hadn't shown you the website, would you have told me?'

'I . . . don't . . . know,' she hiccoughed. 'I hadn't thought it through yet.'

'I wish you'd never told me,' I said, remembering how happy I had been just a few minutes earlier. Now everything was more messed up than ever.

'Really? You'd rather I'd lied?'

'No. No. I just wish none of it had happened. I can't deal with this, any of it.'

She tried to hug me, but I was still too angry with her. 'Leave me alone, Emily,' I said. 'I need to talk to Danny.'

'Please don't hate me, Nay,' she whispered as she left the room. 'Please.'

I don't hate you, I thought. But I was too pig-headed to say it.

I went straight round to Danny's, before I could change my mind or start to rationalise what Emily had told me. I wanted to surprise him, to hear what he had to say before he could invent an explanation. Most of all, I wanted to see him again. It's stupid, I know, but I had the feeling that, somehow, everything could still be all right, that this could all go away.

I let myself into his flat, leaving the door on the latch so he wouldn't be alerted to my arrival. Hearing music playing in the living room, I went into his bedroom and sat on his bed, knowing that he would come in eventually. I was annoyed that I hadn't thought to redo my make-up before I left the house – I didn't want Danny to know what a mess I was inside. It was written all over my face in tear-streaked mascara.

I didn't have to wait long before Danny sauntered in, humming to himself. My heart leapt – in spite of myself, I fancied him as much as ever. It took a moment before he saw me, and then he jumped back on himself, his mouth falling open with surprise.

'Omi! Oh my God! What are you doing here?'

'Hello, Danny.' I smiled. I felt strangely calm.

He looked at me, confused, unnerved. I knew he was wondering if I had come because of his message or because Emily had told me what happened. He was trying to work out why I had hidden myself in his room, rather than call or text him to say I wanted to see him. My smile revealed nothing.

'Omi, it's so good to see you,' he said, rushing over to me. 'I've missed you so much.' I felt the sensation of his mouth on mine and I couldn't help but kiss him back. It was familiar and comfortable and yet new and exciting, all at the same time. God, I had missed his kisses.

Don't forget why you're here, Naomi, I told myself.

I pulled away. 'Missed me? Not that much,' I said cryptically.

He knew, then, that I knew. His voice rose by an octave. 'What do you mean?'

'Why don't you tell me what happened at the party last night? Or should I call Emily and get her to come round here.'

'What's she been saying?'

'Don't play dumb. She told me what happened. She said you kissed her. Why did you do it, Danny?'

'You've got it wrong,' he said. 'She's lying.'

'She's my sister. Why would she say it if it wasn't true? She wouldn't lie to me.'

'No? Never? And I would?'

How would you prefer to die, Naomi, by hanging or the electric chair? It's weird how your brain summons up long-buried memories at times of crisis. It was a game I'd played as a child, with the little boy who lived next door: decide which was the worse of two evils.

I don't want to die at all.

But you have to, Naomi.

Who did I want to be the liar: my only sister or the love of my life?

I'll take the forfeit.

Danny was right – Emily had lied to me before. She had lied about borrowing clothes and make-up and whether she'd stolen chocolate from the newsagent. Could she be playing some kind of sick game to make me finish with Danny?

It didn't make sense. Emily had nothing to gain by telling me about Danny's kiss – and everything to lose. I'd seen how painful recounting the kiss had been for her, knew that she had squeezed out every last, honest detail. But if Emily wasn't lying, then Danny must be. Hard as it was to admit it, I had known it all along, hadn't I? Why couldn't he simply have confessed and told me how sorry he was? Was his pride more important to him than the risk of losing me?

Danny took my silence to be my answer. He turned his back on me and began pacing the room. 'I can't believe you don't trust me. After everything we've been through, you still don't trust me.'

'It's not as simple as that. I want to trust you, Danny, but I'm so confused.'

I caught up with him, positioning myself between his body and the wall so that he had nowhere to go, so that he had to look at me.

'It is simple,' he said, shoving me out of the way and turning sharply, so that he had his back to me once again.

'Either you love me or you don't. Either you believe me or you don't. Yeah?'

I said nothing. There was nothing left to say.

It was over.

Chapter 19

That should have been the end of the story. In many ways, I wish it were. But nothing was ever neat with Danny; there were never any clear beginnings, middles or ends.

Of course, I didn't have the benefit of hindsight then. I left Danny's, certain that our relationship was over. I was broken and empty and exhausted and shattered, and all the other adjectives that don't quite express the indescribable pain of leaving someone you love. Most of all, I was terribly, terribly sad. Despite everything that had happened, I still loved Danny and I didn't know how I would ever stop. I knew that all I had to do was to go back and tell him that I believed him, and he would take me in his arms and everything would be all right. He still wanted me and I still wanted him – the fact that we couldn't be together was illogical. But how could I be with someone whom I didn't trust, someone who had looked me in the eye and lied?

I didn't allow myself to think about his reasons, to wonder whether he hadn't been able to help himself because he was hurting so much, or because he was on autopilot to self-destruct. What was the point? It would only cause me more confusion, more pain and more guilt. If he had done it because he was ill, then I had deserted him when he needed me most – and what sort of a person did that make me?

Somehow, I knew instinctively that the only way I could survive was if I thought of the relationship as dead. And so, when I arrived home, I found myself carrying out my own little mourning ritual. I got out all my photos of Danny and, one by one, took a last look at each image before putting it away in my bedside drawer. I was saying goodbye to my memories, filing them away in the past. Danny posing on stage: gone. Danny pulling a silly face: gone. Danny, his arm protectively around my shoulder: gone. Funny how the colours already seemed less vivid, our smiles ghostly. I could barely remember how I had felt in each captured moment, couldn't recall what had been said in the instant before the shutter clicked shut and the flash exploded. Even the photos taken only a month before now appeared years old – a lifetime away. There would be no more gigs, no more hugs, no more kisses; the realisation struck me like a hammer to the chest.

I took my favourite photo of Danny out of its frame and studied it. It felt as if his eyes were following my gaze, his unfathomable expression begging me to reconsider, to help him. 'Stop torturing me, Danny,' I said aloud, but my conscience refused to obey. I kissed his face, before putting the photo away with the others. Then I cried until there were no tears left in me.

Afterwards, I felt numb, empty inside. The fog of emotion had cleared and, at last, I was able to focus, to think logically. I decided to write a list of all the reasons I'd ended the relationship, to help convince myself that I'd done the right thing.

1. Danny lied to me. *Can I ever trust him again?*
2. Danny kissed my sister. *And then tried to blame her. Ditto.*
3. Danny cuts himself. *It scares me and, no matter how much I want to, I don't know how to help him. I'm not wise enough, or strong enough.*
4. Danny is lazy. *He's barely done a day's work since I met him and he can't even be bothered to rehearse.*
5. Danny bitches about my parents. *But I love them and it makes me feel bad.*
6. Danny makes me question what I want to do with my life. *He confuses me.*
7. Danny hates his mum and dad. *OK, they're not the best parents, but I don't know if they've done anything to merit such vicious rage. It makes me uncomfortable.*
8. Danny is moody. *It puts me on edge.*
9. I never know quite where I am with Danny. *Ditto.*
10. Danny turns everything into a drama. *It's exhausting.*
11. My parents don't think I should be with Danny. *I'm sick of fighting with them.*
12. I'm supposed to be going away to university in

the autumn. *If I stay with Danny, I won't want to go.*

I couldn't think of any more. It was enough, wasn't it?

Then, almost inevitably, I suppose, I found myself composing a list of what was good about Danny.

1. I love Danny and he loves me. *There's no better feeling in the world, is there?*
2. Danny is my soulmate. *I might never find another.*
3. Danny is gorgeous. *Just looking at him gives me butterflies.*
4. Danny is spontaneous. *Being with him is unpredictable and exciting.*
5. Danny is clever and interesting. *I've learned so much from him. He's so stimulating.*
6. Danny makes *me* feel clever and interesting. *Nobody else has ever done that.*
7. Danny a) writes amazing songs and b) has an incredible voice. *He's so talented – he could be really successful one day.*
8. Danny is generous and thoughtful. *He's given me the most amazing presents.*
9. Danny makes me laugh. *He even laughs at my jokes.*
10. Kissing Danny.

I read through my lists several times. I had to acknowledge that there were more points in the negative list than in the positive, and that, collectively, the negative points outweighed the positive. However much I enjoyed kissing Danny, loved hearing him play, laughed at his jokes, these things couldn't make up for his problems, his lie. It had come down to a simple mathematical calculation: I couldn't be with Danny because there were too many obstacles in our way. Following my heart had got me nowhere, so perhaps it was now time to follow my head.

Finally, I decided to write Danny a goodbye letter. I can't remember the exact words I used – I don't have a copy – but it was four pages long and detailed all the points in both my lists. I didn't know if I was doing the right thing, or how he would react, but I had to be honest, to articulate everything I had been unable to say before. It wasn't fair not to tell him the truth, was it? So I told him that I loved him, and that I would always love him, but I couldn't be with him. Maybe, one day, when I had finished university and he had sorted out his problems, we might try again. I wanted to say, 'Please wait for me, Danny,' but I knew it wouldn't be fair to ask that of him. I signed it, *Forever, Omi*.

As I sealed the envelope, I imagined the look on Danny's face when he read my letter and remembered how desperate I had felt when I'd received his. I wished that I could be there to hold him and wipe away his tears – the possibility that he might have another – more violent – reaction was too horrible to contemplate. I prayed he wouldn't hate me; I couldn't bear that.

I posted the letter in the postbox at the end of my street, waiting until I had heard it flutter down and hit the bottom before I turned and walked away. Now it was too late to change my mind. Danny's fate lay in the hands of a faceless postal worker.

I didn't tell my parents it was over with Danny until the next day. Mum said she would be there for me if I wanted to talk and reassured me that the pain I felt would fade. Dad just patted me on the back and told me I was being very mature. 'One day,' he said, 'you'll look back on this relationship and wonder what you ever saw in Danny.'

His blasé attitude irritated me. I wanted to ask him how he could be so sure. He had never known, and would never know, what it was like to have a soulmate, to share that once-in-a-lifetime connection that is beyond words.

I told Emily that I believed her and had forgiven her for the kiss, but try as I might, I couldn't remove the image of her with Danny from my mind. It was there when we chatted, when we hugged, when we laughed. Something fundamental in our relationship had shifted; it would take many months to repair it.

And so, I got on with the business of living without Danny. I kept myself as occupied as possible, working late and taking books and papers home to read. I e-mailed my friends abroad and rang Debbie for a long heart-to-heart. Aching for company and consolation, I told her I'd like to come up and stay with her for the weekend. I got back in touch with Dee and planned a summer holiday with her, after her A-level retakes. I even enrolled in an evening class in photography.

Of course I couldn't erase Danny from my mind

entirely. Everything reminded me of him: bus journeys, music, TV programmes, other couples holding hands. They taunted me, forcing me to recall what I had once enjoyed and to acknowledge what I had now lost. Crying became as natural to me as eating or sleeping – I couldn't remember a time when my eyes hadn't been sore and puffy. But I discovered that I was far stronger than I had realised. I didn't break. Whenever I felt upset I would look to the future for comfort – to new adventures at university, new places and new friends. Life would go on without him, propelling me forwards. Grateful as I was, it was depressing to accept that the future was unstoppable. As far as the universe was concerned, Danny and I were just specks of matter, tiny and insignificant.

And then Danny had to go and spoil it all with one last, dramatic performance. How could I have forgotten that he never left the stage without playing an encore?

Chapter 20

The call came at two p.m. on a Saturday afternoon, not quite two weeks since I'd last seen Danny. He hadn't replied to my letter and I had finally stopped expecting to hear from him. I no longer jumped each time my phone rang.

But, for a split second before my mobile began to vibrate, I saw a clear image of Danny in my mind, and I *knew* something was very wrong.

The number was unfamiliar.

'Naomi, it's Mike – you know, the keyboard player from The Wonderfulls.'

Why was Mike ringing me? How had he got my number?

'Mike? Hi, how are you?'

'Yeah, all right.'

I could tell from his anxious tone that he wasn't calling to make small talk. 'Listen, Naomi, I'm sorry, but I've got some really bad news.' He took a deep breath. 'Maybe you should be sitting down, or something. Danny's in hospital.'

'Oh God,' I said. I felt my legs buckle. 'Oh God.'

'He's at St Hilda's. I thought you'd want to know.'

My mouth was suddenly so dry that I could hardly speak. Had there been an accident? Was Danny ill? Had he hurt himself? 'What's happened? Is he OK?'

Mike took a deep breath. 'He took an overdose, Naomi. And he's cut himself up pretty bad. But he's OK. I'm going to see him this afternoon and I know he wants to see you. Would you like a lift?'

'Yes, please. I'd really appreciate that.'

I felt completely numb after our conversation, as if, subconsciously, I had been expecting this news. I was neither scared nor anxious – I wasn't aware of any emotion, or any sensation at all. And then, the strangest thing happened. It must have been the shock, but all I could think about was what to take Danny in hospital. What do you give somebody who's taken an overdose? Grapes? Chocolates? Magazines? Who could I ask? Danny had felt so desperate that he wanted to die – almost certainly because of me – and all I could worry about was whether to run to the corner shop and buy a pound of red seedless or the *NME*. I was driving myself mad with the simplest, most inane decision.

Mike rang the doorbell an hour later. I waited until he was standing on the doorstep before I told my parents where I was going, so they wouldn't try to stop me. I knew they'd never argue with me in public, in front of a stranger.

'Oh, Naomi,' said Mum sadly as I left. 'I do hope you know what you're doing.' Then, as an afterthought, 'Give Danny our best.'

The car journey was uncomfortable. Here we were, two people who hardly knew each other, thrown together by something unspeakably horrible. I wondered if Mike knew that Danny and I had split up and, if he did, whether he blamed me. Was it my fault? Had Danny hurt himself because I'd left him, because I sent that letter? *What have you done, Naomi, what have you done?*

'Have you brought him anything?' I asked. Anything to break the silence, to stop the guilty voices in my head.

'No,' he replied, glancing over at me. 'But I took him his iPod this morning.'

'You've already seen him?'

'I was the one who found him, Naomi – last night. I didn't want to call you until I knew he was all right. And it took some time to get your number.'

'You found him?'

'Yes. He called me yesterday afternoon, saying he wanted to rehearse. I thought it was odd; we never rehearse on a Friday and we haven't got together for weeks. I was the first to arrive. The door was on the latch and I found him lying semi-conscious on the living room floor and called an ambulance.'

'How awful,' I said, remembering the shock of Danny's blood on the carpet. Poor Mike. This must have been far worse.

He nodded. 'It wasn't nice.' He paused, evidently visualising what he had seen. 'He must have meant for me to find him. He'd taken some pills and cut a kind of circle into his arm, with a knife.'

'He cuts himself, Mike. He's done it before. Did you know that?'

He didn't flinch. 'Everyone knows Danny has problems. They've got worse since we didn't get the record deal.

To be honest, it's caused the band a lot of hassle. We were talking about winding it up.'

'Winding up The Wonderfulls? Oh my God. But you're so good.'

He smiled and shrugged his shoulders. 'Cheers for that. It's all getting to be too much like hard work, though.'

'Do you think it's my fault, Mike?'

'No!' He laughed. 'Of course not. You're the best thing that ever happened to him.'

He had meant to be kind, but hearing that made me feel even more guilty.

'I dumped him, Mike. A couple of weeks ago.'

'Oh, Naomi, he didn't tell me – I had no idea. I wouldn't have called if I'd known. He asked for you – I assumed you were still together.'

Danny hadn't told his friends we'd split up? Hadn't he understood my letter? How could he not believe it was over?

'No, no,' I said, shaking my head. 'I'm pleased you did. I still love him. I'd hate to think of anything happening to him and nobody telling me.'

We had arrived at the hospital. Mike parked and came round to my side of the car to open the door for me. *He's a gentleman*, I thought, *just like Danny*. We walked into the building together in silence and Mike called the lift. 'He's in a ward on the third floor,' he said, squeezing my shoulder. He had noticed that I was starting to shake. 'Let me go in for a couple of minutes first and then I'll come out and get you.'

I paced the corridor. St Hilda's is an old Victorian hospital,

Gothic and grand on the outside and dilapidated on the inside. The walls were yellow-white, the curtains faded and tatty, and the fixtures and fittings chipped and outdated. Thankfully, there was no smell. That's what I dreaded most about hospitals – the stench of urine and chlorine and sick all mixed together like the devil's perfume. My grandma had reeked of it when I went to visit her, a couple of years before. She had died the next day. Now, whenever I thought of her, I caught a whiff of it in my nostrils again. I didn't ever want to associate that smell with Danny.

Mike came to find me a few minutes later. 'He's OK,' he said. 'He's looking forward to seeing you. I'm going to get off now.' He kissed me on the cheek. 'Good luck.'

He pressed a piece of paper into my hand. 'My number – in case you need to call me.'

So Mike had only come back to bring me? What a kind thing to do. Perhaps, if things had turned out differently, we could have become friends. Now, I would probably never see him again.

I steeled myself before I pushed open the double doors and walked into the ward. *Daisy Ward*, it was called. *Danny would hate that*, I thought. It wasn't exactly rock and roll. I had no idea what to expect, what state Danny would be in, what he would look like.

A nurse stopped me. 'I'm here to see Danny Evans,' I said.

She smiled kindly. 'You must be Naomi. He's at the far end.'

I walked past rows and rows of beds: old men, dozing or

coughing; middle-aged men hooked up to machines and drips; young men staring vacantly into space. Some looked up at me expectantly, perhaps hoping that I might have come to visit them. It wasn't until I had neared the end of the room that I saw Danny. My stomach lurched. He was propped up against some pillows, wearing a blue hospital gown, with tubes coming out of his hand. His hair was lank and greasy and he had at least three days' growth on his chin. He didn't look like Danny – this guy was much older, much smaller in build. If I hadn't known he was there, I might have walked straight past him.

'Omi,' he croaked as I approached his bed. 'It's so good to see you. Thanks for coming – I knew you would.'

Did he?

He beckoned me to sit down beside him, moving his tubes out of the way. Now I could see that his arm was covered in a large dressing and there were black marks on his chin, remnants of the charcoal the doctors used to pump his stomach. He held out his hand and I took it. It was like holding hands with a ghost.

'Sorry about the wires,' he said. 'They've got me on an antibiotic drip, to stop infection.'

'Oh, Danny, what have you done? I've been so worried about you.'

'I'm sorry, Omi,' he said flatly. 'You shouldn't worry.' Then his voice became more animated. 'Look – I've got something to show you.' He dropped my hand and started to unwrap the dressing on his arm, wincing with pain as he did so.

'Don't,' I said. 'Please don't.'

But he ignored me. He pulled away the bandages and pointed to his arm. 'See it, Omi? See it?' I forced myself to look. There before me, on his forearm, was a large, deep, angry wound, in the shape of a uneven circle, just as Mike had described.

And then it hit me. It wasn't a circle. It was an O – O for Omi.

'I did it for you,' he said, almost proudly.

It was too, too horrible. I felt a rushing in my ears and, for a second, everything went black. I gripped the sides of the bed and breathed deeply, until the room came back into focus. How could I not have realised how ill Danny was? He was out of his mind. Even now, he was playing games with me. Just as he had planned for Mike to find him, so he had known that if he did something desperate I would come running back to him.

I couldn't look at him. 'No, Danny, no. This wasn't what I wanted. Don't you understand? It's not that I don't love you, it's just so difficult for me. And doing this doesn't help – it makes it worse.'

'I wanted to show you how sorry I was, how much I love you,' he pleaded. He tried to re-dress his arm, folding the bandage back over itself. But the ends hung limply, rolling outwards again and exposing his wound to the air.

'I'll get the nurse,' I said.

'No, stay and talk to me for a bit first please.'

'OK.' I took his hand again. I didn't know what to say.

'You could have just got a tattoo, like anyone else

would,' I said eventually. It was a feeble attempt at black humour.

He laughed, in spite of himself. 'That's what I love about you, Omi. You always speak your mind. Everybody else has been fussing around me, scared to say the wrong thing. How could I have let you go?'

'You kissed my sister,' I said, my voice suddenly serious.

He hung his head. 'I know and I'm so, so sorry. I'm sorry I did it and I'm sorry I lied. But I did it because I love you. I was missing you so much and then I saw Emily at the party and she reminded me of you and . . . it just happened. It was you I wanted, not her.'

It was an explanation, an apology, of sorts. *Too little, too late.*

'OK, Danny, I understand – kind of,' I said. 'But if you'd just come clean when I came round, we could have sorted it all out then. Maybe.'

'Don't you think I know that?' he said angrily. 'It wasn't till I got your letter that I realised what I'd done, and then it was too late.' His voice softened. 'All I've thought about for the past couple of weeks is you. You are the most important thing in my life, Omi. I don't care about my music, The Wonderfulls; none of it matters without you. Please give me another chance to prove it to you.'

He was so earnest, so desperate, that I felt my resolve beginning to slip. Maybe it was possible to make this work. Nobody would ever love me this much again, would they? Or was everything he was saying merely part of his illness?

'But you need help, Danny,' I said. 'You're not well.'

'I know,' he said, quietly. I could tell that it was a big deal for him to admit it. 'But if you're with me I can get better. You can help me get better. I'll stop cutting myself, I'll make us both happy. I need you, Omi – please help me.'

My head was spinning, my mouth parched. I got up from the bed. 'I need some air,' I said. 'I need to think. Give me ten minutes or so and I'll come back and see you. I will.'

He grasped my arm. 'OK,' he said, his eyes piercing into mine, as though he thought that if he tried hard enough he might be able to decipher my thoughts. 'Promise me.'

I didn't bother to wait for the lift. I ran down all three flights of stairs as fast as I could, unconsciously holding my breath until I reached the bottom. It wasn't until I had pushed through the hospital's front entrance doors that I stopped and leaned against the railings, gasping for air.

'Naomi?'

I looked up. It was Mrs Evans. She stood in front of me, dressed as immaculately as ever, in a slate grey suit and black stilettos. She was done up for a business meeting, not a hospital.

'Mrs Evans? Have you come to see Danny?' It was a stupid question, but as I've said before, she made me nervous.

'Yes,' she said, with a trace of sarcasm. 'Have you been in to see him already?'

'Just now,' I said. 'He's in a bad way – he showed me what he did. It was horrible. I think it's all my fault.'

'I doubt that very much, Naomi.' It was said not with kindness, but to make me feel that I was an irrelevance. 'It's not the first time this has happened and I dare say it won't be the last. Danny is a very troubled young man. He has been for several years.'

I was confused. 'What do you mean?'

'Come on, you're not telling me you thought you were dating Jiminy Cricket? Danny may be very intelligent and talented, but he's also oversensitive and his ego gets the better of him. He has a self-destructive side.'

She hadn't answered my question. 'What do you mean, it's not the first time this has happened?'

'He started cutting himself when he was thirteen – though, I grant you, he's not hurt himself as badly before. You must have seen the scars.'

I nodded. 'But the pills?'

'He tried that once before too, when he was fifteen. He didn't take enough pills to do much damage – then or now. He did it for attention, Naomi. Everything Danny does is for attention. When things don't go his way, he can't deal with it. It's always been the same. When he was ten, at his sister's eighteenth birthday party, he deliberately slammed the door on his hand because he felt left out and wanted everyone to focus on him.'

Sister? Danny didn't have a sister. He'd told me he was an only child. Was it another lie?

'His sister?'

'Stepsister,' said Mrs Evans. 'Danny didn't mention Sally? From my husband John's first marriage. She lives in America now.'

'Oh.'

'You're not the first girl to get sucked in by him. Lucy,

the girlfriend he went travelling with, she couldn't deal with it either. She left him in Colombo.'

I'd assumed that Danny had gone travelling with friends, not a girlfriend. He'd told me I was the only girl he'd ever loved. Had he told Lucy the same thing? Imagining Danny with anybody else made me feel sick to my stomach.

'I have no doubt he truly believes he loves you,' said Mrs Evans, as if she were reading my mind. 'But he'll use you as a crutch and eventually drag you down with him. Has he asked for your help, told you that you can save him?'

I nodded. *How did she know?*

She smirked. 'You can't help him, dear – he needs professional help. I should tell you that John and I have decided to pay for him to go into a private clinic, so he can get full-time care and intensive counselling. I tried once before – that's probably why he dislikes me so much. This time we won't take no for an answer. He won't get very far if we take away his trust fund, will he?'

'Oh,' I stuttered. 'No.'

It was all too much to take in. The sister, the ex-girlfriend, the trust fund: three fundamental aspects of Danny's life that I had known nothing about. Now I understood where he had acquired the money to pay for my gifts, for our expensive meals out. He didn't hate his car or his house, he hated himself for accepting them. He hated his parents because, without them, he would have had nothing.

Were omissions the same as lies? Danny may not have volunteered this information, but I had never asked. Had I been too scared of the answers to ask the right questions? Or was it his reaction that I'd feared?

Mrs Evans was suffocating me; I wanted her to leave me alone. 'You should go up and see him,' I suggested. 'I'm going to sit out here for a while and then I'll go back to the ward.'

She smiled, slyly, and proffered her hand. 'Goodbye, Naomi.'

I ignored her gesture. I no longer cared what she thought of me. She was a hateful, bitter woman – no wonder Danny was so messed up.

'Goodbye,' I said. *And good riddance.*

When she had gone, I found a bench in the hospital grounds and sat myself down, pushing my fingers in between the slats. The world was topsy-turvy and back to front. It even smelled different, the atmosphere heavier and darker, as if it had been laced with tar. Somehow, I had found myself in a parallel universe where Danny was a sick and needy stranger. However much I wished it wasn't true, *this* was the real world after all. The strong, confident Danny – the guy I had fallen in love with – had been an illusion; he had never existed.

Spiteful as she was, Mrs Evans was right about one thing: I couldn't help Danny. I wanted to, but what could I do? I wasn't a doctor or a counsellor, and I didn't want to be. Danny had been ill for years – what if he never got better? I was going to go to university, to become a lawyer or a pho-tographer, or whatever I decided, one day. I didn't want to spend my life in dingy pubs, applauding Danny, soothing his ego when things didn't go well, putting antiseptic on his cuts. If I stayed with him, that might be my reality. And then it struck me: I didn't want to be his muse, I wanted to be *someone* myself, and I wanted a partner who could support me and be strong for me too. Danny needed time alone, to figure out who he was.

If Danny doesn't know who he is, how can he be my soulmate?

And if he is my soulmate, doesn't that make me as damaged as him?

Sometimes, the more you think, the less you understand. My mind was plagued by interference, like a radio caught between stations. I wished I could shut it up, switch it off.

I waited until I saw Mrs Evans leave the hospital and then I took the lift back up to the third floor. As the doors opened, I noticed that a slender girl was standing by the ward doors, with her back to me. There was something familiar about her posture, her colouring.

'Debbie?'

She turned round, startled. 'Naomi! Your parents told me you'd be here. I was starting to worry that I'd missed you.'

'I was just outside, having a think.' It was so good to see her. 'Oh my God, what are you doing here?'

She hugged me, tightly, and the warmth and familiarity of her embrace made my eyes begin to brim with tears. 'Your mum called me and told me what had happened. I was in the town centre already, so I just got straight on the next London train. I thought I should come down to be with you.'

I blinked hard. If I let myself begin to cry now, I might never stop. 'You came all the way down from Manchester just to see me?'

'Of course I did. You'd do the same for me, wouldn't you?'

'Yes, definitely,' I said, pleased that she'd want me to. Not that I could imagine that Debbie would ever find herself in a situation like this. 'Oh, Debbie, things are such a mess.'

'Do you want to go somewhere to talk?' she asked.

'Yes, please. Just give me a second – I need to say goodbye to Danny first.'

'Do you want me to come with you?'

I pondered her offer. While I welcomed her support, this was hardly the time to introduce the two of them. I didn't want to upset Danny, or embarrass him.

'No, I'll go in by myself, if you don't mind waiting.'

She hugged me again. 'Of course not.'

Danny was sitting up in bed, a half-read magazine lying open across his lap.

'You've been ages, Omi,' he said impatiently. 'I thought you weren't coming back.'

'I promised I would, didn't I?'

'I know, but you were so long that I was starting to get paranoid.' He laughed at his choice of word. 'Then again, I guess I'm entitled to be, considering everyone here thinks I'm a mental patient.'

He noticed that I wasn't smiling and his bravado

vanished. 'I wish you hadn't gone,' he continued. 'My mum was here – I told the nurse I didn't want to see her.'

I decided it was best not to mention my encounter with his mother.

'Don't be paranoid, Danny,' I said gently. It was best to come straight out with it. 'But I can't stay. Debbie's turned up. I need to spend some time with her.'

'Debbie?' He looked bemused. 'What's she doing here?'

'She came down to look after me.'

'Oh, I see.' But it was obvious that he didn't. The thought that I might need looking after because of what he had done was incomprehensible to Danny. I could tell he was thinking, *Hey, I'm the victim here.* He truly had no idea how much his actions had hurt me, how much I was hurting now.

'I was hoping we could spend some time together, talk about things,' he said. He looked so pitiful that for a moment I just wanted to forget about Debbie and hold him.

I steeled myself. 'We can. Just not today. I'm sorry.'

'Oh, OK.' There was desperation in his voice; he feared he was losing me. 'I was thinking – when I'm better I want to teach you how to play the guitar properly. And maybe we could go travelling together.'

'That would be nice, Danny.' I didn't mean to patronise him, but I couldn't deal with any more confusion – I had to get out of there. I kissed him lightly on his cheek. 'We'll talk about it tomorrow.'

'OK.'

As I turned away, he sank down in the bed and pulled

the covers over his head. I can't be certain, but I think he was about to cry. He didn't want me to see, and I didn't want to witness it.

Debbie stayed the night. We locked ourselves away in my room and talked for hours, just as we had always done before she went to Manchester. There was so much to tell her, all the anecdotes and details that I had missed out before, the things that would help her to understand why it was so hard to let Danny go. I took out my pictures, the notes, the song and the gifts he had given me, and we studied them in detail, as if we were collecting evidence for an autopsy of my relationship.

Some of what I related to her – such as our first date, the picnic – seemed to have occurred so long ago that it was like talking about another couple. It made me sad to realise that my memories and feelings were now coloured by what had happened later and by what I had learned about Danny. Why couldn't I have read between the lines of his lyrics and seen the anguish behind them? Had he really thought me special at all, or had he just seen in me a need to be wanted? I wept, often – tears of grief for what I had lost and for what might never have been.

Later, I made up a bed for Debbie on the floor next to mine and we carried on our conversation in the dark. It was easier to be candid when we couldn't see each other's faces.

She asked: 'How do you feel about Danny, Naomi?'

'You know how I feel – I love him.'

'That's too easy. I mean how do you really feel about

him – *now*? After everything? Do you still feel the same way you did? Honestly?'

'I don't know,' I said. 'When I looked at him in his hospital bed, he seemed so small and weak, so needy. I felt like I wanted to protect him and look after him.'

'Do you still fancy him?'

'Yes, of course. He's still gorgeous. But nobody's sexy when they're in hospital, are they?' As I said it, I realised that part of Danny's allure had been his strength, his mystery. Was he as attractive without them? I couldn't say it out loud, but I had to acknowledge that he wasn't.

Debbie hesitated. 'Don't take this the wrong way, but that makes it sound like you want to be his mother.'

I bristled. 'No, not exactly. If you love someone, you want to be there for them.'

'Sure,' she said. 'But what's in it for you?'

'I get to be with him. And perhaps . . . I don't know, when he's better maybe everything might be great again.' I pictured myself with Danny – saw us smiling and laughing – and, once more, my eyes brimmed with tears at the memory of what we had shared.

'You don't know that, Naomi. Will you really just be able to forget everything that's happened? And what if he doesn't get better? How long will you give it before you finally give up on him? A few months? A few years?'

'I don't know,' I sobbed. 'I haven't thought about it. Right now, I just want to help him. Just help him, you know?'

'Oh, Naomi,' she said, in her sweetest voice. 'Please

don't be upset again. It's not your fault. You can't make him better – he's the only one who can do that.'

'I know,' I croaked. I was gulping back the tears now, breathing too fast, my head growing light.

'Shh,' she cooed. 'Shh. It's all right, honey. It's going to be all right.' I sensed that she was moving and heard the rustle of her duvet. 'Budge up,' she said. She climbed into my bed and snuggled up to me, stroking my hair and smoothing the tear-dampened strands away from my face. Feeling her warm body against mine was such a comfort; for the first time in many weeks I didn't feel alone. We lay there, silently, until my sobs had subsided.

'I wish you weren't away in Manchester,' I said.

'I know. But I'm still here for you.'

'Thanks,' I said. 'That means a lot.' It meant the world to me. I felt that we had reached an understanding. Even if we couldn't share experiences first-hand we could still support each other. And, at last, I knew that despite our differences, our friendship could move forward.

'I think I pushed you away, Deb,' I said. 'I didn't intend to.'

'It's OK. It's my fault too. I was so caught up with uni and you were so caught up with Danny. It happens.'

'I'm not sure I can cope without him,' I said. 'I'm scared, Deb.'

'I know you'll be OK, whatever happens. Don't forget that you'd finished with him – you were getting on with your life. You were making plans. You're tougher than you think.'

'I wasn't happy, though. It felt like a big part of me was missing. I think I knew, deep down, that it wasn't really over – that something else would happen.'

Debbie was quiet for a moment. 'You know that John Donne poem about the compass, the one we did at school? Maybe that's how you should think of things with Danny. Maybe you have to let him go. If you really are soulmates, if you're really meant to be together, then, somehow, you'll find your way back to each other.'

Long after Debbie had fallen asleep, I lay awake, thinking about what she had said. Perhaps she was right. Perhaps the only way I would ever find out whether Danny and I were meant to be together was if we were apart.

> *If they be two, they are two so*
> *As stiff twin compasses are two;*
> *Thy soul, the fixed foot, makes no show*
> *To move, but doth, if th' other do.*
>
> *And though it in the centre sit,*
> *Yet when the other far doth roam,*
> *It leans and hearkens after it . . .*

By the time I waved Debbie off at the railway station, the following morning, I had made my decision.

Chapter 21

Isn't it weird how the truly significant days of your life often begin as the most banal? Isn't it? Debbie took the train back to Manchester, Emily got on with her homework and my mother cooked Sunday lunch. My bus took its usual route to the hospital, the traffic was as busy as ever, the other passengers as impatient and uncommunicative. Nobody asked me how I was or where I was going. And no one took any notice of the small rucksack I carried on my shoulder. The sky didn't fall in and the world kept turning.

The nurse grinned at me as I came into the ward. 'Hi, Naomi. I just need to let you know that we're moving Danny today, to the psychiatric unit.'

'That's OK,' I said. 'I'm only popping in for a minute.'

Danny's eyes lit up when he saw me. I noticed that he had washed and shaved and combed his hair, in preparation for my visit. He resembled the old Danny again, and it made my heart skip a beat. I had been a fool to think this would be easy, to believe I could control my emotions.

I swallowed. 'How are you?' I asked. 'You look better.'

He nodded and smiled and I looked at him, as if for the first time, taking in his beautiful eyes and the curve of his nose, trying to memorise the detail of his features and the way that he moved.

And then I kissed him. It wasn't a passionate kiss – the setting and the situation didn't allow for that – but it was a deep, slow, satisfying kiss that embodied all the emotions I felt but couldn't explain: hurt and regret, sorrow and fear, love and affection, loss and hope – all rolled into one wordless expression. I didn't want it to end.

Danny was the first to pull away. 'You're saying goodbye, aren't you?' he asked, his voice no more than a whisper. He looked into my eyes with a gaze so intense that I knew he had read my mind, that our connection remained as strong as ever. It was agonising. I had promised myself that I wouldn't cry again, but my tear ducts refused to obey. Salty water cascaded down my nose, into my mouth and my hair.

'I'm so, so sorry, Danny,' I said, forgetting the long speech that I had prepared. Quoting words from a poem seemed trite, telling him that he was in the best place, that I wasn't qualified to help him, patronising. Nothing I'd meant to say seemed relevant or important now. All I could muster was, 'I can't do this any more.'

I don't know whether it was arrogance or delusion, but he would not accept it. 'You're seriously giving up on us?' he asked, with a strange, guttural laugh that unnerved me.

'Yes, Danny,' I said. But I wasn't 'giving up' – that made it sound so easy. I was fighting every instinct and feeling that I possessed, trying to do what I thought was right.

'What – that's it? *Finito*? You're going to walk out on me when I'm in hospital?'

He was playing the guilt card. Of course he was – I should have anticipated it.

Be brave, Naomi, I told myself. *You're not a bad person. You're doing the right thing.*

'Yes, Danny, I'm sorry.' I couldn't look at him – it hurt too much. I wanted this to be over now. Clumsily, I unzipped the rucksack that I had brought with me. It contained some CDs, books and a sweater he'd lent me. 'Look, I've brought your things.'

'I don't want them,' he said, turning his head away. 'Hang on to them until I'm out of here and then we can talk about it.'

'No,' I said. 'There won't be another time. It's over.'

'You're kidding yourself, Omi. What we've got is too important for you to just walk away. You need me.'

He still didn't get it. Why didn't he get it? Was I going to be there all day, going round and round in circles, until I couldn't bear it any more and gave in? Why wouldn't he let me go?

'But I don't really love you any more,' I said. I hadn't intended to say it – at least I wasn't aware of any conscious thought process – the words just tumbled out of my mouth of their own accord. It was a lie more terrible than any I had ever told, a lie far worse than any of his. I half expected a bolt of lightning to shoot in through the window and strike me down; I almost wished it would. But, at the same time, I knew it was the right thing to say, the only way I could ever put an end to this. Danny needed to be adored; he wouldn't want to be with anyone who didn't love him absolutely. The slightest doubt about my feelings would be enough to make him loosen his grip.

'I don't believe you, Omi,' he said. 'I know you love me – I felt it in your kiss.'

'Believe what you want.'

Lying to Danny – and to myself – had freed me. Now that I was acting, my true feelings buried, I could say whatever needed to be said. 'The fact is,' I continued, 'I don't feel the way I did.' I remembered the words Mike had used when I'd asked about The Wonderfulls, and added, cruelly, 'Being with you is too much like hard work.'

Danny flinched. 'Tell me right to my face that you don't love me,' he dared, still defiant.

I took a deep breath. It was harder to say a second time. 'I'm sorry, Danny, but I don't love you.'

He began to shake and I couldn't tell whether it was from fear or anger. He had grown so pale that for a moment I was scared he might pass out. Then his face hardened. 'Go on, then,' he said coldly. 'But remember this: no one will ever love you the way that I love you.'

'It's not enough,' I said. And that, at least, was the truth.

I turned and walked away from his bed, as fast as my legs would carry me, but it felt as if the end of the ward was growing further away with each step. Every patient I passed seemed to have Danny's face, to wear his pained expression. Their eyes bore into me, hating me, accusing me.

When I reached the doors, I glanced back. Danny was still sitting up, his eyes vacant, his lips parted as if he were about to speak.

I hesitated. *Just call out my name*, I thought, *and I'll take it all back.* But I knew it was far too late for that. The best that I could hope for was that one day, when he was well, he would understand my reasons and realise that I wasn't a terrible person. He would see that I did love him after all. Painful as it was, I had to believe that.

He said nothing.

So I pushed open the doors and walked out into the cold, brightly lit corridor to see what life without Danny had in store for me.

Epilogue

I never saw Danny again.

Mike kept in touch with me just long enough to let me know that Danny had gone to the private clinic his mother had told me about, and that he had done well there. The last I heard, he was planning to go back to university and finish his degree.

I hope he is still writing songs and playing, somewhere. It's possible, I suppose, that he has given it all up and joined the rat race he so despised. Maybe he now wears a suit every day and goes to work for his father's company. I'd like to think that isn't true, that at least some part of the person I loved remains.

For a long time, I would watch music shows on TV with some trepidation, in case the next new band to be featured was fronted by Danny. I know it's selfish, but to my relief, it never happened. I often think how awful it must be to have loved someone famous, to have constant reminders of them forced upon you every day.

Perhaps it makes no difference. Once a lover has imprinted himself on your mind, it is impossible to wipe him clean. I can go for weeks, months even, without thinking of Danny and then something – a phrase, or a smell, or a joke – will conjure him up again, as clearly as if I'd seen him the day before. Occasionally, he will feature in my dreams, and I will wake wondering if I did the right thing, feeling guilty for abandoning him, hoping that he has forgiven me. I'm happy now, but if things had turned out differently, could I have been happier?

If I know anything at all, I know this: I will never forget Danny. He has left a D-shaped scar on my heart, just as real as the O-shaped scar he will always wear on his arm.

Acknowledgements

Many thanks to: Brenda Gardner, Yasemin Uçar, Melissa Patey and everybody at Piccadilly; my agent, Janice Swanson at Curtis Brown; Celia Duncan, Diane Leeming and everyone at *CosmoGIRL!*; Bibi Lynch for being my first critic; Nula Bealby for putting up with me; Mum and Dad for the peaceful writing week in France; Matt Whyman for his wisdom and experience; and all my friends for listening and being there. Love and thanks to my husband, Steve Somerset, for the song lyrics for 'Take It Now'. And finally, a bittersweet thanks to all the Dannys I have known, loved and lost.

Love Divided

To Tristan

*Thanks to Celia Duncan, Ehsan, Hannan,
Brenda and Ruth*

Vanessa St Clair

Love Divided

Chapter 1

Oh God, why oh why did this always have to happen to me? I was walking back from school, minding my own business. At least, I *had* been minding my own business, until I noticed a bunch of kids in front of me, on bikes. They couldn't have been much older than my brother, around ten years old. They'd just dropped all this crap they had been eating – burger wrappers, polystyrene cups – in the middle of the pavement. I hadn't been going to say anything. I mean, normally I'm one of these people who just looks the other way. I'm much too awkward to draw attention to myself. But I'd just been thinking about this boy I used to date and how *awful* he'd been and I was feeling a bit cross. And these kids practically dropped their crapola on my favourite shoes – a drop of Coke splashed right on my leg. Maybe they hadn't realised. Before I could think about it I heard myself say, 'Hey, I'm really sorry, but would you mind picking that stuff up? It's just really dirty, and I've got to walk through it and . . . I've got new shoes on . . .'

I trailed off.

They were looking at me as if I had another head growing from my stomach.

'Oh, it doesn't matter. Sorry.' I wished I hadn't said anything. They had that look about them, like they were trying to think of something to say. And I could bet I knew what it was.

I am an *idiot*!

I've got red hair see, dark red, which around here is enough to mark me out as a freakazoid. Obviously, I don't have a right to say anything to anyone. Added to which, I attract embarrassment, like flies to . . . fly-zappers. I'm a total klutz for one thing. I'm tall for my age and I'm always spilling things or knocking things over. And I have this uncanny ability to attract crazy people. Like, I'm always the one person that the crazy old guy on the bus will sit next to. Not that I mind crazy old guys, I just wish I had the same skill with the young and cute ones.

The kids finally found the power of speech.

'Oi, ginger!'

'Ginger minger!'

'I bet she smells weird!'

'Eeeww, better watch out, she might get really angry!

She might explode!'

Cue crazy laughter. They obviously thought they were being *hilarious* – it's amazing, the self-delusion of some people. And even though it's happened a zillion times before I was still worried I was going to blush, and because I was worried I was going to blush, I could feel myself doing exactly that. My face went bright red, sunburned tomato red, right up to the tips of my ears. Then I couldn't think of a suitably withering response because I was concentrating so hard on keeping my face pointing down at the pavement. If there's anything worse than having red hair, it's the fact that my cheeks go up in flames and everybody can see what I'm feeling. It's like having subtitles over my head: *JUST IN CASE YOU MISSED IT, LUCY BROOKS IS EMBARRASSED.*

I was just bending to pick up the rubbish myself when I heard a voice right behind me. I recognised it, but I couldn't get to the name right away. A boy's voice. Very in control sounding, which was a relief because I was *not* very in control at this point.

'Why don't you get back on your bikes?' the voice said. 'That is, if you know how to ride them. I'm surprised that kids with as few brain cells as you have learned how to balance, actually.'

The chubbier of the boys, who also happened to be

the leader, got this tortured look on his face, like he'd got a stomach ache. But he'd obviously just been having a thought, because then he exclaimed, 'Oi, onion bhaji!' It was Mally – only the coolest boy in school.

'Right,' said Mally. 'Onion bhaji. I don't even know what you mean by that.' Then he paused and pretended to look surprised. 'Oh, you mean I come from a place in which people *eat* onion bhajis. And you know where that is? *England!*' Mally shook his head. 'Go on, why don't you just piss off?'

The chubby boy went, 'Oh!' in a tone that was probably supposed to suggest that he'd still got the upper hand but actually came out like he couldn't think of anything to say. 'C'mon, let's go. This is pointless.'

He was trying to sound tough, but actually he just sounded pathetic.

'Yeah, for once it looks like you've got the right idea,' said Mally.

The others all looked a bit sheepish and couldn't meet my eye. Then they turned around and followed their leader up the street.

Wow, Mally was so damn cool! But then I knew that already. And *I was* a complete idiot. God, this was awkward. Quick, I had to think of something to say!

'What stupid, weren't they . . . I mean losers! Some people have the brain of a gnat.'

'Yeah,' said Mally. 'They were only kids though. Probably it's their parents who are the real losers. It was actually pretty childish of me to resort to their level. It was the first thing that came into my head.'

'I thought it was . . . you were . . . cool!' Nice one Lucy, way to go. First Law of Thermodynamics: never tell a cool person they are cool. It makes you look uncool.

I'd known Mally for ages. Not *known* known, but he'd lived a couple of streets away from me for as long as I could remember. His dad runs the Indian restaurant that everyone goes to and Mally was at the same school as me. His kid brother was even friends with my kid brother; they're both quite nerdy so they got on pretty well. But Mally and I, we'd never really *clicked* before. It might have been his age – he's two years older than me. But it was more likely the fact that I'd found him a bit intimidating. He always seemed to have his iPod clamped to his ears and he dressed quite a lot in black. On top of which, he was really brainy. He was wearing an old black T-shirt now, though I guess it did suit him because it clung in all the right places. His arms were nice too – smooth with just the right amount of muscle, so there was that yummy line on the inside of them when he flexed.

'Anyway,' said Mally. 'I probably should have left those kids to you; I mean I know you can handle yourself, but, well, there was only one of you and four of them.'

'No, I'm glad you got rid of them. It's fine. I mean, *it's* not fine. *I'm* fine. Are you fine?' Oh God. I couldn't stop saying fine!

'I'm fine,' Mally flashed a brief smile at me, which made his cheekbones look even higher . . . Oh God, at least he hadn't heard the whole rubbish incident. I'd forgotten all about the rubbish. I couldn't very well *not* pick it up after all this business. But I'd lose any shred of cred by picking it up in front of Mally. But, thinking about it, it was too late for that. If I was standing next to a cool-o-meter, the arrow would be pointing to *COMPLETE AND UTTER LOSER*.

I crouched and picked up a corner of greasy paper by the edges of my fingertips.

'You pick up rubbish? Cool! Weird . . . but cool,' said Mally, bending down to help.

Then, *of course*, there wasn't a bin for about twenty miles so we both had to walk down the street holding out pieces of crap in each hand like some kind of rubbish-munching daleks. This was definitely the new Number One on my Most Embarrassing Moments list (and I have *a lot*). This one would be hard to beat.

'Are you going . . .?' I gestured up the street with my head.

'Yeah.'

After about a thousand years we found the bin and let go of our rubbish, then I lost the ability to speak for a bit. Mally must have taken off his headphones without turning his iPod off because I could hear music still coming out of them. It sounded like it was being played by a tiny band in a matchbox.

In desperation I said, 'What . . . what are you listening to?'

'Oh. Umm . . .' Mally fumbled with the wheel and the music stopped. 'The Thrillers. Do you know them?'

'I think I've heard of them. Are they American?'

'Yeah, from the Mid-West or something. I'm not really into them though.'

There was another pause.

'I've just discovered Jeff Buckley,' I said desperately. 'He's amazing. He died – drowned, I think.'

'I know – in the Mississippi River. He *is* amazing. Do you know that song "Hallelujah"?'

'Yes! I bought it on iTunes yesterday! It's so beautiful. It makes my spine tingle. It makes me feel as if I'm the only person in the world who's feeling . . . well . . . who's feeling like that,' I ended lamely. How could I describe my favourite song? It's as if it was written just for me, and the writer knew my innermost thoughts, and it made me feel special and uplifted and a bit melancholy at the same time. But I couldn't say all this because Mally would think I'd gone completely bonkers. I didn't know him *that* well, even if we were managing to have a conversation. Plus we were almost at the door of my house.

'I can't believe you like Jeff Buckley. He's so unusual,' said Mally.

'Oh, and I'm not?' I said. I was *not* flirting because I don't know how to flirt, at least according to Rachel, and to be honest I still felt pretty awkward. It was just the first thing that came out of my mouth.

'No! That's not what I meant. You are. You are very unusual. You pick up other people's rubbish – that's pretty unusual.'

'Oh, so I am a freak. I knew it.' I was laughing now and Mally gave me a great wide grin that illuminated his whole face.

'OK, you're a freak,' he said.

'That's what those boys thought,' I said, embarrassed again. I walked right into that one. Probably Mally *did* actually think I was a freak with my stupid red hair and freckles and tallness. 'Thanks, by the way, for earlier.'

'Oh, no, it's nothing. I like your new haircut.' Mally

was standing there with one finger tucked into his waistband. For one crazy moment I thought he might actually be looking me up and down. My hands shot to my hair. It had been very long and straggly but I'd had it cut to shoulder-length, so on a good day it was tousled. On a bad day it was just a mess. I doubted this was a good day though, so . . . was he taking the piss? But he was just standing there looking at me. I didn't think boys noticed things like haircuts.

'Thanks??' I said idiotically.

'It's a pleasure.' Mally flashed me another smile, put his headphones back in, then he turned on the heels of his beaten-up trainers and was gone.

I shut the front door. I had to call Rachel and tell her what had just happened. I felt like I was going to burst. But Mum got to me first.

'*Loo-cin-dah!*' She is practically the only one who calls me by my full name and she only does that when she's cross.

'Yes?'

Mum poked her head over the stairs. 'I notice the dishwasher hasn't been unloaded even though I asked you to do it this morning. And you need to take your wet clothes out of the washing machine.'

'Sorry, Mum!' Mum had asked me, it was true, but I'd been late and I couldn't decide which tights to wear and I forgot about it. 'Can I please just —'

'No, you can't!'

'But you don't even know what I'm going to say!'

'I don't need to. And don't forget to feed Socks. You know what happened last night.'

'Yes, Mum.' The previous evening I had forgotten to feed Socks and he had started barking really loudly at eleven o'clock. Mum had had to get out of bed and give him some food.

Mum gave a theatrical sigh. 'I know you're sixteen, but really, darling, sometimes you're more like a six-year-old. Before you even think about using the phone, or your computer, can you do your chores?'

Mothers are *so* annoying. I stuck my lip out and flounced into the kitchen.

My little brother, Herbie, was sitting at the kitchen table, bent over his plate and sawing at something with a knife. He looked up when he heard me. 'What's wrong with you?'

'Nothing! Nothing that a pickaxe wouldn't cure anyway.' I bent down and started unloading the dishes noisily. 'What are you doing – or shouldn't I ask?'

'Seeing how many little squares I can make from my sandwich,' said Herbie.

'Right, geek brain.'

'A sandwich is a rectangle, so the number wouldn't be infinite, as it would in a square. My knife is too blunt as well. I've got nine so far.'

I was still full of my encounter with Mally and so desperate to tell Rachel about it I clattered the plates down on the shelves.

'You're going to break those if you carry on like that,' said Herbie.

'Yes, Mini-Mummy,' I said.

Herbie glared at me. I threw the last few into the cupboard and literally ran to my room, dialling Rachel's number as I went.

'Hello? Rach. Guess what just happened to me. You won't believe it!'

When I had finished, I had to hold the phone about a metre away from my ear, Rachel was screaming so hard.

'YOU MUST HAVE DIED!'

'Embarrassing is not the word,' I said.

Rachel has the kind of gorgeous dark brown hair boys come up to admire rather than to mock, and I wondered for a second if she could understand what it felt like to be me. Now she was making vomiting sounds down the phone.

'I mean, I've had to put up with that kind of stuff

before,' I said, a little defensively. 'And by the sounds of it, Mally has too.'

'Yes, I know, sweets, I'm your best friend, remember? The one who's known you for about a million years. Those kids were just jerks. I mean – you must have died when Mally came along. He is *so* cool! And, like, drop-dead gorgeous!'

'He is not! I mean, I can see that he's cute, I suppose. But he's not my type.' As I said it I could feel myself starting to blush – for no reason at all. Luckily we were on the phone and Rachel couldn't see me.

'Not your type?' she said. 'What's not to be your type? He rescued a damsel in distress – that's one major plus over the losers round here. Plus the dreamy eyes,' Rachel put on a sing-song voice. 'The lean muscles. The tousled hair. The strong but mysterious —'

'All right, all right,' I interrupted her. 'He *is* quite cute. I'm not denying that. But I've known him for ages. He's practically the boy next door. Plus, as you well know, I am Officially Off Boys.'

'Apart from DG.'

'Apart from DG.'

Rachel and I were always talking about who we were going to fall in love with, our Dream Guy. He changed every week. His current incarnation was a motorbike-riding lead singer of an Indie rock band who looked like that model in the Hugo Boss ads. We would meet our DG in some totally random but fateful way, like on holiday when he was taking a break from his touring commitments, and had spotted us across a crowded restaurant, and just knew we were The One. Or The Ones, as there were two of us. Though probably, knowing Rachel, she'd get there first. Maybe he could have an identical twin left over for me.

Come to think of it I was getting *way* too into this DG thing.

'But you know, babes, it might be time to let go of the anti-boy thing,' said Rachel. 'I know the Evil Quin was a total jerk, but that was ages ago now.'

'Not ages ago. Three months and three weeks ago.'

I knew exactly how long because the Evil Quin still made me mad. I'd never really fancied him, but he was the first boy to properly ask me out and I was so surprised I'd said yes. He had taken me to the cinema to see a scary film. I HATE scary films, but I think Quin picked it on purpose because in the middle of it, just as the heroine let out a big scream, he snaked his hand along the back of my seat and started pressing my shoulder. I couldn't believe I was living in such a cliché. And then, on the way home, he made a lunge for my lips. And the maddest thing was that because he had paid for my pizza I felt as if I couldn't really stop him.

It was my first proper snog and I'd always thought it might be like something out of James Bond – all soaring music and melting into his manly arms. It wasn't though. It was actually quite boring and uncomfortable.

After that we seemed to be 'an item'. Which seemed to consist of snogging a lot and never actually talking. Which was bad enough, except for one day I felt his hand creeping up my thigh, slowly, like a tarantula. I was wearing a pair of giant pants but that wasn't the reason I was so freaked out. I just didn't want him anywhere near *there*. I wasn't ready! And I'd never *be* ready, at least not with Quin! I leaped out of the car – I could feel myself going the *deepest* red – and started stammering out excuses about having to get home right away to complete some T-shirts I was designing.

I had to finish it – I mean, I should never even have begun it. But it was horrible. I was so obviously crap at this sort of thing that I couldn't tell Quin the truth – I thought I'd hurt him too much. So I said:

'I'm really busy with my T-shirts.'

'My little brother needs help with his homework.' A lie – Herbie *never* needed help with his homework.

And lamest of all, 'My mum says I'm not allowed to hang around with smokers.'

Quin went really quiet and said, 'If you don't like me, just tell me.'

I realise now that I hurt him much more by not being honest. Because Quin was so furious with me he spread it all round school that I was frigid. Mum said to ignore what everyone said, that I had made the right decision. She said 'frigid' was just a word boys used when they were trying to put girls in their place, but it was old-fashioned and had no power any more in the real world. In the end she was right – it all blew over when the gossips found something new to talk about. But the whole episode was enough to put me Officially Off Boys, that's for sure.

'But you know the longer you stay Officially Off Boys, the longer it'll hurt,' said Rachel, at the other end of the phone. 'You need someone to get you in the groove again. What's wrong with Mally? It sounds as if you had a *thing* going on today.'

'If by *thing* you mean a *thing* never to be spoken of again, yes we did. A thing of complete humiliation, of utter —'

'OK, OK, I get your point! Actually you're probably right. You and Mally are quite different.'

'What d'you mean?'

'I mean he's all cool and mysterious, you're a total klutz. And you can be quite loud,' said Rachel.

'You're much louder! Besides, I'm only loud when I'm with my friends! I'm really shy otherwise.'

'I know, I know. And I *am* louder, it's true. That's because I haff to haff vayz off making you do vat I say,' she said.

'If that is meant to be a German accent, it's terrible.'

'Plus you're totally into fashion,' Rachel continued without listening. 'Mally's into saving the world. Mally's the kind of guy who speaks in debates about global warming. B-double-O-ring.'

'I *am* into saving the world, thank you very much. I just wouldn't speak about it in debates. I'd go puce.'

'Anyway, it gives you a chance to see him again.'

'What does?'

'The debate, idiot! It's on Monday. You can see Mally again, your eyes can meet across a crowded room . . .'

'Stop it! We're different, as you said. He obviously saw me and *took pity* on me. Which I suppose is quite nice considering he's so cool, but it definitely is NOT a good beginning to a love story. "Oooh, Lucy, you're so sexy when you get picked on by boys!"'

'Whatever! Maybe on Monday something will happen to change your mind.'

'Yeah, maybe I'll grow a new head by then, but I doubt it,' I said.

Chapter 2

To be honest, I was with Rachel on this one. I thought the debate about global warming was going to be a total waste of time. It's a really important issue, I know, but these school things are usually lame. Apart from it being compulsory, our teacher had also said, *It's for your own good*, which is usually a guarantee it's going to be *bad*, or, at the very least, *boring*.

When we arrived the hall was packed and full of noise. Everyone was mucking about and screeching and elbowing each other. The headmistress had to clap her hands above her head for about a minute before anyone paid her any attention. When she spoke she said that this was the most important issue facing our generation *blah blah blah* and that the motion was: *Global Warming – It's Not My Problem*.

The side that agreed with the motion started first, and fair enough, they did have a tougher argument to win. They said there was no such thing as global warming, that it was some conspiracy to make us all stop doing what we wanted. The planet had always got warmer and colder – look at the last Ice Age. We didn't have to worry about flying abroad on holiday or bother about washing out cat-food tins for recycling. It sounded much easier in fact, and I was halfway to believing they were right.

Then Mally stood up. This time he didn't look at all cool. He looked quite upset. He ran his hand through his hair so that it stood straight up. He didn't sound pompous like the other side had; he spoke quietly, but there was something in his tone that made everyone listen. Then he brought out a trillion facts and figures – the sea-level had risen $X + Y - Z$ amount quicker than natural warming, polar bears in the Arctic were now finding it impossible to hunt and were dying – until we were all completely convinced. His hair kept falling into his eyes and Mally kept giving this little toss of his head that said, *Get out of my way, hair, I've got more important things to worry about, even though you do look impossibly cute falling into my eyes.*

Mally's family was from Bangladesh. His cousin was a schoolteacher who lived in Antarpara, on the bank of a river. But the river kept overflowing. Global warming was melting the ice caps and putting extra water into the sea, which got pushed up into the rivers. His school was flooded and they had nowhere else to go. The crops had failed too because the river was so salty. They were now hungry and homeless. The crisp packets had stopped crinkling in the hall and no one moved. Mally's voice had dropped very low. We were so lucky in England, he said. But it is countries like ours that were causing global warming, while countries like Bangladesh suffered. But just by doing a few simple things – recycling, turning off lights – we could massively benefit people in poorer countries. Global warming, he said, was our problem, and our responsibility.

When Mally sat down, there was silence for a moment then everyone broke out into crazy applause. 'That was pretty good,' said Rachel in my ear. 'Though Mally did have an advantage.'

'What d'you mean?' I said.

'The whole sob story.'

I poked her hard in the ribs. 'It's not an *advantage*.'

The headmistress hardly had to count up the votes: it was obvious who'd won. Mally – by a mile.

I wanted to go up and tell him how GREAT his speech was, but Mally's hipster friends who were all older than me, had got there first and I didn't feel like pushing through them. Then all these girls from the year above came over and were saying how brilliant he was, and putting their arms around him and standing really close. His mate Raj was there too, looking super-relaxed and jokey. Rachel and I hovered around the edges. I was just about to give up when Mally looked over and saw me.

'Lucy!'

He gave me a massive smile that made the hairs on my arms stand up. I'd had this little speech planned in my head, but now that it came to it, it sounded too cheesy.

'You were great,' I said. Nice one, Lucy, top marks for originality.

'You were amazing,' said Rachel.

'Thanks. It wasn't really me though – my argument was easier to win.' Mally stopped smiling.

'That's what I said!' said Rachel.

'*Rachel!*' I was bright puce.

'Oh, I mean, it's obvious that global warming does exist,' said Rachel. Even she looked a bit awkward now. 'But you did a great job of, ummm, bringing it home.'

'Thanks,' said Mally. 'I think.'

Great. Now he thought my friend and I were total tossers. 'I thought I might do something, maybe, to help?' I said, but before I could say anything else, Raj said to Mally that he'd better make a move, otherwise they'd be late.

'Yeah, OK,' said Mally. 'Look, sorry, Lucy. Raj and I

have to see the Head about our applications to uni. Thanks to Raj here, my timekeeper.'

Raj gave me a big wonky smile. 'The brainbox is only trying to get into Cambridge!'

'Maybe we could speak tomorrow? Or sometime!' said Mally.

'Yes,' I said, over-brightly. 'Sometime!'

Sometime! That was the lamest arrangement ever. I should have at least pinned him down to this week. I just wanted to tell him about an idea I'd had during his speech. I could do something useful that wasn't totally crap (like confronting kids on bikes). I would customise T-shirts. I'd been doing this for ages for friends – just bows and sequins and stuff. But now I could maybe put on a stencil of a polar bear, or a whale. But were whales victims of global warming? I hoped so, then I could make a sequinned spout. But if they were maybe they'd be global-warming winners? More water to swim about in . . .

Hmmm.

This was the kind of thing I needed advice on. I was just so totally clueless. Also I needed a good slogan. *The polar bear needs you! . . .* Hmm. *I'm hot – global warming's not.* A bit confusing. *I'm hot – and so is global warming, but not in a good way.* Hmmmmm.

What else?

What else?

I sat with my fingers poised over my laptop. Long minutes passed.

As I was trying to think, this other voice just tapped away at the back of my brain like a woodpecker. *Why,* tap tap tap, *don't you email Mally* tap tap tap *for advice?*

No! He said *sometime*. He'd think I was pushy.

But you're not after him. It's just for advice.

But still, I shouldn't really email him first. It was up to the boy to email the girl. Also, he'd think I was stupid and trivial – T-shirts!

But you're planning to sell them and donate the proceeds to the school fund. Doesn't that make it un-trivial? Just ask Mally. He's not that serious anyway. He can be quite funny.

He could be quite funny, it was true. Sometimes, when I dropped off my brother at his house, he'd answer the door with a really good impression of Mr Biggs, the science teacher.

Oh God, Mr Biggs had been chair of the debate. I'd had a go at Rachel earlier for being such an *idiot* in front of Mally, but she'd only accused me of sexual tension, which she'd just read about online. Apparently if you had it, you went red in each other's presence and couldn't think of what to say. Basically, she blamed *me* for her being an idiot, said the atmosphere had been tense and she'd just blurted it out, which I thought was a bit of a cheek.

But obviously there had been no *sexual tensity*, or whatever it was called. Mally had been surrounded by other girls and he hadn't even been looking at me, until right at the end.

Which was why, I thought with a little stab of excitement, I *could* email him. We obviously didn't fancy each other so there was no way my email could be misinterpreted. It would just be as one . . . activist . . . to another.

Right.

I could email his school address – we all had one in the same format for when the school wanted to get hold of us (no escape from the evil eye). Just a quick note and then I could get on with the design of the T-shirts.

What should I say?

From: Loocee@blueyonder.co.uk
To: m.khan@stmarys.co.uk
Subject: Hi!

I deleted the exclamation mark. Too keen.

Subject: Hi.
Hi Mally,
Just thought I'd write a quick note to say how great
I thought you were today.

I'd already told him I thought he was great. God, I was boring! Plus, 'great' – it was like saying 'nice'. I took out 'great' and put in 'brilliant'.

Hi Mally,
Just thought I'd write a quick note to say how brilliant I thought you were today.
What you said was amazing.

I wanted to write that I'd known about global warming before, in a vague way. It was the reason Mum went to the local farmers' market, when she could afford it, so the vegetables didn't have to be driven as far. But I hadn't actually *understood* it before now. The people in countries like Bangladesh had seemed so far away, but Mally's speech had made me realise they were just like us.

I didn't write any of this down. I tried to, but it sounded too cheesy, so I deleted it all.

After literally an hour, this is what I came up with:

Hi Mally,
Just thought I'd write a quick note to say how
brilliant I thought you were today. What you said
was amazing, you really made me think. I thought
I'd make some T-shirts about global warming. Is it
OK to run some things by you?
Thanks,
Lucy

I wasn't that pleased with it – I sounded pretty lame. But I hit *send* anyway and then surfed the web for a while. I wanted to be online in case Mally emailed me back.

But one hour later, Mally had *not* emailed me back! My eyes hurt. Better go and have dinner.

One hour forty-three minutes later, Mally still had not emailed me back! I didn't really know what to do. Watch TV I supposed.

... OhmyGod, three hours ten minutes later and Mally *still* had not emailed me back. I knew the precise time because I was checking it at the top of my screen every three seconds. I kept thinking that three hours wasn't such a long time to wait for a reply. He might have gone out. He might have a life! Then again, it was a school night and it was the evening and ... oh Jeez, I was so *humiliated*! *Why* had I had to bother him with my stupid stupid T-shirt idea? He obviously thought it was not even worth replying. I was a total fool. Mally was far too cool for me. Who did I think I was?

OK, OK, during the last three hours fifty-five minutes and twenty-four seconds, I had been forced to admit it. I did like him. Just a little bit.

I'd got no chance though.

I hit *sleep* on my computer. Then I remembered I should turn it off. I might have lost the boy but I didn't have to lose the planet too.

In the morning there was still no email. I checked it as soon as I woke up, even though I had to admit it was quite unlikely Mally would have sent one in the middle of the night. Then I had to go into school, and of course, as soon as I walked in, there he was. Mally was at the top of the stairs and I was at the bottom, but luckily I spotted him before he saw me. My heart gave a giant lurch and I spun round on my heel, bumping into some Year Sevens in my eagerness to get out. I had to skulk around in the yard until the bell rang, pretending to all my friends that I had a really important text to send.

I skipped lunch and ate three packets of Twiglets instead. Not so good for my diet – not that I was on a diet, I just wouldn't mind losing some weight, just a couple of pounds. Mum said I was mad, but I felt too big, especially compared to the girls I saw in magazines. But even breaking my non-diet diet was better than risking the utter humiliation of bumping into Mally.

Rachel could see immediately that something was wrong and she didn't launch into her usual mad routine. When I told her I had sent an email to Mally but hadn't got a reply, even this morning, a whole thirteen and a half hours later, she put her arm round me.

'You like him, don't you?'

'Yeah, OK, I admit it. You were right. But now I've completely blown it, oh God, and it's sooooo embarrassing.'

'Sweetie! His email might not be working,' said Rachel.

'I've thought of that. About a thousand times. But whenever someone doesn't reply that's what I always think, and they've always got it, they've just been really slow at answering.'

'I don't know . . .'

'It's far more likely that he just doesn't want to answer.'

Rachel squeezed my shoulder. 'Then he's an idiot.'

'Yeah, an idiot,' I said. But what I really thought was

that he was probably pretty smart, not wanting to be involved with me. Awkward, blushing, litter-picking-up me. Why would someone like Mally be interested? 'I've scared him off, haven't I, by emailing?'

'But he doesn't know that you like him. He just thinks you're a friend at this point. And if one of your friends didn't answer straight away, you wouldn't be upset, would you?' said Rachel.

'Great. I'm a friend. That's just what I need.'

'I didn't say that! But . . .'

'What?' I said.

'Well, have you thought that maybe you just *think* you like him because you think he doesn't like you?' she said.

It was true that I hadn't admitted to myself how much I fancied Mally. But I had liked him even *before* I sent him the email. If I was honest, that was *why* I had sent him the email. 'I don't think so,' I said. 'I like Mally because he's so different from the rest of the boys round here. Most of them are so full of front.'

'Tell me about it,' said Rachel. 'Though sometimes *some* front is . . . a tiny bit sexy, right?'

'Not to me,' I said.

'No, you're right,' said Rachel.

'I thought Mally was full of front. Until he rescued me and helped me pick up rubbish! Though he did tell those kids where to go. But that wasn't front, exactly. Then, you know, the debate, he was just so, so passionate and not cool at all . . .' I trailed off.

'You should have asked my advice!' said Rachel. 'I'm the expert when it comes to boys! Seriously though, hon, it's not all bad. At least you can be friends with him now you've got to know him a bit. You can hang out with your brother as a foursome.'

I pulled a face. 'A foursome! You mean, me and three boys, one of whom is my *brother*?'

Rachel and I burst out laughing.

'OH MY GOD!' said Rachel. 'Don't take me there! That would have to be the least appetising foursome in history.'

My mind kept wandering all through afternoon lessons. My brain was completely trying to do me in, because it *kept on* turning to Mally, even though he was the last thing I actually wanted to think about.

Here's what my brain sounded like: *Do you think Mally saw me on the stairs? Then he would have seen me running away and – STOP! Think about something else. Hmmm, OK, looks like spring is finally arriving. Leaves on trees at last, ice-creams! Swimming. Bikini shame! Bet Mally'd look pretty cute in a pair of – STOP IT.*

Chemistry, chemistry, periodic table; what is technetium anyway? Sounds like the name of an online super geek. Oh God, why did I have to send Mally that email? STOP IT STOP IT, PLEASE STOP IT.

I was quite depressed by the time school ended, and utterly sick of myself. Rachel wanted to walk back with me, but I said I'd be OK. I just felt like going home and watching TV.

I was heading out of the playground when I saw Mally and Raj loitering around the school gates, as if they were waiting for someone. Oh blimey, now I had no protection! But if they were waiting for someone, why were they walking over to me? There was absolutely nothing I could do to escape. Most of the other kids had gone home. It was just Mally, his mate and me and a giant expanse of concrete.

I hoped it would be over quickly.

'Howya doing, Lucy?' said Raj, with his trademark cheeky grin.

'Fine, thanks,' I mumbled, looking down at the ground. Raj was wearing a giant pair of old school trainers, not the sort you could get in shops round Redworth.

'Cool. OK, catch ya later, yeah, bro?' he said to Mally, with a wink.

Now it was just Mally and me.

'I'm sorry I didn't get to talk to you after the debate,' said Mally after a silence. 'I felt like I was a bit rude.'

Why was he apologising about that? He probably felt sorry for me. 'It's OK, it's fine,' I said. I was blushing right up to the roots of my hair and I had to drop my head down and pretend to be looking for something in my bag. Why wouldn't he just *go away*?

'I think you said you wanted to do something, I dunno, to help? After the debate. Maybe I didn't hear you properly.'

Oh bloody hell. I was boiling over with confusion. What about the email? I didn't know what else to say, so I just said, 'Yesss,' as if I was thinking loads of deep thoughts.

'I mean, you don't have to!' said Mally. 'I'm not pushing you. I just, I just wanted to apologise, I guess.' He stopped and thrust his hands into his trouser pockets.

'I was thinking about T-shirts,' I said. 'Did you . . . get my email?'

'Email? No. When did you send it?'

NO!!!

'Oh, around seven,' . . . thirty-six, I added silently.

'I wasn't online after six yesterday. I had a tonne of maths homework. What did it say?'

HE HADN'T GOT IT!

'Oh, it was no big deal,' I said. 'I just thought I might make some T-shirts for the school fund. I've made them before, just silly ones, but I thought I'd make some for global warming.'

'That's a great idea,' Mally said. Then he gave me a smile that made my skin goosebump. 'I was kind of hoping you might email me actually.'

He *was*? I flushed up to the roots of my hair. Bloody hell, Lucy, stop being so awkward!

'Really?' I said, only my voice came out all weird and wobbly.

'Yeah, really,' he said, with the same slow smile. 'I was going to text you, only, if you can believe it, I don't have your number.'

'Oh.' I stood there, rooted to the spot, but staring and staring at him with a feeling of incredible excitement.

'I was going to ask you if you wanted to meet up tomorrow afternoon. We could talk about your T-shirt idea then, if you like.'

'Yes! I'd love to. Only . . .' Oh *no*! *I'd forgotten about Socks!* '. . . Only on Saturday afternoon I have to take the dog for a walk. It was kind of a bargain my mum and I made when we got him.' God, I sounded lame.

'That sounds great,' said Mally, turning towards the school gates and giving his hair a little shake. 'If that's OK?'

He really was impossibly cute.

'Really? You want to come on a *dog walk*?'

'Why not? The weather is just getting good, and if that's what you're doing, I'm in.'

OHMYGOD. I'd just made a date with Mally. If you could call a dog walk a date. Which I could and I would!!!

When we reached my house we stood awkwardly, looking at each other.

'OK then, Lou-ceee . . .' said Mally.

Just the way he pronounced my name, long and slow, gave me the shivers.

'OK then, Mally.'

'I'll see you tomorrow.'

Mally arrived early. I knew because I was still upstairs applying mascara and the doorbell gave me a shock and I smudged it on to my eyebrow. Then I heard his footsteps in the hall and the sound of muffled voices. After a moment I heard my mum laughing. Lordy, what was he saying to her? I had to get down there.

I still wasn't happy with my outfit – I hadn't wanted to look as if I'd worked too hard – no high heels; but I'd also wanted to wear something that didn't make me look fat, so no baggy pair of old cords. Which left . . . not that much really. I finally settled for my favourite jeans with a pale green cotton tunic top. For once I didn't mind my hair or my pale skin – the colour of the tunic seemed to suit them. I fluffed my hands through my hair – aiming for tousled – then I rubbed off the mascara. It would have to do.

I ran downstairs.

I was in such a hurry that I collided with the doorway on my way in but I pretended it didn't hurt. And *there* was real-life Mally in *my* kitchen, leaning on the table, with one long leg bent up against the table leg, waiting for me.

The kitchen suddenly seemed much too small.

Mum smiled. 'Ah Lucy. Mally was just telling me you're going for a walk.'

I hadn't wanted Mum to know Mally coming over was a big deal, just in case it wasn't. I loved my mum and everything but I know what she's like. She'd be full of questions and then she'd say something really embarrassing like, *Where are you going on your date?* And then she'd probably ask me if I'd finished all my homework, or hassle me about something I'd forgotten to do. I know I can be scatty, but at the same time Mum can be quite bossy and go on at me a lot.

So to avoid mother-shame, I had said something vague about Mally coming round to take Socks out because he was helping me with something for school. Mum had had some work she'd brought home for the weekend and she was screwing up her eyes at it when I told her, so she just nodded.

'Socks!' said Mally, rubbing his neck. 'Good to see you again!' Socks was in heaven, pressing himself against Mally's legs. I knew exactly how he felt.

He looked up. 'Hi Lucy.' My heart skipped a beat. He was wearing a great pair of jeans, not too baggy, not too tight. His legs looked very sexy and I could see the perfect brown skin of his hip bone above his waistband. His retro trainers and beaten-up navy blue coat looked old, but not at all grotty. Mally caught me looking him up and down and winked at me, in a really *naughty* way that gave my heart a little electric shock. The kitchen was growing tinier and tinier until I felt as if my head might explode.

I had to get out of there.

'We should probably go!' I said, a bit breathlessly.

'Well, have fun,' said Mum. 'Are you sure you're going to be warm enough? It's quite cold outside.'

'Yes, Mum! The sun's out.'

Mum looked doubtful, but before she could grab my arms and manhandle me into a coat I sped out of the front door.

* * *

I loved taking Socks down by the river. Down there you'd never know that a huge bustling town was just around the corner. For a start you couldn't hear anything but water whooshing by. You couldn't see many houses at all through the trees, and the banks were covered with daffodils. Daffodils are great, they mean summer is just around the corner. Though it wasn't that hot today; Mum might have been right about the weather. Still, it smelled lovely, damp and fresh.

I let Socks off the lead and he scampered about, shoving his nose in clumps of grass. I suddenly felt incredibly happy. It was spring and I had the cutest boy in school walking next to me.

'So,' said Mally. 'You wanted to ask me about T-shirts?'

'Oh – yeah! Well, I thought I would put an animal on the front, one that was threatened by global warming, and then a tag line. Only, when I thought about it more, I wasn't absolutely sure which animals were in trouble. The polar bear, of course, but is the whale, or the dolphin?'

'Loads of them are but the polar bear is probably your best bet,' said Mally. 'It's the most instantly recognisable in terms of global warming.'

'Right. But all the tag lines I thought of are incredibly cheesy. Like, *It's hot, I'm not. It's hot, and so am I.*'

Mally burst out laughing. 'That's actually pretty good. I can see that last one on you.'

'Can you?' I said, raising my eyes to meet his, for once. I couldn't believe I wasn't blushing.

We talked some more about ideas and different things I could do and I found myself having new ideas on the spot. Mally didn't mock me or say they were crap. He actually seemed to be listening to me.

'How about *Global warming is not cool*?' I said. 'Short and to the point.'

'That sounds perfect!' said Mally, smiling at me. 'You're not just a pretty face. Though you *are* pretty, that's for sure. Gorgeous, in fact.'

I didn't know what to say, so we just stared at each other, smiling, our eyes drawn together like magnets. I kept thinking, *I can't believe this is actually happening*. None of my fantasies had ever matched up to this. And we'd probably still be standing there locked together if Socks hadn't started barking and I'd finally had to look away.

'Socks!! Come back! Sorry, he loves chasing squirrels.'

'I don't blame him. If I was a dog, that's what I'd like too,' said Mally.

'Do you know that dogs have a sense of humour? They've recorded these really high-pitched sounds dogs make when they're playing; it's like laughter.'

'Really?' said Mally, taking my hand in his. 'I'm sure it's true. I always think the next-door neighbour's dog is laughing at me when I go to school in the morning. He's just so perky, and I'm just so . . . not.'

I was trying to keep on being normal even though I could feel Mally's hand burning through my skin. I couldn't believe that Mally ever looked anything less than gorgeous, even first thing. He looked gorgeous now. He had the most ridiculously long eyelashes. And the most perfectly formed nose.

'You know, you have a nose Michael Jackson would kill for.' It was my turn to flirt – very unlike me, but this whole thing was very unlike me, and it felt *great*.

'I'm glad you like it,' said Mally. 'It cost me almost as much as it cost him.'

'Really? You mean you've had . . .' I realised he was joking. 'You mean, I'm on a date with a rich man?'

Mally's face broke out into a grin. 'Imagine if I told my dad I was getting plastic surgery. Oh no, Maladhar,' he said in his dad's voice, 'don't be like the Big Brother. I didn't come to England for this!'

He really was pretty good at voices. I didn't dare ask him to do me.

'When did your parents come over here?' I asked. It was crazy that I'd known Mally all these years but actually I didn't really *know* anything about him.

'They came in the Seventies. Lots of Bangladeshis came then. In search of a better life and all that. Initially they lived in London; my cousins have a flat there. But they didn't like it – they wanted a safer place to bring up us kids. Then my dad heard about the restaurant here and even though he'd never run a restaurant before – he didn't even know how to cook – he decided to move us all out to Redworth.'

'Wow, pretty brave,' I said.

'Yeah. Mad, some might say!'

I knew Mr Khan's restaurant. It was on the High Street and it was always bustling. 'But Khan's is really successful.'

'Dad works hard. When we were kids he used to work fourteen-hour days. That's not even unusual when you've come from rural Bangladesh. I guess we all understand the value of hard work. Tareque's at Cambridge University, where I intend to go. Dad wants to give us what he never had growing up. Nice house, nice car, all that stuff.'

I was impressed. I'd always thought the value of hard work was, I don't know, about 15p. I preferred to take it easy. 'But your dad has already given you what he never had; your house is really nice.'

'Yeah.'

'Gravel drive! Very posh. We can only manage crazy paving. And a cat statue.'

'I noticed that. What is that?'

'You mean, *who* is that?' I said, mock-angry. '*That* is Cheshire. Dad found him on his travels. Needed a good home, he said. Though I think he was pretty heavy to bring back in his suitcase.'

'I can imagine. He must really like cats.'

'He did. I always liked dogs more. But Dad said cats were less effort, more independent. He said dogs were too desperate.'

'My parents don't like dogs either. In Bangladesh dogs carry disease. Even though I've told them a million times it's different over here, they still don't get it. I love dogs.' Mally bent down and scooped up Socks, planting a big loud kiss on the top of his head.

'Mum got Socks for me just before she and Dad split up. He's grown up with me, haven't you, Socks?' I ruffled his grey muzzle. 'He's a rescue dog though, so he wasn't a puppy when we got him. He's probably pretty old now.'

'Old dogs are the best. They're like wise old men,' said Mally, straightening up. 'Do you still get to see your dad a lot?'

'Not so much. My dad is completely different from your dad. Even when he was married to Mum he wasn't around. I mean, not properly.'

My voice had dropped and I saw that Mally was looking at me.

'I'm sorry,' he said, really gently.

'It's OK. He used to drink too much, when he was with us, so when Mum kicked him out it was a bit of a relief. Then he stopped, and then he found a new wife. I've only met her once, so I don't see him so much, no.'

'That must be tough,' said Mally. He squeezed my hand.

I really don't mind that Dad doesn't make the effort to see Herbie and me very often – at least I tell myself I don't mind. But now, with Mally right beside me, I suddenly found myself blinking back tears.

'It is tough, yeah.'

I couldn't believe I was telling him about my dad – I hardly knew him. But somehow it seemed OK; I felt safe with him, as if I could tell him anything.

'I can't imagine anyone not choosing to see you as often as they could,' said Mally, bumping me gently with his shoulder. 'I know I would.'

I blushed. Then I remembered that Mally had lived a couple of streets away practically our whole lives and we'd barely exchanged more than a few words. I said this to him.

'Yeah,' said Mally, 'but for most of those years I was just a child. I always thought you were pretty, but it wasn't until that afternoon with those stupid kids that I realised how truly gorgeous you are.'

Gorgeous; that word again! But hold on a minute. 'Why on that embarrassing afternoon, of all days?' I asked him.

'Because you looked so, so . . . vulnerable. Not that I only like vulnerable women! But before that I always thought you were a bit of a . . . fashion vixen . . . I guess.'

'*Fashion vixen?* That's how I used to think of you! I mean, not the fashion part.'

'Or the vixen part hopefully,' said Mally, laughing. 'More a fox. Or a wolf?'

'Yeah!' I laughed. 'No, more a . . . cool, umm, cat.'

Mally laughed. 'Really?'

'Too cool for school. I was a bit in awe of you,' I said.

'But I was a bit in awe of *you*! That's why I never stuck around your house for long.'

How *anyone* could be in awe of me I couldn't imagine. Boys were often scared of Rachel, especially when she was being loud. But not me.

We smiled at each other.

'Is that why you said, "See you sometime," when I came up to you after the debate?' I said.

Mally cringed. 'I kept thinking about that. That was so utterly lame. But I didn't want to sound too keen.'

'You know, when I sent you that email, I obsessed about it all night, waiting for you to answer.'

Mally stopped walking and pulled me towards him. I could feel the buttons of his coat pressing through my tunic. I shivered.

'Are you cold?'

'No. I mean, maybe.' But I wasn't shivering because of the cold.

'Here, take my scarf.'

Mally unwound it and hooped it round the back of both our necks. Then he wrapped his arms tightly round me. He smelled good, of lemons and soap and that warm boy smell, as if he'd been running. His arms felt tight around my back.

'I'm glad,' he said.

'Glad?'

'Glad you obsessed all night. I can't believe someone as beautiful as you would do that over me, but I'm glad.'

I wanted to tell him I wasn't beautiful – had he seen my

thighs? But it was good that he thought it, and at that moment I almost believed him, staring into his eyes.

'I didn't obsess *all* night,' I teased. 'I did manage to get some sleep. Not much, but some.'

'Good. Because I was up. I should have been working, but instead I was thinking about you.'

'Really?'

'Mmmhmm.'

I was finding the conversation increasingly hard to concentrate on, what with Mally's lips centimetres from mine.

Kiss me, please kiss me, I thought. He was just too close, my heart was racing.

Then he kissed me.

Mmmm, warmth and softness and this incredible tingling sensation right up to my scalp.

I wished we could stay like that for ever.

But the next thing I knew, Socks was scrabbling at my leg with his muddy paws and we broke apart, flushed and laughing.

'I think he's jealous,' said Mally.

'He should be,' I said. 'He's got competition now.'

Mally smiled. 'Really? I'm honoured.'

'Good,' I said softly. Then Mally put a hand on either side of my face and brought my lips to his again and kissed me harder. This time the world spun around and around until I was about to pass out.

When I opened my eyes again I knew everything would be different.

Chapter 3

♥

Pretty soon after Mally and I started seeing each other it was the Easter holidays, which meant we could spend the whole day together. Yes, that's right, Mally and I were *seeing each other*. Seeing each other every day, all day in fact, and I was so happy I was walking on air. People always say, 'I was walking on air', but up until then I hadn't known what they'd actually meant. Shiny bubbles of happiness were bouncing around inside my chest and I wouldn't have been surprised if I'd looked down one day and seen the whole of Redworth spread out beneath my feet.

Mally was the most perfect boyfriend I could ever have dreamed of. Every day he'd do something romantic, like pick me a bunch of wild flowers, or leave me a sweet message in my coat pocket, or text me a dirty joke. OK, so the last one wasn't exactly romantic, but it made me laugh. When we were together I couldn't keep my hands off him; I always wanted to sit on his knee, or kiss his face, and he seemed to want to do the same. Now I knew where another cliché came from too – 'joined at the hip'. Or in our case, the lips. Did I mention that we kissed? Well we did, *a lot,* and every one of them made butterflies to go with the bubbles until I could hardly feel the ground at all.

At night, when we had to go back to our separate houses, I lay in my bedroom with the phone pressed between the pillow and my ear, talking to Mally for hours. We had only just said goodbye to each other, so we didn't have anything new to say, but it didn't matter. We talked about *everything,* and it was just so amazing to have found someone who listened to me, who got me totally, and who on top of all that was so incredibly sexy.

One evening Mally mentioned that his family were having a get-together on Sunday at his house and asked me if I'd like to come. Would I ever! Mally had told me so much about his family, I couldn't wait to meet them. His brother Tareque would be down from Cambridge and his cousins from London. It was no big deal, he said, but it was to me.

I spent hours deciding what to wear – I didn't want to look too smart but at the same time I didn't know if everyone else was going to be dressed up. Would they be wearing saris? Or full headscarves? God, would I stick out like a sore thumb?

In the event everyone was really nice to me. We all sat around a big table in the dining room (Mally's house actually had a dining room!) with everyone talking over everyone else and reaching across and helping themselves to enormous silver dishes of different coloured food. It all smelled incredible. I'd never even seen some of them before. There was so much noise and action that it didn't matter that I sat next to Mally not saying much. Mally's mum never seemed to sit down; she was wearing a headscarf that covered her hair, even though Mally's aunt was not, and she was constantly in and out of the kitchen, taking away empty plates and bringing new ones in. I wondered if Mr Khan would help her, but he never seemed to. He was too busy talking.

Even though it was Sunday Mr Khan still looked very smart. He was sitting very upright in a suit, and his hair looked as if it had been sculpted from wood. I was a little in awe of him and I was dreading him asking me any questions. When he spoke he addressed the whole table as if he were a public speaker, and everyone else fell silent. He seemed pretty impenetrable, but I noticed that when he looked at his kids his face broke into a huge smile. Now I knew where Mally's smile came from.

'Tareque,' he said, beaming, 'has joined the

University Law Society, have you not, Tareque?'

'Dad, I'm sure they don't want to know all my business,' said Tareque.

'Oh, don't worry – we know all about your business already! Your father makes sure of that!' said Aunt Shefali. I liked Aunt Shefali; her eyes twinkled when she spoke and she had a way of making us all part of some kind of conspiracy.

'But do you know about Tareque's society, eh? You'll soon be head of it, yes, Tareque?' said Mr Khan.

'Dad! Let's not get ahead of ourselves! I've only just joined.' Tareque smiled and looked down at his plate.

'Ah, but Tareque always gets made the leader. Do you remember at school, you'd only just joined the Law Society there, and you were made head?'

'Dad, that's slightly different. There were only three people in the Law Society at school. It was hardly an achievement.'

'Getting into Cambridge is an achievement! First of your school to have done so,' said Mr Khan.

'I don't know about that, Dad.' Tareque was older and shorter than Mally, with a neat side parting. I could totally imagine him as head of the Law Society, but he wasn't like one of those flashy lawyers on TV. He was very still and calm and when we'd been introduced he had taken my hand and shaken it, as if he was about forty years old. He seemed nice though.

Uncle Rafiq laughed. 'Ah Tareque, you are too modest. But that's a good thing too, is it not? And you, Mally, I hear you were a winner too, eh, in your school debate?'

I was beginning to feel like a serious loser. I hadn't done anything recently except . . . fall in love. A slow smile immediately crept across my face, which I hid behind my napkin. *Except fall in love?* But falling in love was the most amazing thing I could ever do!

The conversation had turned to Mally and the debate, and they were asking him what else he planned to do. Meanwhile Aunt Shefali looked at me.

'Lucy, you are at school with Mally, is that right?'

Oh God, I was going to have to speak. I felt myself grow hot. 'Umm, yes, different year though.'

'Ah, so you don't spend too much time together,' she said.

'Oh yes, we do. We spend quite a lot of time together.' I smiled at Mally, who smiled back.

'I see. So, you are good friends?'

It was on the tip of my tongue to say, we're more than good friends, but I held back. I didn't know what Mally had said to his parents. I mean, it was pretty obvious that something was going on; my mum had guessed it straight away, as soon as I'd come home wearing a massive grin. But Mally's family might be different.

'Lucy lives a few streets away,' said Mr Khan. 'Ehsan is friends with her brother. She is a neighbour.' He gave me a short smile.

Then the conversation moved on to Ehsan, and what genius things he'd been doing at school and the whole thing would normally have bugged the hell out of me if it had been any one else's family. But Aunt Shefali kept asking her questions in such a teasing way, and Mr Khan was so pleased that it didn't seem so much like boasting, but more like a good kind of pride. I wished my dad would be half as proud of me.

Mally's cousins were there too: Huseyn, who looked about fifteen, and his two younger sisters, Leena and Nanda. Neither of the girls said a word through the whole of lunch, except to answer questions about school. I couldn't believe how well mannered they were compared to most kids their age.

I had eaten a tonne of food. I could feel Mally's leg pressing against mine under the table and I reached under and squeezed it. Even though Mally's family was completely different from mine and I hadn't said much, I felt happy and relaxed because Mally and I were together and it was the best thing that had ever happened to me.

Nothing could touch me.

'And how about Cousin Nina?' Mally, who had obviously been following the conversation better than me, asked.

'She's very well,' said Aunt Shefali. 'She's enjoying life.'

Her husband snorted. 'Enjoying life, yes, you could put it like that!'

'Come come Rafiq, we are in England now. She's bound to do what the English do. She *is* a student after all.'

'Why, what is it?' said Mr Khan.

'She is dating someone, Father, that is all,' said Tareque.

'Someone? Who?' said Mr Khan, his eyebrows almost in his hairline.

'I believe he is very nice. Martin someone-or-other.'

'Martin someone-or-other? An English boy then. Do her parents know?'

'Oh yes, they know,' said Uncle Rafiq. 'She had this Martin to stay with her – in their own house.'

'They are fine with it. And why should they not be?' said Aunt Shefali.

'He is a nice boy,' said Uncle Rafiq, pulling a face that might have been either a grimace or a smile.

'Exactly!' said Aunt Shefali.

Then Uncle Rafiq and Mr Khan started talking together in a language that had to be Bengali and everyone looked embarrassed. I had a feeling I was missing something. But then they switched to English again and I was too full and happy to think about it properly.

After a while it started to grow darker outside. I looked at my watch. Blimey, I'd been at Mally's house for hours! I'd better go. The rest of Mally's family didn't look like moving for a while.

I stood up a bit awkwardly, my chair scraping on the wooden floor. 'Well, I'd better go, I think. Thank you so much for having me!'

Everyone's faces turned towards me and I started to blush. But then Mrs Khan spoke; it was the first thing she'd said to me all day.

'Thank you very much for coming, Lucy. It has been a pleasure to meet you,' she said, bowing her head. 'It is always good to meet one of Maladhar's friends.'

'Great to meet you too, thank you, it was all so delicious.' I smiled at Mally's mother and gave a vague wave to everyone else.

'I'll see you out,' said Mally.

* * *

As soon as we were out of the door Mally pulled me towards him. I giggled.

'Careful, your parents might see us.'

'They won't,' said Mally, gesturing behind us. The porch was made from thick coloured glass. I guess he was right – no one could see anything through there.

'Do you not want them to see us?' I said, teasing.

'I don't care. Come here!'

His arms felt so strong and warm around my waist and his lips still tasted faintly of the pudding we'd had.

'Mmm, that reminds me,' I said, between kisses. 'What did we eat in there? It was delicious.'

'There were loads of things. Mughlai lamb biriani. Naan, alu-jira. The minced chicken was reshmi kebab. What else, there was a lamb kalia and for pudding there was Bangladeshi egg haloa and some shemai. Mum really went to town.'

'Wow. I don't think I've had any of those things in a restaurant. It must have taken her hours.'

'Yeah, she started days ago. Dad doesn't cook in the house.'

'My mum isn't a bad cook. But she usually doesn't start a meal more than an hour before we're going to eat. Why don't you come over?'

'I'd love to.'

We decided Mally would come next Sunday. Then he could get to know my mum too and we'd be fully introduced to each other's families like real-life grown-ups.

'Perfect. But I'll see you tomorrow?' said Mally, looking at me from under his adorable floppy fringe.

'Try and keep me away. And by the way, thanks. I loved today, meeting your family. Thanks for asking me.'

'Thanks for coming. You weren't too bored though? You seemed a bit quiet.'

'Bored? No! I was just a bit . . . shy . . . that's all.'

'I don't know what you've got to be shy about. You have so many talents,' said Mally, kissing me all over my face. 'You're multi-faceted.' I imagined 'multi-faceted' must be something good, from the way he was nibbling on my earlobes. I'd have to Google it when I got home.

'You're sure you don't want me to walk you back?' Mally said.

'I'll be fine. You should go in.' It was ridiculous the way I hated leaving him, even if it was just to go to sleep. But I could still feel his teeth marks on my ears and his lip prints on my nose as I walked off down the street, and that helped. It helped a lot.

Chapter 4

♥

I met Mally in the hall of my house and gave him the biggest kiss ever. Well, maybe not the *biggest* kiss ever. Herbie and Mum were in the sitting room and I didn't want to be in full snog with them basically just two metres away.

'Come through,' I said.

'Oh, hello again, Mally.' Mum stood up and smoothed down her skirt.

Herbie was lying on the floor playing on his Xbox. He was surrounded by all kinds of crap – empty crisp packets, abandoned comic books, smelly trainers. Even if he *was* a nerd, he still had a rubbish-making super-power, just like every other ten-year-old.

'Herbie!' Mum said sharply. 'Get up, please!'

Herbie pushed his glasses further up his nose and twisted round. 'Oh hi, Mally. Have you come as Lucy's date?'

'Herbie, do you have to?' I said.

'Yes, I have come as Lucy's date,' said Mally with a smile and sat down next to me on the sofa.

'And how's school?' said Mum.

'Fine, thanks,' said Mally.

Mum seemed at a loss.

'Something smells good,' said Mally after a moment.

'Yes, it's roast beef. Oh God! You do eat beef, don't you?'

'Yes, don't worry. It's pork we don't eat,' said Mally.

'Oh, that's right, yes. How silly of me.'

Herbie rolled his eyes and turned back to his Xbox. This was a lot more awkward than I'd expected; but I'd never had a boyfriend round for lunch, so I didn't know what I was expecting really. I never used to think I wanted my boyfriend and my mother to get along, but now that I actually *had* a boyfriend I realised how important it was. The only one who seemed relaxed was Socks, lying on his back on a turret of cushions. I wished I was a dog.

After about a million years Mum said lunch should be ready by now and we all went through to the kitchen. She brought out a great hunk of roast beef from the oven, surrounded by a landscape of vegetables.

'Well, tuck in, all of you.'

Mum poured herself a glass of wine and for a while the only sounds in the kitchen were knives and forks scraping against plates. This wasn't going well.

'So Lucy tells me some of your family still live in Bangladesh,' she said.

'Cousins, yeah.'

'I hear they've been devastated by floods and so on.'

'Yeah, it hasn't been good.'

'How terrible. It must be so difficult for them.'

'*Mum.*' I was blushing, I didn't know who for. Mum was basically being really uncool, in the way mums are. But Mally didn't seem to mind.

'It is difficult, yes. But I don't know that, you know, it's exactly like you imagine. I mean, not everyone's miserable, eating, like, dirt or whatever. A couple of years ago Bangladesh came top in the World Happiness Survey.'

'Is there such a thing?' asked Mum.

'It was done by the London School of Economics,' said Mally.

'Where did Britain come?'

'Thirty-second,' said Mally.

'But that doesn't make any sense,' I said. 'Why would they be happy when they've got nothing and we've got everything?'

'I know, it's weird. But I think that's exactly the point. Over here we're always wanting more when we don't actually *need* anything. Over there, if people have what they need, they don't particularly *want* anything else.'

'But still, their situation is pretty crappy,' I said.

'Yeah, materially it is. But there's a lot more acceptance of their situation than there would be over here. The most important thing to everyone is that their family is happy. They don't think they should go out and be a celebrity or whatever.'

'Well, maybe you should spend less time reading those celebrity mags of yours, Lucy, and more time thinking about the happiness of your family,' said Mum.

'Yeah. You can stop hogging the bathroom for a start,' said Herbie.

'*Herbie.* As if.'

'What were you doing this morning? You were in there for hours,' he said.

'*Herbie*, thanks a lot. I wasn't long at all.' Great, I really needed my bathroom habits to be discussed in front of Mally.

But Mally just smiled at me. 'At school in Bangladesh every child learns the fable of the king who is hugely rich but still unhappy. A wise man tells the king that he will only recover if he wears a happy man's shirt. Ministers search everywhere, all the big mansions, all the successful men. But they can't find one. At last they come across a man working in the woods; he has no house, no money. But he says he is happy.'

'So the king is cured, right?' said Herbie.

'No, because the man has no shirt,' said Mally.

We looked at him blankly.

'I think it means that only the poor, who can't afford to wear a shirt, are happy,' said Mally.

'What a lovely story,' I said, secretly thinking that having no shirts would seriously suck. 'Does that mean shirts are bad?'

'I don't think it's meant to be taken literally,' said Mally.

'Phew!' I said.

'Oh, I get it.' Mally grinned at me. 'I love your T-shirts. I love all your clothes. They're very cool.'

After lunch Mally and I went upstairs and lay on the bed in my room. I felt a little self-conscious to be honest. My room was looking pretty bare. I'd taken down the cheesy posters, but I hadn't got round to replacing them with anything else. And I felt full and fat.

Mally was lying next to me, propped up on one elbow. I sucked my tummy in.

'Mally, you don't think I'm shallow, do you?' I asked. I was fishing for compliments but I needed reassurance.

'Shallow?' Mally burst out laughing. 'You are the least shallow person I've ever met. You're thoughtful and kind and you care about things. Why can't you care about what you look like too? I know I do.'

'I knew it! I knew that look had some planning behind it. All those just-tight-enough black T-shirts, and jeans that fit you perfectly. You must have gone through about fifty pairs to find them.' I punched him playfully on the shoulder.

'Yeah yeah,' said Mally, rolling me on to my back.

'What else d'you like about me?' I said. Now I was *badly* fishing for compliments, but ... I'd never had a boy be so amazing to me before. What's a girl supposed to do?

'I like the fact that when I'm with you I feel free,' said Mally. Then he paused. 'Free from all ... the rest of my life. I never thought I'd fall so hard for anyone right now. It just wasn't part of my game plan. I thought I'd have my head buried in a book for the last year of school. But then *you* came along and I realised what I'd been missing. I don't have to be *only* serious and hard-working, I can have a laugh too, just goof off. It's not a question of absolutes.'

'Huh?'

'I mean, I can do both. You're the best, most funniest

person I know. And after I've been with you I feel refreshed, so I can work even harder. It's a win-win situation!' Mally kissed me playfully.

'Great,' I said with a pout. 'I'm just the good-time girl. And FYI, "most funniest" won't win you any gold stars in your father's book.'

'Most funny. Funniest. Hell, I'll say what I want,' said Mally, burying his face into my neck until I was screeching.

'OK, OK, say what you want – I give in!'

'Do you? Do you give in?' said Mally, still growling.

'Yesss. Yes I do.'

Then we kissed and everything went dark in my head, except for a few bright points of light that spun around and around. When I opened my eyes again I found Mally already looking at me.

'You know the amazing thing though?' he said.

'What?' I said, blinking exaggeratedly, like a silent film star.

'If I tell you, you'll think I'm weird.'

'No, I won't! I mean, I think you're weird already, so it won't make much of a difference. Tell me.'

Mally pulled me close to him and sighed. 'It's a bit of a long story. But I've never told anyone – any girl – about it before.'

'Tell me,' I said again, torn between glowing with pride and being upset that we weren't going to kiss any more.

'It's about going back to Bangladesh when I was ten. My "identity update" I call it.'

'Go on,' I said, snuggling closer. That would have to do instead of lip action.

'I hated it at first. Everyone was so poor. They were filthy, nobody had any shoes on. This was where my parents came from, the place I had always been told was home, but it felt so . . . it felt so foreign.'

'I can imagine,' I said, even though I couldn't really.

'It was hot out there and I mean *really* hot. No electricity, no fans or air-con, nothing. One morning I went to the mosque next to the house because I'd noticed how cool the floor was. It was made of marble, I think. I lay on the floor all day. I felt so peaceful. Everything just seemed to drop away. Every day after that I went into the mosque first thing in the morning, before anyone, and lay there for hours. Tareque was on at me; he said I was showing off by pretending to be a devout Muslim, but that wasn't it.'

'It wasn't?' I said.

I must have looked a bit worried because Mally looked at me and said, 'I knew you were going to think I'm weird, a fanatic or something.'

'No no! Of course I don't,' I said. But if I'm totally honest, I did feel a bit weird. Mosques and Muslims were usually something I saw in the paper and usually to do with something bad. 'Sooo, you're a Muslim then?' I asked.

'Yeah, I'm a Muslim. Don't look at me like that! I'm not going to put you in a veil or anything. It's me, Mally!' He kissed me on the nose. 'But that's exactly my point. I felt different over there, but when I came back to England I realised I was different from everybody here too.'

He paused for a minute.

'And that's what's so amazing. When I'm with you I forget about all that stuff. It doesn't matter if I'm Bangladeshi, or British, or brainy, or stupid. Whether my favourite dinner is reshmi kebab or fish and chips. It doesn't matter. When I'm around you I just feel like I'm . . . me. Does that make any sense?'

My anxiety dropped away. 'Totally! I feel exactly the same. I mean, I'm just plain old English with some Scottish thrown in, but I feel like I can be *me* around you. Even though we haven't *properly* known each other that long. I feel like I've known you all my life.'

Mally kissed me again. Then he drew back and stared at me. He looked very serious all of a sudden. My heart started to beat very loudly.

'I love you,' he said.

It was exactly what I had been feeling.

'I love you too. I love you!'

I reached up and kissed him. I wanted to drown in him.

'You know that happy man in your story? I'd be happy like him, if I had no shirt, no house or anything. As long as I had you.'

Chapter 5

♥

When summer term started, Mally and I couldn't see each other all day, every day, as we had in the holidays. But we tried to squeeze in as much time together as we could. I wanted to be with him all the time. I knew how a drug addict felt. I went into Mally-withdrawal during lessons (there should be posters up at school: *Parents, beware, keep your children from the dangerous new drug* Mally!) and found it really hard to concentrate. So by lunchtime I was desperate for a fix. The only problem was that Rachel came to meet me too and I had to tell her that I couldn't hang out with the usual gang at lunch because I was spending it with Mally. But I was sure Rachel understood – I was in love. If I'm completely honest, any time spent apart from Mally right then was time wasted, and that included my friends.

Exams were very definitely starting to loom on the horizon and Mally sometimes put in a couple of hours of homework in the library in the evening. I had to work too, although I wasn't under quite as much pressure as Mally. We sat beside each other as the light outside faded to darkness. Sometimes I used to rest my head on my arm and let myself daydream: Mally and I grown up and married, both working in jobs we loved and coming home to sit side by side, not talking, just happy to be together, just like we were now. What would our kids look like? If they were half as cute as Mally . . . then I'd glance sideways at him and blush a little. We hadn't talked about any of this stuff; even if I did write *Lucy Khan* in curly writing down the side of my notepad, I made sure he didn't see it. It was just a daydream . . . wasn't it?

It was shocking to discover that, even when I was so happy, things could still go wrong. The day started off badly. First Socks knocked an entire glass of orange juice over my new T-shirts that I'd made for global warming *and* my chemistry homework. Then Mr Skelton didn't believe me, and he gave me *more* homework, as well as making me redo the last lot.

When I went to meet Mally at lunchtime he'd had a crappy morning too. He had got a B in an economics essay – hard to believe but that's what made up a crappy morning for him. We were both pissed off, sitting on a bench outside the school gates with Ehsan – who loved it when, occasionally, Mally hung out with him for lunch – munching dolefully on our sandwiches. We badly needed cheering up.

Here's how the fateful conversation went:

Me: Let's go to Barbados!

Mally: Or Skegness!

Me: Skegness? London would be better than Skegness.

Mally: London *would* be better. Why don't we go to London?

We both looked at each other. We knew we could go to London quite easily: it was only half an hour away by train. We'd both been there loads of times before and it meant we could spend the whole afternoon together. Only we had lessons. Mally had economics. I had English.

Me: London could be part of our education. Dickens lived there. It's the economic centre of the world.

Mally: It'd be wrong *not* to go!

Ehsan looked at us both like we were mad. But he was only ten, what would he know? So we walked him back to his school and then went straight to the train station.

So that's how we came to be standing outside Buckingham Palace at three-thirty p.m. on a Wednesday, taking pictures of each other trying to stroke the guardsman's hat. We had decided to be tourists for the day; we figured that just because we had both been to London before didn't mean we couldn't be tourists. I mean, neither of us actually *lived* there.

So we did what tourists do. We walked across St James's Park holding hands and sharing an ice-cream even though it was spitting with rain. In the middle of the park Mally turned around and gave me absolutely the longest kiss *ever* and told me he loved me. I thought my heart would burst out of my chest with happiness.

By the time we got to the Houses of Parliament we were starving, and there were no cafés anywhere. We eventually found a picture of a man wearing a sign that said *CAFÉ*, only it seemed to point straight into the ground. Then we saw an ancient heavy door beneath the street. We looked at each other and shrugged; after all, we *were* on an adventure. Inside there were no windows and the whole place smelled of damp and we were just beginning to get freaked out, but we turned a corner and suddenly there was the *sweetest* old lady standing behind a huge tea-urn. Another equally old lady came to take our order; by now we didn't feel like tourists at all, but People of the Overground who had stumbled in on an ancient subterranean world. The best thing of all though was the dessert, which was huge and called a Double Chocolate Fudge Sundae Surprise, with ice-cream and cream and chocolate sauce and a flake all crammed into a tall glass. It came with two long spoons, and Mally and I kept clashing spoons trying to get to the most chocolatey bits.

I'll remember this moment for the rest of my life, I thought.

Usually I just carry on with life and only realise I've been happy when I look back. But this time I knew it then and there, and I wanted to make time stand still so I could feel this way for ever.

'I love you,' I told him.

'I love you too.'

We didn't seem to be able to stop saying it.

When Mally and I came blinking out into the sunlight we decided that the only way we'd really see all the sights was to be among our own people again – the Tourist People. So we caught an open-topped double-decker bus. It'd be educational, I said, though actually I hadn't given skipping my English class a second thought. And it *was* educational – in a way. The guide explained the history of the landmarks we were passing, how the original London Bridge had been sold to an American and was now in Arizona. Sometimes he threw in some cheesy jokes –

'You won't see any animals at Piccadilly Circus,' type stuff and everyone groaned.

It had started to rain but it was still hot and muggy. It felt as if we were floating above London in a ship. Mally looked so beautiful. The rain had spiked his hair and stuck to his eyelashes. It ran in miniature rivulets down his skin and made his T-shirt cling to his chest. I stared at him; he almost looked too real, as if he was in a movie.

'What?' he said.

'Nothing,' I said. 'Just that you're beautiful.'

'YOU are beautiful,' Mally said. He reached for his camera. 'Don't close your eyes like you usually do! Seriously. The rain really brings out who you are. Like it's washed you and made you shine.'

I smiled. Then he threw his arm around my neck and held the camera out in front of us.

'Perfect!'

It wasn't too bad, I suppose: my head was tilted up and my hair was in wisps around my face. I was half smiling, half wistful. Mally's beautiful almond-shaped eyes shone and he was looking straight into the camera.

He pulled the ring from the Coke can he'd been drinking from and slipped it on to my finger. It could have been the cheesiest thing, but in that moment it was so romantic. 'I want to be with you till I'm eighty,' he said.

'I want to be with you till I'm eighty-five,' I replied.

'Oh yeah? Well you've outdone me again.'

Then we kissed, and the whole of London passed by before we looked up again.

I was still wearing the Coke can ring Mally had given me on the bus, only my hands were thrust into my pockets and it was pressing painfully into my skin, when Mr Khan began to shout.

It had been a bit of a shock to see him in my kitchen when we got home. Mr Khan wanted to know where we'd been, though he already knew we'd been to London – Ehsan had told him. But Mr Khan wanted to know *precisely* where we'd been, and he made us tell him, though with each place we said he grew increasingly angry. My mum was cross too, though not as furious as Mr Khan.

'It is all very well going to *London*,' he leaned on the word with disgust. 'But what about your lessons, eh?'

'*Sorry*, Dad, it was only one lesson and it was revision. I can catch it up from Raj.'

'But it is not the same as being there, is it? *Is it?*' said Mr Khan.

'Not exactly,' said Mally, shifting from foot to foot.

'I really don't see how you could have been so

irresponsible to have missed lessons. Exams aren't far away. What could you have been thinking?'

Herbie had come into the kitchen. He'd obviously heard all the noise. 'What's wrong, Mum?'

'Nothing, sweetie,' said Mum, reaching out for him and pulling him in front of her. 'We're just having a discussion.'

'The trip was my idea, Mr Khan. I'm very, very sorry,' I said, trying to hold back my tears.

'No, it wasn't. It was my idea,' said Mally. 'Dad, please, can we just go?'

'IN A MINUTE, MALADHAR. Let me finish, please.'

Herbie looked really upset. He put his glasses back on and scrunched up his face, the way he does when he doesn't want to let anything bad in. But Mr Khan didn't notice. He spoke more quietly, but if anything it was more scary than before.

'Forgive me, Mrs Brooks, if I speak out of turn. But whilst you may be willing to let your daughter run around London on a school day, *I* am not willing to allow my son the same privilege. He has most important exams coming up, and all the family is most keen he should join his brother at university. If he should forfeit his place because of your daughter, it would be most . . .' Mr Khan seemed to search around for the right word, '. . . *unsuitable*.'

'But I'm not trying to make Mally forfeit his place!' I burst out. 'I want him to do well.'

'Well, you are certainly not showing it,' said Mr Khan, giving me a horrible look.

'Let me talk now, Mr Khan,' said my mum. 'I did not know that the two of them were in London this afternoon and I resent the implication that I am not strict enough with my daughter. You know nothing about me, or how I choose to bring my children up, and you are in *my* house. I think it's best if you and Mally leave now.'

Mally and I could only look at each other silently. Then I went up to my room and burst into tears.

Mum grounded me for two weeks. She was pretty angry with me. I understood why, so I didn't make too much fuss about being grounded. But it had all been worth it, in my opinion. I had had one of the best days of my life. Obviously Mally's dad was even more angry than my mum. A lot more angry. He grounded Mally for *three* weeks and during that time he hired a tutor to give him extra lessons *after* school too. Apparently he thought Mally wasn't taking his A-levels seriously enough.

I don't know where he got that idea. We might have

bunked off for one poxy afternoon, but if he'd known Mally like I knew him, he never would have thought he wasn't serious. He was incredibly dedicated and hard-working; he just happened to love me too.

Mally apologised a lot for his father. He said that his dad only wanted the best for him, but that he didn't know how to rein in his temper.

'But is everything OK now? I mean, your dad doesn't still hate me, does he?'

Mally laughed awkwardly. 'Oh no, it's fine. Honestly. He's still a bit angry with me though, and he's probably right. I can't afford to waste an afternoon at this point in my life.'

A little sliver of ice pushed its way into my heart. 'Is that what you thought our trip was, a wasted afternoon?'

'No, Luce, I didn't mean that! We had a great time. I just meant, we probably shouldn't have gone, at least, not now. I've never done anything like that before.'

'But I thought that's what you loved about me, the fact that you didn't have to be your old self all the time!'

'I do, Lucy, I do.' Mally put an arm around my waist. 'I'm just saying we probably shouldn't have gone, that's all.'

'Well, I'm *glad* we went,' I said, with a quivering lip. 'I had an *amazing* time. I would have given up my last day on earth to go to London with you. Obviously it's not the same for you.'

A thought flashed into my mind: *I miss my best friend.* I needed to speak to Rachel about this.

Mally spun me to face him. 'Lucy, don't be like that. I love you. I just need to work right now. It's different for you. You only have GCSEs and you . . .'

'And I what?'

'Nothing.

'And I don't care as much anyway?' I said, my voice trembling with anger.

'I wasn't going to say that exactly. Just that you probably don't want to go to Cambridge.'

'How do you know where I want to go? I'm just as ambitious as you are! I'm just not going to be a lawyer, or a doctor, that's all!'

'It's OK. Look, I'm sorry. I didn't mean it. I know you're going to be amazing. You are amazing!' Mally stroked my hair as if I was a child. 'I had a fantastic time in London. I'll remember it for ever. I love you. Let's just forget this conversation, OK?'

But I couldn't forget it. And we didn't say much else as we walked to the school gates and went our separate ways.

Chapter 6

Exams were steaming towards Mally and me like a runaway train. Most of our lessons were revision, but then there were revision essays, and some of the books I had been supposed to read the first time round, I hadn't, so I had new stuff as well. Mally didn't have that problem, of course, but there was massive pressure on him because he was trying to get into Cambridge and he had to get three A's. And he had a load of extra-curricular activities too, to put on his CV; mainly projects he was doing on global warming.

I'd thought about it and I had to admit Mally might have been right – an afternoon off *did* have more consequences for him than it did for me right now. I tried not to worry about how we would keep our relationship going when Mally was away at university – Cambridge wasn't that far and they had super-long holidays. Love would find a way, I thought.

The weekends were our precious time together – our time to do whatever we wanted. Which was usually nothing, just lazing about in my room together, kissing and listening to music. It was just nice to relax.

On this particular weekend though I had planned to surprise Mally with something special. I'd read in the local paper that they were showing a Bollywood film in a cinema nearby. It was quite difficult to get tickets – it was in an arthouse cinema that never seemed to answer the phone and it didn't have a proper website to buy them on either, so I had to go all the way over on the bus and buy them from the box office. The film starred a new Bengali girl who was meant to be fantastic; she was a big heroine in Bangladesh. Mally always complained that there weren't enough Bengali stars in England so I figured he'd be really pleased to see her. I was so excited about my surprise I nearly blurted it out a thousand times, but I made myself wait until just a few days before the weekend so that the surprise would be even greater. I just couldn't wait to see the look on his face – I knew he'd be totally over the moon.

'I have got an amazing Saturday night lined up for you, Maladhar Khan,' I said in my best game-show voice. 'First we travel by five star coach – well, it's the bus really – over to Brinton. A quick change, and then it's off to —'

'Lucy, I'm really sorry, I can't make Saturday.'

My heart plummeted and I nearly dropped the phone.

'Oh . . . but . . . it's all planned. I mean, I thought you'd be thrilled. I bought tickets to the new Bollywood film, especially . . .

'I'm really sorry, Loooceee,' he said, in the teasing way he usually used to get round me. 'I'd love to come, you know I would, only I can't. One of my cousins is getting married.'

'Oh, right. Where?'

'At Aunt Shefali's house in London.'

'What – is her daughter getting married? She didn't mention it!'

'No, it's her sister's – my other aunt's – daughter. They live in a tiny flat, so Aunt Shefali is having the wedding at her house. Well, in the garden, really.'

'Right.' My first thought was: *Why didn't you tell me about this earlier?* And right on the heels of that: *Why didn't you invite me?* Even though I didn't know the bride, I knew Aunt Shefali and Uncle Rafiq. And I thought Mally would want me there. But maybe the wedding was really small. 'How many people are going?'

'Oh, not many. About two hundred, I think.'

'Two hundred! Wow! That's many in my book. It's . . .' I paused.

'It's annoying, I know. I'm really sorry,' said Mally.

'No, I mean, it's just quite weird you didn't mention

this to me before. I've gone to all this trouble with the tickets, and I wouldn't have bothered if I'd known you were busy.'

'Yeah, I know, it slipped my mind – stupid of me . . .' Mally sounded awkward.

I bet lots of people were bringing their girlfriends. If it had been the other way round I would have been desperate to have Mally there.

Mally seemed to know what I was thinking. 'I didn't ask you to come . . . I mean . . . I didn't think you'd like it. You'd know hardly anyone and it would be weird for you. It's not like an English wedding.'

It sounded like just the kind of thing I'd love.

'You'd probably get bored. It goes on the whole weekend and —'

'I love weddings. I've heard so much about Bengali weddings. They sound amazing,' I said, thinking I was making it really obvious.

'Mmm, I don't. All that eating and sitting around.'

'Yeah. That's what's great about them.'

'Mmm,' said Mally again. He sounded even more awkward now. 'Perhaps we could go another evening? To the cinema. Another weekend I'm totally at your disposal.'

'I've already bought the tickets for *this* weekend.'

'Of course. Look I'm really sorry, Lucy. I promise you, the weekend after this we'll do something really special, OK?'

After I'd put the phone down I almost burst into tears. I didn't believe him when he said I would find it boring. I'd told him I loved weddings. It was really weird of him to have forgotten to tell me. And I'd made such an effort to treat him to something really special. Now the tickets would go to waste.

Usually Mally and I talked about everything. This was just the kind of thing I'd normally go to him with for advice. Only this time, it was *about* him.

Maybe I could persuade Rachel to come instead, but I didn't know if she even liked Bollywood films. And I hadn't seen her in a while; I just hoped she wasn't busy too.

'A *Bollywood* film?' said Rachel. 'Why aren't you taking Mally?'

'It's a long story. Do you fancy it?'

'I don't know.'

'Please come, Rach. Please please please!'

'I haven't seen you in ages,' she said, accusingly.

'I know and I'm really sorry. I'll buy you dinner!'

So, by blatantly bribing my best friend, I got her to come. I realised that over the last few weeks I'd missed phoning Rachel at any time of the day or night. Even though I was totally over the moon and besotted with Mally, at least some of the pleasure of that feeling was sharing it with my best friend.

Before the movie we had a cup of tea in the cinema café. Rachel was a bit quiet at first, not her usual noisy self. So I just came right out and said it.

'Look, Rach, I'm really sorry we haven't been hanging out so much. I've missed you.'

'It's OK,' she said, in a way that obviously meant it *wasn't*.

'Really?' I said. 'Are you sure?'

'Umm. It's just, I feel a bit second best. I mean, you only asked me tonight because Mally couldn't come. Whenever he's around you don't want to know.'

'You're right. You're completely right,' I said, blushing with shame. 'It's just that, I don't know, being in love has taken me over. It's like, I don't have room for anything else. Or I didn't.'

'But I've been out with loads of boys. Have I ever not included you?'

'Weeeell,' I thought about it. 'There was that time we were meant to be going to the cinema. With Dan, wasn't it? You kept me waiting forty minutes . . .'

'I know, I know, and we missed the film. That was

Dan's fault. His car broke down. But I showed up.'

'And then there was that time we were meant to be going out for my birthday, only you brought Cato along.'

'But Cato was really sweet!'

'He was sweet. But it was meant to be just us. I felt like a gooseberry; he kept trying to snog you on the way to the toilet. And then there was Andrew; we were meant to be going shopping that time —'

Rachel burst out laughing. 'OK, OK, point taken.'

'Look, I've realised that friends are really important too, and you're the most important friend I've got. And I promise to call you from now on, even when Mally *is* around.'

Rachel gave me a big grin and flicked her hair back over her shoulders. 'OK. You're forgiven. Anyway, I have something to confess too.'

I looked at her quizzically.

'I've been avoiding you a bit too.'

'Oh God, Rach! What, because you were so pissed off?'

'No, silly! I have to admit, well, I was a little bit jealous.'

I was amazed. 'Jealous? Of me? But you always have loads of boyfriends!'

'That's just it. I always have loads of boyfriends but they're all crappy. You have lucked out on the very first one.'

'Second one – Quintin Tiptree, remember!'

'Second one then. But I've had about a million and I've never felt serious about any of them. I mean, I'm not serious about Sam either.'

'*Sam?*'

'Haven't I told you? My new boyfriend, in the year above.'

'Oh, *that* Sam!' I said, even though I had no idea who he was; our school was pretty big. 'But that's great!'

'It's not serious though. It just happened the other day.'

'Oh . . . but still . . . it's exciting.'

'Yeah. I don't feel the same as you feel about Mally, but I like him. It's cool.'

'I don't know that . . . I mean, you're only meant to fall in love once or twice in your whole life, right? I might have used mine up on the very first go. You've got ages.'

'Yeah . . . So what's it like, being in luuurve?' said Rachel. 'I mean, we've watched so many movies about being in love – is it like that?' It was really strange *her* asking *me* about this stuff. Usually she was dispensing advice. I could see it was strange for Rachel too. She was fiddling with her hair and looking at me sideways.

'It is the same as in movies, yeah. When I think of Mally my heart feels as if it's soaring over the clouds. Sometimes if I'm just doing something boring like walking down the street I've got this great big orchestra playing in my head.'

'Or maybe you've got your iPod on!'

We laughed.

'I think of him at least once a minute when I'm not with him – everything seems to lead back to him and then it's as if my heart gets a tiny electric shock. I don't know how I went through sixteen years without him.'

'Wow,' said Rachel.

'But then, you know, it doesn't mean everything is perfect. I was really upset he didn't invite me to the wedding this weekend.'

'Maybe he thought you'd be bored.'

'That's what he said. I wouldn't have been though.'

'But by then it was probably too late to invite you along,' said Rachel.

'Maybe. All I know is, *I* wouldn't want to go anywhere without Mally by my side.'

'That's a good thing though, right?'

'Yeah. I just hope there's not something weird going on,' I said.

'No! Like what?'

'I dunno. Probably nothing. I'm just a bit worried that Mally's family is totally different from mine. He has so many more family commitments.'

'But you and Mally are soulmates, right? That's all that matters.'

'Yeah, I guess.'

'I know Mally should have been here with you today, and he isn't,' said Rachel. 'But I'm glad you asked me to come instead.'

'You don't mind missing out on a Saturday with Sam?' I said.

'Sam? No, it's cool. And you're not missing Mally too much?'

'Not now that we're solid again,' I said, kissing her on the cheek.

Chapter 7

♥

With just a few weeks to go until exams I sat down and made a timetable. Every day would follow a strict routine. Get up at seven a.m. and do an hour's work before breakfast. From nine a.m. to one p.m. I was either in lessons or revising in the library. Lunchtime – one hour off. Two p.m. till four p.m. – in lessons or revising in the library. Break until five p.m. Then working at home till six p.m. when I would collapse in front of the TV.

Most lunchtimes I'd text Mally, or he'd text me, and we'd meet in our café. Believe it or not, I'd grown quite fond of cappuccinos. They helped my concentration. Then I'd test Mally on some fiendishly difficult maths or economics question that *obviously* I wouldn't know the answer to, and I'd have to skim through the whole of his files to find it, which took hours. I didn't think I was being very helpful, but Mally said just having me around was helpful enough.

Some lunchtimes I'd meet him and he'd have black

circles under his eyes. He said he was fine; he wouldn't say what time he'd stayed up till the night before, but I had a feeling it was late. On those days I worried for him – I mean there is such a thing as working *too* hard. Mally drank a lot of coffee and sometimes his hands shook – too much caffeine, he said. But when I said he was working too hard, he smiled and shook his head. There was no such thing as too hard, he said. He really wanted to do something with his life; what was so wrong with that? Nothing, I said, nothing at all. Then I'd put my hands over his and lean into him and let his head rest on my shoulder. He smelled so good, of shampoo and pencils and an indefinable Malliness that I wanted to bottle up and keep next to my bed for ever, and I'd feel all his stress drop away and I'd know he still needed me.

This relationship was the REAL THING. Mally had turned out to be so much more than any Dream Guy I could have thought up. He wasn't like those boys (cringe) that I used to have on my bedroom wall, all chisel-jawed and ripped pecs. He didn't have a motorbike, or even a car; he didn't have a record deal. We hadn't met in a trendy, crowded bar – far from it! He could be quiet, even moody. Occasionally he had spots. But I loved him. I just wished it could be pure and uncomplicated, like it had been in the beginning. I wished Mally didn't put himself under so much pressure. I wished he could just be mine, away from all his other commitments. It was selfish of me, I know, but a tiny part of me wished he had a small family, just like mine, that made no demands on him. But he didn't, and there was nothing I could do about it.

When Mally and I needed a break we went to the football field. My bum was so numb from all that sitting, and my legs were crooked like an old lady's, and I'd just want to run and shout to release some of the pressure. Then Mally would grab my hand and we'd sprint about, laughing hysterically.

So you see, even though there were exams and everything was crazy all around us, we were still happy.

One afternoon I really really didn't feel like going to the library. I know it meant breaking my routine but I was sick to death of the sight of it. So I asked Mally if we could go to his house to revise – we could do just the same amount of work there *and* we could have a cup of tea at the same time.

'Oh yeah. Sure,' he said.

'Great!'

'Only, hang on a minute. I think my dad's home and there might be, you know, some cousins coming later. I actually think it might be a bit mad over there to work.'

'Oh, OK. But shouldn't I see your dad again? I don't think I made a very good impression last time.'

'You did! I mean, it's fine. Though you two should meet again, definitely. Only maybe not today. He's got a lot on.'

In the end we went to the library. Again. We spent so much time there we should have our own chairs with little plaques on them.

When I got home I realised I hadn't been to Mally's house since I went over for lunch that time. I was on the computer, pretending to work, but actually I had done so much revision that day I just wanted to chill out. I noticed Rachel was on MSN.

Hey yooooooo. How goes it?

Looo C. Wot you doing MSNing me u shld be WORKING?

I KNOW I've had it for today. Can I ask you a q???

Go ahead . . .

I've never been to Mally's house to revise. Izit weird?

It's a bit weird.
Actually not that weird.
I've hardly been to ne of my X's houses.

O ok.
But I asked if we could go round today and Mally
said NO.
Relatives were ova.

Then DATS why you couldn't go you FREAK.
Wots problemo?

Don't think his dad likes me.
After THAT row.
Wot u think??????

Then I just stared at the cursor blinking on and off. I
stared at it until my eyes burned, thinking about Mally's
dad.

Where r u? I typed finally.

Hang on sweeeeets Ian jus texted.

Ian?????

Ian my new boyfriend.

Wottt?????? I didn't even know Sam was out the window, let alone Ian in.
Wot bout Sam?? I typed.

It's ova.
Wosn't going newhere.
I'm seeing a new boy now.
Ian.
South End Ian.

Wow. This was pretty quick, even for Rachel. I had heard of the South End Crew. They hung about in tracksuits (not a look Rachel usually liked), talking like black guys, even though they were all white. I was a bit surprised . . . maybe she was on the rebound. Then again, nothing ought to surprise me about Rachel.

Gr8, I typed.
Is it cooool??

Yeahh.
It's fine. He's fit.

When did it happen?

2day!!!!! He kissed me in bus shelter waiting 4 da no.
52 bus. Row Man Tic ehhhhh???

Wowjeeeee. Did u heart go PITAPAT??

Kindaaa. He's got big arms.

Awwwww.

But you should go ova 2 Mally's.
Surprise him.
Dress nice and make nicey wiv Mr Khan then you
don't hav 2 worry that u've neva seen his house NE
MORE.

You think??????

TOTALLY.
Mally's dropped over unannounced 2 u rite?

Mmmhmm.

Then wot's the prob?

DO IT.

Maybe I WILL!!!!!
Can't hurt right?

You know it girl!

Thanks Rach.
U r wicked on a stick.

O I know! Betta sign off now. Hugs n kisses xxxx

I decided to take Rachel's advice. At lunchtime the next day I figured I'd surprise Mally by bringing a takeaway latte to his doorstep – grande, two shots, full fat, just how he liked it. Mr Khan was bound to be at the restaurant. Only, when I reached his house, it was Mr Khan who answered the door. He looked surprised to see me.

'Lucy, isn't it?' he said, and he just stood there with the door half open.

His hair was swept back, and he was immaculately turned out in a suit and a very white shirt and shoes that shone as brightly as a dog's nose. In all the times I had seen him, Mr Khan had struck me as a great big man, but actually he wasn't. He just seemed big.

'Hello, Mr Khan, yeah, it's Lucy.'

'And you have come . . . to see Mally, I presume? Or is it another matter I can help you with?'

'Oh no. Mally. Thanks! I brought him some coffee. To help his concentration, you know, for revising and stuff.'

'I see. Good. Well, you'd better come in.'

Mr Khan showed me into the lounge. I hadn't been in this room on my last visit. It was much neater than the sitting room in my house. In fact it looked as if nobody ever went in there. There was a large beige sofa with cushions arranged on their points, a complicated geometrical rug that obviously wasn't meant for walking on and a big framed picture with Arabic writing on the wall. I sat down gingerly on the tip of the sofa: it would be a nightmare to spill coffee over it. Mr Khan smiled a wide smile – too wide actually; it looked as if his face might break open with the effort of it. Then he left and I heard his footsteps going upstairs. I could hear someone – Mally's mother, I supposed – clanking around in the kitchen, but she didn't come through. Ehsan would be at school. Sitting there I wasn't so sure I had made the right decision coming here after all.

I heard some muffled voices coming through the wall. 'Why mmmphff mmmphff restaurant, Dad? I mean you didn't really mmffshhff home in the first place.'

'I don't want to have any person in my kitchen cupboards! Easier to come home than to explain which pot. Exercise will do me good.' Mr Khan's voice came through loud and clear. 'You had better go and see your friend.'

Then Mally came through the door, looking flustered. 'Hi, Lucy. What are you doing here?'

'I . . . I . . . um . . . came to bring you coffee? Sorry I didn't text you first; I thought, I thought it'd be OK to come over and revise. Are your relatives still here?'

Just then Mr Khan appeared and gave me another stiff smile and motioned for me to sit back down. I wished I hadn't bought the stupid coffee now. I felt too awkward to hand it to Mally but it was even worse trying not to spill it.

'Lucy. How is your revising going?'

'Oh, OK thank you, Mr Khan. Mally's been really useful actually. We go to the coffee house and —'

'Lucy has GCSEs,' Mally cut in quickly. 'She's doing ten subjects.'

'Which coffee house?' asked Mr Khan.

'Umm, Costa? The leather armchairs, they're, umm comfy.' I tried to smile at Mally — we had a private joke about those armchairs. But he didn't smile back.

'And can you concentrate where people are drinking coffee?' said Mr Khan.

'Oh yes, we test each other,' I said.

Mr Khan took a deep breath in before he spoke. 'Test each other. And do you know anything about the subjects upon which Maladhar is sitting his exams?'

'Not too much, but . . .' I looked at Mally.

'It's fine, Dad. We work,' said Mally. 'I go to the library mainly.'

I began to have the feeling Mally hadn't told his dad how much we hung out. But I wished he could have had a CCTV strapped to our foreheads, then he could see we did nothing *but* work. And snog, but that was getting less.

'And what is your favourite subject, Lucy?' asked Mr Khan.

'Umm. Fashion, I think. Or English.'

'Fashion. I see,' said Mr Khan. 'What exactly do you study in fashion?'

'Oh, there's lots of things. History of fashion . . . how to cut a pattern, that kind of thing.'

'How to cut a pattern,' Mr Khan repeated. 'And is that useful?'

Something in the way he said, 'Is that useful?' made me cross. It was as if he was saying that I was use*less*. First he made out that Mally and I did no work when we actually *did*. Now he was saying my subjects were rubbish. I could feel myself starting to blush, but for once, instead of embarrassment, I felt anger. And then whoomphff, there it came, until I was glowing like a red lightbulb.

'Yes,' I said hotly. 'Clothes can be quite useful. You know, for wearing?'

Great, I'd really blown it now. First London, now an argument about the usefulness of clothes. Out of nowhere the story Mally had told us at dinner, about the man with no shirt, popped into my head. Nice one, Lucy, way to pick an argument.

Mr Khan didn't flinch but his eyes narrowed. 'I dare say,' he said in exactly the same tone. 'Fashion may be useful for some. What do you intend on doing with your fashion and English?'

Blimey – what did he want, a full career plan?

'She's quite good, Dad,' said Mally. 'She made some T-shirts at school. Everybody wore them.'

Thank goodness Mally had said something at last – I thought he'd lost the ability to speak.

'Actually I'm going to university to do textile design,' I said, in my poshest voice. I'd just made it up on the spot, but it sounded good, to me at least.

But obviously not to Mr Khan. 'I see,' he said, like he didn't see at all.

I needed to get out and I needed Mally to come with me to explain what the hell was going on.

'I should probably go,' I said. 'Got some revising to do.'

'Oh, OK. I'll see you out,' said Mally.

Why wasn't Mally coming with me? I needed to speak to him. But Mr Khan was right behind us the whole way through the hall to the front door. I didn't say anything. Mally didn't say anything, didn't even kiss me on the cheek as I left. And it was only when I got halfway down the street I noticed I still had his coffee in my hand.

Why the bloody hell had Mally let his father speak to me like that? Had he even *told* his father we hung out? Did Mr Khan even know we were *going out*?

Maybe I didn't know Mally very well, after all.

Mally's dad was so freakin' weird and he made Mally weird. The worst of it was that Mally had just sat there and said hardly anything the whole time his dad was being mean to me.

Work was out of the question and I didn't know what to do with myself. But before a minute had gone by Mally texted me: *Where are you?*

I didn't reply, I just shoved my phone into my pocket. I was fishing around for my keys; I still felt hot and red only now my face was wet with tears. Then I heard footsteps running up behind me.

Mally. He spun me round and tried to hug me. I pushed him off.

'Lucy! I am so sorry. About my dad. He doesn't mean it, he —'

'You haven't told him, have you? That we've been revising together. I bet you haven't even told him we're going out!'

'I have, I have! He knows we're going out. God, believe me, he *knows* you're my girlfriend.'

'But have you told him we've been revising together this whole time? *Have you?*'

Mally looked down. 'Most of the time, yeah.'

'*Most of the time?* What's so wrong with me? Why does your dad hate me?'

'He doesn't hate you – I mean, not you particularly.' Mally looked at his feet and fell silent.

I stood there. 'What d'you mean?'

'Look, Lucy, this is going to sound horrible. You know how I told you you're the first serious girlfriend I've ever had . . . ? You're also the first white girlfriend I've had . . .'

Right. What did that mean?

'The others were friends of my aunt and uncle. I don't think Dad is too keen on the idea that I'm going out with you.'

'But . . . why? Is it because we went to London that day?'

'Oh God, Lucy, this is really hard.' Mally hesitated. 'It's because . . . you're from England.'

'But so are you!' Then I understood. 'Oh, I get it. It's because I'm white.'

'Dad's got loads of white friends,' Mally hurried on. 'Nearly all his customers are white. He doesn't think white people are stupid, or, I don't know, uncultured or anything like that. He loves England. It's just that, when it comes to who his children date, it's different. He's made all these sacrifices so that we can get ahead, but part of the whole future he has imagined for us is that we all marry girls, you know, that he'd approve of.'

'Girls from Bangladesh.'

'Or a British-Bangladeshi, yeah.'

It was horrible – and weird – to hear that somebody didn't like me because of the colour of my skin. I felt so helpless. 'It's like the Dark Ages! And you? What do you think?'

'You know what I think! I love going out with you! But I can't change my father's mind. England is still a foreign country to him. He wants us all to be with someone from home.'

'Which home? What d'you mean – Bangladesh?'

'Yeah.'

'And what about your mum?'

'She likes you – they both like you.'

'But she agrees with your father.'

Mally was silent, which meant yes.

'But why did you let your dad speak to me like that if you love me? It was so humiliating!'

'I'm really sorry, Lucy. My dad was totally out of order. But it's his house. I have to respect that.'

'And that means not respecting me, obviously.'

'It's not like that! You don't understand.'

'So you keep saying.' As far as I was concerned, it *was* like that. 'If you really loved me you would have stuck up for me. Your dad is obviously a weirdo freak who likes to put down people and you just stand there watching.'

'Don't say that, sweetheart, you don't . . . you don't know him.'

'You see, you're *still* sticking up for him even when he hates me!' I started to cry.

'I'm not! I just can't explain.'

'Well, fine. You don't have to! I don't care either way. I'm obviously not worth explaining TO!' I tried to push the keys into the door, but I was crying so hard I couldn't see the keyhole.

'Look, my dad isn't a freak,' said Mally.

'Oh no, I forgot, he's a racist.'

Mally was silent.

I was crying so hard I don't know how I finally got the keys in the door, but I did. And I didn't even look at Mally before I slammed the door on him.

Chapter 8

♥

There was only one person I could turn to. Rachel. And when I phoned her, sobbing hysterically, she was there for me, right away. We met in our old favourite spot, on the bench outside JD Sports in the mini-mall; the inside-out bench we called it, because it tried to pretend it was outside when actually it was inside. I wasn't feeling much like being around people, but I couldn't think where else to meet. I looked a mess. My eyes were swollen from crying and my cheeks were all blotchy and I was basically wearing a pair of pyjamas, which I'd put on after the argument and hadn't bothered taking off.

'Oh my God, Lucy, what's happened?' Rachel put her arms around me and I broke out into fresh sobs.

'It's Mally. It's over.'

'No! Why?'

I was crying so hard people were starting to stare. I drew my knees up and buried my face in them. Rachel held me tight.

'What's happened? Tell me everything.'

It all came out in a rush: how Mally had admitted that his father didn't like me, how mean Mr Khan had been and how Mally hadn't stuck up for me.

'Why doesn't Mr Khan like you?' said Rachel.

'Because I'm not from Bangladesh. Friends are OK apparently, but girlfriends, no. They have to be from where Mally's from.'

'God. That's weird,' said Rachel.

'He hadn't told his dad that we revised together. His dad seemed totally shocked to see me.' I still had more tears left from somewhere and they spilled out on to my cheeks.

'But you know what? Mally must have told his dad you two were serious. Otherwise his dad wouldn't have been so freaky,' said Rachel.

'I suppose,' I sniffed. 'But he could have done a better job of sticking up for me.'

'Yes, you're right, sweetie. You're right.' Rachel still had her arm around me. 'But you can't blame Mally for having a difficult dad. I mean, it's not his fault.'

'But Mally was so *different* around him. The reason I loved him in the first place was that he wasn't afraid to stand up for anything.'

'And he still isn't. He came running after you, didn't

he, just a minute after you left? If his dad hates you that much he can't have liked that.'

'I guess. But then we had a row.' I gave another sob.

'You've said yourself how much respect Mally has for his family. And he did stand up for you a little bit, about the T-shirts?'

'He could have done a whole lot more. He was far more respectful to his dad than to me.'

'Well, I suppose we can't really understand,' said Rachel.

'That's what Mally kept saying. Anyway. It doesn't matter because we're over.'

'But you love him, don't you?'

'Yes,' I said simply. I loved Mally so much it hurt. 'I just wish he'd been honest with me and told me about his dad.'

'And what's he supposed to have said? Gee, Lucy, my dad doesn't really go for you, so I haven't told him that we're revising together? You would have gone mental.'

'I suppose . . . It does feel pretty horrible now that I know about it.' I squeezed Rachel's arm for support.

'Look sweetie, you're amazing. I know that and Mally knows that. It doesn't matter what his dad thinks.'

I had a feeling that it did. But Rachel did make sense. I couldn't really blame Mally for his dad. My own dad was no angel. I wrapped my arms round Rachel and gave her a massive hug. I felt better speaking to her. I'd been pretty self-obsessed recently – I hadn't even asked about her own love life.

'We're always talking about me lately,' I said. 'How's Ian?'

'Ian? He's OK, I suppose. He's pretty fit. But he's not that bright and he's not great company.'

'Why are you with him then?'

'I dunno. Because it's something to do?'

'How does it go – he's not Mr Right, he's Mr Right Now?'

'Totally.'

We smiled at each other.

'There's lots of time,' I said. 'It's not like we're sixty.'

'That's what you always say. Gotta kiss alotta frogs . . .'

'But maybe,' I said, 'you should set your standards a bit higher. You're so worth it. You're gorgeous, and you're smart and you're funny. What boy wouldn't go for you?'

'Yeah – what boy wouldn't?' Rachel puckered up her lips and crossed her eyes.

'You idiot! Seriously though, thanks, Rach. I don't know how I'd live without you, I really don't.'

'You'd be a gibbering wreck, that's how,' said Rachel, and she planted a big kiss in the middle of my forehead.

For a couple of days I didn't text Mally and he didn't text me. But one morning, when I checked my email, I saw Mally's name in my inbox. My heart started beating so loud I was sure Herbie could hear it in the next room. But instead of a long email there was just one line – a link to Mally's MySpace page. Oh God, was he going to dump me publicly?

It took for ever for the page to load up, but when it did, I saw that Mally had a new MySpace page. Instead of the old photo where he was wearing black and looking moody, this one had him in *my* T-shirt, the one I had made about global warming. At least that's what I thought it was at first. But when I looked closer I noticed that he'd changed the words. Instead of *Global warming is not cool* he'd put, *I'm sorry. It's cold without you, Lucy.* Then in brackets he'd put: *(shirts are useful!).* He must have altered the words on the computer. I gave a gulp.

Then the music started to play. It was Jeff Buckley; he had such a gorgeous voice, full of longing and melancholy. He was singing about love and pain and it made my whole body go goosebumpy. Mally had made this whole thing so that everyone could see it! Even his dad, though I doubt he logged on to MySpace much.

Mally really loved me. And I loved him. It was crazy to fight – a love like this only came along once in a lifetime. I grabbed my phone and punched in a text: *I'm sorry too. I love you. Meet in park? x*

I could see Mally waiting for me even before Socks and I turned the corner. He was always on time – that was one of his things. The flowerbeds were a riot of clashing colours but Mally, as ever, wore black. His shoulders were up by his ears and his hands were shoved deep into his pockets. But he still looked super-cute. I started to run, and so did Socks. Then Mally saw me and started running, so we probably looked like that cheesy advert where two people meet in the middle of a beach, only we were in Redworth gardens and we had a grey hairy terrier streaking between us. When we met we stopped short of hugging: it felt too much too soon. Socks obviously didn't feel the same way. He threw himself at Mally's legs like a hairy bomb.

'Ooomph! Hi, Socks!' He bent down and ruffled his head. I was glad that Socks was there to break the tension. 'How have you been, my old friend?'

'He's been OK. Actually he had a weird turn the other

day that I didn't tell you about.' Probably because I had so much else on my mind, I added silently.

'Yeah?'

'Yeah, he kind of went stiff and looked as if he was having a fit.'

'Oh no! Poor Socks.' Mally bent forward and kissed his head. 'Is he OK now?'

'Yeah, he's fine.'

'Good.' Mally stood up and looked at me. Jesus, the power of his eyes! Sometimes they were like laser beams.

'Listen, I am so sorry,' he said. 'About my dad. I should never have let him talk to you like that. Can you forgive me?'

'It's OK. I'm sorry too.'

'Did you log on to MySpace?'

'Yeah. It's the most romantic thing anyone's ever done for me. It was amazing.'

'Good. I love you. I meant every word. God, I hate my father. I hate him sometimes.'

'Don't say that. It's not your fault. It's fine. It's OK.' I stood on my tiptoes and kissed Mally very softly until he put his hands in my hair and pulled me tighter towards him. When I could hardly breathe we broke apart and stared at each other. Suddenly I laughed – it all seemed so ridiculous. Mally and I were meant to be together, end of story.

'What do you say we take a couple of hours off?' he said. 'We've been working so hard. We deserve it.'

'But what about your dad? I don't want a repeat of when we went to London. I mean, does he know you're even here?'

'Yes. I told him. I told him I was coming to see you.'

'And?'

'He has to put up with it. There's nothing he can do. Look, he'll come around in time. He'll understand how utterly wonderful you are. I promise.' Mally threw his arm around my neck and pulled me to his shoulder. His skin was lovely and smooth and warm.

'I just want to be with you,' I said into his neck. 'I don't care what we do. Let's do nothing.'

'We could take Socks for a walk,' said Mally, 'to this special place I know.'

'OK. But is it in the shade? Otherwise I'll just make freckles.'

'I'm crazy about your freckles,' said Mally. 'I wish *I* could make freckles.'

'It's not a skill exactly,' I said.

'Everything you do is clever. Don't be so down on yourself. You're amazing, and I want everyone to know.

LUCY BROOKS IS AMAZING!!'

'SHHH!' I said, embarrassed. 'The whole neighbour-hood will hear.'

'I don't care,' said Mally, taking in another deep breath. 'LUCY BROOKS IS AMA—'

I clamped my hand over his mouth and Mally took it away and kissed me again. Then he led me across the neatly clipped lawn where old people sat with their faces turned up to the sun and walked through the park, over the old railway line, until we were at last in a part of it that most people didn't visit. The grass had been mown recently, but somehow the wild flowers had grown back and were pushing through the hay in clouds of yellow and white. Butterflies flitted about and then the most random thing – when I lifted my eyes higher I could see tower blocks. We were in the town at the end of the universe.

It was perfect.

'Madam, allow me,' said Mally, taking off his jacket.

'Why thank you, kind gentleman,' I said. 'This will be just the protection for my young and tender flesh.'

'Your young and tender flesh,' said Mally, throwing himself down beside me and biting into my neck.

'Aaah, careful! I'll get a love bite and then everyone will laugh at me.' I tried to wriggle away from him. Socks started barking. 'Socks will protect me, won't you, Socks?'

'Socks will try and Socks will fail!' Mally threw his arm around the dog's neck. 'But don't you think everyone's laughing at me already, with my MySpace page?'

'What, is romance embarrassing?'

'You know what boys are like,' said Mally.

'You're not boys. You're different. That's why I love you.'

'You do love me, do you? I was worried for a second.' Mally looked at me with his enormous brown eyes.

'I hadn't gone off you, Mally. I just . . . realised I didn't know you as well as I thought.'

'You *do* know me, the real me. You know me better than anyone in the world. There are just some bits that you'd have to be in my skin to understand.'

'Any chance of that?' I said, snuggling closer.

'Maybe,' said Mally, smiling. Then we kissed for a very long time.

I knew Mally was trying to tell me to chill out, to accept that I could never totally know every little part of him, but that we could still be OK, but it scared me and I had to make a joke out of it.

Actually, Mally was right – I did know the real him. He knew the real me too, the part of me that not even my mum knew. It was scary. I felt as if I was on the threshold of growing up, of starting a whole new life. But a little part of me wanted to hold back, to cling to what I knew: it felt safer. I didn't tell Mally though, and if I'd thought about it, that was a little part of me *he'd* never know either.

'What d'you think we'll be when we grow up?' I said. 'Isn't it mind-blowing to think that soon we'll have jobs and cars and *everything*?'

'I *am* grown up. I'm eighteen, remember? And just about to embark on a great career as a . . .' Mally paused. 'I don't know what. Something useful. I'll need a job before I get to uni, to add to my CV.'

Wow. Mally was right, of course. Sometimes it blew my mind how sorted he was. But I guess, from the outside, I was grown-up too. Although inside I sometimes still felt like a kid. I couldn't imagine leaving home and setting up on my own. But I wouldn't have to, not yet.

'You, what d'you want to be?' Mally asked. 'A fashion designer?'

'Or a textile designer, or, I dunno,' I said.

'You should really go for it, you know? You're really good. You have so much talent.'

'You're a lovely boyfriend,' I said. I wished I hadn't brought up the future. I knew Mally was going off to uni

at the end of the year and we hadn't talked about how –
or if – we would make it work. I didn't know how I
could compete against all those hot student chicks. But I
couldn't face asking him about it now. We were lying in
the shade of a willow tree; Socks was snuffling about in
the grass. Mally had his arm underneath my neck. I stared
up through the branches at the blue sky. Everything was
good. On this perfect blue morning, I didn't want us to
be anything. I just wanted us to be. Together.

Chapter 9

When exams finally happened I enjoyed them, in a weird kind of way. I mean, obviously they were incredibly stressful, but there was something satisfying about concentrating really hard and coming out knowing I'd done my best. There was the occasional bummer – like chemistry – where I sat there hot and flustered not knowing what the hell to do. When I came out of that one I knew I hadn't done very well, but no surprises there. It was also quite difficult after the end of one exam to have to pick up my books and straight away start cramming for the next.

But, one by one, I could cross the dreaded dates off my calendar, until there was one more – English lit – which wasn't too bad except for a question or two . . . and then *no more*. No more GCSEs!!!! I could cut my work up and throw it into the fire if I wanted. Except that I didn't – it seemed like bad karma.

Mally finished later than me. He had fewer exams, but

each one was so much more important. After most of them he seemed pretty pleased, but after the second economics exam he came out looking dejected. I tried to cheer him up but he said he'd messed up. None of the questions he'd been expecting were on the paper and then he'd panicked and answered the wrong ones. By the time he realised, it was too late to start again. I guess he had so much riding on the results he probably felt nothing was good enough. I knew he was a genius. To get into Cambridge he had to get three A's. His teachers had told him that he'd get them, but they were pretty high marks even so.

Now there was nothing but two long months of summer holidays, which by rights should have been mine and Mally's to spend as we pleased. The only problem was that Mum had booked a holiday in Spain for *two weeks*. She'd been saving up for it for ages and I knew I should be pleased, but I wasn't. It would mean two precious weeks away from Mally.

But first we had a week of parties and I was definitely looking forward to *that*. Mally's friends' parties were the real deal: lots of them were going to university at the end of the year and some were taking a year off to travel. It was so weird to think that next year they'd all be gone and Rachel and I would be in the sixth form. Everything was changing. Normally I love change; I can't wait to be grown-up and make a start on life. But now, holding on to Mally's hand as he chatted away to all his friends I realised that these last few months had been the most amazing of my life. Why would I want anything to change – what could possibly get better?

Mally sure as hell could dance. He wasn't one of those arm-flailers or leg-tremblers that it was dangerous to get too close to, and believe me there were enough of those in this town. Mally snaked his hips around in a figure of eight and made this little shimmy with his shoulders that I had tried (and failed) to copy because it was just so damn sexy. Sometimes he twirled me around under his arm and out in front and around behind until I was dizzy and breathless. I felt as if we were the coolest couple on the dance floor, which made me self-conscious and proud at the same time.

But ironically it was the party that should have been the most fun of all that turned out to be the party from hell. I had arranged to meet Rachel and Ian there, and Mally had called up Raj too. It was at a friend's house that we all knew, and Mally had said that he was getting in a massive sound system.

Sure enough, when we arrived, music was pumping out of what, in a previous existence, had been the sitting room. Rachel and Ian were in the VIP room – formerly known as the kitchen. This was the first time we'd double dated – I'd suggested it a few times but Rachel hadn't seemed keen. She kept saying Ian was busy, was with his mates, or down the pub. At this party though, all his mates were there, the South End Crew and, to be honest, they weren't doing wonders for the atmosphere. They stood around in a big baggy-trousered group. They had their backs to everyone and were grasping beer cans in their fists like they were pumping weights. Occasionally one of them swaggered over to the dance floor and pulled a couple of moves that he'd obviously learned from MTV. Then the others hooted at him and punched the air. Rachel stood with Mally and me more than with them, though every so often Ian would come strutting over and run his hands all over her.

I have to say I could see why Rachel hadn't wanted to double date. Ian wasn't one of her best boyfriends – and she'd had some bad ones. Rachel did seem a bit embarrassed and kept backing away from Ian, but he wasn't having any of it.

'Yo babycakes, whassup? You don wanna party?'

'I don't think you've met my friends. Lucy and Mally. And this is Raj,' said Rachel, reversing and turning to face us all.

Ian glanced in our direction. 'Howz it hangin. Listen, superstar, wot you say we fine somewhere more soothin? Me and my mates is thinkin of chippin and I thought yeah we could like go back to your place and chill, innit?'

Raj rolled his eyes.

'Oh, I don't think so,' said Rachel. 'My parents will wait up for me and well . . .' She trailed off.

'I getcha.' Ian's eyes looked glazed and his breath smelled of beer. 'But if it's jus us two, yeah, they ain't gonna have no beef.'

'Well, umm, they might.'

'All right, superstar, whatever, yeah? We can talk about this la'er. Let's dance, yeah?'

'I could do with putting out a few moves on the floor myself,' said Raj to Mally. 'Not with that moron though.'

Mally nodded. But I felt bad abandoning Rachel, especially when she was pointing to a spot beside her on the dance floor. 'Do you mind if I go over?' I said.

'Then we'll all go over,' said Mally.

It was then that it happened. We heard voices shout really loud over the music towards us.

'Hey, Ian, mate. Wot you doing dancing with those Pakis?'

All the blood left my face. Had those idiots really said

that? But they had – I could hear them laughing. Ian smiled stupidly. He didn't say anything.

'Ian!' said Rachel, pulling away from him. 'What are your mates *like*? That's totally out of order! Aren't you going to make them apologise?'

'For what, superstar? You ain't gonna let a bit of loose talk ruin our night, is you?' Ian grabbed at Rachel's hand.

I looked at Mally. I knew he'd heard because his face had a blank look that I'd never seen before. I felt a surge of anger. 'Oh my God, Mally, those *bloody idiots*!' I said. 'I'm going to —'

'Don't worry about it,' Mally said in a flat voice. 'It's nothing I haven't heard before.'

'But I want to just go over and —'

'What's the point?' said Mally.

'Yeah. Let's just go,' said Raj. Raj looked totally unlike himself. His face was closed tight, like a fist. But he started to walk out with his head down.

'But they shouldn't, they shouldn't just get away with it!' I shouted.

'Listen, Lucy,' Mally hissed. 'There's about ten of them and two of us.'

'And me and Rachel!'

'Don't be so stupid. Raj and I are the ones they have the beef with – and you are girls. And if we get aggro they'll beat us *all* up. I know their type. Raj is right. We're going.'

I was so furious I hadn't noticed what was going on with Rachel, but as we went to walk out she was right there in front of us, without Ian.

'I'm so sorry, Mally, Raj,' she said, totally flustered.

As we passed by the South End Crew I let Mally, Raj and Rachel go on ahead. But I couldn't walk by without saying something. 'If you think that being racist is cool, you're wrong. Why are you dressing up like black kids when you're all white? You bunch of utter *wankers*.' I said the last word quite quietly, but I stretched it out and I was sure they could all hear me because everyone had stopped talking.

Mally appeared at the door. 'What the hell are you doing? Do you want to get us all beaten up? *Come on.*'

He grabbed me by the arm and pulled me out. I knew he was right, but I was still glad I'd said something.

On the way home, Rachel kept apologising to Mally. Raj was unusually quiet. It was quite a long walk home and Rachel and Mally drew ahead of us. I could hear her explaining that she hadn't been seeing Ian for long, hardly knew him in fact. Mally was giving short one-word answers, but Rachel didn't seem to be able to let it go.

Raj and I were left walking together. I didn't know what to say to Raj at the best of times, let alone now. I felt awful. At least I had managed to say something to those tossers, and maybe made them think about what they'd said. On the other hand, maybe they were too drunk and stupid to think about anything, and maybe I'd been lucky the South End Crew hadn't come chasing after us.

'I'm really sorry about all that. They were complete losers,' I said in the end.

'I know. It's not your fault,' Raj said.

After another long pause I said, 'I mean, maybe I can understand a little bit. Mr Khan, he doesn't like me, because I'm white. Mally must have told you.'

'He did tell me. He was pretty embarrassed, and it's horrible. It's nothing to do with you, you know that, right? Mr Khan is a difficult old bugger.'

I nodded.

After a pause Raj continued: 'What you said about understanding: you're right in a way. You've known what it's like, once. But Mally and I, we have to go through this all the time. We never know when it's going to come up.'

I blushed furiously. I knew what Raj meant. I thought about the time when Mally and I had been in the café. I had sat down first, but when Mally joined me, these two women nearby looked at him and really obviously picked up their handbags and put them on their laps. And to think I had thought I was in a similar predicament with my red hair!

'I'm, I'm sorry,' I stammered.

'It's OK, I know you mean well.'

We were silent again. Once again I was beginning to wonder whether I understood Mally as well as I'd thought.

Rachel and Mally had stopped outside Rachel's house. Rachel gave me an uncomfortable half-smile and looked as if she was going to say something, but she didn't. She just shoved her hands in her pockets and went inside. I went over to Mally and put my arm around his waist. I could feel his ribs pressing through his T-shirt, but even as close to me as that, I knew that he was still miles away.

Soon we reached Raj's front door. He and Mally embraced.

'See ya later, bro,' said Raj, patting him on the back.

'Later,' said Mally.

Then it was just Mally and me. I felt as if a chasm had opened up between us and to try to stop it I took his hand and squeezed it tight. 'Are you OK?' I said.

'I'm fine,' he said. But I knew he wasn't, and neither was I.

'It doesn't mean anything, those kids . . .' I said.

'It means what it means,' said Mally.

His voice was hard, and distant. I hadn't heard him use that tone before. We lapsed into silence. The sound of our shoes on the pavement was as loud as gun cracks.

Eventually we reached my house. I hugged Mally tight, I wanted to keep him with me for a few minutes longer, and for one instant I felt Mally relax and rest his head on my shoulder. Then he tensed again and moved away from me. I wished I had never let him go.

After that I had to go to Spain. Even though Mally said I should enjoy myself, and that he wished he could go too, he *wasn't* going too, and I knew it would be hard to enjoy myself without him.

Even before I left, Mally was really busy. He'd got a job as an intern in a company that organised car pooling in the local area. Mally had to contact people and convince them to take part. I just knew he'd be great at it – I remembered how passionate he'd been at the debate – but it meant he was at work all day. As well as that, three evenings a week he had to help out in his dad's restaurant.

When I did see Mally it wasn't nearly as easy as it had been – we hardly ever laughed any more. Don't get me wrong, we were still in love. I loved Mally painfully. But since the party he'd been distant, almost as if he was still at work, or somewhere else completely. Then I'd ask him what he was thinking, even though I knew he hated that question. He'd just say, 'Nothing'. But it is impossible to think *nothing*: everybody is thinking of something, even if it's just door knobs and fried eggs.

The worst thing was that Mum had made a real effort with the holiday. She'd got us a nice hotel near the Ramblas in Barcelona, right in the middle of all the action. Herbie was over the moon; there were so many crazy street-performers, he would probably have been happy spending the whole two weeks watching fire-eaters on stilts.

The weather was boiling hot too, just what I usually love (though I have to slap on factor 50 the whole time), and Mum let us go to the beach rather than drag us round museums. And I did try, I really did, to enjoy myself, but all I could think about was Mally.

Mally Mally Mally Mally Mally.

How it would have all been so much better if he were here. How sexy he would have looked in a pair of swimming trunks. How we could have run into the sea and frolicked in the waves.

I reached my arm across the towel and checked my

mobile again. He still hadn't texted. The last text I'd got was the previous morning and I'd sent him three texts since then. He must be really busy at work. Oh God, how was I going to manage nine more days without him? The day after next it'd be a week till we went home. Then I'd be halfway through . . .

Mum broke into my thoughts. 'Do you want me to keep your mobile in my bag? Seems a bit hot out in the sun.'

'No, it's OK.'

There was a silence.

'You'd better make sure you cover up well. The sun is very strong out here.'

'Yes, Mum, I know.'

There was another silence.

'How about going into the sea? You haven't gone in since you arrived,' said Mum.

I squinted across at her. She was wearing a tattered old straw hat she'd pulled out of the cupboard at home at the last minute and a horrible, loud swimsuit she'd probably had since the Seventies. I suddenly felt incredibly annoyed.

'Look, I don't want to go into the poxy sea, OK? Stop hassling me. I just want to be left alone.'

Mum's face hardened. 'Fine, Lucinda,' she said, getting

up and packing her bag. 'Be like that. Just stay here stewing for as long as you like. You've been absolutely miserable ever since we arrived, and to tell you the truth I'm getting sick of it. I'm off to get an ice-cream. Coming, Herbie?'

Herbie shot me a bewildered look and followed Mum, scuffing sand on to my leg as he went.

Great. Peace at last. I slotted my headphones into my ears and scrolled down to Jeff Buckley. He understood what I was going through. I listened to the whole album with tears in my eyes, my heart soaring up above the sea. It was only when I began to trudge back up the beach towards the hotel that I started to think about Mum. Maybe she had the tiniest fraction of a point...I probably hadn't been the greatest holiday companion so far. But I couldn't help it! I *was* trying. I could hear Mum's voice in my head: *Yes, very trying!* Maybe I should try harder ...

Forty-five minutes later, after I'd got lost a couple of times, I finally showed up at the hotel. Mum was in the lobby with a cup of tea.

'Look, Mum, I'm sorry,' I said. 'I know I've been miserable to have around.' As soon as I started to speak a lump came into my throat.

Mum beckoned for me to sit down next to her. 'I just

want you to make a bit more of an effort, darling, for Herbie if not for me.'

'I just miss Mally so much!'

'I know, but you'll see him in a week!'

'I just . . . I don't know . . . he hasn't texted . . . and I hardly see him even when I *am* at home, and I love him so much, you know?'

'Lucy,' Mum gave me a squeeze, 'Mally is a very nice boy. And he's your first love and it's a hugely important thing. I just wish, for your sake, that the relationship could be a little smoother. First love should be pure and joyful and, I don't know, lovely.'

'It *is* pure and joyful! It's just that sometimes the world gets in the way.'

'Yes, well, if you love each other enough, I'm sure you'll find a path through it.' Mum smiled at me encouragingly. 'Well, I'm glad we've had this chat.'

'So am I. Thanks, Mum. I'll try to be better, I promise.' As I said it, I felt just like a little girl.

The second week of the holiday was much better. I had to be very strict with my mind and not let it wander off down Avenue Mally, but when I put a roadblock on any thoughts that were going that way, I found myself having some fun – Barcelona was a really cool place.

Even so, it was great to be back. As soon as I saw Mally I threw myself into his arms.

'Whoa! Lucy! Hey – how are you?' he said, as I smothered him with kisses in the hallway.

'God, I missed you so much, Mally! I didn't know it was possible. I thought of you every day.' I was going to say, every hour, every minute, but I could feel myself sounding a bit mad, so I didn't.

'I missed you too.'

'Did you? Did you really? You weren't too busy at work?'

'What do you mean – too busy to miss you? I *was* busy, but that didn't mean I didn't think of you. I thought of you all the time.'

'It's just that sometimes you didn't text. You're OK, right?'

'Yeah. I'm fine!' Mally stepped back. 'How was your holiday? Meet any nice men?'

'*As if!* I missed you so crazily I didn't even see any other men.'

We went to my room and snuggled together on my bed. It was fantastic to feel his arms around me again and his lips on mine and his hands in my hair and the weight of his body on top of mine. I felt like I'd died and gone to heaven.

But then Mally turned over and lay on his back, staring at the ceiling.

'Are you OK?' I asked, stroking his hair.

'I'm fine. I'm so glad you're back – I mean it. I'm just, well, I can't help thinking about my exam results.'

'Oh, Mally. I know you'll do well. You're a genius.'

'I've just got so much riding on it.'

'I know, baby. Don't worry,' I said, smoothing his brow. 'How can I take your mind off it?'

'I mean, if I don't get three A's, I'm screwed.'

'How about *this*?' I kissed his nose.

'And Dad'll be totally gutted too.'

'Or this?' I kissed his eyes.

'Mmmm.'

'Or this?' I brought my lips down on his and gave him a full-on snog. Finally Mally reacted, putting both his hands on my bum and squeezing it. Bingo!

It was good to see I could still work some of the old Lucy magic.

Chapter 10

♥

When I woke up the next day it was raining again. I could hear it beating down on my window pane – it had been raining for a solid week. Some people were saying it was because of global warming. It seemed like any kind of weird weather was blamed on global warming. I thought of Mally, already working away at his office. He was helping out at the restaurant tonight, so I probably wouldn't see him then either.

With a big sigh I got up, pulled my dressing gown over my pyjamas and went downstairs. Thank goodness Herbie was at a friend's today and I could have the house to myself.

It wasn't until I'd made myself a cup of tea that I noticed Socks was still in his basket. Normally he would have struggled up to meet me, even though his joints were stiff. Something was wrong. I went over to him. He was trembling like he was cold, but it was really warm in the kitchen. He had froth at the corner of his mouth.

My heart gave a great leap of fear.

'MUM! COME QUICK! SOCKS IS HAVING ANOTHER FIT!'

'It's OK, Socks,' I said to him as I stroked his head. He barely seemed to recognise me.

'MUM!!!'

Mum appeared at the door and took in the scene immediately. 'Let's get him to the vet. Now!'

We laid a blanket on the back seat for Socks and drove as fast as we could. 'I was afraid of this,' Mum said.

'What do you mean?'

'This. Those little fits he had before,' said Mum.

'But they were ages ago! He's completely recovered since then,' I said.

'He had another while we were away. Mrs Karposhki said.'

'Why didn't you tell me?' I looked at Mum in astonishment.

'I didn't know how serious it was, darling. I didn't want to worry you, and you were so involved with Mally. I'm sorry, I should have.'

I was sitting in the back, with Socks's head on my knee. He'd stopped shaking now, but he was very limp. He turned his eyes towards me and attempted to lick my hand. Darling Socks! Even though he was so ill, he still wanted to provide me with reassurance.

It seemed like an age that we were sitting in the vet's waiting room, but I lost all sense of time; I was just hugging Socks close to my chest and comforting him, as if by sheer force of willpower I could make him be OK. I texted Mally at one point: *Please call. Socks ill!!* But Mally didn't reply, or at least I don't think he did, because then the vet showed up and what followed next was a bit of a blur.

We laid Socks on the table and he looked so old and fragile I started crying immediately, even before the vet said anything. The vet checked him over and asked a few questions. Had he been drinking a lot recently? Mum said, yes, he had. Then the vet looked at his gums and seemed to sigh.

'And he's been having these fits?' she said.

'For quite a while,' I said, shooting a glance at Mum.

'But today is the worst?'

'Yes.'

'And he's how old?'

'We don't know exactly,' said Mum. 'Probably about twelve or thirteen.'

'Yes, that's quite old for a small dog,' said the vet, patting him gently. Then she looked up at us with a grim expression. 'I'm afraid this is going to be very hard to hear. But I believe Socks has renal failure.'

I looked at her blankly.

'His kidneys have given out. Now, I'm going to take some blood, to make absolutely sure. The results should be ready tomorrow.'

'But can you fix him?' I said.

'I very much doubt it,' said the vet. 'Given his age. I'm very sorry.'

Mum and I took Socks home and we made a nest for him in the living room. He was still really weak and wouldn't eat anything. His breath smelled weird, though I didn't care. I lay down next to him. I was sending messages up to God: *If you let Socks be OK, I'll never go shopping instead of taking him on a walk again!* My brain wasn't working properly, all my thoughts were disjointed and as soon as I said something I forgot what it was. I suddenly remembered Mum should be at work.

'I took the day off,' said Mum.

I still couldn't believe it. When I woke up this morning, everything was fine. Now this. I sent another message to God: *If you let him be OK I'll never leave him alone again!*

Mally called.

'Mally, it's awful! He's just all weird. Like, I don't know, like it's not really him. This all feels like some kind of horrible dream,' I said. 'The vet says it's renal failure.'

'Poor little dog,' said Mally. 'I'm so sorry, Lucy. What happened?'

I told him, and how I felt so bad we'd left him when we went to Spain, and all the times since I'd got back that I hadn't taken him for a walk because he and I had been together.

'It's not your fault, sweetheart,' said Mally. 'The vet told you Socks was old, didn't she?'

'I guess so.'

'Well then, when people, or dogs, get old they get prone to all sorts of things. It might just be Socks's time.'

'Time for what?'

'Time to go.'

I began to cry. 'I don't want him to go!'

'I know you don't, sweetheart.'

Then the phone went muffled and I could hear Mally speaking to someone else. He came back on the line.

'Look, I'm really sorry, Lucy, but I'm going to have to go.'

I was silent. I had been hoping that he could leave work and come over.

'I'm really tied up in here, I'm sorry. I'll call you as soon as I can.'

'You can't leave work early and come round?' I said.

'I can't, I've got so much on. I'm really sorry, sweetheart. Then I've got to go straight to the restaurant. I just . . . I don't see how I can fit it in.'

I looked at poor Socks again. His eyes were closed, he seemed hardly to be breathing. My heart was made of lead. 'OK. Whatever. I just really needed to see you.' I was desperate for comfort and all I wanted was his arms around me.

'Sorry, Lucy,' he said again. 'I'll go into work late tomorrow, OK? I promise. But let's speak later.'

As Mally put the phone down Mum came in carrying a tray. 'How is he?' she mouthed.

'He can't come round,' I said.

'Who d'you mean, Socks?' said Mum anxiously. 'Has he lost consciousness?'

'No, I mean Mally. He's busy at the restaurant.'

'Oh, OK.' Mum put the tray down at my feet.

'Oh God, Mum, I wish he was here and I wish Socks was OK!' I started crying again. I knew I sounded like a baby.

'Oh, darling.' She wrapped both her arms around me. 'I know. It's very hard. I know how much you love Socks. And Mally too, come to that.'

I could feel my bottom lip wobbling and then, I couldn't stop them, tears just started falling down my cheeks. 'Socks can't die! I've had him, I've had him since I was a kid! He's grown up with me! He's like my brother!'

Mum held me until I stopped crying.

'I don't want to leave him tonight. Is that OK?'

'Of course, darling.'

I curled my body round his small furry one. Socks felt small and defenceless. My heart was so heavy it felt as if it was falling straight through my ribcage. I couldn't imagine life without Socks. He was probably the creature who'd been through most with me in the entire world. Without him I'd be all alone.

It was awful breaking the news to Herbie. Even though Socks was really my dog, Herbie loved him and he was just a kid. I watched him trying to take it all in; he took his glasses off and rubbed his eyes very hard.

'Is he going to die?' he said.

'We don't know,' I said. 'He might.'

Herbie burst into tears and rushed over to Mum for a hug.

During the night I kept dreaming Socks was fine, but then I'd wake up and it was like finding out all over again. He had another fit in the middle of the night, his back arching against me and his eyes rolling back in his head.

By the morning I was exhausted. As soon as the office opened Mum phoned the vet. When she put the phone down her expression was grim. 'It's what she thought. His kidneys aren't working.'

When I heard her say that I wondered how I could ever have hoped she'd say anything different.

'What can we do?'

'The vet says that the kindest thing would be to put him down. Otherwise he might live for another week or so, but he'd be in a lot of pain.'

I looked over at Socks and I knew she was right. He seemed to be pleading with me. 'OK.'

I needed Mally so much right now, but when I called him it went straight to voice mail. He couldn't be at work already! He'd promised! Did he have any idea what I was going through?

In the end Mum, Herbie and I went down to the vet's together. I sat with Socks on my lap. Mum had her arms round me. She was crying, which set me off really badly.

'It won't hurt Socks at all, I promise you,' said the vet. 'I'll give him this injection, then he'll drift off to sleep.'

I was stroking Socks's head and telling him everything was OK. That he could let go now, that he didn't need to stay around for us. I felt Socks go all floppy, as if he was finally relaxed. Then his breathing stopped. Just at that moment I felt a tingle in the palm of my hands. Later I thought that perhaps it was his spirit rushing up towards heaven.

It had all happened so quickly. I could never take anything for granted again.

Mally was waiting for me when we got home. But it was too late. Socks was dead. I put him in a box that I'd filled with his favourite things: his old ball, his favourite treats and his lead. Mum and I and Herbie stood around while Mally dug a hole at the bottom of the garden. I said a prayer, which I'd written earlier, about how Socks had helped me grow up, but now his duty was over and he was better off in dog heaven. The fields were greener there and there were plenty of rabbits to chase. I didn't know if I actually believed in dog heaven but I couldn't deal with the fact that Socks had just vanished. Then I put him in the ground and scattered some earth over him. Mally gave me a giant hug but it didn't really help. I was still devastated.

Chapter 11

♥

On the day I knew Mally would be getting his results I called him early in the morning. His mobile went straight to voice mail – was that good or bad? Either he was celebrating or too upset to answer. Over the next hour I must have called Mally thirty times – I know he must have seen my name come up and I know I shouldn't have kept phoning, but I was possessed by some weird phone weevil. I just couldn't stop my finger from pressing redial. As the minutes wore on and still he didn't pick up, or phone me, I began to get a bad feeling. The feeling grew worse and worse until I was convinced that Mally had committed suicide. Which is why, when he finally phoned me back, I was happy just to hear his voice and I didn't realise at first what he was saying.

'I didn't get into Cambridge.'

'Oh God, no! But surely they can't . . . What did you get?'

'Two A's and a B.'

'But you're so close, couldn't you talk to them?'

'Talk to them! Don't be stupid.'

'Oh, OK, but . . .'

'I failed, Lucy. That's all there is to it.'

'But, Mally, you didn't fail. Your results are great. *You're* great. Look, let's meet up – where shall we meet?'

'I can't meet, Lucy, not right now. We'll talk soon, yeah?'

And just like that, he cut me off.

Mally didn't phone me that day. Or the next. Or the next or the next. A week passed and still I heard nothing. I texted him, I phoned him, I emailed him, I MSNed him. Nothing. So I went to look for him. I went to all the places we used to go: the café, the river, the school playing fields, the park with the tower blocks. Come to think of it, there was hardly anywhere Mally and I had not been together. The whole town was one big painful memory of him. Even though I'd grown up here, it was as if when I was with Mally I truly saw everything.

The only place I didn't go to was his house. I hovered around the bottom of his street for a while, then I walked past his house, craning my head to see if he was inside. Over the next couple of days I walked up and down quite a few times, feeling more and more like a stalker, but the house just sat there, its bay windows looking like puffed-out cheeks blowing me away.

Once or twice I walked past the restaurant. The first time there were just a few people having lunch. The second time must have been in the lull between lunch and dinner because the place was deserted. I was just about to walk away when I noticed a figure sitting in the back. He looked like Mally for a second and my heart lurched. But it wasn't Mally. It was his dad. He hadn't seen me; his head was in his hands. There was something about the slump of his shoulders and the press of his head into his palms that looked ... well ... totally dejected. As if he would sit in that chair and never get up. I almost, for a moment, felt sorry for him. Then I walked on: it would be a nightmare if Mr Khan saw me staring in at him through the window.

After that I sat indoors with Herbie, just to be near my computer in case Mally felt like sending me a message. I missed Socks so badly. Comforting me was what he was best at. Herbie and I played computer games; usually I hate computer games but it was just the kind of mindless activity I needed. Herbie was thrashing me as usual.

'I wish Ehsan was here. He's so much better than you at this,' Herbie said.

'Thanks a lot, Herbie,' I said. 'Where is Ehsan anyway?'

'I dunno. I haven't seen him.'

'What do you mean?'

'I mean, I haven't seen him. Not for a month.'

'A *month*? That's a long time. Why?'

'He's not allowed.'

'What do you mean?' I was shocked.

'He emailed me and said he wasn't allowed to come round any more.'

'But . . . why?'

'He didn't say,' said Herbie. 'He just said there were loads of rows at home.'

I sat there in a state of numb shock. It was obviously because of Mally and me. But why the hell hadn't Mally told me about any of this? Didn't he tell me *anything* about his life? Then I felt furious. How bloody dare Mr Khan stop the friendship of two kids?

Herbie was looking at me weirdly. 'Why have you gone red?' he asked.

'I'm just feeling hot, Herb. I'm sorry about Ehsan. Do you miss him?'

'Yeah,' said Herbie. 'He was my friend.'

I put my arms round him and gave him a big hug. I don't know if he felt better. I certainly didn't.

My results were OK, although probably not by Mally's

standards. I got an A in fashion and textile design, an A in English literature and a few others. Apart from that it was B's and C's. The horrible thing was that normally I would have been super-pleased, but with everything that was going on, I still felt gutted.

Mum went to work and came back again to find me still sitting in the same place. She was really sweet; I thought she'd get at me about doing my chores. I hardly ate a thing even though Mum cooked my favourite meals. She didn't usually have time to cook, but she served spaghetti bolognaise, or roast chicken, and it would smell great but I just wasn't hungry. I kept thinking how Socks would have loved all the extra food. Come to think of it, Mum must have left work early to have the time to roast a chicken. Herbie couldn't believe his luck.

I hadn't really told Mum what was going on with Mally. Actually I hadn't really told anyone. Rachel had gone away for a few days to a family thing, and I knew if I started telling anyone else I would begin to cry and not be able to stop. But one evening, after I'd pushed yet another delicious dinner around my plate without eating any of it, Mum asked me if there was anything I wanted to talk about. She looked so concerned and sweet that I started to cry. And then it all came out. How it had been my fault that Mally hadn't got into Cambridge and that

I'd ruined his life. Now he was punishing me by blanking me. How Mr Khan would hate me even more. And how things had been going downhill since the party.

Mum sat next to me on the sofa with both her arms around me. Eventually I stopped speaking and was just sobbing into her chest like I hadn't done since I was a little girl. This voice in my head was saying, *This just isn't fun any more.* When I heard the voice I cried even harder.

Mum wiped away my tears with her thumb. 'Darling Lucy. You've got to stop blaming yourself. This is nothing to do with you. I *know* he doesn't think you ruined his life. You both worked really hard.'

'We did work hard, Mum. We did.'

'Two A's and a B is hardly a poor result.'

'It's not enough for Cambridge.'

'I expect he'll survive,' said Mum.

'I love him so much.'

'I know you do, darling. And first love, well, there's nothing quite like it. I just wish you could have had an easier time with it. Perhaps a boy from a more straightforward family.'

I looked up at her. 'If by straightforward you mean white I —'

'Of course not, darling! I mean that there're so many

other factors at play here. You could love and love each other, but sometimes . . . well . . . love is not enough.'

'What do you mean?'

'Darling. I loved your father as much as you love Mally. I loved him so much I thought my heart would burst. And d'you know what? It *was* enough, in the beginning. When you kids were both very young I felt as if there was no man in the world I'd rather be with. I felt that he understood me in a way no one else ever would.'

'That's exactly how I feel!'

Mum was talking to me as a grown-up. She had never spoken to me like this before. I felt suddenly taller, as if by just speaking to me this way she had actually made me grow up, there and then.

'I know, and it's wonderful.' Mum gave my shoulder a squeeze. 'That feeling carried your father and me through the birth of two children. Even when things started to get bad, I kept hoping for a return of the good times. I tried to ignore the warning signs, when your father would stay out late at the pub and come home drunk. The bottle of red wine after he came home from work.'

'What are you saying, Mum? Mally is hardly an alcoholic. He doesn't even drink.'

'I'm just saying that, even though I loved your dad as much as I did, I couldn't make it work. He had something else that was more important to him, and that was alcohol.'

'And now his new family,' I said, sounding bitter, even though I didn't mean to.

'Oh, Lucy,' said my mum. 'You know what? Your father *will* come back to you and Herbie. For the moment your dad has just replaced the drink with his new wife – I'm sure he loves her, but she's become everything and he can't see beyond her. Maybe, for no reason of your own, you and Herbie remind him of the time when he was still drinking.' Mum paused. 'But I know your father. He is actually a good man, believe it or not. He loves you and he will come back to you. But I know you miss him and I'm sorry.'

Mum gave me a huge hug. When we pulled apart I saw that she had tears in her eyes.

I hadn't let myself admit, except that first time with Mally, that I did really miss my dad. Every time I thought about him it was as if I slammed a door on the thought and locked it up somewhere in my head. It had seemed easier that way. But now Mum had brought it out into the open I felt a lot better. Especially if what she said was right, that Dad would come back into our lives.

'Thanks, Mum. I do miss him sometimes, but I've got you.'

'And I've got you.'

We hugged, a bit tearily.

'But . . . I still don't see how Mally is like Dad.'

'Mally is not really like your father. But in one way he is – they both have something else they love as much, if not more, than us.'

'What do you mean? Mally loves me! He's told me so a thousand times.'

'I know he loves you, darling. I'm sure he loves you very much. But does he love you enough?'

I stared at Mum angrily.

'He hasn't called you at all this week,' she said, very gently.

'He's been upset! His father is probably giving him hell. Maybe he can't.'

'But if you were upset, isn't Mally the first person you would call?' Mum said.

'Yeah, but it's different for him.'

'Different?'

'Obviously!' I was bright red. 'He's got, you know, a different family from me. A different culture, more responsibilities. Plus, of course, his dad is a horrible old man who hates me. He's probably taken his mobile away.' As crazy as it sounds, I had had that thought this week.

'But there are plenty of other ways to get in touch, darling, aren't there?' said Mum.

'Maybe . . .' I had had *that* thought too. 'But our relationship is so much more difficult for him than it is for me. Did you know Mr Khan has stopped Ehsan from coming round here because of Mally and me?'

'I noticed he hadn't been round lately. But I didn't know why. That's terrible,' said Mum. 'Poor Herbie.'

'So now you know how horrible Mr Khan is. It's no wonder Mally hasn't called. There's been loads of rows about us at Mally's house. Herbie's told me. Mally must have stood up for me to his dad.'

'I'm sure he did, darling. I'm not saying Mally doesn't love you. But what about when Socks died – it wasn't his dad who stopped him coming over then, was it?'

'You never know! I mean, it's such a different culture. His dad hates dogs! Anyway,' I added, 'Mally was there at the funeral!'

'Darling, I'm just playing Devil's Advocate. I only want to see you happy. And these last few weeks you haven't been happy at all.'

'Yes I have!' I shouted, even though I hadn't.

'The point of being with somebody you love is that you *share* things with them,' said Mum gently. 'Bad things as well as good. Recently you seem to have been going through an awful lot on your own.'

'We do share things! He understands me, and I understand him!' I was hating this conversation – it was like having my insides stirred about by a hot poker.

'I know you do. But . . . well . . . you don't share *experiences* all that much. Mally just isn't around. He's very busy, and motivated, which is great. But if he doesn't have time for you now, what will happen when he goes to university?'

I was silent. I had had the exact same thoughts. But it was horrible to hear them out loud coming from someone else.

'I wouldn't have said anything, darling, but I've been watching you these last few weeks and I just want to try to help you. You've been putting your whole life on hold for Mally. But would he do the same for you? You can tell me to mind my own business if you like. But perhaps the whole reason that you've been so obsessed with Mally is because you can feel him drawing back.'

My head was throbbing. That kind of made sense. If he'd only called me this last week I wouldn't have gone so crazy.

'Perhaps Mally has been avoiding you,' Mum continued gently, 'not because of Mr Khan – after all, as you say, Mally *did* stand up to him and he knows his own mind. Perhaps he just doesn't *want* to call.'

'You *are* saying he doesn't love me,' I said miserably. Just saying those words cut my mouth to pieces.

'No, I'm not. He does love you,' said Mum, taking my hand and squeezing it very tight. 'Just maybe not as much as you love him.'

Oh God, this was horrible. Horrible. I started to cry again. Recently I seemed to have spent my whole life in tears. 'But why? What's so wrong with me? Am I not good enough?'

'Don't ever say that!' said Mum fiercely. 'This is not about your worth. This is about Mally. Have you heard the saying, "what does not destroy me makes me stronger"?'

'No . . . I don't like the sound of it.'

'What it means is that when you come through all of this – and I know it feels like you never will, but you *will* – you'll be so much stronger than you are now.'

'That wouldn't be hard,' I said.

'Don't say that. You are lovely. You are the very best daughter I could have ever wished for. I love you.'

'Thanks, Mum.'

But nothing could make me feel better. I couldn't stop crying. Some of the things she had said I had been

thinking already, only in a secret part of my brain that I
hadn't really allowed myself to see. Some of the things I
hadn't let myself admit.

But I wasn't ready to give up on Mally yet.

I had to see him again and see if Mum was right.

Love Divided

Chapter 12

Thoughts of Mally wound round my brain like a long piece of barbed wire. I couldn't sleep properly and, when I finally did fall asleep, I was so restless and I dreamed about exactly the same stuff that I spent my time obsessing over during the day, so that I never knew if I was dreaming or awake. After such a long time without hearing from Mally he had grown into more of an idea than a reality. In my dreams he'd at first seem the same Mally that I had fallen in love with, but then he'd turn around and I'd discover he was actually a robot, or he'd be made of glass and crack into a thousand tiny pieces.

So it's fair to say that when he finally texted, ten days after his results had come through, I wasn't as pleased as I'd originally thought I would be. It wasn't lost on me that he'd *texted* either, not even a proper phone call. But I wanted to meet him. I still loved him. Even after everything.

I have something to tell you. Meet at the boats 2 mora?

When we'd first started going out we always used to talk about taking a boat out, but somehow we'd never got around to it. It didn't exactly feel like the best time to be going boating, but I didn't have the energy to think of somewhere else.

And maybe, just maybe, Mally had something good to tell me, for once. Maybe he was going to apologise for ignoring me by whisking me off for a glamorous holiday . . . Or maybe he was going to dump me. Jesus, this was completely bloody mad.

When I arrived at the boats, Mally was waiting for me, even though I was early. At first we didn't have time to say much to each other – we were too busy choosing a boat and sorting everything out with the guy who worked there. Then I got in, wobbling awkwardly and holding on to Mally's hand.

We sat down and Mally started rowing and I looked at him for the first time. His face was tilted downwards and his hair flopped over one eye the way it always did.

Why did he still have to be so ridiculously beautiful?

My heart was stomping around like a wild animal in my chest; I was sure Mally would have heard it if the water had not been so loud. It slipped and slapped the side of our little boat and made our silence not seem so obvious.

Calm down, Lucy. He's only a boy.

After a few pulls on the oars Mally said, 'Lucy. Look, I'm sorry. I know I've been avoiding you.'

Even though I'd rehearsed our conversation a thousand times, when I opened my mouth my words came out strange and stilted, as if I was still in one of my dreams. 'You have been avoiding me,' I said. 'Why?'

'I've been a mess. The whole Cambridge thing.' Mally was now looking somewhere past my left ear. I could see the muscles on his arm flex and relax as he worked the oars.

'What are you going to do?'

'What do you mean?'

'About Cambridge.'

'Oh. It turns out I only failed one module, in economics. So I'm going to retake it, next summer probably. Then I'll reapply. I'll have to have a year off though, which wasn't part of the plan.'

A year off – that might mean Mally would still be around and we could be together . . . Was that what he was going to tell me?

I waited.

'Which brings me to the news I have,' Mally said. He still wouldn't look at me. 'I'm really sorry – God, why am I saying I'm sorry? What I mean is that I'm excited – and – this is the thing.'

Mally took a breath and finally looked at me. God, those eyes! They still had the power to send an electric shock straight to my heart.

'I've decided to go to Bangladesh for part of my year off.'

I opened my mouth, then closed it again. 'Oh,' I said.

'It'll look good on my CV and, well, I might have the chance to do some good.' Mally spoke hurriedly, as if he was afraid I was going to interrupt him. 'I'm going to my family's village. There's a charity there that sets up schools for kids who've been flooded out of their homes.'

'Right.' I hadn't really taken anything in, except that Mally was planning to spend the next year fifteen million miles away. 'Is that . . . is that what you were going to tell me? Is that why you wanted to meet?'

'Yes. I'm sorry, I know it's probably not what you wanted to hear, but, you know, it's an amazing opportunity.'

So he wasn't going to dump me. But he was going halfway round the world without me. I wanted to laugh and cry at the same time.

'How long? How long are you going for?'

'Six months.'

'*Six months!*' That was longer than we'd been going out for.

'They don't really do placements for less than that. It's about making the most out of the experience and well . . .' Mally trailed off.

What about my experience! Have you even, for one moment, thought of me in all of this? I don't think I've ever felt as lonely as I did in that moment, with the boy I loved most in the world sitting right beside me.

'I know, it's all a bit of a shock, Lucy. It is to me too. I'm sorry. You know I love you, right?'

'When are you going?'

'Next week.'

This was all too much to take in. I started to cry. 'How can you do this to me? I love you so much. I thought . . . I thought we were for real.' I was sounding totally desperate but I didn't care.

'We *are* for real, sweetheart. I've never felt for anyone else half what I've felt for you. It's just that, I don't know, there are so many other things going on in my life right now. It's difficult for me to, to, focus entirely on this relationship.'

It wasn't difficult for me. It was all I did, focus on Mally. I was a Mally expert.

Mally leaned forward and very gently wiped a tear from my cheek. 'I've got to do things with my life. I can't just hang around Redworth for a year, waiting for something to happen.'

But that was exactly what he was asking me to do. '*I'm* in Redworth. Doesn't that mean anything?'

'Of course it does. You'll always be my Lucy Luce.' Mally gave me a little smile. He looked like a god sitting there in the sunshine. Beautiful. And completely out of reach.

'Why didn't you call me this whole week? Didn't you ... didn't you think I might like to know about all this, you know, a bit sooner?'

'I know. You're completely right. I was really busy organising everything, then I didn't want to tell you and then not go.'

'Why? Because you thought I'd get hysterical?'

'No, because I didn't want to hurt you.'

'You are hurting me.' I suddenly thought of Quin, and how I hadn't been able to be honest with him and only hurt him more. Maybe Mally was doing the same. 'You know, when you didn't reply to any of my messages I walked all over town looking for you. I even walked by your house. Then I just gave up and sat at home. I haven't eaten. I haven't seen anyone. I've been in so much pain: it's like my leg's been cut off or something. I actually don't know what to do.'

Mally shifted on his seat. 'I'm sorry . . . I guess I kept thinking I'd call, then somehow I couldn't face it.'

'But *why*?'

'I've been thinking about this. I know it's completely unreasonable but I was angry at you. You kept calling me and I just wanted to be left alone. I guess I needed to lick my wounds.'

'But I just wanted to help!' I felt sick. All this time I'd been so worried but Mally had been *avoiding me*. I felt like a bug he'd just squashed against the windscreen.

'I know that. But I didn't need your help.' Mally saw the look on my face. 'I'm sorry, Luce, that sounds mean. What I'm trying to say is that there was nothing you could do. What were you going to do? Help me resit my exam?'

'I meant, help you *emotionally*,' I said, gripping on to the side of the boat. So it wasn't to do with his dad at all. This was like a nightmare. 'I could have been there for you. That's what couples do.'

'Right,' said Mally. 'I know. But I'd put so much stock on getting into Cambridge. When I didn't, I just wanted to be by myself. To process it all. I've had to rearrange the whole of next year and it's been quite difficult.'

'*Quite difficult*?' I shouted. 'WHAT ABOUT ME?!'

How had this happened? How had my beautiful Mally, who I could confide everything in, the only one who had understood me in the entire world, turned into this? Mum had been right. I would have turned to Mally at the first sign of trouble. *Why didn't he want to do the same?*

I still loved him. I loved him more than ever. Maybe because I knew I couldn't have him, at least not in the way I wanted him. If only he had been willing to put just a little bit of his life on hold for me. Like when Socks died. Or even if he'd called me in pieces after his results. And now he was going away and I would be left here. Alone. I didn't know how I was going to deal with it.

'I don't see how this is going to work,' I said, more to myself than to him. 'If you can't be there for me when we live a couple of streets away, how is it going to be when you're on the other side of the world?'

'We can write. Email.' Mally smiled but I looked away from him. He was too painful to look at.

'Yeah, I can just imagine checking the computer every five minutes and you never emailing because you're too busy saving the world.'

'What are you saying, Lucy?'

'I'm saying . . .' I gave a gulp. 'I'm saying that we should split up.'

Saying those words tore my heart out of my chest all over again.

I couldn't bear the thought of my life without Mally.

I had expected Mally to react angrily, to disagree. But instead he reached forward and put his arms around me – which was far worse. 'I'm sorry. I . . . don't know what to say.'

Say you love me! Say you won't let it happen! I thought desperately. *I'd made a mistake – I didn't mean it!*

But neither of us spoke. I remember reading somewhere that to be able not to speak to someone is a sign of true intimacy. Fat lot of use that was now.

'I'm sorry, Lucy. You're my first love. My best love. You know that, right? It's just the timing that sucked . . .'

Oh God! He was actually agreeing with me. What the hell had I done?'

'So . . . it's . . . we're . . . finished?'

Mally looked at the bottom of the boat. 'I really admire you for doing this. It hurts like hell, but . . . I think you're right. I'm probably not at a place where I can commit right now.' He looked up helplessly. 'I love you.'

'I love you.'

I started to cry.

Mally leaned forward and kissed me. His lips felt warm and dry.

But why couldn't he love me as much as I loved him?

I wished this kiss could last for ever. But it ended, like everything did.

'We should probably go,' I said. Suddenly I felt angry. 'A part of me hates you, you know. I would have done anything for you.'

'Lucy, you're right, you have every reason —'

'Stop being so bloody rational!' I shot back. 'Don't you . . . you're just sitting there, when you're going to Bangladesh any second.'

'I have to live my life!'

'Yes, without me!'

'Don't make this harder than it already is. I might look OK to you Lucy, but I'm not.'

'You're doing a whole lot better than me,' I said.

Mally picked up the oars and began to row. I couldn't look at Mally's face. Instead I fixed on the silver studs in his belt and the shift of his T-shirt as he rowed, willing myself not to fall apart.

We were back. I started to cry again. Mally put his oars up and cupped my face with both his hands. 'You know there will always be a part of me that loves you. You're the most wonderful person I've ever met. I know you'll do really well. Be a famous fashion designer!' Mally smiled awkwardly. I hated the way he was envisioning my life without him. 'Goodbye, sweetheart.'

I couldn't speak. There was nothing left to say in any case. I just struggled out of the boat in a blur and ran and ran until I knew that even if I turned around, Mally would not be there.

Chapter 13

♥

Whenever anyone asked me how I was I said, 'Welcome to Lucy's Wonderful World of Pain. Come inside, if you dare!' I had to make a joke out of it; I was seriously beginning to suspect that, if I didn't, none of my friends would call me any more. I was talking all their ears off.

The problem was that every thought led back to Mally.

The whole town, for a start. Then things as random as the summer (we had been together in it), anything to do with rivers or boats, black jeans, sad songs, the whole Indian subcontinent including food, people, global warming, floods. Then there were Muslims, cappuccinos, double-decker buses, London. And all that was only a tiny part of what reminded me of him. You can see how I made for pretty boring company.

A few days after the split I became convinced that I'd done the wrong thing, that Mally didn't want to break up, that I should call him RIGHT NOW and beg him to take me back. It was only Mum hiding all the phones in the house that stopped me. I wrote him a thousand emails and sat there with my mouse on the *send* button. I looked him up on MySpace and Bebo. I could see when he was online and that made him feel so close, just a touch away. I imagined Mally sitting at his computer, completely fine. And there was me, in pieces.

I imagined him choosing what clothes to pack, what he'd put on his iPod for the journey. I wished I could make him a going-away playlist. I couldn't believe that he was embarking on this whole adventure without me. I couldn't believe we turned out to be two separate people after all, when all along I had thought we were two halves of one whole.

I always used to think that you fell in love and that was it, happily ever after. But now I know it's more complicated than that. Mally had loved me, but the timing was all wrong. His dad didn't split us up, but he made things harder.

If we'd met later, would we have had a chance? What if I'd met Mr Right at the wrong time?

I'll never know, and to think like that will only drive me insane.

Mum was being amazing. She came home from work early and sat with me and I literally cried on her shoulder.

'You know, you think this is all about Mally not being

ready,' she said. 'But have you thought about things from your own perspective? I know you feel grown-up but you've still got so much of your life to live. Were you really ready to settle down, for ever and ever, with one man? I know you think you were. But in a few months' time, you'll be at a party, I bet you, and you'll be having fun again. You've got the rest of your life ahead of you!'

But that was what I was afraid of. The rest of my Mally-less life.

'I hope you're right,' I said.

'I am. I'm bigger and older and uglier than you. I have to be right.'

Even Herbie was being sweet: he gave me ownership of the remote control. He even did my share of the chores. But the best thing was that Ehsan had started showing up again. Herbie seemed really pleased – I guess Ehsan had been his best friend. And Herbie being a nerd, doesn't make friends that easily.

And then there was Rachel. Apart from my family, Rachel was the only one that I could talk to without worrying about getting boring. Rachel was single now – she said after Ian she had realised she had to get to know herself before she could get to know anyone else. Which meant we were there for each other 24/7. I phoned her late at night from my bedroom and just talked and talked until my throat got dry. Occasionally we even talked about things other than boys – things like hair, make-up, saving the world. When that happened I stopped thinking about Mally for whole minutes at a time and I realised that, just for that moment, I felt lighter. It had all got so heavy with Mally and so complicated. With Rachel I could just be a girl again – or, as Mum would have said, a woman.

I had to keep busy to stop myself going mad. I didn't feel much like shopping or going out, so at long last I decided to redecorate my room. The little girl who had mooned over posters of boy bands just wasn't me any more. On one of my trips to the second-hand shop I'd found this amazing tailor's dummy, which I'd stuck in the garage. Now I moved it upstairs. The dummy would be good for my new designs – I was thinking I might branch out into jackets. On the wall I pinned up a gorgeous piece of fabric I'd found in Mum's wardrobe – a really bold Seventies pattern. I only had two posters up now. One was of Jeff Buckley swooning over a microphone – OK, I know he's a boy, and he was in a band, but it's completely different from a *boy band*, trust me. The other poster was an amazing picture of the earth taken from outer space. It was there to remind me that the earth is precious and that it's my home and that I share it with everyone else, even Mally, even in Bangladesh. And then I collected together all the precious things from our relationship: the Coke can ring, the CD Mally burned for me, a flower Mally had given me that I'd pressed between the pages of a book and the photo he'd taken of us on the bus in London. I put them in a beautiful box that sat on my desk and I turned the key. I'd keep the key under my pillow until I was ready to let it go.

I was glad I'd got round to redecorating at last. I felt like I finally knew what I wanted in my room, like I finally knew myself.

Even so, I couldn't sleep well that week. I was still dreaming of Mally only to wake up and realise we'd split up. So I put off going to bed. It was on one of those nights that I thought I heard something – or someone – outside on the street. Probably a fox – they were always going through our bins. But I listened again. It was too quiet and too deliberate for a fox.

Immediately my thoughts flew to Mally.

I ran to the window and tore back the curtain.

Nothing.

But . . . I was *sure* I heard something.

I ran downstairs, opened the front door and peered out into the street. A dark figure, the same height as Mally, was halfway down it, walking fast. Whoever it was obviously did not want to stop and talk. On my way back indoors my foot stumbled on something. A stone, and under the stone, a letter.

It *had* been Mally!

I picked them both up and ran back upstairs. But it wasn't until I was snuggled up in bed that I began to read. I wanted to savour every last word.

My Darling Lucy,

As I'm writing this I'm hoping that I'll have a chance to see you tonight for the last time. Then again, if I do see you, I don't know that I'll be able to handle it.

You were incredibly brave to end it and I'll always admire you for it. I couldn't. You did the right thing, sweetheart. I'm so incredibly sorry if I've caused you pain.

I probably don't have the right to ask you to think of me in Bangladesh but I know I'll be thinking of you, every evening at six o' clock. I'll look up into the stars and I'll feel better because I'll know they're the same stars that you're underneath too.

I've left you something. I found the pebble on the bank when I was returning the boat. It looked so beautiful, the flecks of silver in it reminded me of the flecks in your eyes.

You're the only pebble on the beach worth anything to me.

Mally x

I folded up the paper carefully and put it under my pillow. Mally was right, the stone was beautiful. I turned it in the light; the little flecks in it glinted and shone like stars. It was perfectly oval and snug in the palm of my hand. I turned it over – there was writing. Mally had had it engraved: *To one in a million. M.*

I turned off the light with the pebble still in my hand. I was really tired and I had a feeling I'd sleep better tonight than I had in ages.

My Best Friend's Brother

To Andrew and Ellie Nelson,
for inspiration

With thanks to Celia
and CosmoGIRL! team members and readers

My Best Friend's Brother

Laura Ellen Kennedy

Chapter 1

♥

It was the night of the Hallowe'en dance last year and the hall looked amazing. Silver light from the chandeliers glittered off the mirrors and soaked into soft red velvet curtains. Gold-painted chairs and tables completed the illusion of grandeur. After weeks of work and organising, it was the best feeling to see it all finished. Watching the looks on everyone's faces as the function hall at the Broadwick Hotel gradually filled up, I thought I might burst with pride.

I'd been on the event committee and we'd all agreed we wanted to steer clear of all the traditional witches, pumpkins and broomsticks. OK, I'll admit it was probably out of vanity more than wanting to be creative and original – but we hardly wanted to be dressed up as mummies and vampires and lose out on the chance to look glamorous, let alone see all the guys in their tuxes. So we eventually decided on a gothic castle theme. And, not to brag or anything, but we'd done brilliantly with just the money we'd scraped together through ticket sales and fund-raisers.

I'd managed to bribe quite a few of the other art students at college with free tickets and they'd done an amazing job glitzing up the furniture and sculpting fake stone gargoyles and archways. I thought of all those hours we'd spent on the phone, begging and borrowing from local firms and persuading students' friends and relatives to help out – and knew it had been worth it.

Dashing home from helping set everything up that afternoon, so I could get ready before the limo was due, had been a rush, but I was running on excitement. When I arrived back at the hall with my best friend, Sally, her date, Mark, and her brother, Jake, I'd honestly felt like an A-lister arriving at the Oscars – setting the red carpet up outside had been a genius touch.

'Erica, it looks amazing!' Sally gasped as we walked in. She gave me a little hug and added quietly, 'And you look beautiful.' She grabbed my hand. 'We are going to have the *best* night. Come on, let's go and see if we can get the music cranked up – I want to get everyone dancing.'

I couldn't stop grinning. I don't think I'd ever felt happier.

Being the centre of attention wasn't something that happened to me. Neither was feeling pretty, not like I did that night. I had my small group of close friends at college, but at school I was the one who blended into the background – the small, pale, freckly girl people would never remember. Don't get me wrong, I didn't spend my life wishing I was someone else. Going unnoticed can work in your favour sometimes – and all the really popular girls seemed to have to work so hard to please everyone. Besides, if I ever felt hard done by, Mum would go off on a rant, saying I had two arms and legs that worked, I was bright and had a loving family and plenty to be grateful for and that I was luckier than an awful lot of people in the world.

But all the boys loved Sally. Actually, *everyone* loved Sally. And she could look glamorous in anything. She has this long mane of glossy, dark hair. (She swore to me there was no secret to it, but I still made her write a list for me once, of all the shampoos, conditioners and styling products she used, so I could try them one by one, looking for a miracle. But I guess she was just born lucky.) Her clear, olive skin, her womanly curves and beautiful, dark eyes meant people noticed her. Most infuriatingly, she was also the loveliest person I knew. If she'd ever acted like she thought she was perfect or knew the power she had over people, I might have begrudged her, but she had as many days as I did where she looked in the mirror and turned up her nose at what she saw. In a way it made me feel better when she confided in me that she hated her nose or she thought her knees looked podgy – if someone as perfect as her could still find fault with her looks, maybe my own flaws weren't as bad as I imagined. When I longed to be taller or stared hatefully at my pale, un-tan-able complexion, I'd remind myself even Sally thought things like that, and it helped me stop worrying.

For once, though, that night, I didn't feel like the plain-best-friend. I felt like some of the people looking in our direction might actually be looking at me. I'd coloured my hair darker and piled it up in a mess of curls. In the gothic spirit, I'd brushed on as much dark, silver-grey eye shadow as I dared. And I absolutely loved my dress. I had my big sister Tamara to thank for that. I'd gone to stay with her, a few weeks before the dance, in her shared university house in Newcastle.

We'd spent a lovely Saturday wandering around town, shopping and sitting in cafés, and we found this antiquey-looking burgundy dress in a vintage shop. I loved it, but it was at least a size too big. Despite my protests, Tamara still made me try it on. She said it was the perfect colour for me and just wanted to see what it would look like. In the changing room it was heartbreaking to see how lovely it would have been if it hadn't hung off me like some sort of comedy clown suit. For a minute I almost wondered if it might be worth putting on a stone just to fill it out.

I was thinking of all the Green and Blacks I could eat to help when Tamara said she was going to buy it for me. For a minute I thought she'd read my mind and was about to protest I didn't really want to gain a stone, when I realised mind-reading doesn't actually happen. I crumpled my face at her, not understanding. I said I'd never wear it. But she launched into this speech, saying people made this mistake way too often, forgetting you can get clothes altered. She's so bossy.

'How often do you find a dress you love as much as this? You'll look amazing in it – we just have to take it to a dressmaker and get it taken in, that's all. It won't be all that expensive and we'll probably still end up paying less than you would for a new one as nice.' So she paid and then took me to a tailor and they pinned the dress. We left it there and a week or so later Tamara sent it to me in the post. She was so right. When I put it on I felt like a different person. In fact, I was so inspired by the transformation it sparked a new passion: I asked Mum to get her old sewing machine down from the loft, along with all her dressmaking books and patterns, and she taught me some of the basics. I revived loads of my old clothes, customising forgotten T-shirts and adding my own twists.

Anyway, I'm going off the subject (being 'tangential' as

my dad always says while he moans at me for 'lacking focus'). But my point is: the Hallowe'en dance was the first chance I'd had to wear my 'magic' dress. And maybe it swelled my ego just a bit too much, but I thought I'd seen a look in Jake's eyes, when we'd all piled into the limo, that I hadn't seen before. When he said I looked great, I let myself believe he wasn't just being his gentlemanly, lovely self. I thought, just maybe, possibly, he was seeing a new side to me. I was even his 'date'. Sort of. Technically. Well, only because Sally wanted to bring her boyfriend *and* her brother – and I'd given up on having anyone actually officially ask me to the dance long before – so when Sally asked if Jake could be my totally-just-friends-plus-one, while a little part of me was hurt that she'd obviously given up hope on me getting a date too, actually, secretly, if I could have chosen anyone to go with it would have been Jake, so it worked out almost perfectly – and I said of course.

I was in such a euphoric mood, I let all these little scenarios play over and over in my mind – like a montage from some cheesy film – me and Jake giggling together over the punch bowl, Jake complimenting my event-organising prowess and being irresistibly drawn to me because of my talents, me and Jake dancing a slow dance together, staring into each other's eyes . . .

My Best Friend's Brother

As the evening got going, though, I was happily distracted. We had so much fun dancing and chatting to everyone. It was really packed out – as it turned out, probably a little too packed out. Jimmy Burton, who did law with Sally and had a reputation as a troublemaker, had turned up, obviously from the pub, with a gang of his older footie mates. They were being rowdy and messing about, picking on this guy – I recognised him from around college but I wasn't sure of his name, it might have been David. Jimmy had obviously got hold of the guy's wallet somehow and was rifling through it, waving his personal things about and taunting him. Jimmy's chunky, strawberry-blond frame was shaking with chuckles of amusement, and the sound of his laugh carried across the room despite the loud music.

When maybe-David tried to snatch the wallet back, Jimmy just laughed at first, but was then clearly unimpressed when he came close to actually getting hold of it and reclaiming it. So Jimmy decided to start a game of catch. Some of his mates spread out, ready to field the game. Jimmy's closest crony, Alex, was barging backward towards the end of the buffet table, near where Sally was standing close to the punch, chatting with our friend Ruth, and I started to get a creeping feeling in my stomach. As I hurried over, Jimmy sent this wallet flying towards Alex, but powerful as his throw was, it wasn't on target. It was heading straight for the back of Sally's head just as she was sipping punch from a delicate champagne flute (it was only a plastic champagne flute, but it was the sort of thin, tough plastic that could easily crack and cut you just like glass).

It was weird, but I could almost see it all unfolding in my mind, as if in slow motion: the wallet hitting Sally, her face slamming forward into her drink, breaking that brittle plastic into sharp shards which pierced her skin and sent blood running down her chin. Without thinking too much, I sprang into action. Urgh, I still cringe when I think about it but, on instinct, I dived behind her, like some crazed goalie, into the trajectory of the wallet, and my hand made contact! Having always been pretty rubbish at contact sports, there was a fraction of a second then, when I felt very pleased with myself. I watched with relief as the wallet headed off safely towards Alex's face, and wondered if I'd missed a calling to football stardom.

But I hadn't exactly planned what would happen next. I couldn't stop myself falling in time to avoid smashing into the sharp corner of buffet table. We'd had to do things as cheaply as we could, and the tables weren't the sturdiest, so, of course, the entire thing collapsed under me. There was a monumental crash as plates of food and bowls of punch came down on me. I felt a searing pain, first in my side as I hit the table, then in my arm as I landed on it. And there'd been a horrible ripping sound. I tried desperately not to acknowledge that it could have been my dress coming to an untimely end.

It was truly mortifying. The chatter stopped as everyone spun round to look at me then quickly erupted into laughter and shouting. A whole room of people laughing at me. I'm sure I did look funny but I wasn't seeing the humorous side. I was in shock and I'm not sure I could have moved if Sally and Ruth hadn't come straight to my rescue, deftly helping me up and ushering me out of the hall.

I wasn't badly injured but my arm was bleeding a bit and it hurt. I was shaking. There was food and drink all over me, in my hair, on my face and all down my left side; and I had this heartbreaking sensation of air blowing on to my right side, through my lovely dress. I knew it was torn. I could still hear the commotion in the hall and I burst into tears. Sally, bless her, whisked me into the ladies.

'Those guys are such a waste of space!' she growled. 'Don't worry, hon, that cut'll wash up easily – it's not serious. I don't think any of that food will stain, either.'

I sobbed as she pulled wads of paper towels out of the dispenser and filled a sink with water. As she dabbed at me, my head was filled with nightmare flashbacks of all those laughing faces. I stared at my bedraggled reflection and raised my arm to look at the damage to my dress.

'Oh, Erica!' Sally realised what had happened and peered carefully at the fabric. 'Ah, don't worry, it'll fix! It's lucky, it's along the seam – you can sew that up and you'll hardly see it. I bet I can even sort it out pretty neatly for now with some safety pins. Hold on, you keep washing yourself up and I'll go in search of safety pins and make-up bags!' She reached up gingerly and touched the sticky, matted mess that had been my hair, then she looked me in the eyes and smiled. 'Don't you worry, we'll get you sorted out in ten minutes, I promise.' And with a squeeze of my arm she whirled out of the door.

I loved Sally then, always calm in a crisis, with a soothing power only my mum could equal. But there was no consoling me. I dabbed pathetically at my dress for a few moments. As I squeezed the paper towel into the sink, it was like watching all my dreams swirl dirtily down the plughole. I looked into the mirror and the ridiculousness of it all welled up in me. I honestly didn't know if I was going to laugh or cry and what came out was a sort of strangled mixture of both.

Even though I'd barely had a chance to speak to Jake all night, suddenly going back to the party was the last thing I wanted. The loud pounding of the music on the other side of the wall felt alien and oppressive. I needed to escape. So I took all the pins out of my hair, rinsed it deeply under the tap and scraped it back into a bun. Then I swung open the door into the lobby, hurriedly fetched my coat from the cloakroom and rushed out into the night air. There was a bench under a tree just on the right of the hotel forecourt and I claimed it, wrapping my coat tightly round me and hugging my knees. To think, less than two hours before, I'd stepped out of that car with all those expectations and then there I was, sticky and soaked and alone. I stared up at the starry sky and sacrificed what was left of my mascara to more sobs of self-pity.

Chapter 2

♥

If you've ever found yourself looking at a friend you've known forever and suddenly seen them, I mean really seen them, as if it was the first time – as if they were a stranger again and you were rediscovering all the shapes of their features like new treasures – if that's happened to you, you might understand what I felt the day I fell for Jake.

I'd known Jake and Sally since I was eight, from when they moved into our street. Tamara and I knocked on their door and introduced ourselves with that too-young-to-know-better brazenness that kids have. From that day on, we'd all hang out together: me, Sally, Jake – who's just a year and a half older than me and Sal – and Tam for a while, before she went off to uni. I have all these summer memories of running about in our front gardens playing ball games, or hide and seek behind the dustbins and garages.

Sally and I were soon best friends. We started secondary school together, sat next to each other on the bus every day, and in the evenings we'd turn up on each other's doorsteps after dinner and hang out in her room or my garden, depending on the time of year. She was the first person I went to when I was excited about something or needed a whinge or a cry. We got to be like sisters, only we were closer than I ever was to Tamara, because we were the same age and went through everything together.

The evening everything changed was a late-August evening, after seven p.m. I guess, because the light was beginning to turn from evening amber to that inky, dusk colour. Sally and I were lying on a blanket on my front lawn, staring up into the sky talking. We'd gabble constantly, about anything from which was the best chocolate biscuit, to all our deepest philosophies on life. Mum would say she couldn't understand how we still found stuff to talk about, when we practically spent every waking minute together. But somehow we always had as many things to discuss as there are atoms in the air.

Sally had a crush on this boy called Mark, and we were giggling about how she was going to trick him into asking her out when Jake's face appeared in the air above us.

'What are you up to, ladies?' he asked.

'Right now? Getting a better view up your nose than I

ever wanted,' I said, and his hand shot up to cover his nose.

'Well sit up then, and stop lying about like . . . layabouts!' he half shouted and half laughed, and I kicked myself for letting my mouth run off on its own again before my brain had a chance to stop it.

'Sorry . . .' Sally and I dragged ourselves into sitting positions as Jake joined us on the blanket. 'I was just joking you know, your nose is great, er, I mean it's fine, you know . . .' I was no smooth-talker.

Sally tried to rescue me. 'Erica! Shhhhh. Don't stress out so much!' She made a cross-eyed face at me, then turned and started chatting to Jake about some family business or other while I looked down and waited for my red face to fade. What a doofus.

As I glanced back up, Jake laughed at something Sally was saying and this incredible grin flashed across his face. As I watched, the power of it rushed through me and sort of spun me. I don't know how it was possible when I knew him so well, but, as his dark eyes sparkled, my heart skipped. I couldn't tear my gaze away, so I just stared. It was like I was drinking him in. His dark hair was damp because he'd just come back from swimming, and it was getting a bit long, so it curled at the ends and licked at his face and neck.

I was sort of paralysed and hot and spinning at the same time. My heart was racing loudly, but it was like the sound outside me was muted and all I could see was Jake. This new Jake, who had somehow changed from being a big, familiar kid to a nineteen-year-old man in a split second right in front of me. I couldn't help looking at his broad, toned shoulders as he leaned forward, legs crossed, resting his elbows on his knees. He was fiddling with a tuft of grass he'd torn from the ground, and even his hands and wrists were suddenly overwhelmingly gorgeous.

I was properly confused. I'd slipped into some parallel universe where everything was altered – why hadn't anyone else noticed? What was happening? I was terrified that this urge to reach out and touch him would override my brain and my arm would shoot out and grab hold of him before I could stop it.

'Are you OK?' Suddenly I realised Sally was watching me – I was probably goggling like some total idiot. The spell was broken, but I felt as if I'd had an electric shock or something.

'Umm, oh yes,' I mumbled. 'I mean, no, I feel a bit weird suddenly. Er, stay there, I'm just going to get a glass of water. Or something with a lot of sugar in it, or caffeine, or something.' I levered myself to my feet and headed towards the door before I remembered my manners and spun back round. 'Oh, do you guys want drinks?'

But I don't think I listened to their answers. I was kind of terrified, or excited, or just weirded out. Things had changed all at once and I wasn't sure if it was temporary – it didn't feel it. I still can't explain what happened in that instant, but I remember not being able to sleep that night (or for a few nights after that, actually) because I was thinking about Jake. Every time I closed my eyes, I saw him smiling and laughing and being utterly gorgeous – in a totally sneaky crept-up-on-me way, I have to say. Then I'd think about when I'd see him next and it made me smile uncontrollably. But then I'd think of Sally and imagine how grossed out she'd be if she knew what I was thinking, and that made me feel like some sort of pervert. Then the thought of Jake knowing what I was thinking was even more mortifying. He probably thought of me as another little sister. We were practically family, after all – my mum and Sally's mum both said Sally and I might as well be sisters. Oh God. I think I eventually exhausted myself to sleep imagining how hard it was going to be, keeping this secret.

Well, I'd kept it for the longest, most agonising two months of my life. Each day at college, when we'd hang out with our male friends and they were so immature, I'd be comparing them to Jake. Some of the best-looking ones were the worst – they treated girls like rubbish because they knew they could get away with it. Most of the others were just sort of goofy and idiotic. They made me think of puppies, getting over-excited and running into walls or falling over – only not in a cute way. It just confirmed all the things that made Jake different. He never seemed to need to be loud to impress anyone. He was strong, but not macho and idiotic about it like the stupid guys who deliberately got into fights or did dumb stunts to prove how hard they were or how much pain they could handle.

Each time I'd see him, he'd look a little bit more gorgeous than he had the time before, and, every time he was sweet or gentle or polite, I'd think how it was so amazing the way he didn't worry that being nice would make him seem weak, like every other guy seemed to think.

I'd fallen in love with him a little more each day. But as I sat on that bench outside the Broadwick Hotel in semi-darkness, for the first time in those long weeks, I realised what a naive idiot I'd been, holding on to the hope that he might actually come to like me. After that night I was going to be a laughing stock. I covered my face with my hands as the sight of that food avalanche coming down on me flashed through my head again, with the sounds of the shouting and jeering. Thank goodness there was only a couple of terms of college left.

I was just starting to plan how I could get to classes whilst minimising the risk of being seen or spoken to, when I heard someone call my name. I scrunched myself tighter into a ball and stayed quiet. If I closed my eyes hard enough maybe I could just disappear. But then, there was Jake.

'There you are, we've all been looking for you! Sal's frantic.'

I didn't answer, I felt so tired. I put a self-conscious hand up to my bedraggled, scraped-back hair and Jake sat down beside me. When he looked at me his voice softened. 'You're crying. You're not worried about that lot in there, are you? They're having a great time, they've forgotten already . . . Come back inside.' He was being so sweet, as ever, but I couldn't tell him what was really wrong, why I felt so sorry for myself.

'I don't think I can. I'm not worried what people think,' I lied, 'or even that I look a mess. Things didn't exactly turn out as I'd planned tonight.' I tried my hardest to sound jokey. 'But it's fine. I'm just kind of . . . done, you know?' I thought again of how I'd seen the evening in my mind, through a sort of Vaseline-coated lens, me looking like a movie star, dancing with Jake, gazing into his eyes . . . Of *course* things didn't turn out how I'd planned! What a stupid little girl. I couldn't stop myself blubbing again and, when Jake put his hand on my shoulder, this incredible shiver ran through me.

I glanced up at him. He looked amazing in his tux and his face just turned me to jelly. His strong jaw and nose, his soft lips, and his beautiful, gentle eyes, looking at me all concerned and caring, all made me lose my senses for a moment.

'Jake I . . . ' I couldn't believe I was going to tell him, but I knew the words were about to spill out. 'I wanted us to dance together. This stupid dress . . . I wanted you to see me as *me*, not just your little sister's geeky friend. But it all went wrong and here I am looking like a hideous mess and you probably hate me for running out on Sal without telling her . . . '

I looked down at my feet, embarrassed, realising I was going to regret this outburst later. But then Jake reached out and gently touched my face. His fingers curled into a little cradle under my chin, and he turned my head to face him. I thought I might faint. When I looked at his face, his expression wasn't full of pity like I'd expected, his eyes were shining and he was smiling at me.

'Erica, you're not a mess. You look beautiful. You always look beautiful. In fact, weirdly, you're more beautiful than ever right now because your messed-up hair and your streaky face all show you're a loyal friend and you'll always be there for Sal when she needs you. You were worried she was going to get hurt and you stepped in to protect her. That's more important than perfect hair and a lovely dress.' He paused for a second and I think my heart stopped beating too.

'And, I haven't thought of you as just Sal's friend since we were like, fourteen. I was always kind of hoping *you* might think of *me* as more than just Sal's brother . . .' He was half laughing as I tried to get my head round what he was saying. All this time – he'd been waiting for *me* to notice *him*? I couldn't believe it. I didn't want to move or say anything, in case it turned out I'd misheard, or he'd been joking.

I reached up, shaking, to touch his hand, which was still cupping my chin, and our fingers touched. I closed my eyes for a second as he brought his other hand up to my face too. He held my head so softly in his grasp and with his thumbs brushed away what was left of my tears. My skin was dancing. As he moved closer it all felt so unreal, it almost seemed like I was outside my body looking down at myself. He leaned in towards me and his lips just brushed mine. My whole body tingled till I couldn't feel my feet. He softly kissed my cheek, then the other, and then his fingertips stroked down my neck and, slowly, he found my lips again and we kissed. As the cold breeze teased around us, our lips were hot and Jake's kisses were light and then passionate. I was in a new world.

chapter 3

♥

My eyes opened and pinstripes of morning sunlight decorated my bedroom wall through the blinds. Everything seemed the same but I was different. For a split second I imagined the whole of the night before had been a dream. But there was my dress, tattered and torn and blotched with half-mopped food stains, and there was Jake's jacket draped over the hanger.

He'd tried one more time to persuade me to go back in to the dance and, when I'd refused (who could care about a boring dance after a kiss like that?), he texted Sal to let her know I was OK and we walked up to the station to get a cab home. I'd been cold in the taxi, even with my jacket on, and Jake put his round me too. We held hands the whole way home, and I couldn't help staring at our intertwined fingers to reassure myself it was real. Every time I looked round at him, he'd be smiling at me. We paid the driver and Jake had walked me to my door and we'd kissed good-night, the most amazing kiss good-night.

I opened the blinds and stared out into the crisp, autumnal brightness, then jumped back into bed and snuggled up in my duvet, grinning with deep contentment as I remembered my last glimpse of Jake, smiling at me as I'd closed the door.

My phone beeped and I leaped to pick it up and read the text.

Are you free to come over? Nice day for a walk . . . Jxx.

He'd read my mind. I'd got half a word into my reply when there was another bleep.

Hey hon, hope ur ok. Didn't miss much after you left + don't worry, everyone forgot about the incident. Hot choc in town in a bit?

I felt suddenly guilt-ridden. I'd been about to arrange to see Jake, without a thought of turning up on his doorstep like I'd done twenty million times before – only this time I'd be there to see Jake, not Sally. I realised I might not be that impressed if the shoe were on the other foot. Oh God. Like Chandler says in *The One Where Joey Moves Out*: Can: open. Worms: everywhere.

What if Sally didn't approve, or was freaked out? She was the most important person in my life – we'd always been there for each other – but I'd been so swept up in the moment the night before, I hadn't even thought about what my getting together with Jake could mean for

Sally. If things didn't work out with Jake, she'd be angry with me, or angry with him. Even if neither of us did anything wrong, if we split up, there'd be all this awkwardness, I wouldn't be able to go over to hers any more, maybe she wouldn't want to come to mine either or even be friends any more . . . As I got more and more stressed, I realised I had to sort this out right away, so I texted Jake back.

Just made a date with Sal, u free early evening, 5ish?

Jake replied that was cool and he'd come and knock for me, so I replied to Sally: *Genius plan, need to shower, see you outside in 40 mins?*

I was nervous: it was so odd. I was doing the simplest thing I'd done a million times, meeting Sally and driving into town for a drink, and I felt nervous. Outside, Sally was waiting in the car, nodding her head to her terrible dance music, and as she saw me coming she grinned and gave me a cheesy thumbs up. I couldn't help grinning back. I flopped into the passenger seat and slammed the door.

'Hold on to your seatbelt, babe, it's full speed to Coco's for a morning-after, full-fat latte with chocolate syrup!' And with a deft but slightly-too-fast reverse turn, we were off.

We parked by the market square and were walking to the cashpoint when Sally broke the silence.

'You seem quiet; you're not worried about last night, are you? I know it was horrible the way everyone was laughing, but it was knee-jerk, you know. Once the stuff was tidied, everyone was either asking after you, worried if you were OK, or had honestly forgotten about it. Well, everyone except Jo Davy, who was stirring a bit, but then she's just an eternal cow anyway and everyone knows it. We had a really cool time until it happened – try to remember that bit. It wasn't so much fun after you left anyway.'

Bless Sally for bending the truth in the sweetest way to try and make me feel better.

'Oh my God, it was mortifying. I'm sure I'm going to be known as "the-weirdo-girl-who-launched-herself-at-the-buffet-at-the-Hallowe'en-ball" for the rest of my college career. But to hell with it, I can laugh at myself. Anyway, if it gets too bad I can just emigrate. They probably haven't heard about it in Australia yet.' We laughed and linked arms as we walked the last few yards to Coco's.

Coco's is the best little coffee and cake shop in town, and probably the best I've been to anywhere, ever. It's in the more hidden, winding part of town, near the church, and it's shamelessly sweet-toothed – I don't think you can get so much as a cheese sandwich for savoury snacks, but there are freshly baked cakes and biscuits and pastries, and a bigger array of syrups, sauces and spreads than I've seen in any of the big chain coffee places. We pulled open the door and walked up to the counter, enveloped in warm, sweet, milky-smelling air. There was a gentle murmur of chat bubbling under the frothy whirr of the coffee machine.

We were soon sitting down with our drinks and a slab of toffee apple cake to share, and I felt guilty about doing a runner on Sally the night before.

'I'm sorry I didn't come back to the dance last night. Thanks for trying to sort me out, you were great, but I just couldn't face it. I knew I'd need a few hours to relocate my sense of humour, by which time it would have been over anyway . . . '

Sally looked genuinely surprised. 'No, no, don't be silly, I totally get it. Totally. I just feel bad that your night ended the way it did after the work you put into making it such a great time for everyone else.'

'Well, actually . . .' I felt my face burning pink as I said it, 'it didn't turn out to be such a bad night after all.' I couldn't stifle my smile, and Sally's eyebrows shot up mid sip. Taking care not to choke, she put her drink down with a business-like resolution and a quizzical smile that told me I was going nowhere until I'd explained myself fully. This was it, then. No going back.

'Erica Mitford, spill it, right now. What did you do?! Jake texted me to say he was going to bring you right home in a cab. Did you change your mind and go out somewhere?'

'No, no, he did bring me straight home really, it's not like we went out or anything. We walked and talked and stuff, and Jake was really sweet and made me feel better and it was just . . . nice. A really nice end to the evening after all.' I had a lump in my throat thinking about it, I was so happy, and I couldn't suppress my blushes even though I was genuinely worried Sally might not be pleased. I couldn't look her in the face.

'I don't get it, do you mean . . .?' Sally was trying to make sense of my burbling. 'Erica.' She leaned forward to read my face and I looked up, still flushed and nervous. 'You and Jake?'

I couldn't speak. I just nodded and felt so overwhelmed, I had to swallow some tears. What a wuss! But I had to pull myself together; I owed her that.

'Sally, I think he likes me too, we sort of . . . got together – I think.' I shrugged, as if that made it less huge. 'But listen,' I looked her in the eyes and was serious, 'if it's going to be weird for you, we don't have to be . . . I mean I don't want to do anything to complicate things, it's really important to me. I don't even know if it really means anything, it was just a few kisses – argh, I feel so weird telling you!' I clamped my face in my hands and through my fingers searched Sally's stunned expression, which slowly broke into a broad smile and she let out a squeal.

'Erica!' She reached across the table and punched me on the shoulder. 'That's brilliant!'

I didn't want to believe I'd heard right.

'I mean it!' she said. 'I always thought there might be something between you two, but you're both so stubborn and secretive . . . but I think it's great, really. And you worry too much. It'll be fine! We all hang out together anyway, we'll be fine.' She thought for a second and squealed again. 'We can do double dates! It's going to be so much fun!' She grabbed my hands and shook them about in excitement like a little kid. I was so relieved. Then she grimaced. 'I don't know what you wanted to *kiss* him for though, bleugh.' She stuck her tongue out and mimicked sticking her finger down her throat. 'Gross.'

Chapter 4

♥

I was checking the mirror and fiddling with my hair for about the fiftieth time when Jake knocked on the door. My heart was flapping manically like a fish out of water. I ran down the stairs and practically smacked into the front door I was in such a hurry. Smooth.

Jake grinned at me with raised eyebrows as I opened the door.

'I probably would have waited, you know,' he said, 'even if it had taken you, say, a whole minute to get to the door.'

'Shut it.' I blushed and turned towards the kitchen. Mum and Dad were at the table chatting, glasses of wine in hand, amid the warm food smells and pans bubbling on the stove. Mum leaned and peered.

'Well! Hello, Jake.' She started to look worryingly like she might get up, so I hurried through the door, practically knocking Jake off the doorstep.

'Just going for a quick walk, back in a bit!' I called, and shut the door before she could get nosy. She can move pretty fast when she wants gossip.

At the end of the driveway, Jake put his arm round me and pulled me tightly to him. A warm rush ran through me like a head-to-toe smile. I put my arm round his waist and we walked like that, holding on to each other. I looked up at him and he looked back and leaned down and kissed me. It's quite tricky walking like that, though, and the kiss soon dissolved into giggles as we veered dangerously close to a lamppost. It was weird how natural it felt after all the years of being friends, being more. And in the light of day – well, dusk – it felt real. The night before hadn't just been a moment of madness.

'How was Coco's?' Jake asked.

'Good thanks . . .' My nerves returned then, knowing Sally must have mentioned where we were going, because I hadn't. 'Did you see Sally when she got in?'

'Yup. She punched me. She said if I wasn't nice to you she'd strangle me quietly in my sleep.'

'Ha! Cheeky mare!' I giggled. But I couldn't shake my worry. 'She seemed all right though, didn't she? It was such a relief when she seemed happy . . . you know . . . but she's my absolute best friend, well you know that. I'm just so scared things are going to get complicated . . . ' I was burbling.

Jake turned me to face him. We'd reached the gate of the footpath that led through the churchyard, and we were tucked away from the road, standing in the shelter of a little Tudor cottage.

'You worry too much, Erica. Nothing's going to go wrong. I'd never do anything to hurt you, you know.'

'I know,' I said. His sweetness soothed me a little, but I knew deep inside you just can't make promises like that. No one can know what the future holds and people do things all the time to hurt people they love, not deliberately but just because you can't help it sometimes. But Jake rested his hand tenderly in the crook of my neck, his fingers playing in my hair. We kissed again, and I knew he was right. What was the point of worrying about something that hasn't happened?

We walked through the churchyard and up on to the hill, sat on the slightly damp grass and watched the night fall. Somehow I didn't feel the cold. I felt safe and happy and warm as we talked and held hands.

It was nearly eight by the time we got back to our street. I didn't want to let go of him and we just stood for a while, holding on to each other as we talked. He had work the next day. He was taking a year out before university and was working as many shifts as he could in the picture framing and art shop in town to earn cash. But we agreed to meet up in town when he finished at four p.m.

From then on, we saw each other every day, and it was like I had a new home. There was nowhere I felt safer than with Jake. Sometimes I couldn't get my head round how I'd lived my life before, in some sort of black-and-white half-life. Well, I could go on and on about how amazing it was, but basically I'd turned into some soppy girly-girl. And I was loving it too much to be disgusted with myself.

On Bonfire Night, Sally and Mark and Jake and I went to a family fireworks display at the local primary school. I'd had my doubts about the plan – my mum and maybe my dad would be there, and loads of little kids, and their grandparents probably. It wasn't exactly cool. But it turned out to be fun. Mark drove into the village at Sally's command and we did the double-date thing. Sally and Mark bickered jokingly and rolled their eyes a lot at each other while Jake and I quietly held hands as we laughed and chatted with them. At the school there were hot dogs and squares of warm ginger cake. There were marshmallows on sticks you could toast on the bonfire, and really good hot chocolate.

We found a spot to settle against the back wall of the school hall, which faced out on to the field so we had a good view of the fireworks. We all huddled together and the colour-filled, popping and fizzing explosions began.

My pink-gloved hands were clamped cosily around my hot chocolate, but the best feeling was just being there, happily squashed between my best friend and my boyfriend. (Boyfriend! Ha! I was still feeling the disbelieving joy of using the phrase 'my boyfriend'. Even if it was just in my head and I hadn't actually said it out loud to anyone yet, especially Jake!)

I suppose you could say I was a late starter. I'd been out with a couple of boys before GCSEs, but I don't think either lasted more than a week. The first boy, James, was some sort of crazed notch-maker – he got his hands on any girl he could, any time he could. No rules applied. The second boy, Anthony, I'd actually fancied, but it turned out he saw me as little more than a stepping stone, a hand to hold while he worked up the courage to ask out the girl he really liked. Sally. Of course, she sent him packing, like the good friend she was, but it did hurt. Then there was the date with James mark two, just last year, which consisted of sitting on his bed watching a game of rugby on TV and was just about as dull as you could get, datewise. Needless to say there wasn't a second.

I looked up at Jake's face, lit in the bright white of a buzzing Roman candle and he sensed me watching him and looked back. He kissed me on the forehead with a proud smile and none of those other boys mattered any more.

Once the fireworks were over, adults mingled and chatted while the younger kids got tired and ratty, bereft of their sparklers. We decided it was time to make our exit, before our parents could be tempted to come over, emboldened by their mulled wine. We were walking towards the rec, when Mark's mum rang to ask him if he'd come home and babysit his little brother.

'I'll come with you,' said Sally and I felt Jake tense slightly.

'Sally, will you just ring Mum quickly and check she doesn't mind, before you rush off?' Jake's tone was a little exasperated and Sally gave him a look. I felt awkward. I'd seen Jake get fatherly like that with Sally before and I knew she hated him being bossy. I'd always sided with Sally before but now things were different. I could see Jake was just being caring, but it still felt a little like I was betraying Sal, standing by Jake's side, holding his hand while he told her off.

After a quick call to get the OK, Sally and Mark headed back towards the house and Mark's car. Jake and I carried on to the rec and sat together on the round-about, a dark playing-field landscape gently turning around us.

'Your mum seems strict about you going into town in the evenings.' I brought the subject up, because I was still thinking about his insistence on Sally making that phone call.

'Actually, she's pretty cool about not making rules,' Jake replied. 'But I know she worries when she doesn't know what we're doing. I think it's worse because Dad's away so much and when she's on her own she worries more, not having the company to take her mind off it.' He paused, but I didn't say anything, I sensed there was more he wanted to say.

'And I worry when she worries. The last thing she needs is to be stressing about us.'

Jake and Sally's mum, Steph, had been diagnosed with breast cancer last year. I remember Sally having a few days off school – she'd been devastated. But they'd found it early, and she'd had a successful operation. She'd been put through a course of chemotherapy and I know Sally found that hard because Steph was ill with it, and of course she lost her hair and everything, so the physical evidence she was ill was right there to be seen. But once the chemo was finished and Steph's hair grew back – she actually looked great with that pixie-short hair. Good cheekbones, Mum said, and Sally soon seemed to be back to her bubbly self.

'I'm actually having a good year,' Jake admitted. 'Working in the shop, making a bit of money. I get a discount on materials, which is great – I can really work on my portfolio . . .' Jake reached for my hand. ' . . . and of course, now, I've had the chance to get to know you better . . . ' He smiled and squeezed my fingers and I smiled back and went pink. 'But the real reason I put off uni was to look out for Mum, so that's what I'm doing. I think Sally forgets sometimes, that's all.'

I realised then that Jake had shouldered all this responsibility. He was stoic and quiet about it, but his dad, Simon, worked so hard and was away so often, he'd sort of become the man of the house. I'd thought of Steph's illness as being over, because that seemed to be how Sally saw it, but of course you have to wait years to get an official all-clear after cancer, and Steph was still having to go for a lot of regular check-ups, which I imagined could be nerve-racking, and it was Jake who drove with her to the hospital.

It was my turn to squeeze Jake's hand, to try to tell him I finally understood why he had to be bossy, to try to tell him that he didn't have to be strong all the time, that I was there for him whenever he needed me. And I think he understood, because he leaned his head on my shoulder and closed his eyes. I stroked his hair and for

the first time felt that maybe *I* could make *him* feel safe
as well as the other way round.

Chapter 5

Jake laughed at me when I opened the door. We were going for a walk and it was cold.

'What?' I asked indignantly, but clearly he was laughing at my woolly hat with its dangly ear-flaps. I loved that hat. It wasn't like I hadn't checked the mirror but I thought it looked kind of funky. Obviously I was horribly, horribly wrong. I'm the first to admit I embrace my inner geek. But sometimes I give her a bit too much in the way of decision-making power. I felt my face flush hot red and reached up to pull off the offending item.

'No!' Jake reached out, grabbed me round the waist and pulled me outside. 'Leave it on. You look cute.' He kissed me right on the hat and then grabbed the braided wool that dangled from the ear-flaps and yanked down on them, laughing again.

'Why are you laughing then?' I whined. 'Jake, I'm not going out if I look like an idiot!'

'No, no you don't, honestly.' Jake was more earnest

now but still a bit smirky and I didn't know whether to trust him or not. I stood sulking, with my hands on my hips. 'Erica, you don't look like an idiot, you look sweet and lovely. Now stop sulking and come on.' He reached behind me and pulled the front door shut, then grinned naughtily and pinned me against it. He held on to the wool braids again with one hand and pushed at my pouting bottom lip with an already freezing thumb. Then he bent down and kissed me insistently. He still made my feet tingle when he kissed me like that – I don't know how he was so strong and so soft at once.

I screwed up my face at him when he released me, and stuck my tongue out. But I couldn't help smiling too and let him pull me by the hand away from the house. It had been raining, but the sun was out brightly and there was that beautiful combination of winter and summer again. We walked quietly, hand in hand, and I couldn't help thinking out loud, 'I love it when it's sunny and there're puddles. It's like there are little bits of sky all over again, shining up at you from the grey of the pavement.'

Jake guffawed loudly, but before I could curse myself for saying what was in my head, he literally swept me off my feet, picking me up and spinning me round. 'You're so weird!' He said it in a way I knew was supposed to be a compliment. 'I love that you can find joy in puddles.'

I loved that I could totally be me with him and he made me feel good about it.

When we got back, I asked if he wanted to come over to mine, but he narrowed his eyes at me. 'You said you had a film essay to write.'

Darn. What did I have to mention that for?

'I do. But it's not due till Wednesday . . .' I gave him my best puppy dog look.

'I think you should get some of it done at least. I don't want to be the reason you're not doing your work, Erica. Just do a couple of hours on it and give me a call then, OK?' Sometimes I hated how right Jake was all the time. We'd soon worked out a system where I'd take textbooks round and sit at Jake's desk in his room and write my essays on his computer while he drew me. He didn't get a chance to draw life models often like I did at my A-level art classes, and I said I didn't mind him using me for practice – as long as the drawings were flattering! So sometimes he'd mess about and draw me with wings or a halo, or long flowing hair down to my knees, like a Botticelli. But with more clothes on, obviously. He was really talented. I could draw and paint, as in I could get perspective right and make things look reasonably like they did in real life. But Jake had the passion and creativity to go beyond real life and his work had this dream-like, fantasy quality – even his doodles. He'd fill pages of his sketchbook with these strange and beautiful, organic, tangled designs.

When we'd have a tea break, if Sally was around, she would sit on Jake's bedroom floor for half an hour, or we'd hang out in the kitchen and all chat about TV or movies, our college mates or people in the village (everyone knows your business when you live in a village, so you either have to cut yourself off and become a hermit, or just embrace it and join in with the gossip culture). In the evenings Mark would come over and we'd watch movies in Sally's room, or we'd meet up with him in town and go to the cinema, go bowling or just grab a pizza.

But by the end of November, more and more it was just Jake and me. It was really nice to spend time together, just the two of us, but I started to worry that we were leaving Sally out, or even that she was backing off to give us space because she thought that was what we wanted.

One Saturday, I was sitting in my room at my sewing machine, experimenting with the embroidery settings, because I'd decided to sew one of Jake's designs on to a T-shirt for him for his birthday the following weekend and I had a couple of hours before I was supposed to meet Sally and Mark in town. We were going to pick up Jake from swimming and get the train into Cambridge for a gig Jake's mate's band were playing at this Arts Café place. I was just thinking about what I was going to wear and how much I was looking forward to a good night out for the four of us, when my phone beeped.

So sorry guys, M and I can't make 2nite. Explain later. U 2 have fun tho. Sx

I wanted to call her straight back to find out what was going on, and see if I could persuade her to change her mind, but the text seemed odd, like she couldn't talk right then. Jake would probably be in the pool already so I couldn't call him and talk about it either. All I could do was text her back saying I hoped she was OK and to call me when she could. Then I messaged Jake that I'd still meet him at the sports centre and we could walk to the station together, just us two again.

At about seven p.m. Mum dropped me there and offered to take Jake's sports bag home so he didn't have to lug it around all night. He was chuffed at that, and I felt quite pleased too, that Mum would think of it; she obviously trusted Jake to look after me on a night out, but this showed maybe she really liked him too and was happy we were together. Maybe I read too much into it, it wouldn't be the first time – I'm a self-confessed overthinker. I just enjoyed that my parents seemed to treat us like grown-ups.

Anyway, the reason I remember the walk to the station that evening so well, is that when we were halfway there, Jake's friend from the band called to check if we still needed names on the guest list.

'Hello, mate,' Jake replied. 'Ah, sorry, yeah, actually we're two now, not four. My sister's being flaky, but me and my girlfriend are on our way now, so just me plus one would be awesome . . . Thanks, mate . . . Erm, about eight-thirty, what time you on? Cool, yeah see you in a bit. Bye.'

Girlfriend! He used the G-word! Oh, I know it's stupid. It wasn't like I didn't know we were officially going out, but it was the first time he'd said it out loud in front of me and hearing it just felt good. I was grinning into my scarf as Jake stuffed his phone back in his pocket.

'What are you giggling at?' he asked.

'Oh, nothing.'

It was a great night, the band were awesome, Jake's friends were chatty with me and Jake stayed close to me most of the night, as if he was making sure I didn't feel shy on my own. But, looking back, I think that's when things started to change with Sally. She started spending more time in town and I saw less of her. Jake and I talked about it on the train home that night and he shrugged off my worries like he always managed to do. He said Sal was having problems with her grades in politics, and was spending a lot of time studying with this girl from her class, May, and had started staying over sometimes. I'd met May a couple of times and she seemed nice enough, although some of her friends I wasn't so sure about. Still, Jake was usually pretty protective of his sister, so I figured if he wasn't worried, I shouldn't be either.

Then came the distractions of December. Mum still liked to buy me an Advent calendar and for us to decorate the tree together, so I spent much of the evening on Friday 1st doing that (rock and roll, eh?) but it also meant I could finish Jake's T-shirt, because in the morning I wanted to pop into town and get a CD too, so I could go round with all his birthday presents in the afternoon.

The door to Seedies pinged as I pushed it open, and, over the top of the rock section, I spied Mark. I walked round to say hi.

'Mark. What an earth are you doing in *easy listening*?' I said loudly. He swung round and looked only slightly embarrassed.

'Oh, it's my mum's birthday on Monday, she loves rubbish like this. How are you?' He seemed a bit distracted, but I was in a happy, chatty mood so I rambled on.

'I'm good. Hey, that's weird – it's Jake's birthday today as well. I don't know why people have to have birthdays in December, as if it's not hassle enough having to think about everyone's Christmas presents too . . . '

Mark nodded. 'That's right, yeah, I forgot that. You doing anything nice?'

'We're just going for a curry I think, nothing too exciting – you and Sal are welcome to come, I haven't seen you guys for ages.'

Mark turned to face me properly then. He looked confused, and then sort of sad. He glanced down at his feet and sheepishly back up at me through his dark brows.

'Umm. I guess not, or you'd know . . . Sally and I split up. Actually more than a week ago now. I thought you'd have heard, sorry.'

I was stunned and didn't know what to say for a second. He was right, I should have known. But I didn't, and finally it brought home to me how distant Sally and I must have been becoming.

'Oh. Sorry Mark, how embarrassing, I didn't know. I haven't spoken to Sally in a while, college stuff . . . but look, that's no reason you shouldn't come out later if you fancy it – I think a group of us are going. I don't even know if Sally will be there, she's barely been around . . .'

'Thanks, Erica. Actually, I have to go to this family thing tonight anyway – some theatre event, I'm sure it'll be great.' He smiled sarcastically and then backed towards the till, gesturing with the CD in his hand. 'I'd better get this and make a move. Thanks though. Have fun tonight.'

I could have cried. What was going on? Just a couple of months before, it would have been unthinkable that something this huge could happen in Sally's life without her telling me. I thought about that text she'd sent me and wondered how long she had been planning to avoid coming to the gig. I didn't know what to think. Should I be kicking myself for doing something wrong and losing her, or for being too wrapped up in Jake to even know what was happening? Or should I be upset or angry with her because she'd probably confided in May instead of me, and because she'd practically been lying to us?

Seeing Jake's face when he opened his presents cheered me up.

'Erica, it's amazing. Perfect, thank you,' he said when he saw his design on the T-shirt. He hugged me tightly and kissed me all over my face, which made me laugh. But before long I had to bring up that I'd seen Mark, and Jake was stumped too, and couldn't understand why we hadn't heard. But he just told me again that Sally had seemed preoccupied with work and maybe she'd decided to put her social life on hold while she sorted her grades out.

I knew Sally was ambitious about being a lawyer, but I thought about splitting with Jake, the best thing in my life, for the sake of grades, and it didn't make any sense to me. I wondered if he knew more than I did and I was reading too much into it, or if he was in denial of parental proportions. But there wasn't any point spoiling the evening arguing about it. I'd just have to speak to Sally.

So the next night, when Mum and Dad were watching a movie after dinner, I slipped into the dining room and turned on the computer. Just a couple of weeks before, I wouldn't have thought of emailing Sally. If I'd wanted to speak to her I'd have just picked up the phone. But everything was odd. I was worried about her, but I felt frozen out and couldn't tell her what I was feeling over the phone. Somehow it would have been hard, and, weirdest of all, I think I'd have felt I was invading her privacy. So I clicked 'Compose Mail' and wrote:

My Best Friend's Brother

Hey stranger. Hope you're OK, feel like I
haven't seen you in for ever. What you doing
next Saturday? Christmas is looming and I think
some shopping is in order – fancy a trip to
London? We could make a day of it, grab some
lunch and have a proper catch up. Dad said he'd
drop us at the station and even shout us the
train tickets – guess it's got to the stage
where he'll actually pay money to get rid of
me!! Take advantage, I say. Please say yes.

xxxE

Chapter 6

♥

In the morning there was a reply waiting in my inbox.

I was elated that her reply was chatty and normal – and that she'd said yes. But I wasn't sure what I was going to do about broaching the subject of her and Mark. Part of me thought I should wait for the right moment, and not spoil the day, but I also knew I'd be on edge wanting to ask her.

When Saturday came and we were on the platform at the train station, arms linked, braced against the cold, everything felt familiar again and it seemed right to bring it up. I just tried to keep it chatty.

'I bumped into Mark last weekend in Seedies making out he was buying his mum this cheesy coffee table jazz CD, although I'm sure he was eyeing it up for himself.'

I waited for a reaction, but Sally buried her nose

further into her scarf and scuffed her heels sheepishly on the wet ground. The Sally I knew would give in with a little push, so I tried again. 'How come you didn't tell me?' I asked, as gently as I could.

'Oh, there was nothing to tell really.' She sounded sad but philosophical. 'We were seeing each other out of habit as much as really wanting to. We grew apart, you know, all that old stuff. We weren't like you and Jake. I'm OK, honestly, otherwise I would have told you.'

I wasn't sure.

'I don't get it, you seemed happy still, when you were together.' I felt a bit odd the way she'd mentioned me and Jake – the words sounded like they should have been a compliment, but her tone was strained, almost as if she was blaming us or being aggressive. 'But if you're sure you're OK . . . ?'

'Really.' Sally turned to look me in the eye. 'Of course I feel a bit sad, but that's all. It's for the best, I'll be fine, really.'

And that was that. I was relieved. It didn't seem so strange after all that she hadn't mentioned it. I figured it wasn't the sort of thing you'd just text or call to say out of the blue unless you needed to talk, and she seemed to be dealing with it. I did feel a certain loss that she could cope without me though, we'd always gone through these things together. I wondered if it was just that we were getting older.

On the train, we got busy talking shopping and budgets, looking at our *A to Z* and planning the day. Sally suggested heading to St Christopher's Place for lunch and popping into her dad's office to see if he was around. He worked most Saturdays.

'It's really near Selfridges, which we'd want to go to anyway, then maybe he'll buy us lunch and we can save some cash,' she grinned at me. I agreed, thinking for a moment that it would have been nice not to have to be on best lunch-with-the-parents behaviour but hey, why say no to a free meal?

The morning was fun, if a bit exhausting with all the crowds to struggle through, but we were doing well and were slowly becoming laden with all our purchases. By one p.m. we were ready for a rest and some nourishment. We headed to Sally's dad's office but, when the receptionist rang up to his desk, a colleague told her he'd gone out already. We spotted a café just across the street as we headed back out through the revolving doors, and Sally suggested we got some drinks and sat by the window, so we could keep an eye out in case he came back in the next fifteen minutes. I knew she was skint but it did seem a bit odd that she was so intent on seeing him, when presumably he'd be back at home that night anyway.

She must have sensed my hesitation because then she said, 'It just seems a shame to come up here and not say hi – we'd be sitting in a café anyway, so what's the difference?' She'd obviously made up her mind and it didn't really matter to me, so I went along with it.

Well, we did see him come back to the office. Sally was telling me about why Jade Jackson hadn't been at May's party the previous weekend. Nadine had basically decided Jade was after her boyfriend, Max, because she'd been seen speaking to him (gasp) at the football in the morning and, drama queen that she was, she'd blown it up into this huge thing and, because May was Nadine's new best friend, she'd sided with her and started freezing Jade out. Sally was just describing how she found Jade crying in the toilets after law when I saw Sally's dad. Without giving myself time to think, I interrupted Sally and pointed over.

I've wondered so many times since, how things could have been different if I'd kept quiet and waited just a minute, just long enough to see what was happening before I made Sally look . . . by the time she turned round, you could see the woman he was talking to wasn't an ordinary colleague or client. They were holding hands. She was gazing up at him, smiling. As they stopped in a darkened doorway not five metres from the office, they pulled back into the shadow, although not so far that you couldn't see his arm encircle her waist as she tilted her head up towards him and they kissed.

Sally was perfectly still, fingertips still clasping the yellow and white straw she'd been stabbing at the ice in her Diet Coke with, but staring. It may have been the grey winter light seeping through the window, but her face seemed ashen.

For a moment I was just as paralysed. I couldn't do anything but watch as Sally glared, as the couple said goodbye and walked their separate ways, her dad glancing around as he slipped back through those glass doors and disappeared into a lift. Sally didn't speak, so I did. Idiotic nonsense spilled out of my mouth as I tried to second-guess what she was thinking.

'Maybe she's a client. He has to help people who have been through really horrible things a lot, doesn't he? Maybe he was comforting her – or if she's a close colleague and they're good friends but she's having a hard time or something – maybe she's getting fired or something and they're saying goodbye . . . ' But that hadn't been a goodbye kiss or a comforting kiss, and she hadn't looked in the least bit upset. Neither of them had.

'Don't jump to conclusions, Sal. How about we go in, say hello, mention that we saw her – he can explain who she was . . . '

I could see the tears in Sally's eyes and I could see she was swallowing hard against her emotions. Without warning she jumped up, her chair legs screeching against the floor tiles, grabbed her bag and ran out of the café. She wasn't stopping. In a panic, I scrabbled to get all my stuff, and the shopping bag Sally had left under the table, remembered we hadn't paid for our drinks, searched desperately through my pockets for a tatty fiver which I waved at the woman behind the counter and threw on to the table before I clumsily pulled the door open and ran after her, coat and scarf trailing on the ground, not a spare hand to put them on despite the cold. I saw Sally disappear down a narrow side street on the other side of the square, leading back into the throng of stressed shoppers, and cursed under my breath as I lolloped after her as fast as I could.

Back on Oxford Street though, I lost her in the crowd. Scanning up and down the street, trying to work out which way she'd gone, I tried to cross the pavement for a better view, pushing through tutting, shoving currents of people. Just as tears of frustration were pricking my eyes, a bus slowed as it passed me and pulled in at the next stop. Thank goodness I followed it with my eyes, because then I saw Sally in the queue of people squashing to get on. I ran, and reached her just as she was getting to the doors.

'Sally! Wait, please . . .' was all I could say as I tried breathlessly to reach out to her, shopping bags swinging wildly. I was crying. Guilty-faced, she moved away from the bus towards me and gave in to tears too. Seeing a stone bench a few steps away, I took the chance to grab a space to rest, released the bags, beckoned to Sally, and we hugged.

We sat, waiting for the next bus, both knowing it was time to go home. And Sally apologised.

'I'm sorry, Erica. I shouldn't have run off like that.'

'It's OK,' I reassured her. 'It was a shock to see that, I guess, but there could be an explanation you know.'

Sally shook her head. 'To be honest, it wasn't that much of a shock.' She waited for the confusion to register on my face. 'I've sort of known for a while Dad was up to something. It's part of the reason I wanted to surprise him. I'd imagined seeing exactly what we saw, and that I'd confront him with the proof once I had it. But when it really happened it hit me harder than I thought and I was just too weak and pathetic and scared to go and shout at him like I'd thought I would.'

I remembered all Jake had told me about what his mum had been through with her illness and I was angry with Sally's dad for doing this after everything else the family had had to cope with. He deserved to be shouted at.

'We could still go back you know, or we could wait, and go and meet him when he's done for the day. You could still tell him everything you need to tell him – you must be so angry, Sal, I'm sorry.'

'You know, I'm really not as angry as I thought I'd be. More sad, and scared. I wouldn't know what to do if he left, Erica. It can't happen – I have to fix it.'

I was confused by what was going on in her head, but then I saw the bus coming and we had to make a decision. 'Do you want to stay? Or go home?' I asked Sally. She looked so dejected and I was helpless to make her feel better.

'Let's go. I think that's enough drama for one day, don't you?' She smiled weakly and we bundled on the bus just as half-hearted rain started spitting at the windows. We climbed up to the top deck and for a while we just watched, silently, as the streets swarmed with the stressed, frowning people amongst all the over-cheery Christmas glitz below us.

On the train, I admit I pushed Sally to talk a bit more. She seemed lost inside herself, but I needed to know what she was thinking. I used to be able to guess pretty well, but that had changed.

'Are you going to tell your mum?' I asked.

'God, no!' Sally seemed almost angry, and I shrank back a little. She reached for my hand and spoke in an urgent whisper: 'Listen, Erica, this is a secret, OK? I know I can trust you, but you have to know how important this is – no one needs to know about what we saw until I've found out exactly what's happening. And, listen, you can't talk to Jake about this, OK?'

I couldn't understand what she was planning – maybe it was just too hard for her to admit what she'd seen and now she was backtracking.

'But Sal, he's the one person you could really talk to about it, who'd understand, and knows your parents – you could decide what to do together – otherwise you're going through it all alone . . . '

She let go of my hand and held her face in frustration. 'We wouldn't decide together, though, would we? You know what Jake's like – he always has an idea about what's right and he thinks he knows better than anyone. Besides, I know exactly what he'd want to do: he'd go straight to Mum. Sometimes I think he hates Dad, that he wants him gone – but that's fine for him, he's Mum's favourite anyway and he doesn't care what I'd feel like . . . '

'Of course he cares!' She was being so unfair to Jake. 'He'll listen if you just explain to him what you're feeling.'

Sally gasped back a sob then, and I felt confused and clueless. 'Erica, listen to me, OK? I mean this. Jake's different with you . . . oh, never mind. I know you're looking out for me, but this is not your stuff – I mean, it's my family and I know you want to help but you can't understand it, not really. What happened today is my secret, OK, it's not yours to tell Jake – you CANNOT tell him, OK?'

I nodded and mumbled an 'of course' or two. I told her I'd do whatever she wanted, but I was shocked by the way she was about it all. I worried how I'd be with Jake that evening without talking about it. But I couldn't even begin, back then, to imagine how hard it was going to be.

Chapter 7

When Jake came to the door that night, I hugged him hard, burrowing my face in his shoulder.

'You all right?' He looked a bit bemused and stroked away the hair from my face when I finally let him go.

'Yeah.' I smiled and we headed up to my room. 'I'm just glad to see you.'

'How was shopping?' Jake dropped himself on to my bed and I returned to my carefully arranged present-wrapping station on the floor.

'Oh, fine,' I said with a little sigh that maybe wasn't too discreet now I think about it.

'Are you sure?' he persisted. 'Did you and Sal have an argument? She was being moody in her room when I got in and you seem a bit weird too.'

Oops.

'No, no, I'm fine – it was good.' I desperately hoped I wasn't blushing. (Can you take lying classes? If not, they should start doing them. I could really do with better skills in that department.) 'It was just kind of exhausting, you know how the shops can be in London on a Saturday. Anyway, it's a girl's privilege to be moody in her room sometimes.' I smiled my best cheeky smile at him to distract him from the subject. 'She probably had wrapping to do too, with all the stuff we got today. Now, be good while I finish these.' I got away with it I think.

I'd hidden Jake's presents away and had a few family ones to wrap before I could tick them all off my list. I loved the excitement of wrapping everyone's presents, making them look nice and imagining them in their little piles under the tree. I'd just wrapped a liquid eyeliner pen for Tamara and was tying ribbon round it as Jake watched. I reached for the scissors and pulled the flat of the ribbon along the blade so it curled up into a little flounce.

'Are you going to do that with every single teeny tiny little present?' Jake was smirking at me again and I plonked the scissors down in a mock huff.

'Half the fun of Christmas is planning your present-wrapping colour scheme and accessories!' Smirk. 'It's just as important to give as receive, Jake Earley.' I picked the scissors back up and brandished them at him. 'And frankly, if you're not wrapping with love, you're missing out.' I proudly curled the other end of the ribbon and started on the next gift.

He leaned over and ruffled my hair in a deliberately patronising way and then switched on the TV and waited obediently while I finished, but by the time I'd wrapped my last one, a Brahms CD for Dad, he was fast asleep.

I packed up my bows and tags as quietly as I could and moved over to sit by the bed where I could see the TV. But if I'm honest I was more interested in watching Jake's perfect, sleeping face. I think I could have happily just watched him be still for a full half-hour. If I had somehow been able to go back in time to visit my September self, and describe this scene to her, she would never have believed it. Jake was mine, and there he was, dozing comfortably *in my bedroom, on my bed!*

The next day, Tamara arrived home for the holiday and, for all the worrying I'd done about being back in baby-of-the-family mode, it was actually nice to be the little sister again. It was good to sit around the dinner table, all four of us together. Obviously I'd told her about Jake and me and it was embarrassing when he came over and she tousled his hair and winked at him like he was a cheeky toddler. But I knew she approved, and that it was affectionate, so I let her off.

Term finished on December 20th and Jake called that night when he got in from work.

'Wanna come over?' I asked.

'Why don't you come to me for a change?' Jake said. 'I'm knackered. And I'm sure your mum and dad are getting sick of me turning up on your doorstep.'

He had a point. I'd been finding excuses not to go over there. Things had been weird between Sally and me. When we had coffee in the canteen at break, or saw each other at lunch, we'd make small talk, almost like strangers. We were avoiding the real subject. She seemed happier when she was with May and Nadine. So, more and more, I'd sit with Ruth and Charlotte and leave them to it. I was nervous of what it would be like if we saw each other in her house. I couldn't predict how it would be. But I knew it would probably be obvious to Jake something was different. I clearly wasn't getting away with avoiding it any longer, though. I had to risk it, because if I started refusing to go over there without saying why, that would definitely give the game away anyway. I bit my lip.

'OK, sure. I'll come to you. See you in a bit.'

It was noisy when I got there and I had to knock a few times. Steph answered the door eventually, with a dripping whisk in her hand and flour in her eyebrow.

'Hi, Erica. Sorry love, the kiddies are having a bit of a music war up there, I think! Go on up.'

I smiled thanks as she rushed back to her cooking and I braved the stairs. I could just about hear Sally humming along to The Killers as I crept past her room. Then, as I moved closer to Jake's slightly open door, there was a horrible moment of a morphing clash of guitars and drums and then I was listening to Muse.

'Oh! Hey gorgeous. You snuck in quietly.' Jake looked up from his sketchpad as I peered through the door. He beckoned for me to come in. 'I left my door open so I'd hear you knock, but . . . ' He jumped up, charcoal-blackened hands held up in the air, and kissed me quickly before heading out on to the landing. 'I'll just wash these.' I saw Sally dart out of her bedroom and into the bathroom at lightning speed before Jake could get there, and I retreated further back into the room. 'Nice! I'll use the kitchen sink then, shall I?' I heard Jake shout through the door.

A minute and a half later I heard Sally click off the bathroom light and pass Jake on the stairs.

'Erica's here,' Jake said.

'Kind of in a hurry, bro, you'll have to say hi for me.'

When I heard the door slam I didn't know whether to

feel relieved she'd gone, or hurt that she couldn't spare a minute to say hi. Still, I suppose I could have knocked on my way in instead of running straight to Jake's room, if I wasn't such a scaredy-cat.

'Sally says hi,' said Jake as he came back into the room. I nodded but didn't say anything. I felt this wave of sadness hit me and had to grit my teeth against crying. Of course Jake noticed.

'There's something going on with you two, isn't there? What is it?' He sat down close to me and put his arm round my waist. (Why did he have to be so perceptive? I thought men were supposed to be dunces about emotional girl-stuff.) I held on to him tightly and fought back tears. I wanted to tell him everything, so badly. We told each other our secrets. The reason I was so happy when we were together was that we could be totally open and relaxed. I'd never held anything back before and it felt wrong. It felt painful, like I was betraying myself as well as him. I opened my mouth to speak – after this latest snub from Sally I was so close to spilling the whole story. But I didn't.

'Oh, I'm just being silly.' I sniffed. 'Sorry.' I sat up straighter. Seeing Jake's concerned face, I couldn't help putting a hand up to his cheek and giving him a kiss. 'Sally's just spending a lot of time with May and Nadine these days and I'm not really friendly with them so it means we're apart a lot. It's just taking a bit of getting used to, that's all. It's fine.'

Jake seemed satisfied with my answer and pouted in sympathy with me. 'Well, I'm not really friendly with May and Nadine either, so you've always got me.' He gave me a cheesy-grin-and-eyebrow-wiggle double-whammy and got another kiss in return.

Relatives descended on both the Mitford and Earley households on Christmas Eve, and 'family time' meant I wouldn't see Jake for a couple of days – thank the Lord for mobile phones.

On Christmas morning I woke to feel a heavy rustling as I moved my feet. In half sleep, I felt like a little kid again, waking to find a stocking full of presents on top of the covers at the end of the bed, weighing down deliciously on my toes. As I came round properly I looked down – and it was real. There really was a stocking there. Not the hand-knitted Christmas stocking of my childhood though, a red felt one with a proper white-fluff-trimmed top. There was no mistaking it.

Had Mum gone crazy? We hadn't had these since I was twelve. I wondered if she had that middle-aged offspring-flying-the-nest angst thing my dad joked about when Tamara went off to uni. But I knew Mum wasn't that type. Then for a minute I even suspected Tamara too, thinking maybe she'd gone soft, but that didn't seem likely either. So I figured, since my limbs had woken up by this point, there was only one way to get to the bottom of this. Allowing myself some childlike Christmas glee, I reached down, grabbed the stocking and delved in.

The first present was a flat little box about the size of my palm, wrapped in silver and with curly gold ribbon around it. I looked at the tag. It was from Jake! How had he got this stocking on my bed? He'd either colluded with Mum, or Dad was going to have something to say about him sneaking into my room in the night.

For Erica,

This one's from the day we walked through the churchyard and you spotted this and said you liked it because it reminded you of my drawings.

Christmas kisses, Jake.

Later, in a different pen, he'd added at the bottom: *(wrapped with love).*

I laughed out loud. Then I practically cried at the romance of it, looking at all the other little presents, each with their careful curly ribbons and tags. I opened the one I was holding and found the brooch that had been sitting in a shop window as we'd walked past it that day I remembered well. I still loved it. It was plain silver but with an intricate, twirly design.

It was like Jake had bought all these little presents whenever he'd seen anything he thought I'd like and saved them all up just for this occasion. They all had notes attached: the lip balm he knew was my favourite, *To keep you in good kissing order*; some sparkly threads and beads *To make your clever girl-things with*; and my favourite fancy chocolate *'Cos I know you can't last the day without your sugar fix*. And all of them, *(wrapped with love)*.

I hadn't thought it possible that I could love Jake more, but I was aching with the strength of it then. I wanted to run up the street and find him and hold him. I grabbed my phone and turned it on, impatiently waiting for it to be ready. I opened a new message and wrote: *I love my presents. I love you. Thank you. Merry Christmas. Xxxxxxx.*

My finger hovered over the 'Send' button for a moment. It was quite scary – we hadn't said it before, the 'love' thing, but it was what I was feeling and I wanted him to know it. So I pressed.

A tense nine minutes later, there was a bleep.

I love mine too. And I love you too. And Merry Christmas too. Xxxx.

I was soooo happy I can't describe it. I hugged my duvet round me and just stared at that message, practically stroking the phone, for who knows how long, until Tamara barged in with barely so much as two seconds' warning. Mum had told her about helping sneak the stocking into my room and so of course she came straight up to be nosy.

In the afternoon I even got a text from Sally, just saying Happy Christmas. She probably sent it out to her whole phonebook, but I took it as a sign she didn't hate me at least. I texted back and said I hoped to see her soon.

Boxing Day passed in a food-filled blur and, the day after that, Mum and Dad went back to work and Christmas started to feel over, but I had buckets of chocolates and a brand new DVD from my cousin, so I texted Sally and Jake to see if they wanted to come over. Tam seemed up for watching it so I figured it'd be like old times if Sally and Jake came over and we could all have a catch-up and hang out. When Jake replied: *Be over in 15 xx* and I didn't hear back from Sally, I assumed he meant both of them, I don't know why. But when I opened the door to him, he was alone. Sally had gone to May's. And in the end Tam went out to the sales, so it ended up just Jake and me. It was lovely, curled up on the sofa together with the house to ourselves, but it just wasn't the reunion I'd imagined.

<h1 style="text-align:center">chapter 8</h1>

I was really excited about New Year's Eve. Jake's mate Rich was having a party in the village, with loads of people staying, so it turned out a lot of our friends from town were coming over to us for a change and we wouldn't have to worry about lifts – we could just wander up the road, see friends and have a drink, and not have to worry about how much money the cab home would cost. And Sally was coming. She'd actually left me a really sweet voicemail saying she hoped I was going and that it would be lovely to see me properly finally. We'd arranged that I'd go over to her place and we'd get ready together.

I turned up ridiculously early at about six p.m. feeling quite nervous. But Sally answered the door with a big hug, got us drinks and snacks and then rushed me upstairs to help her choose what to wear. When Jake knocked she said it was girls only, just for an hour, and he should 'go play with his toys' until we were beautified. We talked about who was coming to the party, and whether Rich's ex and his new girlfriend would be there, and whether I should wear my hair up or down – it felt so like old times that, for a while, I forgot all that had happened in the past few weeks.

I was so happy walking up the road to Rich's, my right arm linked through Jake's and my left through Sally's. We were all shivering, and although it was freezing I knew, for me, it was partly the anticipation of the night ahead that was making me trembly. After a classic family Christmas indoors it'd be great to catch up with everyone – and dance. Sally must have read my mind, because it suddenly occurred to her to ask about the music.

'Hey Jake, is Rich doing his DJ thing tonight?' she tried to sound nonchalant but there was an obvious tinge of concern in her voice, although I didn't think Jake had cottoned on.

'No, there's quite a lot of people coming and I think he was worried about his decks getting damaged so I think he's just going to plug people's MP3 players straight into the stereo.'

'Oh, that's good,' Sally and I said at exactly the same time, with such blatant relief in our voices that we couldn't help laughing. Jake looked at us though mock-cross eyebrows.

'You women are so evil! He only got his decks in

September. I think he's pretty good, considering.'

'Considering his horrible, horrible taste in music, you mean?' Sally grinned, and I nudged her with another giggle.

We were quite early and there must have been less than ten people when we got there, I think. I managed to calm Sally's impatience by pointing out we had our run of the buffet, which was actually quite impressive, and there was a pretty steady stream of people arriving, so the place was bustling before we knew it.

Rich and his brother James had cleared a lot of furniture out of their massive living room and, once someone had swapped their iPod in for Rich's, loads of people were dancing. Jake and I danced a couple of times, but I was mostly dancing with the girls and catching up with school friends in the kitchen. We had such a good time I'd barely noticed how late it was, but at five to midnight the music went off and we put the TV on, ready to watch Big Ben.

When the chimes were about to start, I scanned the room for Jake but within seconds I felt his arm slip round my waist as he came through from the kitchen behind me. I smiled over my shoulder at him and leaned into him, feeling complete and happy and hopeful. At the twelfth chime, everyone cheered. Party poppers went off and people jumped up and down, hugging each other and shouting 'Happy New Year!'

Jake and I kissed and he looked into my eyes and whispered, 'Happy New Year, gorgeous.' As I grinned at him, Sally came over and hugged us in a group embrace and kissed us both. Then Ruth practically ran into me out of nowhere and enveloped me in a bear hug. While Jake did a lot of manly shoulder slapping with the boys, the music came back on and the shouts died back down into general party noise. That's when I spotted Sally, bundling out of the door with Ed, Munch, Nadine, May and some of their friends I didn't recognise, who looked quite a bit older.

I stepped into Rich's path as he came over towards the kitchen.

'Where are that lot going?' I tried not to sound cross.

'Who?' he shouted over the music.

'Nadine and Munch and that lot.' I nodded towards the door.

'Oh, they're going on to some club in town, I think.' I followed as he pushed through to the kitchen. 'Davy said he reckoned some mate of his who works there'll be able to sneak them in for free now it's gone midnight. Don't reckon it'll be much good though now, just the drunken dregs left, if you know what I mean. You're better off staying here and helping me get through the rest of these sausage rolls – reckon there's only about twenty million left now!' His voice tailed off as his head disappeared into the fridge for another drink.

He sounded like he thought I was jealous and wanted to go to the club. All I actually wanted was for Sally to come back. I didn't trust that lot. Ed and Munch always seemed like they were chasing trouble and, although May was nice when she was on her own, Nadine was a drama junkie. Like all that business with Jade, she never seemed bothered about other people's feelings; she seemed to stir things up deliberately just to create excitement for herself. I felt riled up and had to reason with myself. Maybe I was being unfair, I didn't really know them. But I just couldn't help feeling uncomfortable thinking Sally was out with them. Then it occurred to me, all the time Sally had spent with May lately, this was probably a regular thing – and Sally had seemed fine tonight so it obviously wasn't doing her any harm. What right did I have to get Mumsy about it now, just because I'd happened to see them leaving? Argh. That was the worst thing about it – I felt like such a saddo geek judging them and worrying. Maybe it was *me* I needed to worry about, feeling about ready to go home when it was barely half past twelve.

I found Jake by the stairs, having the end of a

conversation with Ruth as she headed to the bathroom. As I walked up to him, he reached out with a strong arm and pulled me in towards him, kissing my forehead.

'Hey,' I said quietly, feeling really tired suddenly. 'Did you know Sal went into town with May and that lot?'

'Yeah.' He rolled his eyes. 'I had to give her the last of my cash so she can get home. Can't see the attraction myself, but I guess she wants to have some fun before you kids have to go back to school.' He winked at me, trying to get away with calling me 'kid' in the name of comedy, but he still got a girl-punch in the stomach for that.

By the time we left, the house was emptying. As a wave of bodies and noise receded, a mess of cans and cups, ashtrays and dirty paper plates was revealed, like debris washed up on a beach. Outside, though, the air was crisp and cold and clean. The not-quite-full moon was beautifully bright and Jake and I huddled together as we slowly walked home. It must have been about one a.m. The few lights that were still on were shut away cosily inside their warm houses and our little cul-de-sac was silent as usual, despite the occasion. In the perfect quiet I felt like the world was ours, just for a few minutes.

Then I noticed Jake's forehead was furrowed a little.

'You OK?' I asked, squeezing his hand.

'Ruth was asking if there was something going on

between Sally and Ed. I said no, but Sally wouldn't tell me that stuff anyway. Do you know?'

I was genuinely surprised, but I had to admit I didn't know either. 'I don't *think* so. But, you know, when we were having such a good time getting ready tonight, it felt for a while like it used to, when Sal and I were so close – but I guess it was sort of an illusion. Before tonight, I can't remember the last time we really sat and talked, so I don't think she'd tell me either – she didn't even tell me when she and Mark broke up, remember? I just don't see that much of her at the moment.'

'That's what Ruth said too,' frowned Jake. 'I just figured she'd been hanging out with May – but I didn't know she was mates with Ed. Rich hates him – I think they've got some history or something. I never really paid much attention before, but I'm not sure how I feel about Sal being with him. And Ruth seemed worried too, like Sal was going off the rails or something. Am I being blind, Erica, is there something going on with her?'

I felt sick. My heart was thumping. Of course there was something going on with her. She was terrified her family was falling apart and she was trying to deal with it. The thought of it made me sob and I couldn't stop myself.

'Oh, oh, I'm sorry, I didn't mean to upset you.' Jake swept me into a strong hug. I had to tell him.

'She won't talk to me about it, Jake. I don't know what to do . . . ' I cried. But he misunderstood.

'I know. I'm sorry. I don't know why I'm quizzing you like that when you don't know any more than me. Don't worry. I'll talk to Rich about Ed. I'm sure it's fine. He's probably just better at football – Rich is such a kid about that stuff.' He held my face and smoothed my hair out of my wet eyes, and kissed me. 'Don't worry,' he repeated. I was shaking. 'You're freezing, come on, I'll walk you to your door.'

I stayed quiet and just said 'Happy New Year' again when Jake did, and 'good-night' when Jake did; and I went to bed queasy with confusion. I'd come so close to betraying Sally's trust. So close, I was ashamed of myself. But now that Jake was starting to worry about her too, it was harder to pretend everything was fine. And it was so hard to lie to Jake. And even though I *wasn't* really lying to him, it felt like I was, and it felt horrible.

Term started on Wednesday 3rd, and on the Friday Ruth threw a dinner party at hers as a kind of commiseration on being put to work again. I'd said I'd drive Sally because Jake was going into town too for a night out with some mates, and was taking their car and staying overnight. When I knocked on their door, Steph answered. She looked tired. She said Sally would be ready in a minute so we sat in the kitchen together while Sal clattered about upstairs. Steph was drinking some sort of evil-looking green sludge, wheatgrass and ginger something-or-other I think, so when she offered me a drink I instinctively declined, although I'm sure she would have poured me a water or made tea.

'What are you up to tonight then?' she asked.

I told her just dinner at Ruth's, not a late one, and just as a puzzled look flickered across her face, Sally skipped down the stairs, grabbed her bag and went straight for the door.

'Sorry Erica, I've made us a bit late – you ready? We should probably get going. Hey Mum, see you later, don't wait up!'

I hesitated for a second, then shrugged at Steph and followed Sally, who was already at the car with her hand poised on the handle. She had on chunky high heels and a teeny tunic dress. Her hair was big and backcombed and she had loads of black eye make-up on. She looked amazing, but a bit overdressed for dinner at Ruth's, and I had a sinking feeling as our seatbelt fasteners clicked into place and we drove off.

'You look nice,' I said, hoping she'd offer an explanation.

'Oh, thanks hon,' was all she said.

'Ruth'll be flattered you've made such an effort,' I said, humourlessly I admit, because I knew what was coming.

'Oh, I'm meeting up with May and Nadine after dinner. I'm not sure where we're going, so I thought I'd better not wear jeans and trainers just in case . . .' She looked down at my black skinny jeans and Vans. 'Er, but if we don't end up going anywhere special, you know, with a dress code, you're welcome to come . . .'

I knew she didn't mean it.

'I think I'd feel a bit underdressed anyway, though – maybe next time,' I said. I thought about what she'd said to Steph as we'd left her house. 'Does your mum think you're coming home with me?' I asked her.

She was the worst liar. 'Erm, no, I don't think so. I did say I'd be out late. I'll make sure I tell her if I have to get a taxi back, don't worry.'

Dinner was embarrassing. We tried to ignore Sally's obvious impatience to leave – she was practically still chewing as she walked out of the door – but I felt bad for Ruth after all the effort she'd made. Her parents had even made themselves scarce for the evening so we could have a proper gossip. And to be honest, I felt bad for me too. I didn't like feeling angry with Sal, I didn't like that she wasn't interested in spending time with us any more, and

I didn't like that the Sally I *did* like seemed to be slipping away.

It was a nice evening once she'd gone; we watched some TV but mostly chatted about our uni applications and our plans for next year. Ruth and Charlotte were excited about how little college we had left, how soon they'd be moving out of home and starting new lives. Of course, I was too, but a part of me hadn't quite acknowledged yet that it was all going to be so soon. I was morbidly nervous about what would happen. My first choice was Brighton, and, although Jake had his place at Edinburgh to take up, I knew he wasn't sure if he wanted to go back into studying. He was actually pretty happy working at the shop because it meant he was well connected to get his work sold and exhibited locally. He was already making money from his paintings, so there didn't seem to be much reason for him to keep training as long as he was doing as well as he was. As I drove home alone, I felt isolated and nervous about the changes that seemed to be going on around me. It all seemed beyond my control.

chapter 9

♥

I shut my eyes against the tingle of tears. I couldn't be crying just because Jake was going away for a week! I couldn't have turned *that* soppy. I wasn't jealous at all that he'd be skiing in France while I was stuck at home – I'd been skiing once and it had been embarrassing enough to last me a lifetime. But we'd been together over three months and this was the first time he wouldn't be just round the corner if I wanted to see him. And with things going wrong with Sally, and the winter blues and all, I guess it all got a bit much. That's my excuse anyway. Thankfully, Jake was being pretty soppy too.

'I kind of wish I wasn't going now,' he said, squeezing me tightly.

'You do not,' I said, finding it easier to be tough while he was being so cute. 'You'll have a great time. Besides, I've driven you to the flipping airport now, so if you don't get on the plane I'm going to charge you petrol money.'

His mates had flown out early that morning, but Jake

was a late addition to the group because he'd had to work during the day, so he was stuck for a ride to catch his later flight and I said I'd drive him. I waited while he checked in, just to draw the whole thing out, and we hugged goodbye again at the bottom of the escalator up to departures. We kissed and Jake held my face in his hands.

'I'll miss you,' he said. God, I almost cried again.

'I'll miss you too,' I said. And, having to joke to keep my senses, said 'Now sod off!' I pretended to push him on to the escalator and he pretended that I could actually push him on to the escalator if I wanted. He stuck his bottom lip out and waved at me as he disappeared backwards and upwards. I laughed and waved back, then slowly turned and headed towards the car park. Thank God I was going to Anna Harrison's party that night, or I'd be properly moping. As it was, I had to rush back, shower and make some serious wardrobe decisions.

Mum said she'd drop us off and pick us up to save us driving or worrying about cabs, so I texted Sally at seven-thirty and told her to be outside for eight. She was leaning against the car when we came out of the house, dressed all in black and looking great, but tired, and as if she'd lost weight.

The party was at the function hall at the Broadwick Hotel, where the Hallowe'en ball had been, and, as we drove up, there was 'our' bench. It pulled at my heart to see it but made me smile too. I obviously wasn't going to be able to forget about Jake tonight.

It was packed and noisy inside. The music was great and we had loads of fun to start with. I didn't see much of Sally, but Ruth and Charlotte and I were dancing loads. By eleven-thirty I felt tired. It was half an hour till Mum was due to come and get us, but I was keen to get outside in plenty of time so I went in search of Sally to see if she was about ready. I couldn't find her. As I came out of the Ladies and walked through the lobby, I felt like some air, so went outside to sit on the bench for a bit. I was thinking about Jake anyway so I figured I might as well indulge myself.

Well, there was Sally. She was leaning against a wall beside the car park, smoking, and Ed was with her, his hand on her bum, kissing her neck. She didn't look all that interested but she wasn't exactly fighting him off either . . . and I was sure he had a new girlfriend. I was rooted to the spot. This was a different girl to the Sally I knew. What was going on?

Munch and Nadine appeared round the corner and the four of them seemed to huddle for a moment before making off towards the town centre. Nice of Sally to let me know she didn't need a lift after all. I felt like giving up on her right then, on just deciding if I wasn't important to her any more then she wasn't worth my time. But the feeling didn't last long before I started to blame myself. She was keeping this huge secret, terrified her family would be torn apart. I was the only person who could help her because I was the only other person who knew. She was going through all this pain and I was about to abandon her. No matter how strangely she was acting, she was still Sally, my best friend for what felt like our whole lives.

When Mum pulled up I had to explain Sally had gone. We drove back and forth through the town centre for a while, but there was no sign of them and Sally's mobile was going straight through to answerphone, which made me think she'd either run out of battery or they'd gone to The Studio, a notoriously rough basement club where she wouldn't have any signal. Mum called Steph and while they were chatting Steph got a text from Sally, from a number she didn't recognise, saying they were at a party and she'd be staying at May's. I didn't know how much of the truth she was hiding but at least we could go home.

'What is going on with that girl, Erica?' Mum asked.

'I don't know, Mum, I really don't.' All my emotion came pouring out. 'I don't know what I can do – I hardly really see her any more anyway. I mean we go out together, but she's not really there, and then after a while she goes off with May's crowd . . . '

Mum could tell I was worried and her voice softened. 'Don't worry, love, it's not up to you to sort her life out for her. But maybe you should tell her you're worried about her, that we all are. You've got all this history, I'm sure she'll listen. There's nothing more we can do tonight anyway – short of gate-crashing that party.' She smiled at me and looked pointedly down at her slipper-clad feet. 'And I'm not really dressed for a night on the town.'

I woke up late the next day and still felt tired. I lay in bed for a long time, thinking. Dad had brought me tea, his way of saying, in the nicest possible way, it was about time I was up. I checked my email and read a sweet message from Jake – he'd got up early to write before they all went out and hit the slopes. He said the resort was cool and they were having a nice time so far, what they'd had of it, and that he was thinking of me. Then I showered and took my time getting dressed, knowing that when I was done I had to go and talk to Sally.

I knocked a few times on their front door and was just stepping back to look up at the house, thinking they must be out, when Sally's messy head appeared at her window and she waved feebly. She disappeared and I thought she'd come to the door, but instead the next noise I heard was the same window opening up. I stepped back again.

'Hey lady,' she croaked. 'I'm in bed still. Come up though,' and with that she threw her keys out at me and flopped back down out of sight. I let myself in and made two cups of tea before I headed up the stairs. Sally had managed to prop herself up as I pushed her door open.

'Hey. Oooh, you're amazing, thanks,' she said as she reached gleefully for her tea.

'You got home OK, then?'

'Oh, yeah, I crashed at Nadine's, and Ed drove me back this morning. I've been in bed since, I'm totally knackered. Mum wasn't best pleased; she's gone to the supermarket in a huff, I think. She'll be hours, I've never known anyone who could pass so much time happily just reading food labels . . . How was the rest of Anna's party?'

What was she talking about? 'I left about the same time as you, Sally. Mum was picking us up, remember?'

'Ohhh, sugar. Yeah, sorry about that, I kind of lost track of time. Are you cross with me?'

I stared into my tea for a second; confrontation wasn't my thing normally but I was cross with her and I wasn't going to lie about it.

'A bit.'

I looked up at her and she was rummaging through her bedside table drawer for lip balm. The fact she didn't seem to be listening emboldened me. If she didn't care if I was angry I might as well tell her.

'You never would have done that before you started hanging out with May and Nadine. Look, Sally, it's none of my business who you hang out with, but I'm worried . . .' Sally was out of bed now, scraping back her tangle of hair and looking around the floor for jeans to throw on. 'You're so different. If it's just that you like hanging out with them, and if you genuinely like Ed, then that's great – but I'm worried that you're going out late to avoid thinking about your dad. I wish you'd talk to someone about it. Sally, you don't have to go through it on your own. If you can't talk to me I understand, it's family stuff, but I'd listen, any time. Or talk to Jake, please, don't bottle it all up, it's not good . . .'

'I will NOT talk to Jake.' Sally swung round from the wardrobe where she'd been looking for a jumper. Her face was screwed up with rage. I'd never seen her look like that, and my heart leaped in my chest as I realised how my good intentions had enraged her. 'And you'll keep quiet, do you get me?' She pointed a sharp finger at me, jabbing with her arm, almost as if she was mentally stabbing me. 'You. You think you know better than me what's going through my own head? You don't have a CLUE, with your perfect family and your perfect life – and your PERFECT boyfriend who you can't see is selfish and stubborn and just thinks of himself. And it IS none of your business who I hang out with. AND, if you must know, I AM thinking about Dad. You can't even imagine – I've found out exactly who that woman is and next time he goes on one of his "business trips" I'm going to find out where she lives, too, and I'm going to have it out with her and put an end to this thing before people find out . . . ' She'd gone back to looking through her wardrobe and was muttering to herself. It was so weird, sort of unhinged, like she'd forgotten her tirade at me the moment the words were out of her mouth, and now she was thinking about her crazy plan and it was like I wasn't there.

I had pain in my throat from forcing myself not to cry. I was shaking from the venom Sally had spat at me. I recognised nothing in the friend I thought I knew so well. I was out of my depth. I couldn't think of a thing to say and, even if I could, she needed to calm down before she'd hear anything, just as much as I needed to calm down before I said it.

I put down my unfinished tea, my fingers stiff with

tension from gripping the mug so hard. I tried to say I thought I'd better go, but no words would come out. So I slipped out of her bedroom silently, ran down the stairs, out of the front door, all the way to my front door, up my stairs, into my bedroom, and, as I shut the door behind me, all the tears I'd been holding on to flowed freely.

Chapter 10

♥

It was freezing that week. When I left for college on Monday, everything was frosted. Hundreds of usually invisible spiders' webs had suddenly appeared in glittering strings and lattices of white. The pavements sparkled with the hint of ice.

I had to drive so slowly and carefully I was late for my first class and, as I got close to the door, I could hear they were watching some sort of film, so I decided instead of interrupting I'd wait in the library and join them after break. There was a lovely email from Jake when I logged on to a computer and opened my messages.

```
Hey gorgeous,

Still missing you, but having a great time - is
that allowed? Our instructor is amazing (quite
scary, so you have to do what he says or he
looks like he might push your face in! It's
really working though), and even if I do say so
myself, I'm getting pretty darned good. You'd
be impressed, honest! Was thinking, I should
get back quite early on Sunday, and I'd planned
```

to hold on till Valentine's day on Wednesday,
but don't think I can wait (plus everywhere
will be packed out and I didn't book anything!)
so I thought maybe we could go out for dinner
Sunday night istead? What do you think? Can't
wait to see you. All my love, Jake. Xxx

I emailed back yes, and of course after that I was counting the hours even more impatiently until Sunday. By Wednesday we were snowed in. The parties had stopped and it seemed like everyone was hibernating – or starting to panic about work now term was in full swing. I took pictures of our white-covered village with Dad's digital camera and emailed them to Jake – boasting I could probably just pop out of the front door and go skiing myself. I missed him. But part of me was grateful he wasn't at home. Sally and I hadn't spoken since Sunday and I wasn't sure how I was going to explain it if we hadn't made some kind of reconciliation by the time he was back. Staying in touch just by email, with a good-night text now and then, made it easier not to let slip all that was going on. Over and over again, I imagined trying to explain to Jake all my worry for Sally without actually telling him the reason.

It was only a couple of months until study had to start in earnest for A-level exams, and, hard as I tried to get work done, I'd find myself staring at my notes, seeing nothing but Sally's angry face in my low moments, or Jake's welcome, smiling face in my better ones. I cheered myself by picturing his wind-blasted winter tan, and the romantic scene of the welcome-home meal we'd be having on Sunday night.

Sally wasn't the only one pulling the wool over her own eyes. I spent most of the week convincing myself that everything would be magically fixed when Jake came back. First, there'd be the most perfect romantic evening, then we'd have a whole week to spend with each other, because it was half-term and Jake had some extra days' holiday from work. I'd be over at their house all the time, and Sally and I would bump into each other in the kitchen, apologies would come pouring out, we'd hug, and everything would start to heal. I'd made myself believe that this fiction would become reality and by Saturday night I was excited and happy – and impatient to be waking up the next, glorious morning.

I woke up late again, after taking so long to fall asleep in my excitement, and after brunch I warned Mum and Dad the bathroom was mine for at least two hours. I had the longest bath, gave myself a pedicure and manicure, moisturised to within an inch of saturation and put on my favourite perfume.

By five-thirty I'd perfected my make-up and was straightening my hair when my phone rang – the ringtone that meant it was Jake! I was so excited I couldn't stifle a little squeal. But as soon as the words 'Hey, you,' were out of my mouth, I knew from the quiet on the other end of the phone that something wasn't going according to plan.

'Hey you too.' Jake sounded loving but sort of sad. 'How are you?'

I wanted to say, 'Excited. So happy you're home, I can't wait another half an hour, come over now ' but all I could say was, 'Good, thanks. How are you?'

'I'm OK. But listen, I'm so, so sorry but I need to cancel tonight. There's nothing I want more than to go to dinner with you, but there's some stuff going on here and Mum needs me . . . I'm so sorry, Erica, I promise we'll see each other tomorrow . . .'

My heart fell through the floor. Although I knew he must be telling the truth, little demons inside my head were telling me he'd somehow decided, on the flight home, that he didn't love me at all. He'd finally realised he could do better and was trying to let me down gently. I told myself off for being so self-obsessed and tried to think how hard it must be for him.

'Don't worry. It's OK, I understand. But what's

happened, Jake? Please tell me what's going on.'

'I can't really talk now, I'll explain tomorrow. I'll call you as soon as I can in the morning, I promise, OK?'

I think I said OK back, I can't really remember. I do remember unplugging my irons on autopilot, half my hair still a wavy mess, and curling up on my bed, incapacitated by disappointment.

After about two hours Mum must have guessed what had happened. There was the faintest knock at my door and her face slowly peered in at me. She crept in, wrapped me up in her arms and asked if I'd come down and have some food with her and Dad, she knew it wasn't the same but they'd love it if I joined them.

'I'll be down in a minute,' I said dimly, trying to smile.

She nodded, brushing a strand of hair away from my face, and left me alone while I tied my half-done hair back out of the way and pep-talked myself. You'll see Jake tomorrow, I thought. Don't be a baby just because things didn't go exactly how you'd imagined in your funny little head. You just need to wait for things to calm down and it'll all be fine.

After a quiet dinner in front of the TV, Dad went to bed with a book just after ten and Mum stayed up with me and we watched a film. It was just before midnight when my phone rang. Mum reached for the remote to turn the TV down, but I jumped up and rushed into the kitchen. I couldn't have guessed what he'd say but I didn't know if it might be private.

'Hey,' I answered, as gently as I could, and quietly because I knew Dad would be asleep upstairs.

'I didn't wake you, did I?' asked Jake. I said no of course he hadn't, but he was already talking over me. 'Sally's gone. She had a massive row with Mum after she stayed out all night again last night. I shouldn't have got involved, but she was really going off at Mum and it wasn't fair – I guess we sort of ganged up on her.' I could hear the guilt in his voice, but it was quickly replaced with urgent worry. 'We were going to go out to look for her just now, but she's taken the car. Erica, do you have numbers for May or Ed or any of that lot? We tried the number we had for Nadine, but it's disconnected. We don't know what to do – the police don't want to know yet, she has to be missing longer before they can help.'

But I didn't have any of the numbers he needed. 'I'm so sorry, Jake, I don't. I don't know any of them well enough really, I'm pretty sure Ruth and Charlotte won't either, but I can try Anna. Have you tried Rich – he'll have a number for Munch, won't he? He might know something?'

'Of course he will – I'm such an idiot, thanks. I'll call

him now. Can you try Anna in the meantime and let me know? Thanks, Erica.' He hung up. I scrolled straight down my address book and called Anna. No answer, and I knew she wouldn't have credit to pick up voicemails so I texted.

Hi, it's Erica. Sal's missing! Do u have nos for Ed, Munch or May? Let me no. x

I pressed 'Send' and it was then I realised I probably had a better idea where Sally had gone than any of those people. Dazed by the panicked whirl of thoughts in my head, I walked back into the living room, quietly closing the door. I must have had quite a look on my face because Mum got straight up and came over to me.

'Sally's gone,' I said.

'What do you mean?' Mum frowned.

'She's taken the car. They don't know where . . .' A sob escaped from me, my knees gave way and I sank to the floor. Mum crouched beside me and held me.

'She'll be OK, darling, she's not stupid . . .'

'Mum,' I interrupted her, 'I think I know where she's gone – at least, I don't know where, but I think I know what's she's doing.' It all came flooding out then, the visit to her dad's office, the secret I was sworn to keep and the reason Sally had gone off the rails. I remembered the anger in her face, and the way she'd seemed almost insane when I saw her last, and I was terrified of where she might be and what might have happened. I was horrified that it could be my fault. Why hadn't I kept trying to convince her? I was so selfish, thinking of how hurt I'd been, instead of how she needed help.

When I'd finished, the relief I'd imagined feeling when the secret was finally out didn't come. I just felt guilty and ashamed. Mum took charge then. She said we had to go right over to see Steph and tell them what I knew, and we could drive them wherever they needed to go to find her. I was in some kind of disabling shock. She practically had to put my coat on for me and push me out of the door.

Chapter 11

♥

'I thought you might need the use of my car,' said Mum when Jake opened the door. His face was grey and drawn and tense.

'Great! We were just talking about taxis – thanks, come in,' said Jake, leaving us to follow as he rushed in to his mum. Steph had clearly been crying, but the news that they had a car and could go out and start searching got her up and grabbing her shoes.

'Before we go, Steph, I think there may be more to this than just driving into town and trying the nightclubs and friends' houses.' Mum looked at me. 'Are you going to tell them, or should I?' Steph was poised, one arm in her coat, keys in hand. Jake was bent over his trainers on the sofa, lacing up. He looked up at me and I looked back.

'I think she might have gone after your dad.' I stared down at the floor then, so I don't know what their reactions were. Mum must have got the idea I might say something wrong because she took over.

'Sally's got the idea, somehow, that Simon's been

having an affair. She told Erica, the last time they saw each other, that when he went off on his next business trip she was going to confront this woman that she thinks he's been seeing. I assume you called Simon when you knew she'd gone, but it might be worth letting him know she could be on the way to his hotel.'

Steph spoke then, quietly, but with the most dignity I've witnessed in my life so far I think.

'Faye, it's very good and wonderfully diplomatic of you to talk as if it's some fantasy Sally has concocted, but she's not stupid, and neither am I. I suppose we shouldn't have kept sweeping it under the carpet for all this time. Let's get in the car, if that's OK, and I'll call Simon as we drive – hopefully, if Erica is right, Sally will be with him by now.'

We made for the door and I watched Jake lay the gentlest, supportive hand on his mum's shoulder as she walked ahead of him, but his face was straining, as if his jaw was clenched so hard all his teeth might fracture under the pressure. He stared determinedly ahead. I wasn't there to him.

The front door was about to slam behind us as we rushed out into the frozen night air, when a shrill alarm sounded, shooting through me like a knife and making me jump. The landline was going. Steph threw herself back into the house and grabbed the receiver.

'Hello? Yes, this is she . . . ' A shaking hand raised to her mouth and, as she squeezed her eyes shut tight, her face crumpled and a tear caught the light from the porch. We all held our breath. 'Is she OK? . . . Yes, I see. We'll be there in fifteen minutes. Thank you.' She gasped in a breath with a shudder as she gently dropped the receiver back into place.

'There was an accident, a crash – she's OK, well, no, she's hurt – Faye, could you take us to the hospital?' I felt my heart stop in my chest and the breath run completely out of me.

'Of course,' Mum said, but before we could move I felt a jolt of pain in my arm and I think I let out a yelp. I turned to see Jake had grabbed my arm.

'You KNEW!' His voice cracked in a strange growl. His face was so full of pain, there were tears in his eyes, those eyes I loved so much. I wanted to hold him, to say sorry, but he hated me with every inch, I could see it clearly in his face and it terrified me. I felt cold and clammy. He shook me and pain shot through my arm. 'You knew, and you said NOTHING! She could be dying . . .'

'JAKE!' Steph screamed, crying like I was, like Jake was. 'That's ENOUGH!' I felt Jake release me and

Mum's arm was round me, holding me up, holding me together. 'We can't run through every "if" and "but". Let's just get to the hospital. *Please*.'

That drive to hospital was the worst fifteen minutes of my life. I sobbed the whole way, trying to stay silent, staring out of the window so Jake wouldn't see me and think I had no right to cry over what I'd caused. I huddled as small as I could make myself in the corner of the back seat, wanting to disappear. I didn't turn to look at him, I didn't dare. I could see his livid, glowering hatred every time I closed my eyes. Most of all, I dreaded finding Sally bloody and badly hurt – or worse. How could this night – that I'd been wishing would arrive – have ended like this? The world was crumbling under my feet.

Chapter 12

I felt nauseous as we pulled into the car park, and it wasn't just the sickly, chemical glow of the hospital lighting bleeding out into the murky night. Part of me wanted to rush into the hospital and find Sally, another part of me dreaded seeing her. I felt ashamed and frightened and so I hung back as the others rushed into reception.

It was chaos inside. Clearly a lot of drunken nights out had ended here, and I imagined how depressed it must make the staff, having to clear up the mess everyone had got themselves into. But I was thankful for all the noise and rushing people – it meant fewer eyes were on me.

Mum stayed in the background with me as we followed Steph and Jake through to the cubicle where Sally was being treated. Mum was practically dragging me along. My hand was over my mouth as I got a glimpse of Sally. She was awake, thank goodness. There was a brace around her neck and a large, vicious cut on her head, which had been cleaned and stitched but still looked terrifying. It ran from near her hairline right down through her eyebrow and scarily close to her eye. Steph let out a little cry and rushed over, obviously wanting to scoop Sally up in her arms but holding herself back for fear of hurting her, she was so battered and bruised.

I think Sally saw me and gave the slightest smile. But it seemed right to leave the family alone together. We waited back at reception to hear more news. Mum had gone to get us some hideous machine tea, just for the sake of something to do I think, when I saw Simon arrive. His face gave little away. I saw him have an exchange with a receptionist, who gestured for him to go through to the cubicle. I watched him disappear in the direction we'd just come from. I stared after him, into the corridor, wondering what Sally's reaction would be when she saw him, or Steph's. Or Jake's. Hopelessness rushed through me again as I thought of Jake, but I had no energy left for tears.

Then Steph reappeared and I watched her scan the waiting area. I thought she saw me, although she made no move to come over. Perfect in her timing as always, Mum emerged, plastic drinks in hand, and she and Steph spoke. Mum just listened and nodded as Steph spoke and gesticulated shakily for what felt like a very long time, then she said something back. I could see she was worried. She leaned in towards Steph to force her to make eye contact. Steph's hand came up to her face again and she seemed to cry for a moment. Mum did her best to give her a comforting hug while balancing the drinks, and then they exchanged a few more words, nodding with each other, Mum seeming to wait for reassurance Steph would be OK. When she got it, they parted and I watched as she came back over to where I was sitting.

Another driver at the scene of the accident had told the police what had happened. Sally had tried to overtake at the wrong moment. She'd realised her mistake but had left it too late to get back in lane and had veered off the opposite side of the road – and into a tree. Thank goodness the other driver had managed to break in time and wasn't hit or hurt. Thank goodness Sally hadn't been going faster. Thank goodness she'd had her seatbelt on . . . She had a broken leg, a fracture in her wrist, whiplash, and the cut on her head. She had no internal bleeding that they could tell but, because she'd hit her head, she would have to stay in hospital for a day or two so they could keep an eye on her. Mum explained that Steph had said we shouldn't wait because they didn't know how long they'd be – and besides Simon had his car there now. I just nodded. Mum gave me a hug and then we left, abandoning our teas untouched.

I'd like to say I didn't sleep a wink that night. You might think I didn't deserve to. But after Dad forced a cocoa on me, I virtually crawled up to my bed, exhausted. I was drained and numb but sleep was a blessed escape. I remember thinking I didn't care how long I slept for, even that I didn't really care if I ever woke up.

Chapter 13

I came round confused. I could hear clanging and thudding in the kitchen, and voices – the TV on in the living room. But it was dark in my room. The streaks of daylight that would usually sneak through the blind, even on grey days, weren't there – was it still night? We hadn't got home until the early hours, so it couldn't be, and besides there wouldn't be cooking noises. It must be evening. What day was it? Monday? Had I slept for days? Maybe Mum and Dad were just letting me sleep.

It took a few minutes for all the details of Sunday night to come back to me, and each new detail was like another weight on me. Sally's blood and bruises, that horrific cut on her face. Simon arriving at the hospital, Steph leaning on Mum, overwhelmed by all that was happening. Jake's hand crushing my arm in hate, his pain and rage-filled eyes. It didn't have to be real. All the noises of life I could hear in the house, if I could just ignore them and stay where I was, cocooned in darkness and in my duvet and in sleep – none of these things that had happened had to be real if I could just hide.

The phone rang downstairs and I heard Mum's voice, but the conversation was muffled and I couldn't make out any words. Once the cordless receiver had bleeped back into place though, I could hear her coming up the stairs. She stopped outside my door, did one of her gentle knocks and slowly eased the door open. I didn't move, but I didn't pretend to be asleep. She sat down by the head of my bed.

'How you feeling, hon?' I shrugged slightly. 'Steph just called. Sally's doing well, she's going to be just fine. In fact, they think she'll be coming home tomorrow. But Steph wondered if you might like to see her tonight – visiting hours at the hospital are six till eight. They're popping in at six but, if you'd like to speak to her on your own, you'd have her to yourself from about half past. It's up to you, darling, but if you wanted to go we'd need to leave in about forty-five minutes. I'll be ready to drive you if you want a lift but you'll need to get up and showered. I'll leave you to decide.'

Bless Mum for knowing I couldn't have stood any pressure just then, and that I wouldn't want to drive to the hospital on my own. But of course I had to go and see Sally. She might hate me for telling her secret. She might blame me for not forcing her to tell it herself, just like Jake. But I had to know, and I wanted to see that she was OK, before she came home, so I could avoid seeing Jake.

In the car, I wondered if Steph had tipped me off on the visiting hours because Jake had said he didn't want me coming to the house. I didn't know if I was being paranoid. At least I could assume Sally wanted to see me, or at least hadn't said she didn't want to, or Steph wouldn't have suggested it.

'How did Steph sound?' I asked Mum. She looked confused. 'On the phone, did she sound angry? Do you think she blames me?' I stared into my lap.

'Listen to me, Erica.' Mum's voice was almost stern. 'You couldn't have stopped this. Sally's got a mind of her own, you can't take responsibility for her, it's too much. Yes, she asked you to keep a dangerous secret as it turns out, but you did what you thought was right at the time. That's all any of us can do.'

Even though she's my mum and I knew she'd say whatever made me feel better, I believed her, and I did feel a little better. By the time we reached the hospital I was looking forward to seeing Sally. There were things I wanted to know about the past couple of months that I hoped she might be able to tell me. When I peeked through the curtain, Sally was sitting up. There was a little TV on an arm coming out of the wall and it was on quietly, but she didn't seem to be watching really.

'Hey.' She smiled when she saw me. 'Come in. I'm sooo bored.'

I smiled back and walked round the bed to sit down. I tried not to stare at the stitched cut on her face, but it still looked angry and painful and I obviously didn't hide my shock too well. Her fingers reached up and touched the cut gingerly.

'The doctors say I'll probably be scarred for life.'

I tried harder to hide my feelings this time and leaned in to whisper to her. 'Doctors pretend like they know everything, but they're wrong sometimes, you know. It'll heal. You'll still be beautiful.'

She shook her head but smiled again for a moment, then the sadness came back.

'Did you see Dad last night?' I nodded. 'He's moving out . . .' I bowed my head. Everything she hadn't wanted to happen was happening and I felt like it was all my fault and, after all the agonising, there hadn't been any point in me betraying her secret in the end – by the time Mum and I had turned up at their house, Sally had already crashed.

'I'm so sorry, Sally.' My voice was shaking. 'When no one knew where you were . . . I thought I was helping . . . telling, I mean.'

She shook her head. 'I know I put you in a difficult place, Erica, I'm sorry. Don't worry about it. It's weird – this is what I was dreading. I imagined it would be the end of my world – but I had a long chat with Mum and she sort of seems actually happier. Sort of . . . stronger than I've known her for a long time.'

I remembered Steph's reaction at the house on Sunday and knew exactly what she meant. 'And I wasn't being fair to her, believing Jake meant more to her . . . ' Sally turned to me and shook her head again. 'You know, she knew. She knew about Dad, so it wasn't really a secret anyway, after everything. There was me thinking I was so clever and important.' She laughed humourlessly and laid back and closed her eyes for a moment. She looked tired, and I thought of Mum waiting outside so I stood up.

'I should probably leave you to sleep, you look tired.' But she reached out to me with her plaster-encased hand.

'No, wait.' I stayed standing. 'It's funny how a good smack to the head and incarceration in a hospital bed can clear your thoughts . . . You were right, you know, about me ignoring things. Nadine and Ed and Munch, even May – they're not real friends, not like you. I'm sorry for the way I was.'

'Don't be silly.' I laughed it off. But secretly I felt happy and relieved that she said it.

'You'll come and see me, won't you? I'm going to be an invalid, stuck in my house for ever. You'll come over and watch movies with me?' I sat down then. She said that like it was so simple.

'I don't know Sally, I want to. But Jake hates me. Really, you should have seen him when we heard you'd been hurt. And I'm not sure your mum's my biggest fan either . . . I just don't think I'd be welcome.'

Sally rolled her eyes. 'Erica, Mum loves you, she always has. She wouldn't have suggested you come and see me if she blamed you for anything, would she? Believe me, it's me she blames. I'm going to have to be on my best behaviour for at least a year to get back in her good books. And Jake – what did I tell you about him? He thinks he knows better than anyone, he's a stubborn pain in the bee-hind. But last night was last night and he listens to Mum. And he loves you too. You know that, come on. I've never seen him so gooey as he's been the past few months. He'll come round. All the more reason you should spend lots of time at ours, being lovely at him!' She fake-grinned at me, acknowledging her pure selfishness in trying to persuade me, and I felt good as we waved each other goodbye, sort of like I'd got my friend back.

I even let myself believe maybe she was right about

Jake, too, that he'd come round and, when I thought of him on the way home, I saw him smiling at me again. Instead of remembering his anger, when I closed my eyes, I felt him sweeping me up in a hug, the warm skin of his cheek brushing mine like that first time on our bench.

Chapter 14

I nbox (1). The next day there was a fresh new white line at the top of my email messages – from Jake! I clicked on it before I'd even thought about what it might say.

```
Hi Erica,

I'm sorry not to say this to you in person, I
know I should, but it's too hard to even think
about seeing you. I think it's best that we
don't see each other any more.
I don't think I'll ever be able to forgive you
for the secret you kept. We'll never know
whether Sally's accident would have happened if
things had been different and out in the open,
but the point is, you kept a secret about my
own family from me, one that belonged to me at
least as much as to you. I thought we were
always honest with each other and I can't be
with someone who can keep such huge secrets so
easily. I'm sorry things had to finish this
way, but I think you can understand.
Jake.
```

My heart was lurching, over and over. I thought I might throw up. I was filled with that horror you get when you've smashed something precious and you're just coming to the realisation of what you've done, before you start to wish with every atom of yourself that you could turn back time, because just a few moments ago you lived in happy oblivion of this moment when all was lost. Did he really mean he didn't want to see me any more – ever?

When I thought of all the happiness I'd had with Jake, I felt a physical pain like it was being ripped away. I felt heavy and breathless as I mechanically closed my email and shut down. I rushed to my room, closed the door behind me, collapsed against it and cried and cried until I was exhausted. I couldn't move and I don't know how long it was until I managed to drag myself into my bed to hide in the folds of my duvet – one hour? Two? Then I slept. It was my only escape from a world where Jake hated me.

Mum left food by my bed when I wouldn't come down for dinner or tell her why, but I didn't eat it. The next day she insisted I'd feel better if I got up, but I walked round in a daze. Occasionally I'd venture downstairs and slump in front of the TV. But of course the day after I got that email, it was Valentine's day and every stupid programme seemed to be about love. Invisible rays of schmaltz would shoot out of the TV and pierce my heart, making me think of Jake and sending me back to my bed in tears. All I could think about was that I couldn't stand him being angry with me. I lived like a hermit, ignoring any texts or calls I got from friends or, when they persisted, sending back the shortest answers I could get away with.

Jake's email had made me feel so small and worthless, I was too scared to read it again, let alone think about replying. But by Saturday the return to college was looming. I knew I couldn't pretend this horribleness wasn't happening. I'd have to face seeing everyone and if I wasn't my normal self – and if I didn't mention Jake in every other sentence – there would be questions. I had to pull myself together and try to fix my life. So I made a strong cup of tea, switched on the computer and prepared to feel the force of the blow again. What could I say to him to make him understand?

But a funny thing happened. Despite how prepared I'd been to explain how sorry I was, how hard it had been for me and how I could understand how angry he was, when I read his words again, I didn't feel sorry.

He hinted he still blamed me for what happened to Sally, but he didn't have the guts to say it openly, even in an email, let alone to my face. He said I'd kept a secret that was more his than mine, well, that wasn't true: it was Sally's and she had asked me to keep it. I'm sure if it had been him who had asked me, he would have expected me to keep it too. But the thing that really filled me with anger – indignant, strengthening anger – was that one phrase: *I can't be with someone who can keep such huge secrets so easily.* Easily?! How dare he think it had been easy? The anguish I'd been through! That one statement made me realise he hadn't spent the slightest bit of effort to imagine my side of things. He was thinking of himself. And the sign-off: *I think you can understand.* Not *I hope you can understand*, but a self-important *I think you can understand.*

All the moral certainty I had thought made Jake so strong and amazing now seemed more like self-righteous stubbornness – and laziness in not trying to see other people's points of view. Maybe I was being too hard on him. Maybe I was being defensive because I did still wonder if I could have saved Sally from her accident if I'd handled things differently. But if Sally could forgive me, why couldn't Jake even try?

There wasn't a single mention in the email of his anger towards me on that Sunday night, either. Not that I didn't understand completely that he'd been terrified and worried at that moment. But I was terrified too and it was truly horrible the way he'd looked at me, and gripped me so hard he'd left bruises. There was no way he could know that, and maybe he didn't even remember, but his ferocity had really frightened me and I thought maybe he might just mention it.

What was the use of me apologising again and again if he wasn't prepared to listen and understand my reasons? He'd already decided that he wouldn't be able to forgive me. I was torn between my anger at his words and wanting to reach out and try to explain my side of the story. So I decided that I wouldn't reply just then. Deciding to wait until I was sure what to say, even though I knew that meant I'd risk losing Jake for ever, felt a little bit like choosing myself, my dignity, over him. And it wasn't easy. I'd leave it at that, and maybe we'd be over. It hurt all over again to think about it. Part of me couldn't believe I was choosing not to reach out to at least try and fix this. But the other part of me knew I had to be true to myself first, even if it meant everything Jake and I'd had would be lost.

Chapter 15

Sally and I emailed or messaged each other almost every day. I kept notes for her in Media studies and nagged her classmates in her other subjects to do the same, until she eventually came back to college to a loving welcome from everyone. Ruth threw a 'comeback' party and this time Sally stayed until the end and we came home together.

Spring sprung. The world came out of hibernation and there was all this energy and colour and sunshine. The earth was turning and time was moving on without me, like a missed bus disappearing down the road. The evenings got longer and warmer and Charlotte and Ruth would invite me into town after class, but I'd smile and say no thanks and that I was going home to revise. I worked hard, right through Easter and into our final term. I'll admit my motives weren't entirely noble – studying kept my mind occupied and if I'd tried to go out and have fun I just would have felt Jake's absence more sharply. So instead I sat at home and imagined sitting in the park with them, seeing Jake arrive through the gates and come over, smiling, to wind his arm round my waist and squeeze hello . . .

So many things made me think of him, and every time he came into my mind I thought about replying to that email. But the once or twice I was brave enough to get as far as just reading it again, I felt the anger still inside me. I didn't want to send an angry reply. It was heartbreaking enough we weren't seeing or speaking to each other. The only thing that could be worse was if we started to hate each other too. So I kept putting it off. I forced myself to think about my work and my future. But Jake had been the voice in my head that spurred me on when I was finding a subject hard or was cross with myself for getting stuck with an essay. Now I had to shut that voice out, because it was angry and accusing. Some days I cried over my desk, feeling like I was only half a person without him and all the strength he'd given me.

The exams were going to happen whether I was ready or not, and whether Jake was there to get me through them or not, and I'd given up so much of my social life to study that actually, in the end, they went well. Except I had one on my birthday, which was a bit rubbish. Sally and Ruth and I had a few afternoon drinks in a pub garden in town to celebrate. I'd been offered a place at

Brighton to do fashion and business, provided I got the grades, so it should have been a double celebration really, but we all either had an exam the next day, or one the day after so no one was up for a big night out. In a way, I was glad. It stopped me thinking about how different the summer, and my birthday, might have been if I'd still been with Jake – well, it stopped me thinking about it *much* anyway. That morning, I'd come down to breakfast to find presents from my family laid out on the dining table as per tradition. I still felt the excitement of seeing the mysterious, wrapped shapes, all for me. But they reminded me of Jake's Christmas stocking and the love that had gone into each beautifully romantic gift.

Sitting there in that pub garden, the sun shining on the colours of the flowers, and warming our skin, the birds singing gently, I should have felt that rush of summer happiness and anticipation. Instead I felt the space on the bench next to me where I wanted Jake to be.

We did a pretty good job of avoiding each other, Jake and I. I saw Sally all the time at college and we met up for extended study breaks at Coco's, so I didn't have to go over to her house, which was better anyway because we'd talk quite a bit about her parents.

Sally's dad had rented a flat in London and she was actually looking forward to being able to visit a couple of weekends a month. She said she liked the glamour of essentially having a crash pad in London when she fancied it. I know things were hard for her and she joked to cover things up a bit, but she did admit that, even though her parents had been careful about discussing things in front of her, her dad had been a wreck. She'd never seen him like that before. He'd promised never to see the other woman again – Veronica her name turned out to be – and begged Steph to have him back. But she wouldn't. I worried when Sally told me that, thinking she might be angry at Steph for letting the family break up, but actually I think when her dad had fallen off his pedestal it gave her new perspective. She and Steph had been spending a lot of time together, just the two of them, talking properly about the split, and how Sally had been feeling about things, and she seemed genuinely at peace with the situation.

One particularly warm day in July, after the exams were over, Sally told me, over a Coco's special double-choc ice-cream shake, that Steph had dropped a bombshell. She was moving to Scotland to live with her sister in Falkirk for a while. So after a brief freak-out Sally had decided she wanted to get into Glasgow to do law, so they wouldn't be too far apart after all. And, she said, Jake was thinking he'd finally be able to take up his deferred place to do an art degree in Edinburgh, now she and Steph might both be headed up to Scotland anyway. I nodded politely and stared into my drink, hoping the conversation would move on quickly. But Sally was testing me.

'You two haven't even spoken since the accident, have you? I can't understand it, you were so close before and you haven't even tried to make up.'

I felt a twinge of irritation at her then. She seemed to have no idea how she'd changed things between me and Jake. It was her who had caused all this, in a way. But I couldn't blame her after the tough time she'd been through. I took a breath in and let the tension go.

'We didn't need to talk for him to make his feelings pretty clear, Sal. Too much changed between us . . .' I held myself back from going into the details – I didn't want to start talking about it, it was too hard. 'You know how it is,' I shrugged, remembering that December day on the platform at the station, when we'd talked about her break-up with Mark. 'It's all for the best.'

She shook her head sadly. 'Jake still mopes about it you know. It just seems sad, to throw that all away, just because you're both so stubborn.'

I felt a flutter in my chest when she said that. He was still thinking about me too? But then she let it go, and started talking about this guy Ruth had apparently started seeing. She'd heard it was getting all hot and heavy and he was going to follow her to Leeds when she took up her university place there.

We finished our drinks and Sally went off to meet her mum. As I drove home I thought about what she'd said. Jake wasn't over me. Maybe she was right and we'd both just been too stubborn. She made me realise how obvious it had been that we were right for each other – people had seen us as this great couple. But I had to bury the feelings she'd stirred up. For my own sanity I'd had to stop myself reading over that damned email. It had taken five months of serious distraction tactics to avoid confronting him. But I found myself wondering what would have happened if it had just been worded a bit differently, or I'd swallowed my pride and replied with a calm explanation. I turned the radio on loudly, found a song to sing along to, and tried my best to shake the thoughts from my head.

When I got home I decided I'd have a clear-out and makeover my room. So for a few days I busied myself filling bags full of stuff to take to charity shops and trying out paint testers. One Monday, I thought I'd try moving my furniture. I plugged my iPod into the stereo and put on my most upbeat playlist, as loud as I thought

I could get away with. I threw open my bedroom window and propped open my door to let the air through, scraped my hair back into a knot to keep it out of the way, and proceeded to spring clean (or summer clean, I guess, if there is such a thing).

But, as the third track faded out, I heard a loud banging at the door that made me jump. I hesitated, knowing I should hurry because whoever it was may have been knocking for a while, drowned out by the music, while thinking at this time of day, in the middle of the afternoon, it was likely to be someone selling something, dishcloths or religion or whatever. Manners got the better of me though and I put the music on pause, skipped down the stairs in my bare feet and swung open the door.

And there was Jake. Seeing him standing there was sort of like being punched in the chest – I actually felt winded. His hands were jammed awkwardly in his pockets and he had an odd expression on, like he was trying to smile through his nervous frown but didn't know if smiling was appropriate.

'Hi,' he said. He looked incredible. I mean he just had on torn old jeans and an even older, faded T-shirt and flip-flops. But he had that easy summer tan already and the tension in his arms squared those amazing shoulders.

In body, he was this beautiful person I still loved, the same face, lips, hands, hair, skin. My instinct was to reach out to touch him. I wanted to hold him and have him hold me, to snake my hand around his torso and feel his warm, strong frame supporting me. I had to fight against the will in my muscles because it wasn't allowed. I don't know how to describe it, there was this barrier – I suppose it was like he was on the other side of a thick glass wall that we'd constructed between us. I don't know how long I just stood there, lost for words.

'Um, I'm driving up to Falkirk with Mum tomorrow – did Sally tell you?' I nodded to let him know I knew his plans, or at least some of them. 'And I have a meeting at the university on Monday and then I need to look around for flat shares and stuff, so I'm staying with my aunt for a bit and I don't know if I'll be back down before . . . well, I don't know if I'll be back – we've already had an offer on the house . . . ' He looked up the street for a moment, as if he'd surprised even himself with the realisation he was really leaving for good. 'So anyway, I thought I'd better say goodbye, I mean I *wanted* to say goodbye.' He frowned deeply and looked away, and I realised I must be staring, and that it must be really difficult for him standing there, explaining his presence.

I couldn't face asking him in though. It was awkward

enough standing on the doorstep with a metre between us, the thought of standing in the kitchen with tea, or sitting on the sofa – it was too much.

'Wow, big changes,' I said, trying to keep the conversation friendly. 'Erm, I was going to walk up to the shop actually – we need milk. It's such a nice day, do you want to walk with me? We could take a detour via the rec or something.'

'Sure,' he nodded.

'Gimme a sec, I'll just put some shoes on.' I left him kicking his feet outside for a couple of minutes while I grabbed some flip-flops, checked the mirror and then wondered why; it wasn't like we were on a date. I switched off the stereo, shut and locked the window, and took a deep breath.

My blood was racing with the excitement of seeing Jake and with the uncertainty of what we'd say to each other. But he'd come to say goodbye. Soon someone else would be living in his house. All the drawings would come down off his walls, all the memories painted over by intruders . . .

I allowed myself a couple of seconds and then headed back down, grabbing my keys on the way out, and my wallet, so he didn't twig that the needing milk story was made up.

'Sally says you're off to Brighton then?' Jake started

off the small talk as we walked slowly. I pulled at strands of my hair, not knowing what to do with my hands and thinking it must be frizzy from being tied back.

'Yeah, as long as I get the grades. So we'd be headed in opposite directions then I guess; you guys North, me South,' I added needlessly. I was desperate to keep talking, about anything, the more boring and less emotional the better. 'It'll be nice you're all nearish to each other still, what with Sally going to Glasgow. Edinburgh will be a great place to be, I reckon. It's really pretty and I bet there's loads of great places to go out.'

We got to the top of the road and I turned down a footpath without thinking then regretted it, because it felt so intimate – a cosy, secret little tunnel cocooned by trees. We had to squash up close to walk and keep talking and I felt Jake's arm brush against mine. It gave me goosebumps.

'Brighton should be fun, too – there's a great music scene, you'll love it.'

I held up my hand to halt him. 'If I get the grades, remember!' I laughed nervously. 'I'm not there yet!'

'You'll get the grades,' Jake said quietly.

Oh. He still believed in me. His soft, sure tone was like a hand reaching into my chest to touch my heart. I was suddenly enveloped in my memories. That feeling I'd had when we were together, of being loved and trusted and believed in, strong and whole, came back to me in a rush. I stopped walking and breathed deliberately, trying to hold myself together. Letting Jake go would be like losing a part of myself, letting it die – did I really have to do it? What if I held on to him now and didn't ever let go? I could visit him in Scotland, and he could come down to Brighton for gigs. Everything new we were going to discover, all the new friends we'd make, we could do it all together as a couple and be happy and complete.

I looked up from the floor and I was gazing into Jake's eyes. Our faces were just a few centimetres apart. I wanted to touch him and kiss him but we were both frozen, looking at each other, not knowing what to say. I wished I knew what he was thinking.

'You never replied to my email . . . you got it, right? I was hoping to hear something back.'

My heart was thumping so wildly I thought I might pass out. He hadn't meant it when he said he didn't want to see me! He just wanted a reply. What had I done, ignoring his plea to talk about what had happened? Had I thrown away what could have been the happiest summer of my life?

'Yes, I got it, I'm sorry.' It seemed ridiculous now that I hadn't replied and I didn't know how to explain. 'I didn't think there was much I could say – it felt like you'd made your mind up.' I tried not to sound too shaky.

'Really?' Jake went quiet for a moment.

I wanted him to say that of course he hadn't made his mind up, he was wrong, he missed me, he wanted me back. I wanted him to lift me up and love me again.

'I was sort of hoping you would reply, though. I thought you might want to explain, apologise . . .'

Apologise? All the wishing and wanting in my head screeched to a halt like a needle tearing across a record snatched from its turntable. I remembered the anger I'd felt when I read that email and found it rising in me again. I had to fight against it with all the calm I could muster. Jake's eyes were searching my face and I wondered if he registered the change in me: it felt too huge to go unnoticed. There we were, head to head on this footpath where we'd been many times before in quite different circumstances. I wanted to go back in time to when I'd just felt love, instead of this swirling, overpowering mix of frustration and hurt and longing.

'Did you ever think how hard it was for me?' I tried to keep my words slow and quiet and questioning, but my voice was cracked and wobbly. 'Can't you imagine how hard it was for me to do what Sally asked me to do? How I wanted to tell you every minute we were together the one thing she'd begged me not to?' It was impossible to hide my emotion. I was quaking. It was all I could do not to cry. 'That night, New Year's Eve, I started to tell you – you didn't understand what I was saying but I hated hiding it from you, I wanted to let it all out.'

'Then why didn't you?' Jake's voice was tensing too. 'You could have, you should have, it wasn't your secret to keep.' I remembered then, that he'd said that in his email, too. It just wasn't fair.

'That's not true, Jake, it's just not.' I felt the tears welling in my chest and crumpling my face, when a man walking his dog appeared round the bend in the footpath and my sentence trailed off. We had to press ourselves right up against the trees to let him through and, seeing my chance to regain my dignity, I followed him out of the lane as swiftly as I could, passing Jake and heading back out on to the pavement.

I kept walking briskly to the little green a few metres away where we could sit down on the bench there. I didn't look back but I could sense Jake following. I reached the bench and sat on the edge, staring down at my hands, and I waited for Jake to sit down too.

'You said in your email that the secret I kept was more yours than mine, but it doesn't work like that.' I couldn't look at Jake; I knew if I looked at him, his face would scramble my brain and I'd melt. As much as I wanted to melt, I didn't want to give in, either. I needed to make him see he was wrong. I needed him to realise he wasn't being fair. 'It's like saying – well, say you painted a picture of that house.' I gestured across the green. 'You wouldn't say the painting then belongs to the house, or even the owners of the house. It doesn't work, because a secret doesn't belong to the content of itself, it belongs to the person who knows it, like a painting belongs to the person who paints it, not to the person or thing depicted in it. It was Sally's secret. She was my best friend and she asked me to keep it. You can't honestly think it was easy for me to do that?'

I looked at Jake then. He was staring at me but I couldn't read his expression. It was thoughtful and intense and could have meant he was realising his mistake, but equally it could have shown he was just waiting for me to finish before he tried to shoot down my argument. Too scared to find out which was true, I kept talking.

'I wanted her to tell you what she was going through, I told her you'd understand, that you'd be the one person who really could. But she was adamant you were the last person I should tell.' I realised, as I couldn't hold the tears back any longer, that I was in danger of bringing Sally's motives into the argument, and that wasn't fair. Blaming her wasn't what I wanted to do. 'Anyway, if you really think it was easy for me, you never knew me at all. That's why I didn't reply.' I turned away, trying to hide my sobs.

'You're right, Erica, I shouldn't have thought it was easy for you.'

That flutter was back in my chest when he sounded sorry. I let myself look at him, still hoping that somehow there could be a happy ending to this. It felt like an eternity waiting for his next sentence – I imagined him saying he'd been wrong, he was so sorry, the summer wasn't the same without me, Sally had been right to forgive me, that I hadn't had a choice in keeping her secret . . .

'But secrets aren't as simple as paintings,' he went on. 'I still think if you'd told me what she was going through, we might have been able to save her from that accident. I wonder every time I look at the scar on her face.'

I thought I felt my heart snap. It was hopeless. Every time he looked at Sally, he hated me. I *knew* he'd already decided not to listen – why had he come to me, after all this time, to make me go through this?

'Exactly!' I cried out. I jumped up, full of turmoil. Why couldn't he just let my guilt be enough without his blame too? Why couldn't he trust Sally's judgement and forgive me? He'd confirmed exactly what I'd been afraid his opinion of me was.

'I could apologise every day of my life, Jake, and you'd never be able to forgive me, because we'll never know what would have happened.' I loved him so much. It hurt to stand there so close to him, but so full of frustrated anger. 'You made it clear enough to me in your email, Jake, even if you didn't realise it yourself, that you'd never be ready to listen to me. I don't know why you had to put me through this, on top of everything.'

I turned to storm off but Jake came after me. He grabbed my arm and I flinched, letting out a little scream before I could stop it. I was surprised at my own reaction, and then I realised I was remembering the last time he'd grabbed my arm like that . . . the night of the crash.

If I'd been honest with myself before, I'd have known it already, but that was the moment I realised it was truly over. I was scared of Jake, or at least I was scared of his anger at me. I saw in that second that he would always be holding on to it, and in the same instant I saw our love dying, like I was holding it in my arms, trying to keep it alive but watching it slip away. We were broken.

'Sorry . . . ' Jake bowed his head. He did remember, as clearly as I did. Tears were running down my face because I knew there was no use any more.

'I knew even before your email, the night of the accident. You pointed all your rage and pain at me, and you really hurt me. Physically and the rest. You terrified me. And I know it was a horrible moment for you, I do, but I was going through it too. I love Sally too.'

'I am sorry for that Erica, really. And I know you love Sally.' He sat back down and I thought he might cry too as he held his head. 'But you're right, I guess we'll never know how things might have been.'

We sat there in silence for a long time, or at least it felt like a long time, until Jake's phone beeped. It was the loudest beep, and hearing it was like waking up to an alarm in the middle of an intense dream. He reached into his pocket and flipped open his phone.

'It's Rich, I'm supposed to be meeting him in The Fox for a leaving drink.'

I stood up, feeling shaken and exhausted. And before he could feel like he ought to ask me along I said, 'Well, I'd better get that milk before the shop shuts.'

I pulled at the bottom of my vest top, straightening myself. Was that it? Were we just going to shake hands as if we'd stopped for a chat about the weather?

Jake stood too and we looked at each other. Then he reached out gently with his right hand, still holding his mobile phone, and hooked his two free fingers around my thumb and into my palm.

'I'll miss you, Erica,' he said softly.

'Me too,' I whispered. For a moment, we were back on our bench, discovering our feelings for the first time, kissing, full of joy at discovering each other. We were turning slowly on that roundabout again, leaning on each other in near darkness that Bonfire Night, fingers intertwined like they were designed to be parts of one whole, loving each other, holding on to each other so tightly, believing we'd never let go. Then it was over.

He turned and walked away and I watched, lost and exhausted like I'd been trampled and beaten and with a deep, debilitating pain in my chest. I still loved him, and I knew that he still loved me. But our love was damaged beyond repair.

I turned away too, then, and walked home alone.

HILARY FREEMAN

Lily believes her boyfriend Jack is perfect, but
wonders why he won't talk about his past.
Wouldn't it be fantastic, she thinks, if she could
talk to his ex and fill in all the gaps?

Lily devises a way to do just that. But
what begins as a bit of fun has unexpected –
and disturbing – consequences . . .

DON'T ASK is a story about love,
friendship and secrets. Sometimes it's better
not to ask too many questions.

The Last Act

LAURA ELLEN KENNEDY

*I stepped out from the deep shadows
in the wings and on to the stage. The others
turned to look at me. Was it excitement or a
renewed bout of nerves making me dizzy?
I tried to speak, but the words stuck in my throat.*

Zoe really comes alive when she's acting,
so she's thrilled when she lands a leading role at
the local theatre. But when rehearsals begin,
strange things start to happen. She has disturbing
blackouts and terrible dreams.

Only Jack, the quiet, charismatic stagehand,
seems to understand what she's going through.
And when Zoe sees a ghostly figure in the props
room mirror, Jack helps her to uncover a
spine-chilling story from the past . . .

ANNA-LOUISE WEATHERLEY

Big house, smart school, horses, swimming
pool . . . Grace Foster-Bryce's life looks like
something out of a glossy magazine. Jay Jones
(aka JJ) is a graffiti artist living on a scruffy
London council estate.

What could bring these two together?

Grace's idyllic life comes crashing down when
her father is jailed for fraud, and she moves with
her mother and little brother to a run-down
house backing on to JJ's estate. When she's
bullied, JJ comes to Grace's rescue and the two
strike up an unlikely friendship and fall in love.

When a crisis occurs, their differing backgrounds
threaten to split them apart. Against all odds,
can their love survive?